**Children of a Broken Sky**

The Redemption Chronicle, Volume I

Adam J Nicolai

**Also By Adam J Nicolai**

Alex

Rebecca

A Season of Rendings (Available 2014)

**Children of a Broken Sky**
The Redemption Chronicle, Volume I
by Adam J Nicolai

Published by Lone Road Publishing, LLC

ISBN 978-0-9849264-2-8



Original Artwork by Adam Paquette © 2013
Cover Element Design by Kit Foster Design and Lone Road Publishing, LLC

For my wife, Joy, who always believed.

I love you.

# Table of Contents

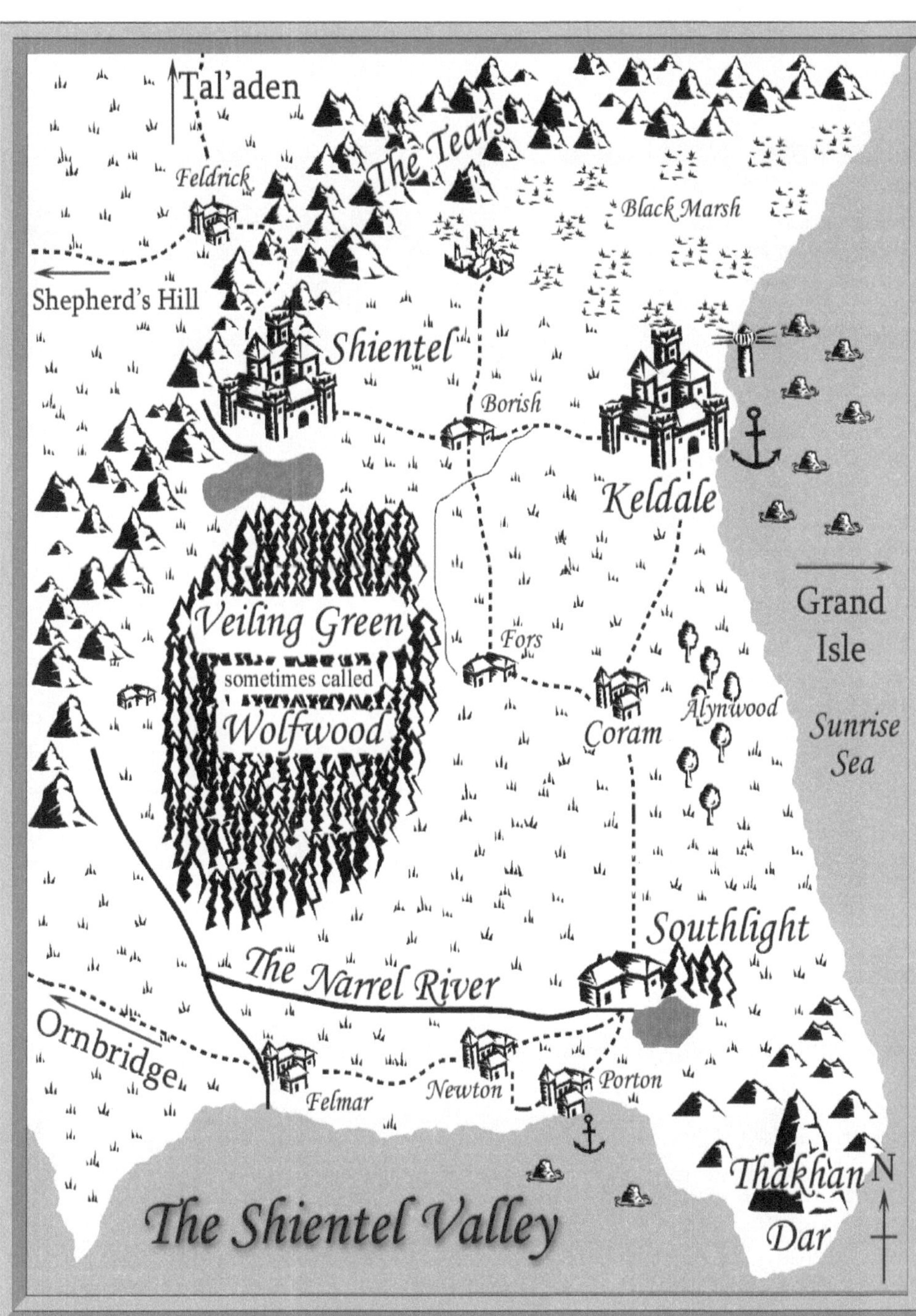
Tal'aden
The Tears
Feldrick
Black Marsh
Shepherd's Hill
Shientel
Borish
Keldale
Grand
Isle
Veiling Green
sometimes called
Wolfwood
Fors
Coram
Alynwood
Sunrise
Sea
Southlight
The Narrel River
Ornbridge
Felmar
Newton
Porton
Thakhan
Dar
N
The Shientel Valley

It's hard to believe, now, how close we once were.

I remember whole summers spent racing beneath a sprawling sky, winters spent slogging through the snow and sniping each other from crumbling white forts. I remember feeling like my skin color didn't matter–not *here,* not with these friends, even if Seth did always call me a nog–and that every grassy ridge, every glimmer from Pinewood Lake, was a mystery waiting to be explored.

Do you remember it, too? You'd make fun of me, now and then, because I romanticized everything–but surely you remember it. A time when no transgression was unforgivable, a time before floods, and silent lightning, and death.

Maybe you really don't remember. Maybe the road we've traveled has stretched so far that you can no longer see back to the beginning. But I know our history makes you who you are, for good or ill. I know the children we were–the ones that laughed and chased each other over the hills, the ones that couldn't imagine anything worse than a frown from our parents–are still here. They are still us.

They always will be.

- *Fragment of a letter from famed historian Angbar Shed'dei, recovered from his quarters upon his death, unaddressed and unsent.*

# Prologue

## The Storm

"Lyseira." Seth's voice, swimming down to her from a hundred miles above. "Lyseira, wake up."

She opened her eyes and saw him crouched next to her, dark hair mussed from sleep, a ragged, greying nightshirt hanging loose from his shoulders.

"What?" she whined. She hadn't meant to whine, it had just come out that way.

He glanced toward the front door. "Come on. You have to see this."

"We can't go out on the Night," she murmured.

"It's dawn. Come on."

"Tired." Her eyes drifted closed, and he shook her.

"Come *on.*" When she tried to roll away, he ripped her blankets off and threw them in the corner. Freezing air doused her.

*"Hey!"* She bolted upright, glaring daggers, but he was already opening the front door.

Beyond she glimpsed an ocean of morning mist, shimmering with color.

She chased him outside, where the mist eddied at her belly. She sank her hand into it, marveling at the lights flickering within. "What...?" she began, but Seth pointed upward, and then she saw.

The heavens bristled with lightning. The bolts ricocheted off each other, carving up the sky; they split the clouds with quicksilver, and sent the remnants skittering. When any bolt ended another sprang out to replace it, bounding through the heavens like a jackrabbit. And the colors...!

Every bolt was a blazing red or yellow, a sizzling green or blue; bolts of pure argent scalded the clouds, intersecting velvet paths of black. Some were indescribable, hues she couldn't even name. Every instant told a breathless tale of fury and light.

Yet the air hung still. The mist was hushed. The lightning, for all its chaos, was silent as a corpse–as though it were screaming a message with its flashing colors that couldn't be heard by any ear on Earth.

Laughter, undiluted and joyous, drifted through the calm. Across the road, she saw little Syntal: beaming skyward as she laughed, arms wide, eyes dancing with the sky's reflected ecstasy. She jutted from the mist at the hips, a creature born of its crackling power.

Something about her made the wonder in Lyseira's chest lurch toward fear. She circled her heart to ward off evil spirits. "I'm getting Mom," she breathed, and Seth nodded, still riveted to the sky; but from behind, she heard her mother's voice.

"I'm here." Mom put a hand on each of their shoulders. "Shhh, I'm here."

Lyseira clutched at her and glanced up. Mom's face was grim, lined with awe but no fear. The sky might be breaking, but Mom wasn't scared, because–

*Because death holds no fear. We are God's people, and if the world is ending, Akir will shelter our souls.*

This insight flooded Lyseira like a steadying breath. In that moment her faith was not hypothetical; it wasn't rote memorization of scripture or learning the proper time to kneel.

It was the bedrock on which her eternal soul stood, and it was unshakable.

# Children of a Broken Sky

## The Redemption Chronicle, Volume I

Adam J. Nicolai

# Chapter 1

## Nine Years Later

*i. Lyseira*

Lyseira Rulano stopped at the church's threshold, her eyes burning.

*Stop it.* She swiped at them, savagely, and wiped the tears on her dress. *You will not walk in there crying. You will not. He will do this for you because he believes in you. Maybe,* she admitted, *because he loves you.*

Not *because he pities you.*

In the fields to the left, past the little row of houses that marked the village's northern border, fire lights danced. Strains of music beckoned to her, whispering of celebration. Her friends were at the festival, she knew, probably wondering where she was. To them, her success was a foregone conclusion.

Of course Lyseira will become a priestess, they thought. She knows scripture better than anyone. With The Abbot going blind, she practically runs the church already. She even speaks on Dawnday.

But they didn't understand that none of that mattered. Every initiate to the Church had to perform a miracle. She hadn't done it, and time was running out. Her friends brushed this off, as if it were a minor detail that would see to itself.

They were wrong. It hadn't. Not after she'd spent years trying, not after sitting with The Abbot for hours of meditation, not after long, secret nights spent begging in prayer. She hadn't performed a miracle, and she had finally realized she never would.

Her heart rimed over with shame, freezing her hand on the temple door. She could still try to pick up the pieces. Meet Keithe at the dance, like he'd asked, and see where their paths led them. Become a housemother, like her own mom had, and raise children. Perhaps one of *them* would be blessed, and work the miracle needed to earn their place in the Church.

Her resolve hardened to steel. *No.* She had given everything to Akir. She had slaved for Him in this church, and done it with joy in her heart, since she was a girl of seven winters. If He refused to grant her this one thing, then she would go around Him.

Performing a miracle was not the only way to join the Church. A few had been admitted through *Básа non-Kasta*: the holy sponsor. A priest, titled abbot or higher, could vouch for a person of extraordinary piety and honor, and secure them entry. It was rare–Lyseira had never heard of it happening in her lifetime–but it was possible, if The Abbot was willing to stake his own position on her merit.

*If he was willing to do it, he would've mentioned it himself.* She'd had the thought a thousand times, but she was past heeding it. She opened the door, and slipped inside the old temple.

"Hello?" It was dark; the candles that normally lit the rows had guttered out. In any other temple, the priests would keep the temple lit at all hours with miracles of light, but The Abbot was the only priest in Southlight, and the strain of such efforts had become too much for him. It was just another way Lyseira had failed him. By now, a real initiate would have been able to keep the holy lights illuminated herself.

"Father?" She lit one of the candles by the door and took it with her into the chapel. Why wasn't he here? Had he gone to Festival? Someone would've had to help him. His night vision had gone first, and that was years ago. Besides, he hated dancing and singing. He wouldn't attend Festival even if he could.

A quiet dread stole into her thoughts, and she hurried into the chapel. "Father?" Her voice echoed off the cold walls, chasing itself back to her. As she reached the altar, she saw him on the floor.

"Father!" She ran to him and crouched. "Father Forthin!" When she shook his shoulder, her fingers brushed his bare neck.

It was cold as stone.

~ ~

Her mother told Lyseira she should give a formal sermon at the funeral. Lyseira refused. It was true that no one in the village would question her, but that wasn't the point. She wasn't a priestess, and to pretend otherwise was forbidden.

Instead she listened as old Willis Mellerson said a few words, and Minda Fletchins led them in hymns. She watched as her own friends–Helix Smith and Iggy Ardenfell, both hulking brutes now compared to the twigs they'd been as children–took up shovels and threw in the dirt. It spattered across the casket, burying the only man she had ever looked to as a father; burying her dreams.

~ ~

The Abbot's replacement came at the end of the month. The evening he arrived he went straight to the temple without a word to anyone, and Lyseira went up to meet him. She found him in the pews, his back turned to her, digging at a scuff in the wood with a thumbnail.

"Father Annish?" she asked.

He turned, his robes dragging against a pew. He must have seen forty or more winters, with a bulging paunch and a sallow face. One of his eyes trained on her but the other was slightly off, riveted to a stray strand of hair above her temple.

"Yes?"

She had never seen a lazy eye before. For one terrible instant she couldn't look away. Then she dropped her eyes, put her hand over her heart, and bowed her head, suddenly thankful Abbot Forthin had occasionally enforced the old formalities. "Lyseira Rulano, if it please you," she offered as she looked up. "I helped Abbot Forthin in his duties as Keeper for many years and wished to welcome you to Southlight." She couldn't figure out how to look at him. She forced herself to look at his good eye, and ignore the other.

"How kind." He crossed to her and offered his hand, palm down. She kissed it; the flesh was clammy and yielding. "Thank you, child."

She straightened to find him gazing at her chest. Her shirt had a modest neck, but perhaps as she had bent to kiss his hand she had embarrassed herself. A flush came to her cheeks. She fought the urge to adjust her collar. "I trust your journey was comfortable? The weather has been–"

"Yes, yes, the weather." He flicked his eyes over her legs–the lazy one seemed to linger–before looking back to her face. He smiled. "I know you mean well. I've just never been one for niceties." The smile faded. "Did Abbot Forthin have an office?"

The abrupt question tripped her. "I–yes. Yes, of course." She gestured to the door behind the altar, at the back of the chapel.

"Ah. Very good. I trust he kept ledgers?"

"Yes, all his books are there." She took a step toward the door, offering to lead him, and he set a hand on her arm.

"I can see the door, child."

She halted. *This is not going well.* "Sorry, Father. Of course."

He flashed her a pained smile; his good eye flicked once more over her breasts. "No, no. I understand. Forthin was going blind, was he not?"

"Yes, Father."

"You were probably used to leading him around like a horse. If I continue your role here at the temple, you won't need to do that."

*If I continue your role...* Lyseira swallowed the sudden lump of fear in her throat. She had come here with some vague idea that this new Keeper's arrival wouldn't change things much; that she could prove her worth to him easily and maybe even pick up where she had left off with The Abbot. In five idle words, he had shattered that idea.

She felt the sudden urge to beg, and choked it to death as it clawed toward her tongue.

"What did you say your name was?" He gazed about the chapel, his lips pursed in mild distaste.

"Lyseira Rulano."

His eyes came back to her. "You can't be a day more than seventeen winters."

"Sixteen, Father."

He nodded. "But you know your way around, I'm sure. I may have some need of you. Though it is too bad you're a girl. Aren't there any boys in town who have interest in serving Akir?"

"I..." She knew female initiates were rare, but this question struck her like a slap. "I've served Abbot Forthin as well as any boy," she retorted, more harshly than she'd intended.

"I've no doubt. But there is weakness in the female flesh that you can't control, and it manifests as you age. You're blooded, I'm sure, and your shape is a distraction. You've spent time with the scriptures? You should know this."

She did, but Abbot Forthin had never raised the concern. *Be careful, Lyseira,* part of her mind cautioned, but as usual, her tongue outran it. "Abbot Forthin withstood my shape well enough. I'm sure you can do the same."

"Abbot Forthin was *blind*," Annish threw back at once. "Apparently in more ways than one, if he tolerated *that* tongue."

*Enough. Stop.* But the words burst from her mouth like a squirrel darting across a wagon rut, throwing caution to the wind. "He was going to sponsor me," she said. "*Básа non-Kasta.*"

She regretted the words instantly. They were presumptuous, arrogant–and worse, they were false. They hung in the air like something obscene.

His lazy eye stared at them, incredulous. Then he began to laugh.

Her wounded pride growled, but this time she kept it in check. *What will Mom say,* she wondered, *when she hears how I've messed this up?* She dropped her eyes, her cheeks burning beneath his mirth.

"Oh, my dear," he managed at last. "Oh, child. That's what this is about? You have no idea who I am, do you?"

The words drew her gaze back to him.

"I've been a Deacon for a month. They promoted me because I was the only one willing to suffer this dirt hole." He guffawed. "You didn't honestly think they'd send another *abbot* here, did you?

"So, you can end the song and dance. You have nothing to prove to me. I couldn't sponsor you if I wanted to. I was an initiate until four weeks ago."

His sallow grin faded.

"I..." she stammered. "I didn't–"

"No," he snapped. "Of course you didn't." He flung a hand toward the door. "Get out of here. I can show myself around."

*ii. Helix*

Helix Smith wiped the sheen of sweat from his forehead and slit another salmon's belly open. Not for the first time that evening, he rued listening to his mother.

*I could be at Pinewood Lake right now, with Minda.* When they'd gone the last time, she had worn a pair of cut-off breeches that had left little of her legs to the imagination. Those legs had been branded in his mind for a week. And she had kissed his fingers, doing this thing with her lips that he honestly didn't remember much of, because where the memory should have been, there was nothing but a white-hot blaze.

For the next time, she had mentioned skinny dipping. The thought of being naked in the water with her arrested his hands in mid-slice, as salmon guts seeped over his thumb.

The kitchen door banged open and Willis Mellerson bustled in, an armload of wooden trays balanced against his ample gut. "How goes it, Master Smith?" he called, dumping the trays into the wash basin with a clatter.

Helix jerked out of his reverie, nearly cutting himself. *It goes well,* he started to say, but a sudden image of Minda Fletchins' nude body shimmering beneath the surface of the lake drew him up short. "Not well," he breathed, trying to sound weak. "It's so hot in here, I... I think I'm getting hotsick."

*Let me go home.* He pushed the thought outwards as if it had the power to compel the man. *Let me go, let me go, let me go...*

"Oh I know, this summer's been a slice of Hel, ain't it?" the innkeeper grunted, without turning around. "Still, can't be any worse than that forge of your dad's. If ya need to sit down for a spell, that's fine, so long as ya get those salmon steaks ready for cookin' by sunset. And don't forget those spices. House secret."

"Yeah," Helix grunted, choking back a surge of frustration. "Of course, the spices." *Don't know why I'm mad at* him, he forced himself to realize. *It was my* mom *that put me up to this.* He resolved to tell her he was done working at Mellerson's little inn when he got home. He was seventeen, for the love of winter–a man grown, by all counts–and he should be spending the last precious days of summer–

*Being responsible*, his mother supplied.

He grumbled and grabbed another fish.

~~

By the time the steaks were lined up, seasoned, and safely wrapped in saltleaf for good keeping, the light from the east window had dimmed. Minda would be long gone by now, probably off with her friends someplace.

He sighed and turned to the dishes. *Tomorrow.*

Mellerson banged through the door again just as Helix grabbed a rag. "You can leave the rest of those, Master Smith," he said. "Thanks for yer help tonight."

Helix threw down the rag he had just grabbed. "Sure," he said, and made for the door to the common room.

"Smith!"

Helix turned around, dreading that the man was going to change his mind and ask him to stay.

"Yer pay," Willis said, laying a silver coin on the wooden counter. "It's a little more than yer mom and I discussed, but ya did good work. Don't be expectin' it every time, now."

*A silver shell?* Helix fought to keep a look of disdain off his face. Money had never been a problem in his family, not with the level of clientele his father kept. That's why it was so bizarre that his mother wanted him to get a job. *Dad was paid a* thousand *of those for his last piece for Lord Locklyn. He talked about it for months.*

He was about to shake his head, dumbfounded by his mother's odd behavior, when he realized Dad had sold that piece three years ago.

*Has it really been that long?*

"Smith?" Mellerson prompted.

"Sorry." Helix stuffed the coin into his pocket. "Thanks," he muttered.

"Yer mom said you could watch the counter in the morning for me, too. See ya at dawn, then?"

"*M'sai,*" Helix agreed off-handedly as he started walking away. Then he turned back. "Wait, *tomorrow* morning?"

"Yuh."

Helix cursed silently. "For how long?"

"Oh, 'til about highsun."

He couldn't suppress a groan. Mellerson chortled. "She didn't tell ya, then?"

Helix shook his head.

"Well, you'd best work it out with her, 'cause I'm countin' on ya now. I'll be here long enough to check ya in and set ya up and then I'm headed over to Brogund's."

Helix sighed. "All right. Don't worry. I'll be here."

"There's a good boy."

~ ~

The common room was busier than usual. He saw Horace Brogund and Old Maid Betsy sharing a table (*That ought to raise some eyebrows,* he thought), Melachi of Locklyn drinking alone in a corner (*As usual*), and at a table near the door–

Helix drew up short. "As I breathe, if it's not Lyseira Rulano at the bar. And with some swarthy Northerner, no less."

Angbar chuckled while Lyseira, who had been hunched forward talking to him, startled straight. "I'm not 'at the bar,'" she said, flushing as she scooped a long curtain of hair away from her face. "I ordered a milk."

"'Swarthy Northerner?'" Angbar repeated. "I like that. Fancy talk for a smith's boy."

"Must be spending too much time around you," Helix threw back, and felt himself returning Angbar's grin. It was always hard not to. "And you may not be *at* the bar," he directed to Lyseira, "but you are *in* a bar, at least, milk or no." Teasing Lyseira was an old, comfortable garment; it slipped right on and put his father's questionable finances and the missed lake trip out of his mind.

Lyseira scowled. "You are a hopeless chunk of meat, Helix Smith."

*Harsh, for Lyseira.* He glanced a question at Angbar, who nodded acknowledgement, wincing.

"Lyseira was just telling me about the new abbot," Angbar said.

"He's not an abbot! For the love of winter, were you even listening to me at all?"

"Right, sorry. He's a–what did you say? A deacon?"

"A deacon," Lyseira echoed.

"Well, that's good," Helix offered. "Isn't it? I mean, a priest closer to your own age will be..." Her look withered the words on his tongue.

"He must be forty winters," Lyseira whispered, glancing around the room. "His left eye wanders. It's bizarre. And he..." Her mouth snapped shut, as if she'd suddenly realized she was speaking ill of a priest. She circled her heart with one hand, then glanced away, her hand darting to her eyes.

*By Akir. Is she* crying?

"Hey," Angbar said. "Come on, it can't be as bad as all that."

"He's not even sure he's going to let me stay on," she murmured. "He thinks a boy would be better. And he keeps looking..." Her lip curled; she shook her head. "He's *horrid*," she hissed.

"A boy?" Helix snorted. "He doesn't want me up there, I can tell him that."

This did nothing to cheer her up. He was about to try to change the subject when Lyseira spoke again.

"I'm getting too old, anyway. Most initiates–"

"Too *old?*" Angbar challenged, incredulous.

She spoke over him. "*Most initiates* start very young, eight winters, maybe as many as twelve, but *sixteen*?" She shook her head. "It's ridiculous. Akir wants me to do something else. I just wish He would've told me before I wasted sixteen winters on this."

Helix's breath caught. He'd never heard Lyseira like this. He looked again at Angbar, helpless.

Angbar's eyes drew into a scowl. "*Rev'naas* take that," he snapped. "You know what's going to happen? He's going to stumble around, blinder than Abbot Forthin ever was, for a few days, maybe as long as a week. Then he'll be at your door begging for help, and you'll have him by the balls."

Lyseira sighed. "I doubt it."

"You said this elderman's got over forty winters behind him, but he's still a deacon?" Angbar scoffed. "Lyseira, come on. If you'd performed a miracle at eight–and I know you didn't, *m'sai*, but if you had–you'd be a deacon yourself by now. He didn't stay an initiate for forty winters by being *good* at anything."

Lyseira considered this.

"I'll put copper on it," Angbar went on, slapping a copper heel on the table. "If he doesn't come crawling after you like a whipped dog in the next..." His hand groped for the right timeframe. "Call it one week, this money's yours."

"Gambling is wrong," Lyseira answered, but she looked somewhat mollified.

Helix fought down a relieved smile. *There's the Lyseira I know.* "No way I'm taking that bet," he put in. "I like my copper right where it is."

"You're both just trying to make me feel better," Lyseira accused.

"If the truth makes you feel better," Angbar rejoined in a mock imperious tone, "so be it."

~ ~

Helix stayed with his friends for maybe half an hour, keeping an eye open for Minda. When she failed to appear, he excused himself and headed home.

He found his mother in the living room, sewing in her favorite chair. His father had gotten it years ago.

For the first time, it occurred to Helix that it was a very nice chair. It was upholstered, with a thick, cozy cushion; its dark green fabric bore an intricate pattern of whorls. No one else in the village had anything like it, except for Mister Mellerson, and Helix's family had *two* of them. At the moment his father was sitting in the other one, smoking a pipe.

*The rug, too,* he thought, taking in the broad runner that carpeted the family room. *Even the front porch. Nobody has anything like them.*

His mother looked up and smiled. "Hello, dear." Father, seated across from her, looked at him and nodded.

"Hi," Helix said, glancing at both of them. He set his things down just inside the door and crossed the room to his mother. "This is what he gave me," he said, handing her the silver shell. A sudden look of apprehension stole across her face; she glanced behind him toward his father. "He said it was more than you asked for."

She slid the coin from his hand, the color slowly draining from her cheeks. "Thank you, darling," she said.

"Bella." The word was a warning. Helix turned to see his father standing, his pipe clutched in one hand.

Mother drew herself up and looked her husband in the face. "We have no *choice*, Kevric. I know how you feel about this, but we have to–"

Father turned to Helix and cut her off. "Where have you been?"

"Uh–up at Mellerson's inn, helping with dishes and such." His father's vehemence took him completely off-guard.

"Oh? And how much did he pay you?"

"A silver shell," Helix answered.

Father whirled toward his wife. "*A silver shell?*"

"And we need every heel of it!" she answered, defiant. "Kevric Smith, you haven't sold a piece in a year and a half!"

Helix's father jerked a finger up in warning.

"We'll be lucky to have enough to buy food for the winter!"

"You are not turning my son into a housemaid!"

"No, you are! Because you weren't willing to do the work yourself!"

Father turned back to him, his face nearly glowing with fury. "Helix, you are not to go back to that place, do you understand me?"

Helix nodded, his mouth agape. Behind him, he heard the front door open. Syntal came in, her eyes taking in the scene uneasily. *Bad timing, coz.*

"And where have *you* been all night?" Kevric demanded.

"I was swimming," she said. "I fell asleep at the lake." She had a black ring that she twisted when she was nervous. She was twisting it now.

Father stared her down. "Get in your rooms. Both of you." Helix immediately obeyed; he saw Syntal scurrying behind him. He ducked into his room and beckoned for her to follow.

"What's going on?" Syntal said as he shut the door.

"I don't know. Mom asked me to help Will Mellerson in his kitchen tonight, and I guess Dad didn't know, because he exploded when he found out."

"What's so bad about you helping at the inn?" Syntal asked. She sounded exhausted; the words dribbled from her mouth like water from a dropped skin.

"Dad doesn't want me doing women's work," Helix said, but he sensed it was more than that. "Mellers gave me a silver shell for doing it. I gave it to Mom when I got home, and when Dad saw it, he got so mad I thought he was gonna pop a cork."

Syntal nodded.

"Mom said we don't have enough money for food for the winter," Helix said. This seemed to wake her up; Syntal locked eyes with him, anxiety painting her face.

There was something strange about her eyes, something that made Helix's stomach twist.

"She should've asked me," Syntal said. "I'd have done it too."

"Syn," he said. "What's wrong with your eyes?"

She glanced away. "What? Nothing."

"They have that weird look again."

"I don't know what you're talking about."

He wanted to grab her chin, to force her to look at him. "Were you looking at the book again?"

Her silence was all the confirmation he needed.

"*Sehk.* Syntal, you promised me."

"Helix, please, I don't–"

"There's a new abbot at the temple. He's not blind, Syn, he's gonna notice. By Akir, it's a wonder Mom and Dad didn't–"

"It goes away overnight. I just need to sleep." Her jaw cracked in a sudden yawn.

"I thought you were sleeping at the lake?" he accused, sharper than he'd intended.

She looked at him. Her green eyes seemed to command the space around them, to drink in his gaze like they were the only real thing in the room.

"It's nothing," she said, and slipped out.

### *iii. Iggy*

Tonight, it would rain.

Some people got a pain in their bad knee when the air was changing. Some could smell a tang in the air. Ignatius Ardenfell could hear it in the wind, as clear as a voice whispering.

He closed his eyes as he stood alone beneath the trees, thanking the wind for the knowledge of the coming rain but trying to listen past it, for the subtle whisper of the saltleaf he was looking for.

*Thanking the wind?* Every now and then, the absurdity of his behavior struck him. He could only imagine what his father would say if he knew. But then, his father didn't understand. Nobody did.

The wind hadn't always spoken to him. He had spent years trying to deny that it was happening, and then years more denying when it had started. But this was the truth: the morning of the Storm, as his parents had stared skyward with terror in their eyes, he had heard the wind laughing.

He'd never heard a sound of such joy, then or since. It had sung and leapt, dancing across the plain like a child on the first morning of spring.

In the weeks after, the wind had whispered things to him and he'd shared its wisdom with his parents. He would casually mention that the horses were hungry, or that the rain would let up by midnight, and they would ignore him in the good-natured way that parents had.

Then Abbot Forthin had given the first of his sermons about the Storm.

The Church called it The Rending. It meant Akir was bringing judgment. The end was coming. *Rev'naas,* mankind's manifest sin, would soon consume everything, and only the righteous would know peace in death. For the rest, there was Hel.

"The world has changed," Iggy remembered him saying. "The world you knew is gone. This one is damned, and only Akir can save us."

Something had told Iggy to be quiet about the things the wind told him then.

The Storm transformed everything. It snowed in the month of Summermorn, and rained in the dead of winter. One day the sun reached its high point and stayed there until midnight, when it abruptly winked out. Iggy remembered wondering if it would come back.

The wolves of Veiling Green turned rabid, striking at travelers from the wood. Crops died overnight, or ripened as fast. For a time, every morning seemed to bring tales of new horrors from abroad, and each week's Dawnday sermon was an island of reason in a sea of madness.

The next year had brought the first stories of witches, miracle-workers who acted without the blessing of Akir and outside of the Church. They were hunted by the Tribunal and put down, no match for the might of the Church, but there were more stories the next year, and the next.

When Iggy was thirteen, as the weather grew stranger still and the insights the wind brought him continued to sharpen, Abbot Forthin had explained to the congregation how to tell a warlock. He read, from the book of Gilleus, the old story of Iis-alac and the witch, "whose eyes were like lanterns before dusk."

Iggy had checked a mirror every day since. But whether due to good luck or Akir's grace, his plain, hazel eyes always stared back at him.

The weather never returned to normal, but there were good years and bad years. The Tribunal's witch hunts grew more frequent. In the worst stretches he would hear of a new one every couple months, though thankfully never in Southlight. It always happened in some far-flung big city: Shientel, or Keswick, or Tal'aden.

All the same, when the world failed to end, life went on. Farmers kept planting, and usually they were successful. Children were born; old folks died; people grew up and moved away. Someone struck by one of the Storm's arbitrary calamities went to the temple for censure, tithed extra, and prayed for better luck the next season. And eventually, Iggy had grown daring enough to mention his insights, though he always couched them in vague references to how the clouds looked or how the air smelled.

*There.* It was quiet, a murmur beneath the clamor of the coming rain, but it was unmistakable. Delicate and beautiful as a spider's web at dawn: the song of the saltleaf.

Putting old thoughts behind him, Iggy hitched up his pack and started into the woods.

~ ~

Saltleaf grew like crabgrass: long and low to the ground, with five thin, forked leaves. He knelt in the patch and pulled out his knife, cutting one leaf expertly from each plant. He left the stem and the other leaves, though he knew his father and others who cut wild saltleaf typically just took the whole thing. The leaves kept longer that way at home, but it killed the plant. He didn't want to do that. There was no need.

He had paused, calculating how many leaves his mother would need for the week, when the wind cried out and an animal roared.

He jerked his head toward the noise. A copse of bushes, sandwiched between two giant trees, rocked like a ship in a storm. The roar dissolved into a tortured yelp.

*A bear.* He heard it in the wind at once. *Its leg is caught in a pair of steel teeth, like a mouth that leapt from a cover of grass.*

He circled the copse and approached from the rear. The bear was a huge black, easily six feet tall, its leg a bloody mess from the rusted metal sunk into the flesh. It heaved, trying to get away, and its roar again became a yowl of pain.

*It's going to tear its foot off,* Iggy thought, and held out his hand. "Stop it!" he called, as he saw the bear crouching to try again. The animal turned to him, desperation plain in its face. "You're making it worse."

The bear's paws fumbled at its leg as a growl burned in its throat. It didn't understand. *Get out of here,* Iggy told himself. *You'll get yourself killed. For the love of winter, it's just a bear.*

Then he caught a hint of the bear's pain through the wind, and realized how senseless this was to the animal. It had sprung a random trap, old and forgotten, and because of man's lazy malice it may never walk easily again. Things like this happened all the time in the woods. Casual injustices, inflicted as easily as men could walk.

Iggy tightened his jaw. Suddenly, he didn't feel ridiculous for wanting to help the animal; he felt ashamed for thinking about leaving.

He held out a hand. *I can help you.* The wind picked up his words, carried them to the bear.

The animal harrumphed once, then let out a bellow of pain.

Furious, it again lunged to the side in an attempt to get away–and fell, panting and moaning, to the forest floor.

Iggy frowned. *Have you had enough, or can I help?*

The beast's eyes were liquid brown, shining like a child's, but when they latched on to Iggy's own, their meaning was unmistakable. *If you hurt me, I will kill you.*

It was the best invitation he was likely to get. Iggy approached, fishing through his bag. *Wurmroot and blackweed. Good.* The herbs would help to dull the pain, once the bear's foot was free, and may even speed its healing.

Getting the foot free to begin with was a different matter.

He rooted through the dirt and underbrush until he found a rock. *I'm going to pry the teeth apart. It'll hurt.* He looked the animal in the eyes. *Do you understand? It will hurt, but it will set you free. Don't struggle, or the jaws may close again, harder this time.*

The animal bared its teeth, but it understood. As carefully as he could manage, Iggy took hold of one of the trap's jaws and worked the rock into the cleft. Slowly, straining against the device's old springs, he managed to pry the teeth apart. *Now, quickly.*

The bear lurched forward, jostling Iggy's hand as it pulled its leg loose. The woodsman jerked his arm back as if it were on fire. The snapping jaws of the trap missed his fingers so barely that he felt the tremor as they clamped closed. The dull *clap* echoed in his ears as his heart fluttered in his throat.

The bear began to limp away.

"Wait!" Iggy took a step toward the animal. "I can still help you." But even though he had freed the bear from its torment, it didn't trust him. *And why would he? He probably thinks I laid this trap here myself.* "See, I have herbs. They can help your wound." Iggy pointed at the bundle of wurmroot lying near his pack.

*I can help,* he whispered through the wind. *I don't know why this happened, but I can treat your wound. Please.*

The hulking creature paused and looked back at him, pain glittering in its eyes, and gave a low grumble.

Iggy scooped up his herbs and held them toward the animal. *Look. Harmless. Let me show you.*

As Iggy approached, the grumbling faded. When he had nearly

reached the bear, it turned suddenly, and Iggy had a flashing vision of it rearing back to attack him. Then it swiveled itself about and gingerly sat its backside on the forest floor, its wounded foot facing him.

"*M'sai,*" Iggy breathed, his galloping heart slowly calming. "Good."

He didn't have a waterskin to mix mud with, so he made do with the dirt from the forest floor. He crushed the herbs and mixed them into a poultice, spitting into the concoction to give it what moisture he could.

The bear's paw was a savaged ruin. The trap had torn past flesh and into bone. If the wound wasn't healed, it would almost certainly draw spirits, and the animal would die of a slow, consuming fever.

He did his best to clean it, then took the poultice and tried to pack it into the cut. Wurmroot was known for its potency against open wounds, but he felt the blood continue to pulse beneath his hands. *No good,* he realized. *The cut is too deep and the poultice too weak.* He crushed more wurmroot into a rough dust and rubbed it in, then wrapped the ankle with his own hands. He felt the blood beating rhythmically against his own flesh, the pulse of the bear's heart straining against the wound. It was a mirror of his own pounding heartbeat.

*The same,* the wind whispered to him. *They are the same.* Now the bear's own blood was moistening the earthy poultice, providing the moisture Iggy could not, helping it to form to the wound. Again the wind said, *The same.*

*All things come from the earth.*

Somehow, Iggy realized there was more to the mud in his hands than the herbs he had crushed into it. Somehow, he drew on that sameness, borrowed it, and shared it with the wound. He felt the bear's anguish slowly ease, like a sea storm spending itself against the shore.

When he took his hands from the animal's leg and wiped away the bloody mud, the flesh beneath was whole.

Iggy sank back, his hands braced against the ground, his mind spinning. The bear leaned forward and stood up, testing its weight on its new foot, then licked him once on the face before loping into the woods.

*Impossible.* Only priests could heal wounds with their bare hands. This surpassed everything that had come before. This was a miracle, but he was no cleric. This–

*This was witchcraft,* his mind supplied.

He scrambled for his pack, his thoughts racing.

*It can't be. I didn't do anything. I didn't* do *anything!*

He tore the pack open, ransacking it, imagining being tied to a stake by clerics as he screamed empty protests. Then he found the mirror and held it up, certain of the worst.

His eyes were normal.

# Chapter 2

*i. Helix*

If he had hoped his father's protests would spare him a Meadowday morning at Mellerson's inn, he was wrong.

Mother had woken him just after dawn and sent him off. It had rained overnight, abruptly dropping the temperature from the sweltering high of the day before into something more closely resembling an honest autumn. He had stumbled in, damp and cold, and Mellerson had shown him where the keys were and how to fill in the guestbook when someone checked in or out. Then the older man had left, and Helix had pulled up a chair and nodded off.

He'd barely slept last night. His parents' fight had lasted halfway 'til dawn, quieting now and then only to flare up again. When he did manage to drift off, he'd see Syntal's eyes, green and hypnotic in the dark, and he'd jerk back awake. Once, he'd even stolen across the hall and peeked in on her, but unlike him, his cousin had been sleeping like the dead.

Now the same images chased themselves through his dozing thoughts–his father's rage, his mom's defiance, his cousin's bizarrely commanding eyes–but they had faded enough to allow flickers of Minda's shy but daring smile. Or the way she would bite her bottom lip and widen her eyes at him, transforming every innocent suggestion into a scandal.

By Akir. He *had* to meet up with her today. It was too cold for swimming now, but maybe–

The bell above the door rang, and a man stumbled through. "Hello," he called, looking toward the empty common room.

"Good morn." Helix waved.

"Ah." The man turned toward him. He had a wild shock of beard and long, bedraggled hair. Except for the pendant of Akir hanging about his neck, he looked like a homeless outcast. A strip of cloth was tied across his eyes, and he clutched a tall walking stick, which he waved back and forth as he approached.

*He's blind.* "Oh. Sorry," Helix said as he jumped to his feet, shaking the cobwebs out of his head.

"What're you sorry for? Did you make me blind?" The man chuckled.

"What? No, I–I just mean..."

The man reached the counter and waved him off. "Forget it. You didn't mean anything by it. I've been walking all night, I'm drenched, and I must smell like a wet dog. Forgive me. Let's start again." He offered his hand, his head tilted slightly askance. "Brother Matthew, if it please you."

Helix shuffled a bit to take his hand. "Helix Smith."

Matthew had a strong grip. He smiled. "Better, I think. Good to meet you, Master Smith."

"And you," Helix agreed.

"If I may get right to business, Master Smith, I need two things. Firstly, I have a letter for my wife in Keldale. I won't be home when she expects me, and I need to get this sent north as soon as I can." He unslung his pack and fished out a rumpled envelope.

"Well," Helix offered, "we do have a courier that comes through every now and again, but it's not often; maybe every couple months?"

Matthew winced. "I need this sooner."

"Well... my father travels to Keldale on occasion on business. I could try to take it to him."

"Bless you. That would be most helpful." Matthew proffered the letter, and Helix took it.

*Great.* He had no idea why he'd said that; his dad hadn't run an errand up in Keldale since last year. *I'll have to just bring it to the courier post. What he doesn't know won't hurt him.* Irritated, Helix stuffed the letter in his pocket.

"Secondly," Matthew went on, "I need a room, and my companion led me to believe this was an inn."

"Yeah, that's right. Are you staying the night?"

"Three weeks." Matthew leaned his staff against the counter and began rummaging through a pouch at his belt. "I need to pay in advance."

"Oh." Helix fumbled with this information. Mellerson had said his customers were typically just passing through. *Three weeks...* He ran the calculation through his head, then gawked. The traveler looked like he could barely afford the rags on his back, let alone the final total. "Ah... twelve silver and three heels," he said, feeling like a highway thief.

"Twelve and three," Matthew muttered. "Twelve and three. This'll do it." He set exact change on the counter.

Relieved, Helix swept up the coins. He hated asking people for money. "So, three weeks," he said as he updated the guest book and grabbed a key. "That's a long stay. You're visiting family here, or...?"

"Oh no, no. I don't know anyone in Southlight, I'm sad to say, though hopefully that will change soon." His smile was warm and honest.

"Well," Helix answered with a smile of his own, "I'd say it already has. Right over here. I apologize; he doesn't have any ground-floor rooms. There's a short set of stairs."

"Stairs I can handle," Matthew grunted as he swung his walking stick out in front of him.

"We don't get a lot of visitors out here. Southlight's pretty small. What brings you out?"

"Akir," Matthew answered, his staff clicking along the rim of the next step. "I go where he sends me."

Helix stopped, his heart suddenly thundering. He glanced back to Matthew's amulet. It was a God's Star, the symbol of Akir. He'd noticed it before, but it never occurred to him that the ratty man could be a cleric.

*Idiot. You shook his hand? You* charged *him?* As he tried to fight down the rising tide of panic, he remembered Syntal's eyes from the night before. *And now, the next morning, some strange old priest arrives in town? What is he doing here?*

"Mercy, Father," he stammered, circling his heart. "I apologize. I didn't realize."

Matthew snorted as he made the top step. "Oh, calm down, son. I'm no priest."

Helix licked his lips; his mouth had gone dry. "You're not?"

"Akir, no. I said I do God's work, not the Church's." He scoffed. "They do not speak for God. Which way, then?"

"Ah... here," Helix answered, but his mind was whirling. *They do not speak for God?* It was the kind of statement that could get you Cleansed. *What does that mean?*

"I was, once," Matthew went on as he followed. "A bishop, actually."

Helix stopped again. "You were a *bishop*?" he blurted. Matthew might have said he was once King Gregor.

"Well," Matthew clarified, "nearly. They offered it to me. I'd been initiated at ten winters, and was as faithful as they come for the next twenty, but then something happened."

"What?"

"What do you think?" Matthew gave the wall a sly look. "A woman."

Helix remembered Minda's lips on his fingers, and surprised himself by laughing. "Yeah," he said. "They do that."

"Not just any woman, of course. A gorgeous, compassionate, brilliant one."

"Of course."

"She works with orphans in Keldale. The children no one else will take, the ones that have nothing. That's *her* calling. Something noble and selfless and wonderful, while I thought mine was..."

He stopped. "You think you know everything when you're young. No, no, don't deny it, I can't see your face, but I know. I was seventeen winters once, too. You think Akir has a plan for you, or your path is laid. You act with certainty. You do what you're told. And then you meet the destiny He meant you for, and it throws everything to Hel." He chuckled.

"I was already thinking about leaving the Church for her when they made the offer. 'Matthew, Akir needs you.' They wanted me to be a bishop of the Tribunal." The mirth in his face faded. "The Tribunal." He stared into his past.

Finally, he murmured, "Do you have any idea the things I've seen the Tribunal do to children?"

"I..." Helix started. *I've heard stories*, he wanted to say, but the haunted look on Matthew's face struck him mute.

"I say that as if I'm innocent," Matthew continued. "As if I've never done what they told me. Of course I have. That's why they wanted me. I had the fire they were looking for." He shook his head. "It makes me sick, now, to think of it, but at the time, I was torn. I went to the docks. I prayed. I meditated all night."

He held out one hand, palm up. "Become anointed Bishop Matthew?" He held out the other. "Or quit everything I'd worked for and marry the woman I love? Which would you choose, Helix Smith?"

Helix hesitated, still nervous. One didn't speak ill of the Church. At best, it was uncouth; at worst, blasphemy.

He groped for a response that wouldn't leave him compromised. When he hit upon it, he nearly sagged with relief. "You said you prayed–how did Akir answer?"

Matthew grunted. "Safe answer, that. But I can't fault you; it's the same one I gave, wasn't it? Too frightened to make the choice myself. Fine. You want to know how Akir answered?

"He answered by breaking the sky. He answered with silent lightning from Thakhan Dar that left me blind.

"He answered with the Rending."

*ii. Lyseira*

The knock came an hour after dawn.

Lyseira heard it before her mother did, and it woke her with a start from some vague nightmare. She sat up in bed, bleary and disoriented, wondering if it had been real or part of her dream.

*Someone at the door,* she mused dully. *Could be The Abbot.* She swung her legs out of bed and reached for a heavy robe crumpled in a pile on the floor. The temperature had plummeted overnight; she was shivering in her gown.

*The deacon, not The Abbot,* she corrected herself, shaking her head. *The deacon.* She pulled the robe on. As she trudged to her door she began the arduous process of pulling her hair, which hung to her thighs, out of the gown she had just put on.

"'Seira?" her mother called.

"It's the door," Lyseira answered. Her throat was rusty; the words tripped in it. She coughed. "I'll answer it." She had worked her hair halfway out of her gown; it hung lopsided, folded in half just below her shoulders. She wished she had time to run a brush through it. Normally she put it up at night so it wouldn't tangle, but last night she'd collapsed into bed without even thinking about it.

A second knock came just as she crossed through the small kitchen and reached the front door. She paused, finally freeing the last few inches of her hair, and checked herself over to be sure she was decent before opening the door.

The man on her doorstep was shaved bald. The contours of his body were lean and hard beneath a loose-fitting, dun-colored outfit. *A Preserver*, she realized. Her last, clinging bits of drowsiness vanished in a jolt of apprehension.

She had only ever seen one Preserver, years ago, but she had never forgotten. They were sacred guardians, each assigned to protect a cleric of a certain rank. They surrendered everything for their training and their charge. Their ancient arts allowed them to withstand extremes of weather, go for days without food, water, or sleep, and perform awe-inspiring acts of physical violence on command.

For a wild instant she wondered if deacons warranted Preservers; if Father Annish had sent his own to teach her a lesson about insolence.

"I'm looking for Lyseira Rulano," the man said.

Something about his voice triggered an itch in her memory, like she had heard it before. The notion was ridiculous. She stifled it, steeled herself, and said, "That's me."

The Preserver opened and closed his mouth once, as if at a loss. Then he extended his right hand and seemed, impossibly, to straighten his posture. "I am Seth."

*Seth?* Her mind leapt. *That's impossible. It must be another who shares his name.* The Preservers had taken her brother years ago; it was forbidden to return. But she couldn't stop herself from searching his face for signs of the boy she used to know.

To her astonishment, they were there. "Seth?" she breathed.

He mistook her words. "I lived here once, many years ago. I–"

"Seth!" He was really here. Her *brother.* A blaze of wild hope lit in her chest.

She threw her arms around him. His proffered hand sank back to his side.

"Oh, thank Akir! We thought we'd never see you again! What are you *doing* here?" She let him go and stepped back, beaming.

"Look at you! You're really a Preserver! Oh, *tíngala!*" She clapped, and marveled again: "Look at you!"

Mom stumbled into the little kitchen. "What is going–?" She halted. "Seth?" she said, an eerie echo of her daughter's voice a minute before.

Seth nodded. Lyseira turned to her, beaming, but she didn't react as Lyseira expected.

"Why are you here?"

"Mother," Lyseira admonished. She knew Mom regretted letting Seth join the Preservers; she'd spoken of it more than once over the years. "It's *Seth.*"

Mother threw her an annoyed look, but when she turned back to Seth, her expression had softened. "Is everything well?"

"Yes," Seth answered. "Don't worry, I haven't run."

*Of course.* Lyseira felt like an idiot. Deserting the Preservers was a sin, punishable by death, and those who harbored deserters got the same. She was suddenly grateful for her mother's caution.

Relief stole into Mom's eyes, followed by confusion. "Then why..." she began, before shaking the question off. "Never mind. Where are my manners? Come in."

He stepped through the door, and Mom's face broke. She swept him into a hug. A bit of the joy Lyseira had felt earlier seeped into her voice. "Oh, Akir. My little Seth. Is it really you?" She pushed him to arm's length and searched his face. "By Akir, look at you. You made it. I won't lie, when you left here I wasn't sure you would." Memories of the boy he used to be danced in her eyes.

Suddenly her expression darkened. "Are you *certain* you're not in any trouble?"

"*Mother!*" Lyseira reprimanded. "Give him a chance, for the love of winter.

"Are you hungry?" she asked Seth.

"A Preserver shouldn't hunger," he answered. Then he admitted, "But if you're eating anyway, I'd take whatever's left."

*Shouldn't hunger?* Lyseira parsed this and turned away to prepare breakfast, marveling. *I barely recognize him. How did they get him to start talking that way?* The Seth she remembered nearly ate them out of house and home.

"*M'sai,* 'Seira," Mother told her. "I'll handle the food. You visit with your brother."

As Lyseira took a seat at the little table, Seth said, "I heard about Abbot Forthin."

"That was a terrible business," Mother agreed as she started logs burning for the oven. "Lyseira had the poor fortune to find him."

"It was his time," Lyseira offered. She didn't like discussing it.

"How did you know about that?" Mother asked. "I know Father Forthin was an abbot, but I didn't think word would travel so far west."

"I visited the temple when I arrived. I met a heretic on my way here and needed to report him. Deacon Annish told me."

"You met a heretic?" Lyseira asked. "In Southlight?"

Seth considered this. "I met him on the road, and accompanied him here. So yes, he is here now. He names himself Brother Matthew." He paused. "He seemed kind. We spoke much on the road. I told him where the inn was before I reported him."

A distant loon's call echoed in the silence.

*A heretic in Southlight?* There had been stories of witches for years, but never anything so close to home. If Abbot Forthin were still here, she would go to the temple this afternoon to find out what was going on. Maybe even send a message north for him, or help escort the heretic to the Tribunal.

She blinked, coming back to herself. "So what is the school like?" she said, trying to move on. "I've always wondered."

He glanced at the wall and then down at his lap. "I have failed to become a Preserver."

"What?" Lyseira leaned forward. "How?"

"I was nearly accepted," Seth said. "I bested each challenger and all physical tests. Master Retash said my combat skill is 'without peer.'" The barest hint of pride glimmered in his words.

Again, silence. Lyseira said, "But...?"

"But a Preserver also needs to know and follow the tenets of scripture." He drew a deep breath, his eyes latched to the wall, his jaw locked. "That is where I failed. In my knowledge of the Church's history and of the history of the Preservers, and in my understanding of the Seven Sacred Principles."

Lyseira absorbed this. "Wait. You failed a *history test*?" She guffawed. "*That's* the Seth I remember!"

"Lyseira!" Mother chastised.

Seth's gaze moved a degree away from Lyseira. *He's ashamed,* she realized. "I'm sorry," she said, her smile fading. "I didn't mean anything by it." *I'm just relieved to hear you're still in there.*

"The Trial can be attempted twice. After a second failure, students are expelled."

"Well, you can study the pieces you missed, can't you?" Lyseira pressed. "They must have a copy of scripture at the school."

"I can't. The words are beyond me." He clasped his hands on the table, still staring past her at the wall. "There are others with that failing, but they can listen and learn. I fail even at that.

"Master Retash arranged for me to leave the compound for a year. He told me to think on my failures and find a way past them. I came to you because you've always been wise with words, and you know scripture. You..."

Lyseira waited while he assembled his words. "You helped me when I was a child," he said at last, "and I had hoped you would help me now."

*Helped me when I was a child.* A pang of old anguish flashed in her heart. She cupped his clasped hands in her own. "Of course I will," she promised. "You're my brother." *And you've no idea how much I've missed you.*

He finally lifted his eyes to her. The gratitude she read in them made her heart ache. *Akir takes Abbot Forthin and my dream of initiation, but returns my brother,* she realized. *I don't understand it, but I'll accept what He gives me. This afternoon, we can go up to the temple–*

"Oh, no," she blurted. "Mercy, Seth. I'm not sure I can help you."

"Why?"

"I... well, I've made a mess of things with the new Keeper." At the oven, Mom turned around and arched a brow. Lyseira stole a glance at her before looking away. "I went up to meet him last night, and he..." She winced, preparing for a tongue lashing from her mother. "He threw me out."

"He what?" Mom demanded.

Seth interrupted. "He asked me to send for you when I came. He needs your help."

Lyseira blinked, struck dumb by this news. Angbar's encouragement from the night before echoed in her mind. "What? With what?"

"He didn't say," Seth answered, "but he asked that I bring you as soon as possible."

She threw a questioning look to her mother, who pursed her lips. "Go on, then," Mom said, waving her off. "Breakfast will still be here when you get back."

~ ~

Lyseira found the new Keeper in Abbot Forthin's old office, seated at the desk, reviewing a ledger. Seth waited in the chapel while she went to the doorway.

"Father." Lyseira bowed her head and waited to be acknowledged.

"Oh, look up." He snapped his gaze to her. "Did you manage these ledgers for Abbot Forthin?" he demanded. His lazy eye might have been quivering with rage. "The man was blind, and this is woman's writing."

A thousand retorts leapt to her tongue. She fought them all back. "He may have been unable to see the ledgers, but his mind was whole. He asked for my help, and I gave it. I wrote only what he asked me to write."

Annish flipped the pages, a curl of disgust on his lips. "This..." He shook his head, flipped another page, then huffed as if he'd spotted a worm on his coat. "This is an abomination. Irregular tithes, and not nearly ten percent from most. I see..." He counted on his fingers. "The Smiths, the Mellersons, and the Rulanos–to your credit. Three." He brandished the count at her. "Three families. Nearly all others tithe less. Most don't tithe every week. And the Shed'deis–there is no record whatsoever."

"Angbar's family doesn't attend–" she started, before realizing her error.

"Their failure to attend temple is a separate sin. Am I to understand it should somehow excuse them from their debts to Akir?" Father Annish snapped.

"No, Father."

"They do breathe the air He made and drink the water He sends?"

She fought to keep her humility. "Yes, Father."

He shook his head. His gaze slid over her breasts before returning to the ledger, where something made him scoff. "And this." He jabbed a finger at an entry. "In his personal journal, he mentions performing miracles of healing, yet the donation in the ledger is far below expectation, if it's there at all.

"'Nellie Ferguson, on the second of Northwind, healed of influenza.' *Influenza*," he repeated, stealing a chance to bore into her eyes. "That can *kill* a child without intercession. And the donation...?"

*Three heels,* Lyseira thought, but kept her tongue.

"Three heels," Annish spat. "Three copper heels. Did Forthin think so poorly of Akir's miracles that he would rent them out like cheap alley whores?"

Her restraint shattered. "The Fergusons are poor shepherds," she snapped, "and old friends. Three heels was half a week's profit for them."

"And a tenth of the expected donation for us! You condoned this?"

*Damn right I did,* she wanted to say, but her brain caught up to her tongue before it could speak. "I would never question the Keeper," she retorted instead.

His onslaught halted. His good eye searched her gaze, while his other regarded her ear. "Fair enough." His posture eased. "You aren't even an initiate. Why would I expect you to keep an abbot in line?"

He tapped a finger on the desk. "I shouldn't tell you this, but you're a smart little thing; you'd probably figure it out anyway. Forthin was not running things the way he should've been. That is probably why he never sponsored you. If an initiate suddenly showed up in Newton who thought it was *a'fin* to heal shepherds without donations because they were poor, and accept low tithes... well, it would come back to him. It *should've* come back to him." He snorted. "Truth be, the bastard was lucky to die when he did."

Lyseira's hand curled into a fist. *The 'bastard?'* She wanted to roar, to slap the man across the face. *You were an initiate for forty years and you dare call The Abbot a bastard? The man who taught me everything I know, the man who was the closest I've ever had to a father?* She was ready to give up everything, to throw away her entire childhood of work, to defend Forthin in that instant. She looked away, fighting to keep control, and met eyes with Seth.

He shook his head.

"No matter," Annish finally continued. "I'm here now, and things will be done according to Akir's plan. *This*"–he indicated the ledger entry for Nellie Ferguson–"will not happen again. It's no wonder this temple looks like a cesspit, when there's no collection of donations."

She ached to confront him. *Nellie would've been lost without Father Forthin's help. Would you have watched her die because her parents were poor?*

"I've decided to give you a second chance," Annish said. "I have a task for you."

Lyseira forced the thoughts from her mind. "Thank you, Father," she made herself say. "What is it?"

"A man by the name of Matthew Rentiss arrived this morning. He was once an abbot, but after the Rending he left the Church to marry a woman." He paused, as if to let the moral of this story sink in. "The man is a heretic. He has wandered Darnoth for years now, spreading lies about the Church.

"I need you to find him and confront him. Make it clear that he's not welcome and needs to leave."

"I..." Lyseira had expected to clean the front entry, or at worst, be sent out to collect on back tithes. She wasn't ready for this.

"Is there a problem?"

"I just... will he even listen to me? I don't speak for the Church."

Annish glared. "Aren't you clever. I'm not going to find you a sponsor, just for this. You'll have to try harder than that."

Lyseira flushed at the accusation. "I'm not–I'm not *trying* anything, I just... isn't he more likely to listen to you?"

"'Never question a Keeper,' you say, yet you've questioned me twice just since you walked in here. Did I make a mistake with you?"

She swallowed her retorts. "No, Father. I'll do as you ask."

"Good. I'll be leaving this afternoon to head to Coram. I have to send a message north. I'll need you to manage the temple for a few days."

Despite herself, she felt a rush of pride at this news. "Yes, Father. I will."

"I'm sure." He closed the ledger and rose. "Lest you read more into this than you should, let me be clear: Do as I ask before I return, or I will request a real initiate for this church." He dragged his eyes over her body. "One who knows his place."

~ ~

"I can't stand that man!" she hissed once they were back on the road, out of earshot. She whirled toward her brother and stabbed a finger toward the temple. "It's bad enough that The Abbot died, but then we have to get *him!*"

Seth said nothing, his eyes dispassionate.

"Why does he talk to me like that? Who does he think he is? I have practically been running this church by myself for the last *two years!*"

"He speaks to you in that way because he's your superior," Seth said, in a voice like stone. "He thinks he's the Keeper of this temple, and he's right."

Lyseira gaped at him. "But how can he just ignore everything I've done for the Church? I've helped The Abbot keep this place running since I was a child!"

"He's not Abbot Forthin. Why should that matter to him?"

"Well, why *shouldn't it?*" Lyseira pounded her fist against her thigh. She felt tears brimming in her eyes and called on her anger, wielding it like a club to knock them away.

Finally, she looked at her brother. "Whose side are you on, anyway?"

Seth returned her stare. "I didn't realize I had to choose."

The Seth she had known would have been supportive, she was sure of it–and probably would have chased the deacon down and hit him with a mudball for good measure. *That was seven years and half a lifetime ago,* she realized with a sudden chill.

*This isn't the same person.*

~ ~

The next morning she went hunting for Brother Matthew, and found him outside Horace Brogund's bakery. It was Mountainday, time for Brogund's legendary apple sweetcakes, and a small crowd had gathered as it did every week. The weather had grown even colder overnight; the villagers were a mass of scarves and heavy winter coats, the words of their conversations coalescing in a haze of fog around them.

Helix and Minda were at the back of the line, laughing as Minda nibbled playfully at Helix's fingers. She was miming eating an applecake, except Lyseira had never seen anyone eat an applecake like *that*.

*Ugh*. Minda Fletchins was a tramp. Lyseira had no idea what Helix saw in her. To be fair, though, it was easy to see why Minda was drawn to him: he was tall and muscular from the hours spent in his father's smithy, with a broad, honest smile and a cap of wild red hair. The freckles he'd had in his youth had faded, robbing him of the childish look he used to have and leaving a rather handsome man in its place. In the summer, he would sometimes wander around with his shirt off, treating the girls of the village to a view of the black hair leading from just below his belly button and into his breeches. This led to rampant speculation among some of the less scrupulous girls as to the color of the hair further down: red or black? Of course, Lyseira had no patience for such nonsense and made herself scarce whenever the topic was raised.

She preferred to wonder about such things in private.

"Miss Rulano!" Cyrus Forester called to her. Now there was a man who had had his fair share of applecakes. "Yer not usually one for Brogund's sweets. Changed your mind, have you?"

She returned his smile and pulled her coat tighter against the chill. "No, Cyrus. Sorry to disappoint you. I was actually looking for someone named Matthew Rentiss."

A scruffy man turned toward her voice. "You've found him," he called in no particular direction.

She wasn't sure what she had expected–someone more sinister-looking, maybe, with shifty eyes and greasy hair–but Matthew was not it. He wasn't *old*, but he was verging on it. He looked like a homeless vagrant, and–

*By Akir. Is he* blind?

He gave an amiable smile, aimed somewhere to her left. "What can I help you with, ma'am?"

Lyseira felt a twist of guilt. Annish hadn't told her the man was a cripple. "Oh, just a word," she said. He extended a hand, and she shook it.

"Just a word?" Cyrus said. He pulled in a sniff of the cold air. "When you can already catch a hint of them cakes on the wind?" He smiled at her conspiratorially. "Let me buy the cake, girl. One cake, and you'll be here every Mountainday morning with the rest of us."

Lyseira shivered as a sudden gust of freezing wind lanced through her coat. She smiled at Cyrus wryly. "How enticing."

Cyrus guffawed. "It's your choice, kiddo. You change your mind around, my offer stands."

"Maybe next spring," Lyseira said. "I'm sorry Matthew, but can you step out of line so we can talk? Just for a moment."

"I don't know." Matthew quirked a brow in mock suspicion. "I'm told these applecakes go fast once they're out, and I've already been waiting some time. You wouldn't be trying to take my spot, would you?"

Cyrus laughed. "Our Lyseira has too much honor for that. You go ahead. I'll hold your place."

"Well, then," Matthew said. "I'd be flattered, Miss...Lyseira, is it?"

She took his hand and led him away. "Lyseira Rulano," she answered.

"Brother Matthew," he returned. "A pleasure."

The guilt chewed at her. He seemed like a nice enough man.

She resolved to get it over with.

"Brother Matthew," she said when they were out of earshot, "Father Annish, our temple Keeper here in Southlight, asked me to come and talk to you."

"Certainly."

"You need–" She halted as he inclined his head, listening closely. "He's asked me..." she started again, but the earnest look on his blind face again stopped her short.

*Rev'naas* take it all, this was harder than she'd expected. She'd planned on coming at him with fire and brimstone, all "heretic" this and "apostate" that, but this man was not the wicked creature she'd envisioned. *Annish couldn't have mentioned he was* blind? She resolved to have a few words with the deacon when he returned.

"I've been through much, girl," Matthew assured her. "Whatever you have to say, spit it out; I promise I'll survive it. I actually have a few suspicions, but I'll keep them to myself in case they prove wrong."

Feeling rather clever and rather cowardly at once, Lyseira seized on this. "No, by all means–share your suspicions."

Matthew furrowed his brows, then shrugged. "Well, if we're talking about the Church, I'm sure the word 'heretic' was bandied about, and perhaps 'apostate' as well."

"They were," Lyseira said.

"Your Deacon Annish wants me gone from Southlight, I'd wager."

"He does." She suppressed a sigh of relief. That hadn't been so bad, after all.

"What do *you* want?"

"I–?" This tripped her up, but she recovered quickly. "I want what the Keeper wants."

"Ah. So *you* want me out of Southlight."

"Well, I... yes. I do."

"Why?"

Lyseira scowled. "Father Matthew, I'm not here to play games with you."

"Brother," he corrected her. "I was never anyone's father, and I'm certainly not now."

She ignored him. "I'm not here to play games."

"Obviously not. I've paid for a three-week stay at your village inn, but you want to throw me out of town. Do you think it's so unfair that I ask why?"

"Father Annish has his reasons."

"But he's not here. *You're* here."

"Yes," Lyseira insisted, growing annoyed. "To deliver the message for him."

"He could just as easily have told me himself."

"He's very busy."

"Too busy to take the time to throw a blind man out of town himself."

Lyseira gritted her teeth. "Yes."

Matthew made a noise, somewhere between a scoff and a chuckle. "Do you even know what I'm accused of?"

*Of being an obstinate horse's ass,* Lyseira wanted to say. "Father Annish didn't feel he needed to tell me."

"Well, it's a few different things, I imagine, though of course it's impossible to say for sure. But this last spring, I was in Northshire. You know where it is?"

Lyseira had never been out of the Valley. "I've heard of it," she said, humoring him.

"They had a rash of redwarts this past winter. It's a nasty business, redwarts. The skin puffs up everywhere into tiny, bleeding pimples. They itch like mad. People–especially children–scratch the warts, and get the blood on others. That's how it spreads. After a couple weeks it brings on fevers and bone-deep pain. If you catch it, you'll be left blind or dead unless you get healing."

"I'm familiar with it."

"It broke out in their poor quarter, in the alleys where the homeless people sleep. It spread fast, there. Then it started showing up in the orphanage."

Lyseira thought of the Fergusons, and their daughter's influenza. She didn't like where this was going.

"Now, Akir can cure redwarts, but for reasons that surpass my understanding, He rarely does so directly. He grants this miracle to the faithful and relies on them to administer it. Do you think they did?"

She wanted to ignore the question entirely, to insist that he get out of town, but she couldn't. She wanted everything: to make him leave, and escape this conversation with her conscience clean. "We've never had redwarts in Southlight. But Abbot Forthin, our old Keeper, healed disease all the time."

"I've heard of him. He was a good man. But I didn't ask about him." Matthew's sightless gaze could've been staring at her. "I was at the temple in Northshire when the afflicted started showing up on the steps. There were old and there were young, but the worst were the children. Have you ever seen the temple in Northshire?"

"Brother Matthew, I don't see what this has to do with anything."

"If you'll spare me the time, I'll make it clear."

She sighed. "No, I've never seen it."

"It's beautiful. The statues in front of the place, alone, are probably worth more than the whole Southlight temple. The God's Star above the altar is tipped with sapphire arrays. It's breathtaking. Not as breathtaking as the *Basica Sanctaria,* but still impressive." He paused. "They turned the sick away. Do you know why?"

*They couldn't pay.* Lyseira was sure of the answer, but couldn't–or wouldn't–give it voice.

"No coin. The priests would let them die before they would bless them for free."

She had expected the answer, but it still stung. Excuses roared to mind, clamoring for her attention. She struggled to keep her face blank, and finally Matthew continued.

"One cleric–I won't tell you his name–was moved by Akir to act. He visited the alleys on his own, and healed those who needed it. He couldn't help everyone–he was only one man, and healing is tiring–but he did what he could. One of the parents he helped came to the temple the next day to thank him. That's how the Keeper found out." Matthew tilted his head. "They brought him before the Order of Judgment, Lyseira. They took his fingers, his tongue, and his eyes, and sent him to the same alley he'd ministered in to spend the rest of his days begging."

Lyseira scoffed. "You're making that up."

Matthew gave her a sad smile. "Lyseira, you've spent your days in a small village, and you've been fortunate enough to have a good man for a Keeper. There are a lot of little villages, with a lot of good men in their temples. And those good men are being rooted out, one by one. The Church is reasserting its control everywhere.

"Church law is clear on the matter of miracleworking. It cannot be done without a donation except with the permission of the healer's superior."

Lyseira shook her head. *He's exaggerating. If these are the lies he's telling, it's no wonder Father Annish wants him gone.* "Father Forthin, our old Keeper, healed others for little or no donation all the time. If what you're saying is true, he should've been executed a hundred times over."

Matthew didn't respond. He let her words hang there, until they soaked through her coat and gave her a shuddering chill.

"That's one story. I have hundreds of others. All I've done is tell them. For that crime, your Keeper would run me out of town.

"On the morning of the Storm, Akir came to me. He gave me this charge. He wants people to know that the Church is not acting on His will. He loves his children. He gave the Church these miracles so that we could be spared the world's evils. But the Church has lost its way. They haven't done the will of Akir in hundreds of years."

The words were the purest form of blasphemy. It was clear, now, why he was branded a heretic. At the same time, though, his story resonated with Father Annish's rebukes the day before. *Is it possible?* she wondered.

Her reaction to this question was nearly feral. *I would wonder that? I would dare wonder that, after all my years serving Akir, after everything Father Forthin taught me? I spend three minutes with a heretic and he has me questioning everything?* Her jaw tightened. She would not be so easily undone.

"What proof do you have?" she demanded. "I have a lifetime of my own experience, and you claim that means nothing, but what proof do *you* have?"

"I was appointed a bishop of the Tribunal, Lyseira. We were charged with rooting out evil, but most of the 'evil' we turned up was poor folk who weren't tithing, or people who had wronged the

Church somehow; even those who were competing with us for land or profit. That was *before* the Storm. Since then, the Tribunal has tripled in size. I've seen the Church commit acts of such atrocity they would keep you awake at night."

Again, her brief discussion with Father Annish fit perfectly into Matthew's accusations; she shoved this realization away and fired back at him. "So you have words," she said coldly. "Just words, and you would have people turn on their Church for that?"

Matthew's face darkened. "What I have is truth." He turned away. "And I'll speak it where I please."

~ ~

Father Annish had returned a few days later. Lyseira had prepared herself for the worst, but when she told him about the conversation with Matthew, he didn't react as she expected: he thanked her for speaking to him and set her to sweeping the front entry. He never went to speak to Matthew himself; instead, he huddled in the temple like a cornered rat as Matthew spoke, day after day, with the villagers.

She'd thought about Matthew's words almost constantly for the last three weeks, but Father Annish had done nothing more to support the accusations. The man might be shallow, but no worse. His actions alone couldn't damn the entire Church. Still, the suspicion that Matthew was telling the truth had sunk into her. She couldn't shake it off.

She was eager for the man to leave, and the feeling to fade.

"I don't need this," Seth said flatly, bringing her back to the present. He set his pen down on the table and looked up at her, defiant.

She had taken advantage of her renewed access to the temple to help Seth study Church history and scripture, but it had quickly become obvious that his inability to read was holding him back. She tried to teach him some of the most basic words so that he could do some studying on his own, but it was like throwing water on a dog. He just shook it off.

Today he was practicing letters at the table. Or he had been, until now.

"You need to trust me," she said, holding back a sigh.

"I don't need to read the books. I just need to know them."

"You need to *study* them."

"Lyseira," Annish said. He was at one of the windows, peering out.

Lyseira looked over. "Yes, Father?"

His lips curled into a satisfied smile. He nodded out the window. "Look."

Four men were approaching on the northern road, leading a wagon that looked like a jail cell on wheels. The lead rider was a soldier in gleaming plate mail, his helmet winged like an angel, his steed white as a fresh snowfall. The God's Star was emblazoned on his breastplate.

"A Justicar," Lyseira breathed, watching in wonder as the holy knight rode into town. Then she saw the man behind him.

The priest rode flanked by two Preservers. His gaze was like a raptor's, watching for prey; his stance was impossibly straight on his mount's back. The symbol on his amulet was unmistakable, even at this distance. A gavel and a God's Star: the mark of the Tribunal.

"He's come," Father Annish said, his eyes glinting with vindication. "Finally, he has come."

# Chapter 3

*i. Lyseira*

Annish hustled down the hill to the road, his shoulders quaking with each bouncing step. Lyseira followed, her brother behind her.

"Bishop Marcus," Annish said, bowing deeply to the priest. Lyseira and Seth followed suit.

Marcus may have seen thirty winters; only the slightest traces of age showed in his face. His Preservers rode to either side of him, their heads shaven, each with the God's Star branded on his forehead. Like Seth they wore dun-colored traveling robes over a simple, loose outfit designed for ease of movement. Neither wore any coat or scarf despite the weather.

Marcus regarded the deacon like an owl hunting a mouse. "Your name?" he said.

"Deacon Kelar Annish, Father."

Marcus looked away. He might have been disregarding a bug. "Where is the Keeper of this church?"

"I–yes, that is me, Father," Annish stammered.

Marcus snapped his gaze back. "I was told Abbot Forthin was Keeper here."

"Abbot Forthin kept this temple for nearly thirty years," Lyseira answered, stepping forward. "But he's been dead for two months now."

Marcus flicked his eyes over her as if evaluating a threat. "Who are you?"

Annish jumped in. "She's of no consequence, Father; little more than a maid."

Lyseira fell silent, her cheeks burning.

Marcus seemed to accept this. "We received your message in Keldale. Matthew had a number of friends in the Church when he left, but their patience for his blasphemy is over. Where is he?"

Annish nodded down the road. "He's staying at the local inn, Father."

Marcus nodded, his gaze latching on to the little building just down the road from the church. "Very good." He indicated the wagon behind him. "We'll leave the jail wagon here. I've already called for a judge; he should be here in a day or two."

"What will be done with him?" Lyseira blurted. She expected the worst, but wasn't sure whether to dread or relish the answer.

Marcus glanced at her in annoyance. "Your maid doesn't know her place, Deacon." He kicked his horse into a trot toward the inn.

Lyseira turned to Annish. "What will be done with him?" she repeated. *Are they going to kill him?*

Annish shrugged. "I don't know. I imagine they'll want to administer justice in private. He was a priest; the bishop will show discretion."

Lyseira's heart burned in her chest. Her discussion with Matthew had been brief, but it had shaken her more than she cared to admit. She glanced toward the inn, then surprised herself by taking a step toward it.

Annish took her shoulder. "Don't intervene."

"I've spoken with him before; I can help them," she said. She couldn't have explained why she wanted to be at the inn when Brother Matthew was apprehended, but her nerves wouldn't let her stand aside. She had no love for the man, but some of his words had rung true, and she wasn't sure he deserved to be silenced. At the least, she felt she should know what happened to him.

"No. Go to the temple."

Lyseira looked again at the inn. The four men were dismounting. She could see the faces of some of the inn's patrons peering from the windows. Her heart was pounding.

She wrenched her shoulder away, glaring defiance at Annish. He staggered and made to lunge for her again; but Seth took a step forward, his eyes locked with the deacon's, and the man drew up short.

She started for the inn.

Annish's voice chased her. "Lyseira, this is *it!* If you go, you are *done!*"

*Done.* All her dreams, everything she had worked for.

To her horror, she stopped.

The Justicar entered the inn, Bishop Marcus and his guardians behind him. *It doesn't matter,* she tried to tell herself. *I can't change the outcome. I don't even really know what's going on.* Her dedication to the Church was too strong; it forced her to turn and march up the hill to the temple, a quiet shame simmering in her heart.

*ii. Helix*

The flour barrel was empty. Silla Tevington had just handed him an order for fourteen flapjacks, and the flour barrel was empty.

Helix spat a quiet curse and rushed through the door to the common room, looking for his boss. He emerged into a cacophony of conversation and clinking silver, the rich aromas of fried eggs and potatoes burgeoning like a fog.

"Helix!" Silla snapped from his right, exasperated. Piled plates and bowls lined her arms; each hand clutched a stack of cups three or four high. "Move!"

He mumbled an apology and stepped out of the doorway. Silla rolled her eyes at him and turned around to bump the door open with her backside.

"Where's Mellerson?" Helix said. "He's out of flour."

The server dipped her head toward the other end of the bar and disappeared into the kitchen, the door swinging lazily behind her.

Helix looked to see Mellerson just coming around the counter, carrying a stack of cups himself. "Smith!" he called over the din. "What are you doing out here? Grab these cups!"

Helix hustled over and obliged him. "You're out of flour," he said, just as a customer inquired about his potatoes.

Mellerson smiled. "Yessir, they're comin'." The patron turned doubtfully back toward his table.

The innkeeper glanced at Helix out of the corner of his eye as he made change for a silver shell. "What was that, now?"

"Flour," Helix repeated. "You're out of flour, and Silla just gave me about a thousand orders for flapjacks."

Mellerson looked up from his money changing, confused. "Outta flour?" he barked. "Can't be."

"The barrel's empty." Helix jerked his thumb vaguely toward the kitchen.

"You check in the back?"

"What back?"

Mellerson grumbled. "The back! With the salt and the like. Or the cellar; did you check the cellar?"

"The cellar's still locked," Helix said, but Mellerson wasn't listening. He was staring past him, toward the front door. Helix followed his gaze and felt his breath catch.

Brilliant sunlight framed the silhouette of a creature in the open doorway, an armored monstrosity with a pair of wicked horns jutting from its head. As the visitor stepped into the room, the door swung shut behind him. In the sudden dimness of the common room, Helix saw the monster was not a monster at all, but a knight: bristling with armor, a longsword dangling casually from his waist, a pair of angelic wings sprouting from his ornate helm.

*Justicar.* Helix had heard of them, but never seen one. They were holy knights, blessed by the Church and tasked with executing its wishes. "Blesséd *sehk,*" he muttered under his breath.

Willis Mellerson dropped the coins he had been counting and hurried to the front of the room. "Good morn, Sir," he said formally, holding out his hand. "I'm Willis Mellerson. I own the place. What can I do for you?"

The Justicar didn't answer. The door behind him opened again. A tall man entered, his head shaven bald with the God's Star branded on his forehead. He moved easily, his lean muscles rippling beneath his simple outfit like a stalking panther's. He didn't walk through the door so much as he flowed through it. His every motion radiated casual menace.

*Syntal.* The thought sent a shock of panic up his back. *Someone noticed her eyes, they must've told, they're here for Syntal. Oh, God.* He wanted to escape, to run home and warn her, but his legs had turned to water; it was all they could manage to keep him on his feet.

Behind the Preserver came a cleric with the eyes of a hawk. His gaze swept the common room in a single pass, then fixed on Mellerson. "Who are you?"

"Willis Mellerson," the innkeeper repeated, dropping his eyes.

"Is this your inn?"

"Yes, Father."

"I'm Bishop Marcus of the Tribunal. We're looking for a blind man who calls himself Brother Matthew. He would be traveling alone. Is he here?"

Helix felt an instant of relief at hearing they weren't looking for his cousin, replaced almost at once by a sudden lurch of fear for Matthew.

"He has a room." Mellerson turned to Helix. The color had drained from his face. "Have you seen him this morning, Helix?"

*Don't drag me into this.* But it was too late; Marcus's gaze had pierced him. He wanted to shrink into the wall. "I... no, not this morning."

"He normally walks around the village during the day, talking," Mellerson offered. "He should be back tonight. I could ask the patrons, see if–"

Marcus held up a hand. "That won't be needed." He lowered his voice. "The man is a warlock; he can see despite his blindness and has been spreading lies about the Church. We've come to bring him to trial; we wish him no harm. Give me a key to his room. We'll return tonight and take him then. Maybe we can spare you any embarrassment or danger to your patrons."

"Of course, Father." Mellerson produced a spare key and slid it across the counter.

Marcus collected it. "If he returns early, or if he mentions plans to leave, come tell us. We'll be at the temple."

Mellerson nodded. "Yes, Father."

Marcus held his eyes, confirming his agreement, before turning away.

~ ~

For once, Helix's thoughts were free of Minda for an entire day.

He was desperate to find Syntal, to warn her to stay in the house. Her eyes had been better lately, but she never kept her promises to him. He knew she was still reading the book, and in his heart he knew what that made her.

He was worried for Matthew, too, and couldn't shake the thoughts from his mind. The man was so friendly and matter-of-fact that it had been easy to forget the full consequences of what he was saying. Seeing the holy men in the inn that morning had been a wake-up call, though. There was a reason people didn't speak against the Church, no matter how legitimate they thought their complaints were.

He kept one eye on the common room throughout the day, hoping to catch a glimpse of Iggy or Angbar so he could ask them if they'd heard the news. Better still would be Lyseira–if anyone would know what was happening, she would. But the day dragged past without any of his friends showing their faces. Finally, an hour before sundown, Mellerson paid him and sent him home.

Outside, he stole a glance toward the temple. A jail wagon stood near the road, a stark reminder of the bishop's threats that morning. Nearby, Lyseira and Seth were grooming mounts.

It was strange, seeing Seth around town like that. Helix still wasn't used to it. The quiet young man pouring oats into a bucket was nothing like the boy Helix remembered. He wanted to go over and say hello, to pick Lyseira's brain about the village's visitors, but he was in a hurry to reach Syntal. And besides, a Preserver was standing on the steps–not the same one Helix had seen at the inn, which meant Marcus had at least two with him. This thought was all Helix needed to turn toward home.

He stole down a side road and cut through Old Maid Betsy's yard. A few quick turns later and he was nearly home. That was when he saw Matthew coming up the road.

His heart leapt into his throat, and his muscles froze.

*I've got to warn him.*

*I can't get involved.*

*I can't just let him stumble into this; he doesn't even know they're here.*

*I need to get home and talk to Syntal.*

He threw a furtive glance around him. It was dinnertime, and the road was nearly empty; Sam Mockling was puttering in his garden, but the old man's hearing wasn't what it used to be. Helix jogged over to Matthew, his brain still warring with itself, expecting at any minute to hear a sudden shout of accusation from the Justicar.

"Matthew," he hissed.

Matthew cocked his head. "Helix! Old Mellers let you out early tonight?"

"Listen to me," Helix pressed, trying to keep his voice low. He threw another glance behind him. He felt like he was trying to steal across the road naked. "You can't go back. There's some priest here from the Tribunal. He's a *bishop*, Matthew. They're looking for you."

"Marcus is here?"

"Marcus, yeah, that was it–and he has a Justicar with him, and Preservers. They came in and asked for you. Mellers gave them a key to your room. You've got to get out of here."

Matthew sobered. A sudden wind came up, making his robe suck against his legs; something about it made him look impossibly frail. He said nothing.

"Matthew?" Helix finally prompted.

"Did you give that letter to your dad?" Matthew asked.

Helix blinked. "What? The letter?" Helix shook his head. "Did you hear what I said?"

"Yes, Helix, I heard you. Did you hear me?"

"I–" The truth was, he'd completely forgotten about Matthew's letter, but that had nothing to do with anything. "My dad isn't heading up to Keldale any time soon. I was wrong about that." He looked around again. *If they catch me talking to him...* "Look, I'll handle the letter, *m'sai?* But you–"

"I can take care of myself. I need you to take care of that letter."

"*M'sai,*" Helix agreed, annoyed.

Matthew grabbed his shoulder. "No. Not *'m'sai.'* Promise me." His voice trembled with need.

"*M'sai,*" Helix breathed. "I promise."

Matthew's grip on his shoulder was unrelenting. Finally, he let him go and pushed past, into the gathering wind. "Get home," he said, feeling his way forward.

"And stay inside tonight."

~ ~

He took the porch steps in two quick jumps and burst through the front door like a gale. Mom started, nearly dropping the pot of stew she was pulling from the wood stove.

"Sweet Akir," she accused. "What *rev'naas* got into you?"

"Sorry. I just–here." He dug into his pockets and set his pay on the table. "Is Syn here?"

"Should be, I just heard her," Mom said. "Are you well?"

"Yeah," Helix said. He forced himself to slow, to give his mother a grin and a kiss on the cheek. "Yeah, sorry. Just excited about something."

Mom rolled her eyes. "Dinner's almost ready."

"*M'sai.*" Helix hurried past her and rapped on Syntal's door. "Coz," he said.

No answer. He knocked again. "*Syn!*"

"What?" She sounded sleepy. Lately, she always sounded sleepy.

"Let me in," he said, irritated.

"I'm trying to nap," she answered.

"It's almost dinner. Mom'll get you up anyway. C'mon."

She opened the door. Her hair, jet black and gleaming when it was clean, was a rat's nest on her shoulders. She glanced away, but not before he caught a glimpse of her eyes, brilliant as emeralds.

His heart clenched.

"Syn," he breathed. "Damn it." He slipped in, shutting the door behind him. *That's it,* he wanted to demand. *Tell me what in Hel is going on.* Instead, he took a breath and decided on another tack.

"There's a bishop from the Tribunal here. He's looking for a warlock." She whirled toward him, her eyes wide. *Oh, do I finally have your attention?* "He has two Preservers and a Justicar with him. If any of them see you like that..."

"It's not that noticeable," Syn protested. "Mom and Dad have never said anything."

"Mom and Dad are idiots," Helix threw back. "They wouldn't see it if it bit them–"

He stopped. This was an old song and dance. It had never gotten them anywhere. "Syn, please. The *Tribunal* is *here."* The words echoed in the room like a thunderclap.

She covered her mouth and sank onto her bed. Her right hand lurched to her ring, twisting it like a compulsion. "*Sehk,*" she breathed.

"Will you please tell me what's going on?" When she didn't answer, he went on: "It's the book, isn't it? Are you still keeping it under the porch?"

She shook her head.

"How did you even get it open? It busted one of Dad's best shears."

She was staring at the floor, her hand still over her mouth. Her face had gone white.

"Syntal, damn it, c'mon. You *have* to talk to me."

"It's a book of spells," she said. "Like in the stories. *M'sai*?" She drew a shuddering breath; her thin frame shook with it. "They're real. They work."

The room could've lurched to the side, threatening to spill him to the floor. He put a hand to the wall, trying to keep his feet.

He'd suspected for months now, but that didn't make the news land any softer.

"How...?" The word tumbled off his tongue and fell to its death. "Well, we have to get rid of it. Is it still under the porch?"

"No." She still wasn't looking at him. "It's hidden. They won't find it."

"They can work miracles, Syntal. Hunting witches is all they do. They can find it. We have to... I don't know, burn it, or something. We can't let them–"

Then, finally, she looked at him. "What are you gonna do?"

"That's what I'm talking about right now. The book–"

"No," she snapped. "You. Are you gonna tell them? Are you gonna tell Mom and Dad?"

There was fear in her eyes, boiling behind that brilliant emerald like a volcano. Panic pulsed in a vein at her neck.

He could feel his jaw working uselessly. He closed it, drew a deep breath through his nose.

"*Sehk,* Syntal," he finally managed. "No. *M'sai?* I won't tell anyone. Mom and Dad will figure it out on their own, and the bishop..." He shook his head. "Look, I'm sorry I scared you, but he's not here looking for you. He's after Brother Matthew. You just... you *have* to stop this. Mom and Dad might be able to pretend nothing's wrong, but this Bishop Marcus... you didn't see him. He's sharp. He won't miss it."

Syntal was nodding. "*M'sai.*"

"Where is the book?"

She shook her head again and made for the door. Mom was calling them for dinner.

~ ~

Night fell clear and cold. Moonlight streamed in through his bedroom window, pooling softly on his floor. He lay still on his bed, but his mind was churning.

Syntal had avoided him after dinner. His parents, as usual, had either not noticed her eyes or chosen not to say anything. Fine. She could try to keep away from him, but he still didn't think she truly understood the danger she was in.

*Witchcraft?* He shook his head. Father Forthin told them about new witches every year, always caught by the Tribunal and put to death. *How could she be so stupid?*

If the book had her spells in it, and she wouldn't get rid of it herself, then he'd take care of it for her.

He threw off the covers and got out of bed. There were only a few places she could be keeping the thing. She'd said it wasn't under the porch, but that had been their secret hiding place since they were little. He'd check there first. He lit the lantern perched atop his dresser, then dug through the top drawer for a warmer shirt.

The lantern's wavering light fell across the letter Matthew had given him three weeks ago.

Helix stopped, still clutching the new shirt, as he stared at the letter. Matthew's words echoed in his thoughts. *Promise me.*

Why had Matthew been so obsessed with it? Helix had just told him the Tribunal was here, that there was a bishop looking for him, and his first reaction had been to ask about the letter.

Had he heeded Helix's warning, and gotten out of the village? Or had he gone back to the inn? And if he had, where was he now?

His stomach suddenly twisted like he was going to be sick. Normally, he'd not spare a second thought for the Church or its witch hunters, but Matthew was not a bad person. He didn't deserve mistreatment. And if even half of what he'd said about the Church in the last three weeks was true...

"I did everything I could," he muttered to the empty room. *I warned him, which could've gotten me killed. I could've just crossed the road and ignored him.*

*I did everything I could.*

He pulled on the new shirt and started for the door. Then, before he could think better of it, he turned back and ripped the letter open.

The script was crisp and brief.

*Lorna, my love -*

*You were right. I won't be able to get back this time. Akir is bringing me home. I miss you. You have no idea how much, but there is no other way. Give the children kisses for me.*

*I love you.*

*I'm sorry.*

He read it again, then a third time. It was a farewell, but why? Did Matthew think he was going to die? Did he know the Tribunal was coming? If so, why wouldn't he run?

Helix dug at his temples. There was too much going on, too many confusing things happening at once. He couldn't make sense of it. But if the Tribunal wanted Matthew, then Helix was sure he didn't want them finding this note.

He wrapped it carefully in one of his seldom-worn shirts, and shoved it as far back in the drawer as he could. He grabbed the lantern, but as he turned for the door, his eye caught on the window.

There was someone running through his backyard.

Helix's breath froze. He sneaked to the window and crouched, his heart racing.

The figure was nearly amorphous in the dim moonlight, flitting through the night like a shadow. Helix squinted into the dark. *Robes*. His pulse quickened further. *And a walking staff.*

His eyes widened. *Brother Matthew*. He was sure of it now: the man was running west, toward the road.

Helix felt a flood of relief. *He listened. I don't know why he's only leaving now, but at least he listened.* He pressed his face to the cold window, craning to either direction, looking for anyone else who might've seen him.

Then a horse and rider burst around the corner of the house, streaking toward the blind man like a javelin.

Helix clutched the window frame. Matthew couldn't see his pursuer. He might not even know he was there.

*I have to warn him.*

*I can't get involved!*

*He's going to get run down!*

"Matthew!" Helix screamed. "Behind you!"

Matthew stumbled to a halt and turned around. The rider hurtled toward him, bent low to his horse's neck.

Helix hurled his bedroom door open and dashed through the house, the lantern spraying wild light across the walls. Somewhere behind him Syntal called his name, her voice thick with sleep.

He burst out the front door like a racehorse, felt the cold air shatter over him as if he'd dived into a lake. He ran to the back of his house in a silence broken only by the mad pumping of his feet and the thunder of his breath.

As he rounded the corner he saw the horse's silhouette come down from a rearing stand, its hooves thrashing. Beneath it, the robed figure crumpled to the ground.

"*Matthew!*" Helix screamed again, his throat raw from the cold. He kept running, hoping to reach them in time, but the two figures were well across the field. He would never make it.

The horseman's shadow leapt to the ground. A weapon appeared in his hand; in the near darkness, it seemed summoned by magic. The figure crossed the distance to the fallen cripple in two long strides, the weapon twirling easily in his hands. Matthew scrambled to his hands and knees, sweeping the ground for his staff.

The figure impaled him.

The blind man pitched forward, collapsing like a gutted fish. A thick, liquid cry gurgled out of him.

His murderer might have glanced at Helix; in the darkness it was impossible to tell. Then he climbed onto his horse, his sword still jutting from the blind man's body.

Numb with horror, the smith's son kept running. Finally, he crashed to a frantic kneel.

"Matthew," Helix wheezed. The man was facedown in the dirt, his bloody fingers fumbling at the blade buried halfway into his back. He tried to say something, but produced only a thin whistle.

Helix tore the sword from Matthew's body, dropping it into the bloody grass. He rolled the man over to find blood welling from his chest like a spring.

"Oh God," Helix heard himself whimper. He was in someone else's body, watching their hands fall to Matthew's chest, slipping through the bloody mess of robes and flesh, struggling impotently to hold in the man's blood. "Oh God. Oh Akir, oh God." Suddenly, one of Matthew's hands grabbed Helix's wrist, latching onto it like a claw.

"I'm sorry." The words were garbled and wet, burbling through the blood on his lips.

"No," Helix whimpered, but he didn't know why.

A horse neighed overhead and Helix looked up dumbly, half expecting to see a second sword flash down for him. It was the rider, its horse rearing as he turned it away. In the perfect frame of the full moon, its silhouette had horns, like some demon made flesh. Then the animal's front hooves dropped to the ground, and it bore its rider into the shadows.

Distantly, Helix heard Syntal call his name.

The smith's son bent back to Matthew. He spread his fingers and pushed his palms hard against the fallen man's gushing chest, trying to stem the river of blood. Prayers babbled from his mouth like nonsense.

"Helix!" Syntal's voice again, closer this time.

*The Abbot can heal him,* he thought.

*The Abbot is dead.*

"Get a cleric," Helix said. His voice had become a wet rag. "He's dying." His voice caught on the last word and he coughed. His hands slipped away from Matthew's wound, sliding across his bloody chest, and he was mortified to see the furious pumping of blood from the wound already abating.

"Hurry!" he shrieked. As his cousin ran back toward the house, he turned again to Matthew and whispered another prayer.

Blood spattered from Matthew's mouth as his breathing slowed. Once more, he tried to speak.

"Yours now," he murmured wetly.

"Shhh," Helix said. "Help is coming. Help is coming."

The man's head flopped weakly to one side. His mouth made a black, gurgling noise that may have been his wife's name.

~ ~

When Helix heard the horses approaching, he was still staring at Matthew's body.

"He's gone," he said without turning. "You're too late."

He heard people swinging off of horses and jumping to the ground. Someone spoke in a tongue Helix had heard only a handful of times in his life, from Abbot Forthin, and the air flared with light. Suddenly, the shadow of Matthew's broken body was thrown into stark contrast: the blackness on his chest transformed into a savage mess of blood, the cold lump of his head an alabaster ruin.

Bishop Marcus knelt easily, looking at the body. His eyes flicked over the wound and the weapon, still lying in the grass. Then he pulled back Matthew's blindfold, glancing cursorily at the white eyes beneath.

"What are you doing?" Helix said, numb.

The bishop leveled his gaze at Helix, his eyes inscrutable.

Suddenly, Syntal and Helix's parents were there, Lyseira and Seth running up behind them. Lyseira stood back, her hand over her mouth and her eyes locked on Matthew in horror.

"Helix!" Mother shouted. Her voice was a pane of glass, shot through with cracks. "Are you well?" She stumbled into a kneel next to him. "What happened?"

"I would ask the same," Bishop Marcus interrupted. "Why have you done this? Matthew was a heretic, but he deserved to be judged fairly. None should make this decision but Akir."

Helix looked at the bishop, uncomprehending. The words might have been gibberish. "What?"

"Seschar! Eldon!" Marcus snapped out the names as if calling dogs to heel. As he rose to his feet, his Preservers flowed into the light.

Marcus gestured at Helix. "Take him to the temple and see that he doesn't leave. I will pray on this, and decide how to proceed in the morning."

The two men nodded curtly and turned to Helix.

"What?" Helix said again, dumbly. Matthew's lips were covered in blood; it was dried in his beard like a frozen waterfall.

"What are you doing with him?" Mother demanded.

Marcus glanced at her. "This is not your concern," he said.

"He is my *son*!" she snapped. "He didn't do anything!"

"Don't test me," Marcus said. "Akir will decide this. Now leave it be."

Helix felt the Preservers grip him under the arms, heaving him roughly to his feet. A glimmer of panic crept into his mind at last. "Wait," he heard his voice say.

*They think I did it?*

Matthew's hands were curled like claws, dug into the cold dirt.

"Wait!" Helix shouted.

His mother said, "No, you don't understand, please–!"

"*Ayen get sil tar'r,*" the bishop answered, the words slithering like vipers. "*Vor kel rushtar'r.*"

His mother crumpled to the dirt, her protest ended.

"What are you doing?" Helix demanded. The Preservers' arms were like steel bars. "*Mom!* What are you doing to her?"

Then one of them struck him in the back of the head, and there was nothing else.

# Chapter 4

## Before the Storm

*i. Helix*

Helix Smith, eight years old, dove behind a tree and prayed for his life.

*C'mon, c'mon, c'mon,* he wished, blood thundering in his ears. *Nothing here, I musta got away, just go on past, just go–*

"Behind the tree!" came a roar. He scrambled to his feet and pounded across the field. His three hunters–taller, stronger, twice his age or older–leapt to the chase like lions closing on a kill.

The prairie grass flapped against his waist and dragged at his heels. He glimpsed a flicker of wood beneath the greenery ahead, and jumped the camouflaged log at the last possible instant. A queasy image of what had almost been–*tumbling to the ground, breaking my ankle, screaming for help as they fall on me like a pack of dogs*–flickered through his head like lightning at midnight. Then he ducked his head and bore down, exorcising his thoughts of everything except tearing toward the growing line of houses ahead.

A startled cry, a muffled thud, and he chanced a look back to see the blond one smashing face-first into the grass, a titan toppled by an invisible log. *Dumb* sehk*!* he exulted. Then he was around the corner, the bullies out of sight.

He darted from house to house, stealing glances behind him. Just as he reached his house, his pursuers burst onto the road four houses back, their faces glowing with rage beneath the hair matted to their scalps. The blond pointed at him and shouted something irrelevant; the other two had already exploded into a renewed chase.

Helix ducked around the corner, wheezing, his momentary victory forgotten. He couldn't outrun them. He couldn't fight. He couldn't even go in his house–they would chase him in.

*So hide.*

His house had a porch, one of the few in the village that did, and where it met the ground at the back corner stood an old, loose board. Helix bounded to it, worked it loose, and slipped through the narrow passage it left behind. Cool darkness washed over him. He leaned the board back into place, hands trembling, then retreated to the middle of the quiet space and peered upward as the porch slats striped his face with sunlight.

It was a huge risk, going beneath the porch. No one knew about it, not Mom and Dad, not his sister Beth, not even Syntal. He didn't want anyone learning it was here.

But he didn't want to get the piss beaten out of him either.

*Here they come.* He heard them pounding up the road before he saw them, panting but not winded, shouting to each other as if trying to corner a rabbit.

"I saw him over here!" That was Esiah, the blond one, the idiot that had tripped on the log. "He's probably behind the houses again, I'll run back and check!"

"He ain't runnin', you stupid cocksuck." Rake's voice, eloquent as always. Helix could imagine his face, even if he couldn't see it: strings of greasy, red hair plastered around a sneer of disdain, a hooked, broken nose that had never set right. Helix himself had red hair, with a shock of freckles to match, and he hated Rake for making everyone believe that all redheads were as devilish as he was. "He ain't runnin'. He's *hidin'.*"

"Yeah." The third voice was deeper, *monstrous,* like some lumbering beast set loose from the depths. Baler's heavy baritone made Helix's dad's voice sound like a chorus of fairies. His single syllable snapped the others into silence.

The porch stairs creaked. Baler's throaty rumble came again. "He went inside, I bet. Probably hopin' Beth's here to save him."

Snickers from the other two. "Why you let that bitch tell you what to do anyway?" Rake accused.

"She don't tell me what to do," Baler snarled, so fiercely that Helix hoped he might start beating on the other kid. But Rake muttered something–an apology, maybe–and the moment passed.

"C'mon," Baler ordered. "Nobody's home right now, except maybe him. Just don't cock up the house. If you find him, bring him out back."

Then his shadow fell across the porch, a leviathan devouring the sun. Through the porch, Helix caught a glimpse of shaggy midnight curls before all three of them disappeared into the house.

*Run back to the church,* part of his mind demanded, *now, while they're inside. This is your chance. Get out and run.*

But he stayed where he was. The cramped space beneath the

porch was damp and dark; as he caught his breath, he listened to the secret whispers of spiders and pillbugs. Inside the house, doors banged and walls rattled as the boys tried to flush him out. Not for the first time, he wondered how in the name of God his sister could possibly have any interest in a stupid brute like Ellic Baler.

"Gone," Esiah said finally when the three of them emerged back on the porch. "I told you he ran. He's probably halfway to the church by now."

"That's fine," Baler rumbled. "I got other *sehk* to do today."

"'Fine'?" Rake challenged. "You ain't the one he spit on!"

*"I got other* sehk *to do today,"* Baler repeated. "It's your own God damned fault you got spit on. Any idiot could've seen him up in that tree. Me and Esiah both did."

"Yeah," Esiah concurred.

"Pf." Rake hawked a gob of spit onto the porch. As it leaked between the slats, Helix stepped carefully sideways to avoid it. "We meetin' by the lake later, then?"

"Piss on the lake," Esiah said, milking the chance to put Rake down. "I want to go back to the tree fort."

"Akir, you're an idiot!" Rake seethed. "What in Hel do you think I was talking about?"

"You said 'by the lake'. The tree fort ain't by the lake, it's in the woods."

"Akir," Rake swore again. "Yes, it's in the woods *by the lake*. How *sehking* stupid are you?"

"Shut up," Baler said flatly. "And quit calling it a tree fort. You sound like a couple of babies. I told you, it's a *garrison.*

"But not until tonight. After dinnertime, like. And remember what I said: you go out there without me, and I'll *sehking* kill you."

They stomped down the stairs, Rake and Esiah still arguing. Helix waited, not daring to believe his fortune, as their voices faded; then he waited some more, just to be safe.

But finally, in the murk beneath the porch, he broke into a giddy grin. *Oh, man,* he reveled, *oh man, oh man.*

He had spat on Rake... and *gotten away with it.*

*I gotta tell Syntal and Seth*, he thought as he lifted the loose board out and slipped, blinking, back into the sunlight. His friends had been near the church when he'd gone home for a quick drink from the well; hopefully, they were still there. *Angbar will piss himself laughing.* He replaced the old slat of wood, then, on a lark, kissed it. It had saved his life again.

High with glee, he flew around the front corner and collided with someone coming the other way–someone who grabbed his shoulders and heaved him backwards, cracking his head against the porch.

"Back already?" Baler marveled. "You're even dumber than I thought."

*ii. Angbar*

*You know, I just remembered something my mom said I had to do today. If I don't get it done, I'm really gonna be in big trouble.* Maybe accompanied by wide, innocent eyes, a serious nod?

Eh.

*Sorry Lys, I'm not feeling well. I better go back home and lie down.* More plausible, at least, but would she even fall for it? Maybe she was only seven, but she was sharper than most of the adults in Southlight.

*Lys, I changed my mind. I'm gonna head home. The truth is, I'm scared to death of that church, and it always feels like everyone there hates me–The Abbot most of all.*

Ah, yes. The direct approach.

Angbar frowned. He wasn't a big believer in the direct approach.

*Rev'naas* take all! She was two years younger than he was! How had he let her talk him into this?

It had started innocently enough, with her asking why he and his family never came to church. He'd even told the truth, more or less: because they were *Bahiri.* Northlanders. *Infidels,* the back of his mind offered, and while he didn't know exactly what the word meant, he'd heard it whispered behind his back often enough to guess.

Lyseira said that was fishguts. Having darker skin was no reason to skip church. Akir was *God*–why would He care if His people were brown, purple, or polka dot?

The thought of polka-dotted people had made Angbar laugh, so when Lyseira had suggested that he come to church with her, just to meet The Abbot and look around, he'd agreed.

He hadn't realized she was talking about *this afternoon.*

The road drew shorter, the church looming on the hill drew closer, and Angbar sighed. It was *Blessday,* for the love of winter, and a gorgeous one: not blistering with heat like last weekend, nor raining like the one before. *Church?* he thought incredulously. *We should be going to the* lake.

He considered this, kicked it around, stared at the back of Lyseira's bushy, brown-haired head and weighed its chances. *The lake.*

*Definitely.*

"Hey, Lys!" Angbar exclaimed, as if he'd just learned why the sky was blue. "You know where we should go today? The lake!"

She whirled toward him, grinning, those striking grey eyes of hers glittering, and he felt a spark of hope.

"You mean after we leave church?"

The spark flickered and died.

"Yeah, that sounds like fun! Maybe Helix and Syntal can even come with!" Her smile faltered. "But... we probably won't have time today. We'll be at the church for at least a few hours. By then it'll be getting a little late to head out to Pinewood."

She resumed their grim march toward the church on the hill. Angbar sighed. Maybe he could feign sickness after all. He'd never had redwarts. He could say he was coming down with those. That should scare her off, at least.

"Oooooh!" Lyseira suddenly squealed, her Dawnday dress fluttering as she bounced in the road. "I can't wait! You promise you've never been to church, Angbar?" She had turned back again, beaming at him.

Her excitement was contagious. He realized he was returning her smile, and fought to smother it. "Nope."

Lyseira giggled and bounced again–even *clapped.*

"Um... is that a good thing?" Angbar asked.

"No! Of course not!"

"Then why are you so happy?"

"Because I get to bring you! If I want to be a priestess, I need to convert a heathen." She screwed up her face, ticked off the other requirements on her fingers. "And learn First Tongue, and do a miracle. And do some other stuff, but they're easy." She waved them off. "I learned my alphabet already, and I know Akir will let me work a miracle when the time is right."

"Oh." Angbar tried again. "I'm just... you know, it's so nice... maybe today's not a good day for it."

"No, Angbar, you need to go today! Do you know what happens if you die without going to church?"

Angbar nodded, wearily. "Yeah. You told me–"

"You wind up in Hel! The Seven Sacred Principles say you have to go to church to live a holy life, or your *rev'naas* will take over your soul."

Angbar sighed, shifting from foot to foot. "I don't know, I've never been to church, but I feel fine." *Wait!* "I mean, actually…" He coughed experimentally. "I don't feel so good. I think I should go home and lie down. I think I have redwarts."

Lyseira's eyes lit with excitement as she grabbed his hand. "Then you *have* to come to church! I've seen the Abbot work miracles before – I bet he can ask Akir to make you feel better!" Thrilled by this prospect, Lyseira pulled Angbar along with renewed vigor. "Come on, come on, we're almost there!"

*Crap.*

Angbar's mind churned through new excuses as they covered the last few steps to the church, climbed its cracked, stone steps, and made the porch. He came up with nothing. Lyseira stepped reverently to the door, glancing back to be certain Angbar was still there. He sighed, resigning himself to his fate, as she reached for the door handle.

"Ha! Killed ya!" a boy cried from behind the porch rail.

"You did not, I didn't even feel anything!" This from an indignant but giggling girl.

"I did too, I stabbed you right..." A pause, punctuated by more yelping laughter. "There."

"Did not!"

Angbar ran to the side of the porch. Lyseira glared at him, her hand nearly over her head, grasping the church's doorknob. "Hey!

Are you still coming?"

Angbar ignored her. He knew those giggles. "Syntal! I thought you were at Helix's place!" The word *Helix's* was a mouthful of mushy sibilants, but he was always pleased with himself when he managed them.

Syntal was on the ground, wriggling as she tried to get up, but Seth ruddy and barefoot–had a long stick jabbed into her breastbone. "Angbar!" he said, grinning, then indicated his fallen prey with a tilt of his head. "Ain't she dead? Look, I stabbed her!"

With a squeal and a fresh round of laughter, Syntal rolled over, jerking the stick out of the boy's hand and scrambling to her feet. She pointed an accusation, green eyes dancing against the frame of her raven hair. "Nope! You're gonna be the worst pazerver ever, Seth!" She launched past him in a wild zigzag.

"You take it back!" Seth demanded as he gave chase.

"Run, Syn!" Angbar shouted, tearing down the stairs toward Seth.

Lyseira was outraged. "Hey! *Angbar!*"

"You'll never get away!" Seth cried, bare feet pounding through the grass. "Every step you take only means I'll kill you more!"

"*Everybody stop!*" Lyseira shrieked.

Everybody did.

"Kiir, Lyseira," Seth muttered. "I wasn't *really* gonna kill her."

"Don't use God's name in vain!" she retorted from the top of the stairs.

"I didn't, I said 'kiir'."

"And that comes from *A*-kir and it's just as bad as saying His name. And I don't care if you play with Syntal, but *I* was playing with Angbar!"

Seth shrugged. "*M'sai.* So play. What's the big deal?"

*I'd rather play with you lot,* Angbar wanted to say, but Syntal saved him the trouble. "Oh!" she said, panting. "What were you gonna play?"

"Well..." Lyseira furrowed her brows, and Angbar chuckled. *Even she can't say visiting church is playing.* "We were gonna visit The Abbot. Angbar was gonna get censure and stop being a heathen."

*Whoa. Censure?* Angbar's friend Helix *hated* censure. He'd told Angbar about it before. You had to sit, and tell The Abbot everything you'd done wrong, and then he gave you punishments. The punishments were worse if you left anything out on purpose, or if you hadn't seen him for censure in a long time.

Since Angbar had never been in for censure at all, he'd probably have to cut off a foot or something.

"Uh... you never said anything about that, Lys," he said.

"How else could you start living a holy life, Angbar?" She might have been explaining that the sun set in the west. "Oh!" She brightened. "You lot could come too!"

Seth recoiled. "To *church?*" He blew a raspberry.

Syntal stared at the grass.

"You don't want to?"

Angbar marveled. *She looks honestly confused.* "Lys, come on," he wheedled, sensing an opportunity. "Syntal's a guest. She's only visiting Southlight for the summer. Shouldn't we do what *she* wants to do?"

Lyseira glanced back at the church, her eyes earnest. "But–"

"The church isn't going anywhere," Angbar pressed. "I promise!"

"We were just about to go back and look for Helix," Syntal said. "He was here before, but he went home for a drink and hasn't come back yet."

Seth dropped to the ground and started picking at a scab on his knee. "Think he ran into Baler? I saw him around there this morning, lookin' for Beth."

"He's not supposed to come by there," Lyseira said. "I heard his mom say it."

"Think he cares about that?" Seth spat on a caterpillar making its way across the grass. As if this had triggered a thought, he peered back at Angbar. "He'd beat you especial, I bet. Baler'd love beatin' up a nog."

Lyseira scowled. "Seth! It's not nice to call Angbar a nog!"

"But he *is* a nog," Seth replied, perplexed.

Angbar shrugged. He'd been called worse. "C'mon, Baler wouldn't do nothin' to Helix. He likes his sister and all."

Lyseira's frown evaporated, replaced by a silly grin. "Oooooooo," she sing-songed. "Baaaaaaler and Beeeeethany, foreeeeeeeever."

Syntal looked worried. "I don't think so–don't you remember last summer when Baler almost beat him up right in front of her?"

Seth shot Syntal a withering glare. "You don't know nothin'. Angbar's right. He won't do nothin' to Helix. ‘Sides, I'm gonna bring my stick." Seth hefted the shaft of wood he'd pinned Syntal with earlier.

Syntal snorted. "Ooh, Seth has a stick. You're so stupid, Seth." Seth stuck out his tongue.

At some point during this exchange, they had started walking down the road. The threat of the church fell away behind them. Angbar drew a deep, happy breath as he listened to Seth and Syntal bicker.

*Now* it felt like a Blessday. No school, no chores, and heading *away* from that god-awful church.

"You think Baler's gonna be afraid of some stick?" Syntal needled.

"No, he's gonna be afraid of *me!*" Seth mustered a grimace. "If he tries sumthin'–POW! –I beat him in the head!" He flailed the stick, repelling a wave of invisible attackers. "And if he's still comin'–CRACK! –I rip out his guts!" Seth leapt and cracked his weapon against a nearby tree. With a splintering crunch, the stick split in half.

Angbar chortled. "You can't hit anyone with it now! It's too short!" Syntal giggled with him.

Seth regarded the broken stick with dismay, then thrust it aloft. "Now I have a spear! I'll *stab* him!"

"You better not," Lyseira chimed in. "I'll tell your mom."

~ ~

Helix's place was on the far side of the village from the temple. As the hike dragged on, Angbar's mind wandered, as it often did. *We* should *go to the lake though. I feel like a swim. We could play pirates. Seth is hysterical at pirates, and we could make Lyseira walk the plank.* In the distance, the little house with the attached smithy finally came into view. *I wonder how we could make a plank though. Maybe there would be a stick big enough in Pinewood.*

"Hey, what... what's all that?" Lyseira asked, pointing at a churning cloud of dust in the road.

Seth peered ahead. His eyes lit up. "A fight!" he cried, and burst into a mad run, broken stick pumping as he tore down the road. Angbar gave chase at once, craning to get a good view; over the boy's bouncing shoulder he saw flailing punches and a head slamming into the dirt, caught flashes of red hair and freckles.

*Helix!* A sudden surge of allegiance made him redouble his pace. No one would beat up his friend and get away with it! They'd be sorry, whoever they were, Seth would help for sure and maybe even Syntal, they'd outnumber him four to one and then he'd have to–

*Oh no.* The strength went out of Angbar's stride as he made out Helix's rival: a tower of lanky muscle piled beneath a pair of broad shoulders, with a boar's jutting jaw and the sloped forehead of an ogre. Angbar could stand on Lyseira's shoulders and barely reach this monster's shaggy crown.

Baler.

His bravado bled away as fast as it had come on; his run dropped into a brisk trot that slowed to a walk. He was suddenly in no hurry to reach the fight. *Baler? I mean, if it was anyone else... but* Baler*?*

Helix had somehow gotten the monster to his hands and knees and was now straddling him, smashing his fist repeatedly between the larger boy's shoulders. Unfazed, Baler rolled to the side, heaving Helix hard on to his back. Helix made a great whooping sound, as if all the air in Southlight had suddenly disappeared, and fumbled at the dirt as he fought for breath.

Baler climbed to his feet, locked eyes on the smaller boy, reared back for a kick–and Seth was on him, letting out a great whoop of his own. He whacked his spear across Baler's back. The stick fairly exploded, hailing the older boy with splinters as he pitched into the road.

The attack tripped something in Angbar–some sense of shame or loyalty–and he broke into another run, racing to help Helix to his feet while Baler was still down. Roaring, Seth hurled himself at the bully, but Baler jumped aside and caught the charge with his foot. Seth hurtled through the air like a tossed cat.

More surprised than harmed, Baler regained his feet. He backed to the edge of the road to face all five of them at once, his sunken eyes flashing murder.

"These your friends come to save you, Smith? A runt, a filthy nog, and some little girls?"

Syntal licked her lips and took a few steps back as Lyseira marched up to the bully.

"*You're* in lots of trouble!" Lyseira barked, jabbing an accusing finger upward. *Like a mouse challenging a bulldog,* Angbar winced. But Hel, it was more courage than he had. "I *know* you're not supposed to come here! I heard your mom *say* it!"

Baler sneered. "Get out of my face."

His defiance only enraged the girl. "I heard her! She said to stay away unless you were going to see one of your friends! And *we* aren't your friends! I'm gonna tell your mom you're here!"

Baler snorted. "Go ahead, she don't care. Hel, she already knows I'm here."

Lyseira's jaw dropped, scandalized at the older boy's casual curse. Then she drew herself up, eyes flickering with triumph. "Fine then," she snapped, "I'll tell *my* mom you're here." As Baler paled, she turned smartly and began running toward home, just across the road.

"Lys, wait for me!" Syntal yelled, sprinting after her.

"Let's see you take all three of us, Baler!" Seth challenged. He had clambered to his feet, his hands balled into fists.

Helix's freckles were streaked with dirt and blood, and a nasty split bulged on his lip, but at Seth's words he nodded.

*Nuts. Both of them.* Angbar wondered if he wouldn't have been better off at the church with Lyseira after all. *Except that if The* Abbot *had decided to beat me up, I doubt Seth would've been there to help.* He got a sudden image of Seth whacking the Abbot in the back with his stick, the old man flailing helplessly as he toppled forward, and chuckled despite himself.

Baler glared. "Sumthin' funny, nog?"

"Don't call him a nog!" Seth shouted.

"Nothin'," Angbar said, shaking his head. He chuckled again, somewhat frantically. It was a bad habit, one that had annoyed his parents for years, but he couldn't help himself. It happened when he was nervous–and nobody made him more nervous than Ellic Baler.

Baler glanced up and down the road, saw no one, and pulled a knife. Angbar's breath caught in his throat.

"Sometime when you ain't lookin', nog," he leered, "I'll give you something to laugh about."

"You have to get past us," Seth retorted, like he was acting a part in some drama play. *Seth, hush!* Angbar wanted to say. *Can't you see he has a* knife*?*

"Ellic Baler!" Lyseira's mother burst out her front door, furiously drying her hands on her apron. "Your mother told you to stay away from here!" Syntal and Lyseira jogged along in her wake.

The knife disappeared. "She said I could come see my friends, Missus Rulano," Baler yelled to her.

Corla Rulano came to a halt. She was a petite woman, barely as tall as the boy, but her flashing eyes granted her stature beyond her frame. Those eyes darkened upon hearing Baler's words, and the woman gathered such an air of authority about her that she could have towered to the heavens.

"Don't you give me that tripe, Ellic. After the stunts you've pulled, you've no friends in the Smith house."

"That ain't true, Missus Rulano," Baler replied, suddenly a model of courtesy. "I came to see Beth. We was gonna take a walk in the woods."

"'We *were going to,*'" she corrected him. Behind her, Lyseira glowed. "That girl has no interest in a bully like you. Kevric and Bella are good folk and raised a better daughter than that."

"We gone out together before, Missus," Baler argued. From her safe position behind Lyseira's mother, Syntal rolled her eyes. Lyseira stuck out her tongue at Baler, triggering another round of nervous giggling from Angbar, which he wrestled down as if it were a thrashing bear.

Lyseira's mom stared daggers, out of patience. "Enough. You must think me a fool. She's not even here; she's gone with her father up to Coram for supplies. But that doesn't matter. You've no call to come beating up on Helix here. You're twice his size."

"He jumped me!" Helix shouted, but Corla snapped her head toward him and raised a finger, and he stopped.

"Now I don't know why your mother hasn't got enough sense to keep you in your place," she said, turning back to Baler, "but if I catch you messing with these kids one more time, I'll take you to The Abbot myself. Now get gone or I'll think better of it and take you up there now."

Angbar had to admit, the idea of returning to church to see Baler get censure was far more appealing than going there for his own.

Baler met her stare, defiant, but it didn't last. "If she ain't home I don't want to be here anyhow," he muttered as he turned away and started down the road.

Lyseira's mom shook her head and let out a sharp sigh, then turned to the children. Her eyes fixed on Helix at once. "Helix, you poor dear," she fussed, kneeling. "Let me see your face. Where is your mother?"

"She's at Iggy's place, ma'am," Helix said as he tilted his face up.

"Come on with me, then. Lyseira, run and pull some water for this cut. We may have to take you up to The Abbot," she said to Helix, wincing at the gash on his bottom lip. "Syntal, run down to the Ardenfell's farm and let Bella know you're here and what happened. Tell her Helix is at our house–"

"OW!" Helix yelped.

"On second thought, tell her we're heading up to the church first," Corla corrected. "Come along, Master Smith."

*iii. Helix*

The worst part of getting into the fight with Baler, Helix thought, was being forced to go to the temple afterward. Every Dawnday he came to this place with his family, kept his head low, and counted the minutes until he could get out.

Now he sat on the altar's worn, velvet-covered steps in the rear of the little building. Silence stagnated in every inch of the room. Looming windows sliced into the walls, letting the light in only as towering panes of dancing dust. Between these obscure boundaries the endless rows of pews languished in murk.

Abbot Forthin knelt next to him, his dingy cleric's robe rustling as he applied a wet cloth to the cuts on Helix's lower lip. The old man's hand trembled and his unkempt white hair bobbed absurdly as he peered into Helix's eyes.

"You say it was Ellic Baler that did this?" The Abbot asked Lyseira's mom in his grating, old man voice. It echoed dully off the stone walls, an intruder to the temple's punishing stillness that was quickly quelled.

"It was!" Seth answered, jumping to his feet from the steps next to Helix. "He was–"

"Hush, child!" the Abbot returned, his face sour. "I did not speak to you."

"It was," Lyseira's mother answered. "Saw him myself, Father. That boy and his little gang of thugs are the worst bullies I've known since before I was married."

The Abbot nodded, then put his hand on his knee and winced as he straightened up. Missus Rulano hurried over to give him a hand.

"He will survive." As The Abbot gained his feet, Helix suppressed a sigh of relief. The old man's rheumy eyes and rotting breath made his skin crawl. "It's a nasty cut, but it will mend."

"You're not going to... pray over it, father?"

Forthin looked at Lyseira's mother. "Unless I'm mistaken, you don't need to be making any extra donations to the Church just at the moment, Corla. Surely you agree."

Corla bit her lower lip and glanced at Helix. She caught him feeling at the cut with his tongue and wincing. "No," she said. "I suppose I don't."

Abbot Forthin searched her eyes. "Then again," he murmured, "Bishop Jelhennar hasn't come by to check on the coffers in some time. The only one who would know would be Akir, and if you won't mention it to the bishop, I'm sure neither will He."

Lyseira's mom gave him a tight smile. "I know the Smiths would appreciate it, Father."

Forthin turned to Helix and held out his hand. "Come on, son. Stand here next to me."

"You're gonna heal it?" Helix asked. He'd seen The Abbot work miracles of healing before–once, when he was little, Beth had broken her ankle–but had never been healed himself.

The Abbot's expression soured, as if the question offended him. He nodded impatiently and beckoned with his trembling hand.

*That's all right,* Helix was tempted to say. *It doesn't hurt that bad.* Anything, really, to avoid having to getting so close to the old man again. But he didn't want to talk back to Lyseira's mom, let alone the priest, so he drew a deep breath and braced himself. As he approached, the cleric took his chin and tilted his head up.

"Do you have faith in Akir, child?" the Father asked. Helix nodded, looking past him at the wall, not wanting to look into those filmy eyes. The question was pointless, anyway; Helix knew there was only one acceptable answer. Things like this were exactly why church was so dull.

The Abbot kept silent until Helix glanced at him. The old man caught and held his eyes, staring with the mild disdain of a scholar examining a bug. Helix tried to meet his gaze, but it made him feel small and guilty. Finally, he squirmed and looked away, and Forthin said, "I remember last week at congregation, you were throwing pebbles at Silla Tevington."

Helix froze. He *had* thrown a few pebbles, but Silla had stuck her tongue out at him first–and besides, The Abbot hadn't even been in the chapel when it happened. How could he have known?

"Do you believe Akir wants children acting that way in his holy house?"

"No, sir," Helix offered, licking his good lip and fidgeting. *What does he want from me? Can't we just get this over with?* "I–I won't do it again, sir–Father," he finished.

The Abbot, still gripping his chin, grimaced. "See that you do not, Master Smith."

Then he spoke, his voice quiet but powerful, uttering alien words that Helix could only assume were of the First Tongue, the language of the Old Clerics. They slithered into his ears like long, dark worms, as if *they* were hearing *him*, rather than the other way around. He licked his cut again and tried to move his head, but the old cleric's eyes held him captive and the grip on his chin was unrelenting. Suddenly, he felt a burning sensation in his chin and lip, as if his wounds were being torn anew. He gasped and jerked backwards, raised his hand to his mouth – and found his bottom lip whole.

The pain disappeared as quickly as it had come. The Abbot stopped speaking, his hand still hovering where it had clenched Helix's jaw a moment before. "Akir's patience for misbehavior is finite, my son," he said. "But today He saw fit to aid you. See that you avoid Ellic Baler in the future. It's been some time since I saw you for censure, as well. I expect that will change, yes?"

His eyes wide and his hand over his lip, Helix nodded.

*iv. Syntal*

Syntal hurried up the path to the church, Lyseira at her heels. "Helix's mom was pretty mad, huh?" she said, and heard Lyseira harrumph behind her.

"Of course! Baler's always getting into trouble! The only reason he gets away with everything is 'cause his mom never punishes him."

Syntal didn't feel it was her place to comment on that, but she did know that Baler scared her. She only got to visit her cousins Helix and Beth a few times a year, and the summer visit was always her favorite–but during the past few visits, Baler had gotten steadily stronger and meaner. She loved visiting, but she didn't want to get beaten up.

"Do you think she'll punish him this time?"

Lyseira blew out a sigh that sounded just like one of her mother's. "Who knows? I hope so, but if she hasn't yet, why would she start now?"

Syntal frowned, trying to think of something to say to this, when the boys emerged, blinking, from the church.

"Did it hurt?" Angbar asked Helix in awe as they came down the front steps. "It looked like it could hurt."

"Nah. What's to hurt about it? Look, my lip's all better."

Seth grinned. "That's why the pazervers are so powerful. Even if you hurt them, a priest just heals them and then they come back for you. If you have a pazerver coming for you, you might as well just die! There's nothing you can do–*no one* can stop a pazerver!" He jumped down the last few steps and raised his fists at the approaching girls. "Wa-aaah!" he cried, battering an invisible opponent with punches before leveling an extravagant kick at nothing in particular.

Syntal flinched. Seth could be fun to play with sometimes, but he could really get carried away. Ignoring his display as she jogged up, she dutifully delivered her message. "Helix, your mom said we're supposed to wait at home until she's done at Iggy's place."

"Aw, why?" Helix whined. "That's fishguts! Baler ain't gonna come after me twice in one day!"

Syntal shrugged. It hadn't been *her* idea. "I don't know, but that's just what she said."

"Where is my mom?" Lyseira asked. "Is she still inside?"

"Yeah," Helix answered. "She said to go on ahead, she has to talk to The Abbot some more."

Lyseira's eyes widened as she saw his lip. "Helix, your cut's all better!" she squealed. "Did you get prayed on?"

"Yeah." Helix grinned and stuck out his bottom lip. "See?" he mumbled.

"I wish I could've been there!" Lyseira lamented, shielding her eyes from the sun to get a better look. "You can't even tell you got hit!"

"Well, if you and Syn have to go home," Angbar said to Helix, "can we come with? We could play over there for awhile."

"That would be fun," Syntal said. She liked Angbar. He was funny, and hardly ever teased her.

"Yeah," Angbar said. "Otherwise I'm just gonna go out to the lake by myself. I don't feel like going home yet."

"I'll come with to the lake," Seth said.

Helix scoffed. "Forget all that. I ain't done with Baler yet."

Syntal felt a spike of trepidation. *Oh, Helix, come on...* "Your mom sounded pretty serious. I don't think–"

Her cousin waved her off. "No, no, listen. Before Baler caught me, I was hiding under–" He shook his head, started again. "I was hiding, and I heard him and Rake and Esiah talking. They have a tree fort, in Pinewood somewhere. Someplace by the lake."

"Whoa," Angbar breathed. "Really? A big one?"

"I *think* so. They sounded pretty excited about it."

"In Pinewood?" Seth asked, looking southeast. Syntal followed his gaze, but all she saw was the houses of the village against the distant backdrop of Thakhan Dar, its peak lost in the clouds. She'd played in the woods with Helix and his friends last summer when she came to visit, but couldn't remember how to get there.

"We should go find it," Seth urged. "Right now."

"Seth!" Lyseira said, scandalized. "What if Baler's out there, and Rake and Esiah too?"

"But that's just it," Helix pressed. "They won't be. I heard 'em talking about how they were gonna go out there *tonight.* After sunset, like. And Baler said if either of the other two went out without him he'd kill 'em both."

Syntal's frown deepened. Was that supposed to make her like the idea more?

Helix looked at her. "What do you say, Syn?"

"I don't know," she answered, shaking her head. "Your mom..."

"Come on! If we go right now, we can probably get home before Mom even knows. She's gonna be at Iggy's all day, you know she is."

"But... why not just leave it alone, Helix? I mean, maybe if we just leave him alone, he'll–"

Seth spat. "Baler don't work that way. He probably wants to finish beating the piss out of Helix still."

Again, this didn't make Syntal feel any better about the idea.

"But if we go out to the tree fort first," Seth went on, "maybe we could... I don't know..."

*Get killed?* Syn thought to say, but Angbar was quicker. "Break it?"

An evil grin broke across Helix's face. "Yeah," he murmured.

That wicked smirk was irresistible. It had suckered Syntal into misbehaving more than once, and despite herself, she felt an answering grin break across her own face. It *would* be nice to get back at Baler. She didn't get to visit often, and every time it was always Baler-this and Baler-that; it felt like she spent more time cowering from the bully than she did playing with her cousin and his friends, sometimes.

If they could really get to the fort without running into Baler at all, and still get home before Aunt Bella...

An idea dawned on her. "We could trap it, somehow, so it would break when they go on it."

Helix's grin widened. "Now you sound like my cousin," he said, and she felt a flush of pride.

"No," Lyseira insisted. "The fifth Sacred Principle says, 'In all things, thou shalt seek the righteous path.' *Your mom,*" she said, pointing at Helix, "said you're supposed to go home. The book of Zian says that part of the Principle means obeying your parents."

Lyseira was always quoting scripture at them; it drove Syntal crazy. This time, though, she had an answer. "But the Seventh Principle says, 'Mind your brother's sin like it was your own'," Syntal rejoined. "We have to go and see if Baler is going to do anything else bad today."

"Baler ain't my brother!" Helix protested.

"Not yet, maybe," Angbar quipped.

"Never mind that," Syntal insisted. "I know my Canon too, Lyseira. You're not the only kid who listens at church, you know."

"Yeah," Seth put in.

"But, what if Baler is up there again, with his friends this time?" Lyseira pled, exasperated. "We'll *all* get beaten up then."

"Lyseira, you don't have to come with," Helix said in a consoling tone. "But if you don't, I'll tell your mom what you said last week when you fell in that mud puddle."

Lyseira's face burned. She crossed her arms as Angbar snickered. "Fine," she said tightly. "Fine, let's go."

They chatted and teased each another as they made their way through town. Syntal did her best to keep up with the banter, but she was the outsider. Helix had always been nice to her, but she didn't know his friends as well as he did. She fell silent eventually, watching the houses trail past with longer and longer stretches of empty grass between them, until she recognized the old Samson farm: a long-abandoned ruin that marked the southeast edge of the village. Something about the place, slowly crumbling beneath the sun's glare, gave her a sudden pang of homesickness.

*Dad would laugh,* she thought. *I beg him for months to let me come visit, and then my first week here I want to go back.*

With the village behind them she finally saw Pinewood, lazing in the breeze on the other side of the road. Thakhan Dar looked even taller here, brooding over the forest like a stern father. She had hoped that passing the Samson farm would help ease her longing for home, but it didn't; the unbridled wilderness, the disappearance of civilization, only made her more wistful. *It won't be long,* she imagined her mother saying. *You'll be back before you know it, and then you'll start missing Helix and badgering us to give you a brother. So enjoy it while you can.* The mental scolding helped, a bit. She drew a deep breath, and tried to put on a brave face.

Seth and Helix were first off the path, pelting toward the ragged line of trees. Helix got there first, crashing through the underbrush like a wild gorilla. Syntal raced after him, not wanting to be the last one in.

Within the wood, the murmur of the distant village faded to nothing. Faded green sunlight drifted through the tree cover like a waking dream. Only an occasional glimpse of Thakhan Dar, looming beyond the branches, confirmed she was still in the same world.

"How are we even gonna find it?" she said, picking at a burr caught in her dress. "Do you even know where it is?"

Seth pursed his lips and peered through the underbrush.

Angbar glanced at her. "Helix said it's by the lake, right?"

"Yeah," Helix muttered, ducking under a low branch. "That's where we're goin', I think. I didn't know it was so far! I never been this deep in the woods before." He squirmed. "I gotta pee." He glanced at a likely tree. "I'm gonna–" He cut off abruptly, staring.

"Ha!" he cried.

A dark clearing spread out just beyond the tree. The ground, mostly bare dirt, was littered with pine needles and fallen branches. A great oak towered from the middle of the small meadow, making the dappled light dance across the ground in time with its waving branches. A few feet up, its trunk split into three gnarled, winding boughs, each ascending in its own direction. One bore a ladder made of crude, wooden boards, leading up and along the side of the massive trunk to a hand-cut wooden ledge broad enough to support everyone.

Angbar laughed. "That's it! Look, there's a ladder on it! This is it! This is their secret hideout!"

Helix grinned and started forward, his bladder apparently forgotten. Syntal grabbed his arm.

"*Shhh!*" Suddenly, coming here seemed like the stupidest thing they could have done. "They might be up there!"

Seth ignored the warning and burst out of the tree cover. He was already up the first two rungs of the makeshift ladder when Helix broke free of Syntal's grip and bolted after him. Hanging from the side of the tree, Seth shouted back, "It seems strong enough!"

"Seth!" Syntal hissed, but the rest of the kids boiled past her and into the clearing. Syntal followed, her eyes darting around the meadow. Baler and the others weren't supposed to be here until nightfall, but she kept expecting them to appear at any second.

Seth clambered up the remaining wooden rungs, wincing once as a sliver stuck into his thumb. The diagonally-leaning ladder didn't look safe–every board wobbled as he scrambled over it–but he reached the ledge quickly enough. Gritting his teeth, he grabbed onto the available branches and pulled himself up onto the tree house floor, then grinned in victory.

"Seth!" Helix panted. The smaller boy reached down to give his friend a hand.

Syntal watched Lyseira and Angbar climb up next, but didn't follow. Constantly throwing glances from one end of the small clearing to the other, she sneaked to the tree's far side and leaned against one of the massive trunks, cringing as excited chatter rattled from the ledge above.

"Look! They got buckets up here for water 'n' stuff!" Angbar exclaimed.

"We could stay up here forever, as long as we did hunting," Seth declared matter-of-factly. "No one would find us."

"Hey." Lyseira was quieter, apprehensive. "There's some more boards here, and nails. You think they're still working on it?"

Syntal's ears pricked at a rustling from the woods. Twigs snapping, maybe? And...

Her heart leapt into her throat. *Voices.* "Helix!" she whispered.

"We should take all this stuff," Seth said.

"Pf," Angbar scoffed. "Take the nails and leave the wood. That'll leave 'em up a creek."

Lyseira was indignant. "I didn't show it to you so you could steal it."

"*Helix!*" Syntal repeated. The voices from the forest were louder now. One of them was a deep, rumbling baritone.

Finally, Angbar's head popped over the edge of the fort above her. "Syn! What are you still doing down there? You gotta see this! They have buckets, and extra wood... even a basket of apples!"

"Angbar!" Syntal hissed. "*Baler's here!*"

*v. Helix*

Helix picked up one of the nails and peered at it. "You think this is one of my dad's?" he asked Seth, who shrugged.

"No other smiths in town," he said around a mouthful of apple.

"If they've been stealin' from my dad–"

"Syntal says Baler's here!" Angbar exclaimed, a sound somewhere between a whisper and a gasp.

Helix's blood went cold.

"What? Where?"

"I don't know–down there!"

Helix took a tentative step toward the edge, crouched like a burglar, to see if he could make anything out–and froze at the sound of laughter.

"What a cocksuck," Rake said. "So he ran right into you?"

*I shoulda listened to Syn,* Helix realized. *We shoulda just gone home, but now we're trapped here, and all three of them are down there, and Lyseira's mom ain't gonna save us this time.*

He cast about for some way down. Taking the ladder was too slow. If he jumped down, he'd probably just break his ankle, plus they'd hear him. Maybe it was safest up here. If he waited until they were on the ladder, coming up, maybe he could ease over the side, and–

"What in Hel?"

Helix whipped toward the voice below, and saw Baler staring right at him. Rake and Esiah glanced up, slack-jawed.

"*Smith!*" Baler roared. "*I'm gonna* sehking *kill you!*"

"Run!" Angbar cried, breaking for the ladder. Baler and Esiah bolted beneath the ledge, while Rake leapt into the nearest gnarled bough, a sheet of red, greasy hair swinging behind him.

"Grab a board!" Seth ordered, hefting one of the loose planks. "Grab a bucket!"

Helix snapped up the basket of apples and lobbed it at Rake. The redhead turned away, wincing, as the spinning volley of fruit pelted him–then swung upwards on his branch and grabbed the next one.

Angbar recoiled from the ladder. "Baler's coming up!" he squeaked. "*Baler's coming up!*"

"Jump!" Helix screamed, his heart racing with panic. "Run!" He lurched toward the edge, ready to take his own advice, but drew up short at the sight of the ground swimming dizzily below. *It's too far. Sweet Akir, I can't jump that, I–*

Lyseira suddenly shrieked behind him, and he whirled around to see a square section of the fort's floor burst open. *A trap door?* he thought in sick horror. *I didn't even see–*

Esiah's head popped through the hole, his face contorted with rage, and Lyseira kicked the door closed, squealing. It smashed into the back of his skull and bounced back to her foot, so she kicked it again, squealing some more. He wailed in pain and fell away. The door dropped shut behind him.

At the ladder, Baler crested the ledge, swung one leg over the side, and flinched as Angbar bounced a wooden bucket off his skull. "*Sehking* nog!" he thundered. Seth swung his board down like a sledgehammer, crashing it into the monster's thigh, but Baler grunted and heaved himself upward.

Seth's follow up caught him full in the face. He plummeted backward, screaming.

"Nice, Seth!" Helix heard himself yelling, giddy, then felt the whole ledge tremble as Rake leapt from his branch and landed, snarling, right behind him. He whirled around, thought too late to duck, and saw the world explode as Rake's fist connected high on his cheek.

The blow spun him from his feet and crashed his face into the wood.

Somewhere beyond, Esiah exploded through the trap door again. Lyseira shrieked and kicked at the door, but this time he caught it on his hand and shoved back. It smashed into her shin and knocked her on her butt with a stunned shout.

Behind her, Baler's hand shot back onto the ledge. This time, it was clutching a knife.

"Lyseira!" Helix called, scrambling to his feet just in time to catch Rake's knee full in his gut. He doubled over, dropped to the floor in a sea of pain, and felt a kick blast into his back.

As Helix fought for breath, the world spinning, he saw Esiah climb through the trap door–but Angbar loomed behind him with a board just like Seth's. It caught the blond on the back of the skull, clapping his teeth together and shoving him downward with a surprised *woof.* He caught the edge, though, hanging by his fingertips–and Lyseira again slammed the door shut, this time jumping on it with both feet as she tried to jam it closed.

*"Eyeaagh!"* Esiah shrilled. Lyseira jumped back off the door like a burnt cat, horrified, and he fell away.

Helix heard him crying beneath them as Baler's other arm swung over the ledge. Seth kicked at it, knocked it loose so the monster was hanging by the hand with the knife, then hammered his board into those fingers until they spasmed and dropped away, leaving the weapon on the floor. Seth stuffed it into his waistband.

Gasping, Helix tried to lever himself to his feet, and saw Rake towering over him once more. He flinched, braced for another blow–and Seth hurtled into the monster like a bull, roaring, bearing him over the fort's back edge. Both boys disappeared.

"Seth!" Angbar screamed.

Helix dragged himself to his feet, still fighting for breath, and got to the ledge's far side in time to see Rake deliver a savage kick to Seth's stomach on the ground below. The ruddy boy rolled in the dirt, clutching at his gut and whimpering.

"Seth!" Helix called, a hoarse echo of Angbar. Rake snapped his head up, then ran for the ladder.

"Baler's coming again!" Angbar whimpered, peering down at the ladder. As Helix limped over to join him, Angbar lifted his board over his head and hurled it.

"No!" Helix shouted, but too late: the last weapon they had clattered dully to the ground.

"Missed! *Crap!*" Angbar squeaked, throwing a wild, searching look at Lyseira and Helix. "What're we gonna do?"

Baler was halfway up the ladder, eyes burning with murder. Rake was right behind him.

Helix blanched and whipped his eyes around the fort, but there was nothing left. It was hard to think. He hurt all over, and he *still* had to pee–when Rake had kicked him in the gut, he'd thought he was going to burst.

Then he had an idea. The best idea he'd ever had in his life.

Grinning, he pulled down his breeches.

Lyseira backed away, her eyes widening. "What–what are you *doing?*"

"Hey Baler!" Helix called down the ladder. The bully looked up, snarling. He locked eyes with Helix.

A shot of piss took him in the forehead.

Helix barked laughter as Baler screamed, revolted. "Agh! You little *sehk!*" He sputtered and jerked up a hand, but Helix swayed the attack all over his face and chest, being sure to share some with Rake. There was no escape.

Baler's other hand slipped off the ladder. He pinwheeled backwards, his hind end smacking into Rake's face behind him. Both of them crashed to the ground.

Angbar howled in laughter, chortling so hard he was gasping for air. Helix crowed as he kept the flow coming. "Eat *sehk,* Baler! You seem to like piss well enough!"

"Agh!" Rake squealed. *Like a girl,* Helix thought. "God! Agh!" He broke toward the lake, spitting and pawing at his face.

"Rake!" Baler roared as he stood up, but the redhead didn't stop. "Smith! I am gonna kill you!"

"By yourself?" Seth wheezed from the ground.

"I'm not–" Baler began, but cut off suddenly. Rake was gone, driven by his disgust to the lake; Esiah's whimpers were still echoing back from the woods as he floundered toward home, nursing his broken fingers.

"*Sehk* on you, Smith," Baler hissed, still trying to wipe his face and neck. "This ain't over."

"Probably not," Helix rejoined. "Angbar could probably manage a piss, too." They locked eyes again, just long enough for Helix to start wondering if his final taunt had been one too many. Then Baler turned with a dismissive grunt and walked away.

As Helix brayed laughter at Baler's back, Syntal ducked out from behind a moss-covered tree stump and hurled a rock at the fleeing boy's head.

It cracked into his skull with a sound like splitting timber; a fine mist of blood burst from his scalp. He staggered forward a step before crumpling to the dirt.

Helix's laughter turned to ash in his throat. Syntal covered her mouth.

The only sound was the twittering of birds in the trees.

"What...? By *Akir*, Syntal," Helix breathed. "What'd you do that for?"

Syntal just stared.

"Why'd you throw the rock at him?" Angbar accused. "He was running away, you didn't have to kill him!"

"I just–I didn't mean to... *he* came after *us!*" Syntal protested.

"He was running away, idiot!" Seth yelled.

"Shut up, Seth!" Syntal yelled back.

"Shut up, everybody!" Lyseira screamed. She barged past Helix, climbed down the ladder, and knelt by Baler's body. As she held her hand near his mouth, she announced with a tremor, "He's not dead–he's still breathing."

"See?" Syntal whined.

"Good," Helix said as he swung down onto the ladder. "We can just leave him here then. When he wakes up he won't know what happened anyway–he didn't see Syntal hit him, maybe he'll think he just tripped."

"Maybe his whole memory will get forgot," Angbar said, following Helix. "That happened in a story my dad told me once. And then he'll become nice."

"That's good," Seth said as Helix jumped to the ground. "Yeah, now we don't have to worry about him."

Lyseira shot to her feet, her dirty dress twirling as she turned to face them. "We can't leave him here if he's alive! He got hit in the head–he could be in a longsleep!"

Helix shrugged. "C'mon, Lyseira–if he's in a longsleep, we can't help him anyway."

"The Abbot can! 'Thou shalt not slay thine fellow man' is the second Sacred Principle–if we left him here it would be like killing him, that's what the book of Golath says."

"He ain't a man anyway," Angbar pointed out. "He's only sixteen."

"Yeah." Helix started to chuckle at the joke, but his eyes snagged on the slowly darkening dirt around Baler's head, and the laughter died.

Lyseira's eyes flashed, her bottom lip quivering. "Fine!" she barked. "Fine!"

She stalked toward Seth, who started to back away, and snatched the bully's knife from his waistband.

"I'll take him back myself!" she snapped, marching back to the unconscious body. "But if you think no one's gonna know about this, you're wrong!" She knelt next to Baler's head, smoothed her dress out in front of her, and started awkwardly trying to cut out a swath of it for a bandage.

"I'm going to tell my mom, and all your moms," she seethed as she sawed at the hem. Abruptly she stopped and glared at Helix. "And you can tell my mom I said 'poop' if you want, because I don't care, and Baler's going to die if you leave him here, and Akir will send you to Hel!" she shrieked.

"*M'sai*, Lyseira. Calm down," Angbar said.

She kept cutting at her hem, finally tearing off a ragged strip. She wrapped the makeshift bandage, grimy with mud, wood slivers, and urine, around Baler's head wound and tied it tight.

Syntal came over wordlessly and extended a hand to help her up. Lyseira grabbed it. "Are you gonna help?" she demanded. Biting her lip, Syntal nodded.

"We might as well help her," Angbar said. "She's gonna tell everyone anyway." He grabbed Baler's hands, grimacing at the weight, and looked plaintively back at the other two boys. "He's heavy."

Seth shrugged and went to help.

Helix sighed. "Better than he deserves," he drawled, "after stealing my dad's nails."

# Chapter 5

*i. Lyseira*

Lyseira did not sleep.

Behind her closed eyelids she heard Bella Smith screaming at the bishop's back, and, worse, her abrupt and total silence. She saw Syntal, struck dumb, cowering in the shadows. She saw Kevric, Helix's father, begging Bishop Marcus to reconsider, and Helix himself, pale and shaking, as he mounted a Preserver's horse without resistance. Matthew's dead gaze and gaping mouth permeated all of it, glazing the memories in a red sheen.

Bella had been Bound by Marcus, and when the miracle had finally broken, she had asked Lyseira for help–*pled* with her for help. Marcus had left strict instructions that none should follow them back, but Helix's mother hadn't cared. She was a wreck. She had looked at Lyseira like a drowning woman begging for a rope. *The Abbot is gone,* she'd cried. *Lyseira, you're the only one who knows him. You have to make them understand.* Kevric had finally reeled her in, and under cover of her hysterical sobs, Seth and Lyseira had escaped.

"He didn't do it," Lyseira had said to Seth as they crossed the road toward home, her voice threatening to shatter. It had started snowing. She had floated through the drifting flakes, untethered and numb. "You know he didn't do it, this is Helix.

"This is *Helix.*" There was no more absolute denial.

Seth was untroubled. "The Church will try him. I'm sure he'll be freed." His blithe certainty gave way to the wash of blood caked into Matthew's beard, and the cycle of nightmares began anew.

An hour before dawn, she dressed and left for the temple.

~~

"Lyseira," Annish said when she entered his office, bolting up from behind his desk as if he'd been bitten by a snake. "I'm glad you're here." It was the first time Lyseira could recall him saying anything nice to her.

"Father," she said curtly. "I want to talk to Bishop Marcus about Helix. Where is he?"

Annish's eyes flicked behind her. "Close the door."

"Is he outside?" Lyseira said as the latch clicked into place. "I thought he would be staying in the temple."

"Father Marcus is very busy this morning, Lyseira, you understand."

"I also want to speak with Helix. Are they together? Where is he keeping him?"

Annish winced and stood up. "All right. Marcus is a bishop of the Tribunal, not a dog. He doesn't come when you call. And Helix is a prisoner of the Tribunal."

"But he shouldn't be," Lyseira pressed. "That's why I'm here. He had no reason to kill Matthew. He would never do something like that. He–"

"That is for the Order of Judgment to determine. Marcus had already requested a holy judge, for Matthew; he's on his way now."

*There will be a trial, then.* Lyseira's wild bravado abated. *That's something. That's important.* Once, the Tribunal had been the Order of the Church that had both sought out wrongdoings and punished them, but hundreds of years ago, those duties had been split apart. The Tribunal had kept its name, even as it became the arm of the Church responsible for hunting down and capturing heretics. The task of judging and punishing those the Tribunal discovered fell to the Order of Judgment. However, the Tribunal would often have a cleric present at the trial who could present the evidence they had gathered. Such would probably be the case in Helix's trial.

Annish came around his desk. The office had always been small, but now, stuffed as it was with odds and ends from around the temple in order to make room for the bishop's entourage, the little space felt particularly cramped. The deacon put a clammy hand on Lyseira's shoulder and mustered a smile. It didn't touch his bad eye.

"Lyseira. You must understand that you've no call to speak with the Father about this. If he wants to hear you, he'll seek you out. You must trust in Akir and let Him do His work."

Lyseira bit her lip. He was right, but he hadn't heard Helix's mother begging. He hadn't seen the terror in Helix's eyes.

"Let me see Helix," she said. The words sounded like a plea.

"Girl," the deacon said, "you know that's impossible." His one-eyed gaze glommed on to hers and held it. Her throat hitched as she swallowed.

He smiled again. "All the same, you've done much for me and the Church. I'll speak with the bishop about both of your requests–to meet with him and to be initiated–and find you with his answer. I don't know when I'll have the chance, but I'll do it as soon as I can. I can promise you that much."

His mention of initiation snapped around her neck like a collar. She felt her hopes of helping Helix diminish abruptly, dimming from the dazzling force she had felt upon waking to a faint glimmer, more painful to acknowledge than ignore. She nodded dumbly.

"But I do still have need of you. Go to the back and find Galen Wick, the Justicar. The holy judge will not arrive alone, and Sir Wick is setting up the camp for his entourage. He has a list of requirements you can help with. I've cancelled morning sermon, which will give you the rest of the day to complete his tasks. It ought to be plenty of time."

He turned back to his desk and ignored her until she left.

~ ~

Galen Wick put Seth to work assembling tents and preparing camp. Lyseira was made to clean the temple, dusting and polishing every inch of it. Her work took her outside occasionally, where she could see a tent had been erected over the jail wagon. Helix was inside. She wanted to sneak in to make sure he was well, but one of Marcus's Preservers was posted outside it at all times. She wouldn't be able to get past him.

The holy judge arrived a few days later. The rumble of approaching hooves made Lyseira hurry to the window, her heart suddenly leaping into her throat. She had expected him to have a Preserver or two, like Father Marcus; maybe a Justicar, as well, for additional protection on the road. Instead, he had brought a small army.

The black mare at the head of the procession bore a Justicar. To either side of him rode a banner-bearer, one with a griffon and a lance–the sign of King Gregor–and the other with a God's Star.

Behind these three, the group was thick with priests and their Preservers, knights of Lord Locklyn, and soldiers.

*So many soldiers.*

Father Annish, who had been cleaning nearly as much as she had, turned from the books he'd been dusting and rushed outside. Through the window Lyseira saw Bishop Marcus sweep out of the prison tent, one of his Preservers gliding behind him.

The group parted and a cleric rode to the front: Holy Judge Gideon Elmoor. He was balding, aged, and plump, a vision of Father Annish in twenty years, but he carried himself with more dignity than Lyseira had ever seen Annish muster. His two Preservers followed behind him, each unarmed, on twin dusty brown stallions. He and Bishop Marcus exchanged a few words.

Then the group began dismounting and making its way into the field behind the temple, where the camp Galen Wick had been preparing suddenly felt far too small.

~ ~

Three days after Elmoor's arrival, she and Seth were hauling two giant buckets of water down the hill. As Lyseira's eyes fell on the campsite, she grimaced. Tents, tethered horses, and spent campfires pockmarked the field behind the church. It reeked of horse manure and smoke, languishing under the grey sky like a festering sore.

Sir Edward Kalbear had a tent in the middle of camp. When they reached it, Lyseira sighed and dropped her buckets, sloshing water to the ground. She paid it no mind, wincing as she rolled her shoulders and stretched her arms.

Seth set his pails gently next to hers and waited.

"You could do this all day, couldn't you?" she accused as she massaged her right bicep.

"I have, many times," Seth answered. "This is much like life with the Preservers." His eyes flicked across the campsite. "Dirtier," he added, with a trace of disapproval.

Sir Edward emerged from his tent. "The water," he said, nodding at the buckets. "Good. When you have an opportunity, my horse also needs to be brushed down."

Lyseira seethed, but didn't say anything. Such requests were, in her opinion, beyond what should be required of her, but she hadn't been able to speak to Father Annish about them. She saw Seth nod humbly, and it only annoyed her more.

The knight started away, his boots slopping through the mud, but he stopped and turned back. "Lyseira, is it?"

"Yes," she answered carefully. She was tired and still frightened for Helix. Every muscle in her body burned. The last thing she wanted from this man was another task. The sun had nearly set, and already she had enough work to keep her running around until well after it did.

"Father Annish asked me to direct you to the church if I saw you. He wants to speak with you."

"Thank you." Lyseira's mind scrambled, trying to reassemble the list of complaints and requests she had for the deacon. "I'll see him at once." The knight grunted and turned away.

"I can brush Sir Edward's horse," Seth offered.

Lyseira could've sagged with gratitude. "Thanks. I'll find you when I'm done." She left and headed for the temple, dodging people she recognized along the way who might have chores for her.

She found Annish just inside the chapel, speaking with one of Elmoor's initiates. The boy couldn't have been more than fourteen winters, making him at least two years her junior. The sight of him was a shock–an acute reminder that she would never be initiated–but she tried to squelch her shame. She had too much to say, and agonizing over her failures wasn't going to make finding the words any easier.

"Father," she said briskly as the boy scurried away, "have you been able to–"

"I've asked for Marcus to speak with you. He's waiting in my office."

Now?" she stammered.

"Yes, and he's been in there waiting for you for some time. I've been trying to find you all evening, but you haven't even been on the grounds."

"I was bringing water for Sir Edward," she said, knowing as she did that the excuse meant nothing. Thinking fast, she thanked him and walked away before he could find something else to berate her for.

Her thoughts whirled as she marched toward the door to the deacon's study. Suddenly, she couldn't remember anything she had wanted to say to Bishop Marcus. For several hours after her earlier meeting with Annish, she had rehearsed and refined her words, trying to prepare. That had been almost a week ago. Now, with only seconds left before the meeting, the only words left were, *Helix is innocent.*

Marcus's Preservers loomed to either side of the closed office door. She drew a breath and stepped between them, knocking briskly before her nerves could get the better of her. A clipped voice from inside answered at once.

"Enter."

Bishop Marcus sat at the deacon's desk, where he had strewn a motley assortment of papers, anchored at either end by a giant book. Lyseira recognized them as the temple ledgers.

"Close the door. Sit." He rolled up a scroll and set it on a nearby shelf; she obeyed. Once again, the tightness of the space leaned in on her. The creeks outside would freeze in a week or two if they weren't already, but inside the cramped room she was nearly sweating. She tried to gather her thoughts about Helix, but the words she wanted kept flitting away, chased off by her quivering nerves.

Then Marcus's stare fell on her like a mountain. When his eyes latched onto hers, the words she had been chasing didn't just escape. They vaporized.

*Bishops control whole regions of the kingdom, not just one temple. This man is probably responsible for the Tribunal's actions in all of the Shientel Valley. He reports directly to the Archbishops of the Tribunal.*

*And now he is looking at me.*

"Deacon Annish tells me you wish to become an initiate."

She had expected to discuss Helix. "Yes," she answered, marveling at how level her voice was. "For many years."

"Yet you've performed no miracle."

The accusation came like a knife. There was no argument

against it.

"No, Father," she said. The heat in the stuffy room seemed unbearable. Her face felt like it was glowing.

"Akir chooses those who are most faithful to be miracle workers. Only they receive the divine blessing, which is why only they may be initiated."

Lyseira swallowed. The motion of her throat took forever. "I know," she said.

"Then what made you think to ask?"

The words were flat and factual, devoid of curiosity: another accusation. That quickly, her dream had slipped beyond her grasp, but she wanted it too badly to let it go. She fumbled after it reflexively, a baby rooting for milk. "Some are initiated who can't work miracles."

The bishop's eyes widened as if she had cursed him. "Such as Eoler Squirehand? A man who spent his entire life devoid of coin and devoted utterly to the Fatherlord's works, for *years* before receiving his recognition? Or Elynor Highlund, who was crippled taking a blow from a knight errant who meant the strike for her abbot? You, a girl of sixteen, compare yourself to these?"

She wanted to flinch from the words. They struck her like darts.

"The deacon has told me you would sooner have this temple fall into ruin than do your duty as it would be commanded by the Fatherlord. That you would waive the peoples' donations for the privilege of Akir's counsel and aid, and that you resist when given even the simplest requests."

*Annish,* she thought. *He's twisted everything around.* Before her shame could stop her from speaking, she snapped, "That's not right."

Marcus arched a brow. "Are you calling the deacon a liar?"

"What you said is not right. He's exaggerating it." Everything was spiraling out of control. Sehk, Lyseira thought, too angry to even be surprised at the curse. *If you're going to condemn me, at least condemn me for what I've actually done.*

"You honestly expect that I should take the word of a peasant over one of Akir's chosen?" Marcus said.

"What about the fact that I have practically run this church by myself since I was eight years old? Did he mention that?" *Lyseira,* some distant part of her said, *don't yell at the bishop.* But the voice was lost in the flood of desperation. "Or the fact that Abbot Forthin once said to me that if he could, he would initiate me himself?"

Coldly, Marcus answered, "Forthin is dead. You would do well not to mention him again. There are discrepancies in his records that shame him in his grave." He squinted at her, the intensity of his stare focusing even further. "Or were those your doing?"

"I don't know what discrepancies you're talking about."

"Of course you don't. What else?" he said.

It took her a second to realize what he was asking. "After Father Forthin passed, I conducted the affairs of the temple until Deacon Annish arrived. Some of the townspeople felt that I should even give the Dawnday sermon."

"Did you?" The words settled in the air like a trap.

"Of course not!"

"Do you believe the peasants of Southlight should determine who is initiated?"

Lyseira parsed the question. "No–"

"Nor do I," Marcus interrupted. "So you have cleaned the mud from the floor for many years, and even earned the respect of your peers. Which of these things compares to the sacrifice of Elynor Highlund?"

Lyseira's mouth opened, but she had nothing to offer. As quickly as it had come, her burst of furious courage withered.

After her silence had spoken for her, Marcus pursed his lips. "Helix Smith," he said.

"Yes, Father." The change in subject was a book slamming shut on the other conversation, an abrupt death to her lifelong dream that left her no time to mourn. She tried to gather what courage she had left to face this new topic.

"The deacon tells me you have something to say about him."

Her thoughts whirled, the remnants of her week-old rehearsal ricocheting off each other as they tried to scramble into place. *I want to speak with him. His parents should be allowed to see him. I would like him moved indoors, where it's warmer. I wish to speak with Father Elmoor.*

She managed to stammer, "Helix… he's innocent."

"Were you present when Matthew was murdered?"

"No, but I – "

"You did not witness the deathblow."

"No! Let me finish!" Marcus's eyes widened at her insolence. Her face flushed. *I'm sorry, Father,* she thought to say, but smothered the words. This could be the last opportunity she would have, and she meant to seize it. "I've known Helix for many years, since we were children. He's never harmed a soul. He is a gentle and decent-hearted young man, if a bit shallow." Lyseira winced inwardly. This wasn't helping. Damn her nerves! "He has learned a small bit of swordplay from his father, but nowhere near enough to– "

"To murder a blind man?" Marcus nodded. "Very well. You've known the boy for years. That is your testimony. Yet my Communings with Akir have revealed that he did this thing. A moment ago you expected me to take your word over the deacon's. Now you expect me to take your word over God's?"

Lyseira felt her face sagging with shock. *His Communings?*

Communion was a rare gift, even among priests. A cleric in Communion was said to hear Akir's words as if they were in a room with Him, able to gain knowledge from the most divine and pure of sources. It was said that at times the knowledge could be incomplete or misunderstood, but it was never false. Any failings of a Communion were the failings of the priest who initiated it, not of Akir. If a Communion had revealed to the bishop that Helix was guilty...

"He was found with the weapon in his hands, covered in blood. He has claimed, upon questioning, that the murderer rode a horse that attacked Matthew, but we've found no such wounds on the body. And, Akir has made it known to me that Helix did not act in this alone."

Lyseira's heartbeat thundered in her ears. All words had abandoned her.

"I…" she started. The word trembled ominously. Furious with herself, she cleared her throat and tried again. "I don't know what to say."

"Akir has revealed that Helix had an accomplice." He peered at her. "But I don't need to tell you that. You already know. You overheard them discussing the plan, but since no names were mentioned and Helix is your friend, you assumed it was some game they were playing and mentioned it to no one. Your failures have caused Matthew's death, but they are understandable and the Church may forgive them."

Lyseira shook her head, the room's heat dragging at her cheeks.

"Judge Elmoor does not possess the gift of Communion. He can't divine the truth of what happened on his own. It's the Tribunal's sacred trust to pursue evildoers and present the case to the Order of Judgment." The bishop settled forward. His eyes glinted in the lantern light. "Tomorrow, you must tell the holy judge what you heard. There will be no doubt of Helix's guilt then. As you said, you are respected in this village. If you tell what you heard, the villagers also will believe you. It will make the news easier to bear if it comes from someone they trust."

Finally, Lyseira found her voice. "Father, I heard no–"

Marcus leaned back again. "I have been questioning Helix all week, Lyseira. He continues to claim his innocence, but he has unwittingly dropped bits and pieces of his plan that have allowed me to understand my Communion. I wish to use these pieces to weave a tapestry that can be presented to the holy judge, but if I cannot, I will return to questioning Helix. Tonight. And I will continue until the morning.

"I've been a bishop of the Tribunal for a long time, girl. There are ways to make him tell the truth about what he has done, believe me. But none of those options are as clean as this one.

"I lay this choice at your feet. You can speak tomorrow and reveal what you know. Or I can return to questioning Helix until he tells me the truth, using whatever means are necessary."

*This can't be happening.* A drop of sweat trickled slowly down her back; her stomach roiled with nausea. "Bishop, I'm sorry," she said at last. "But I… I'm having trouble recalling the conversation you referred to."

"I understand," he said, and he sounded as if he truly did. "I know this is hard for you. You said you've known this boy your entire life?" She nodded. "And you have now discovered that he is a cutthroat, this childhood friend of yours. Furthermore, if you had only reported the conversation you overheard to your temple's Keeper, the murder may have been averted. So the sin of it falls on you as well.

"Admitting these things to the judge will be painful. They require you to set aside your pride and your mortal loyalties, and profess to a greater calling. Doing such a thing would be a tremendous sacrifice for the good of the Church.

"A sacrifice as great as Elynor Highlund's."

Lyseira dropped her eyes, her feelings churning. Her outrage at the bribe should have towered like a storm, but cutting through it, insidious with surrender, was a small voice. *Maybe it's true. If Akir told him in a communing, maybe it's true. He'll be found guilty no matter what I say, anyway.*

*This is my only chance.*

"I understand, Father." She didn't recognize her own voice. "I'll do as you ask."

His smile made her want to retch.

*ii. Helix*

Helix jerked awake from some formless nightmare. He sat bolt upright, his eyes wide.

His body retaliated with a cry of protest. His legs and arms were stiff as boards, and bent nearly as well. The sudden burst of stale pain in his muscles sent him to his back with a groan.

He hadn't stretched in days.

They had put him in a jail wagon on the night Matthew had been killed. Little more than a barred cell on wheels, the wagon had probably been meant for Matthew. The only break in the tiny chamber's floor was a small hole in the corner, cut to allow use of a chamber pot below. While the cell looked rough, the construction was as sturdy as any castle's dungeon.

Helix knew; he had tried everything he could think of to get out.

The next morning, they had erected a small tent around him. Helix hated it – it blocked out the sun and made it harder to tell what time it was – but he imagined waking under a mountain of snow would be worse.

Deacon Annish pushed through the tent flap, pouring sunlight into the darkened cell. Helix recoiled from the sudden brightness.

"Good morn," the Father said. He wore a heavy winter cloak, and carried a modest tray bearing Helix's breakfast: bread and cheese. This he pushed between the bars, and stepped back from the wagon to wait.

Helix grabbed the hunk of bread and bit into it. The meal had been the same all week, but by the time he got it each day, he was too hungry to care.

"Father Elmoor asked me to speak with you. He arrived four days ago."

Helix knew something had changed; it was louder beyond the tent, and the few times he had stolen a glance outside, he'd seen tents and soldiers.

"Who is that?" he croaked.

"Your judge."

A burst of fierce hope rippled through him, but Helix kept his tongue. He must have protested his innocence a hundred times in the last week. He'd resolved not to say anything else until his trial. His calm was a mask, though; inside, he was terrified of being found guilty.

*Impossible,* he thought for the hundredth time. The holy judges were supposed to perform a special miracle, one that let them know a lie when they heard one. *This is all just a misunderstanding. He'll* know *that I'm not lying. I just have to wait for the trial.*

He swallowed his cheese, and said, "When?"

"The trial will be this afternoon. Father Elmoor will have the truth of it. It would be best for you to admit what you have done now, and ask forgiveness. If he learns that you protested your innocence, the punishment will be more severe."

*I didn't do anything!* he wanted to scream, but he refused to give the new Keeper the satisfaction. Instead, he gave him a vicious glare and bit off another mouthful of cheese.

"It will go easier for you, and your family."

Helix chewed, staring at the wagon's floor. The solicitations died off.

When Helix had finished eating, the cleric stepped to the cage again and slid a tiny cup of water through the bars, which Helix downed at once. It was cool and fresh, and gone far too soon. He set the cup down next to the bars and scooted away. The deacon took it and left.

This time Helix stole a look outside before the tent flap fell, but nothing he saw changed his situation. The light snowfall had almost completely melted away, and tethered horses and other tents still packed the field outside.

He stretched his stiff legs as best he could. The little wagon was too short for him to stand upright, but if he lay on his back he could nearly manage to stretch out fully. It felt good to work out the kinks in his legs, but it wasn't enough. *If I don't get a chance to* walk *soon, my legs will shrivel up and fall off.*

He spent the day rehearsing what he would say at the trial, forced to act on the assumption that the holy judge would be just. He didn't see any other option; if the man was like Marcus, unwilling or unable to see the truth, Helix was doomed anyway. But if he were fair and Helix assumed otherwise, he'd be stuck in a cell like this one for the rest of his life.

*Or worse,* he thought grimly. If Marcus had his way, he'd undoubtedly have Helix killed. The bishop hadn't touched him–a fact Helix was profoundly grateful for, after what Matthew had said about the Tribunal's methods–but he had badgered him constantly, demanded to know who his accomplice was and why he'd done it. He was convinced of Helix's guilt. Again and again, he'd rejected Helix's version of events.

Once, Helix had snapped. *You came here to jail him anyway,* he'd accused. *Quit acting like you care who killed him.* Marcus had scribbled this into a book as though capturing a confession.

The glow of the sun was favoring the tent's western side when the flap was finally lifted again. One of Marcus's Preservers flowed like a shadow into the canopy, followed by Marcus himself, his other Preserver, two soldiers, and a knight of Locklyn. Earlier, Helix had entertained the notion of attempting escape when his captors came for him. In an instant, any such delusions were broken.

The first Preserver unlocked the cage. He regarded Helix as a cat would a mouse, and opened the door.

"Step out," he said.

Helix slid his feet to the ground, testing to be sure his legs would take his weight. The muscles felt like baked mud suddenly exposed to rain, but he didn't falter.

The soldiers took his arms.

"Can you walk?" Marcus said.

"Depends on where we're going," Helix answered.

Marcus didn't smile. "See that he keeps up," he said to the soldiers. "He may have trouble on the hill." With that he and his Preservers left, and the soldiers fairly hauled him outside.

In the failing light, Helix could finally make out the full size of the camp. A motley collection of tents was strewn about the area behind the temple, with soldiers, initiates, and the odd knight dicing, fencing, or eating. The space had been a grassy slope a month before; now, the turf had been trampled down everywhere, and clots of mud littered the grass. The smell of horse manure clung to the air like a wet shirt.

The tent housing his jail wagon stood at the edge of the camp, just off the road. Helix guessed that position would make it easier to get moving again, rather than driving it through the beaten grass and lumpy earth to somewhere more secure. *But it also means I'm close to the road–very close.* Visions of escape burst in his mind like sunspots, but then the soldier on his right jerked him toward the hill, and the sudden, aching flare in his legs forced his attention to more immediate matters.

By the time they had climbed the hill and reached the temple, his legs felt like they were burning off. He struggled not to let the pain show on his face and forced his legs to bear his weight. He refused to be dragged to his own trial.

Several of the pews had been moved from the floor to make room for a table and some chairs, and a little desk rested on the altar for the judge. In the back some pews remained, and he saw Lyseira as he entered, wearing her finest Dawnday dress. She caught his eyes with her own, and he read a glimmer of surprise or shame there before she glanced away. *Do I really look that bad?* he thought ruefully, and then figured that he must; in the week since she had last seen him he hadn't shaved, bathed, or eaten a full meal once.

It wasn't until he was seated at the long table near the altar at the front of the room that he thought to wonder why she was there at all. His family wasn't present, though he had hoped they would be; nor were any of his other friends who might be able to vouch for him. He craned his neck to look around. Knights and soldiers ringed the room, each of them armed with a longsword, and a small huddle of junior clerics gathered in the pews along with a boy of roughly Helix's age that he didn't recognize, but the only friendly face he saw was Lyseira's.

Then the front door opened again, and Galen Wick entered. The Justicar wore a heavy, velvet-lined cloak over light leather armor festooned with the sigil of a tiger, as well as the five-pointed God's Star. He glanced around the room, then strode down the aisle between the remaining pews and approached Bishop Marcus.

Helix watched the Justicar as he passed by, his stomach twisting at the sight. Sir Wick's sword hung at his side, swaying easily as he walked. Rich, mahogany leather wrapped its hilt, and below that its cross guard was fashioned to look like twin angel wings, the symbol of the Justicars. A similar adornment had been mounted on the knight's helm, Helix remembered. When he'd entered Mellerson's inn, for a second they had looked like...

*Demon's horns.* Finally, the memory that had been tickling at his mind all week burst into his thoughts as if he were seeing it for the first time. *It was the wings!* his thoughts screamed. An image of the murderer above him, framed by the moon as his horse reared, flashed through Helix's mind in an instant comparison with Galen Wick coming through the door of the inn, the sun blazing past the wings of his helm and twisting them into horns as he entered the dark interior. *He was the only Justicar in the village. It was him! It had to be him!*

He leapt to his feet and screamed, "Marcus!" He shot a finger at the Justicar, who whirled toward him. "It was him!" Helix yelled, his heart racing. "It was–"

He didn't even see the bishop's Preserver move. In an instant the man had grabbed Helix's outstretched arm and twisted it behind his back; at the same time, he flashed a sharp kick into one of Helix's aching legs. He felt a burst of pain from his tailbone as he collapsed back into his chair. The fall twisted his arm up behind him, and he gave a wounded shout. When the man released his arm, Helix clutched at his elbow, wincing as he tried to keep the pressure off his shoulder.

A gravelly voice cut through the din.

"What is this?" Father Elmoor demanded. He stood in the door to the Keeper's study, behind the altar. The bishop was an older man, his thin, grey hair receding from his forehead like a low tide. His eyes held a hint of indignation or disgust as they trained on Helix. "You will have your chance to speak, Helix Smith. Rest assured. And you, Seschar." He flicked his eyes toward Marcus's Preserver. "The boy has been caged for a week and has no weapon. I think there is no need to beat him." From the corner of his eye, Helix saw Bishop Marcus nod. In a heartbeat, the Preserver had returned to his bishop's side.

Judge Elmoor walked stiffly toward the table that had been assembled for him on the altar, and seated himself. His Preservers towered behind him like pillars of stone.

"We are gathered because of a man named Matthew Rentiss, a lost sheep of Akir's, who was murdered as he passed through Southlight just a week past. It is ever the hope of the Church to discern the truth in matters of justice, and that is why I'm here. Akir has blessed me with his gifts, and by his divine voice, as spoken by our Fatherlord, I have been granted the honor of presiding over such trials as this." He raised his left hand palm up, the sign to pray.

The pain in Helix's arm slowly subsided. The urge to hurl accusations at Galen Wick buzzed in his thoughts, but he forced himself to calm down. He had decided days ago that the best decision would be to speak his grievances during the trial, he reminded himself. He would be given a chance to speak. With a tremendous effort, he closed his eyes and lowered his chin.

Bishop Elmoor's prayer was in the First Tongue, as all ritual prayers were, and so Helix had no idea what he said. It was the longest prayer Helix had ever heard.

When it finally ended, Father Elmoor said, "Bishop Marcus, proceed."

"This need take little of your time, Father," Marcus said as he rose. "It is a simple matter, made simpler still by the words Akir has shared with me. First and most greatly, I have Communed with Akir regarding this matter, and He has spoken to me in certain terms, saying that the boy Helix Smith is guilty of this crime. His divine wisdom has granted me the knowledge that the act was premeditated, that Helix expected payment for his deeds, and that he did not act alone."

The words slammed into Helix like bricks, forcing him to his feet to defend himself. "Father, that's a lie!"

Again Marcus's Preservers' eyes snapped to him, but this time neither of the men moved. The soldier to Helix's right dropped his hand to his sword.

"Helix Smith!" Elmoor snapped. "I will tell you but one more time. You will not speak until I ask it of you! If you talk out of turn again, I shall make my decision without listening to your words at all!"

Helix swallowed and sat back down, his cheeks burning and his pulse racing. Sehk, he thought miserably. *Shut up, Helix! You're going to get yourself killed!*

Marcus had never looked away from the judge. When Elmoor nodded to him, he continued. "As you know, however, mortal minds are weak and may not be able to hear the voice of Akir accurately, and so I have determined other ways by which you may determine the boy's guilt as well.

"Firstly. I found him on the night of the murder in a stupor next to the corpse. He was covered in Matthew's blood and held a bloody sword in his hands, which he had no doubt used, moments earlier, to deliver the death blow to Matthew's chest. It is my belief that Helix had never killed before, and after having committed the deed was so aghast at the strength of his *rev'naas* that the force of it sent him into shock, leaving him too senseless to flee before being caught. I have seen this happen to many men in my years in the Tribunal, Father. When faced with the true magnitude of their own evils, most men are struck dumb."

Helix breathed deeply and looked away, forcing himself to stay calm. *You'll get your chance,* he told himself. *Stay quiet.*

"Secondly, the boy claims that a mysterious horseman murdered Matthew, and that he arrived only in time to witness the killing. He says this horse struck Matthew with its hooves, causing him to fall, and that it bore the murderer away after the deed. Yet when we examined Matthew's body there was no sign of the wounds a horse's flailing hooves would leave, nor, when we searched the earth behind Master Smith's house, did we find any sign of horses other than our own. Whether these fabrications are delusions Helix created to spare himself the misery of the truth, or simply outright lies, only you can determine. But clearly they are not the truth."

No tracks? No wounds on the body? There *had* to be wounds on the body; Helix had seen the horse strike Matthew so hard the man had crumpled from the blow. *That's impossible!* he wanted to shout, but again, he clamped his teeth shut.

"Finally." Marcus gestured toward the rear of the room. "The girl in the back is named Lyseira Rulano. She has tended this temple for many years, and I understand that Abbot Forthin thought to recommend her for initiation before his death. She is well known and well trusted among the villagers here, and has known Helix Smith since they were both children. She came to me last night and told me of a plot she overheard between Helix and his accomplice, which she would like to share with your court."

A wave of vertigo crashed over Helix. *No,* he thought limply. *Lyseira.* As he heard the rustle of Lyseira rising to her feet, he felt paralyzed. He wanted to face her, but his muscles held no strength.

"Father," she said. He could hear the slightest hint of a tremble to her voice. *Bitch,* he thought impotently.

The holy judge nodded twice. "Proceed."

"I..." she began, then stopped. A sudden silence engulfed the room. Someone coughed.

"Say what you have to say, girl," the judge prompted again.

Something in her voice made Helix twist to look at her. She stood in the middle of the room, in the center aisle between the pews, her hands clasped. The pulse in her neck was so fierce he could see it. *Lyseira...*

"I heard no conversation," she said, and Bishop Marcus gestured immediately. Two soldiers, standing at either side of the main entryway, started up the aisle behind her. "Helix didn't kill Matthew and Marcus has been lying since he opened his mouth." Her eyes flashed. "I don't believe the Communing ever happened."

"Lies," Marcus said. The word was quiet, almost casual. "I ask your leave to have her escorted outside. I can deal with her treachery after the trial."

The judge nodded.

"The tracks were there when I arrived!" Lyseira protested. "Marcus had them covered somehow, removed... I saw the wound on Matthew's head myself!" She started toward the front, but one of the soldiers caught up to her and grabbed her arm, yanked her around. "Helix was–" she screamed, but a gloved hand clapped across her mouth.

"Why can't she speak?" Helix cried. "Let her speak!" He was on his feet, pushing away from the table, but a soldier yanked him back, driving a spike of pain up his arm. He collapsed into his chair with a whimper.

"Peace!" The holy judge shouted, his face contorted in disgust. "There will be peace!"

*No! Let her speak!* Helix tried again to lurch to his feet, but there were now two men behind him, and they held him down easily. Somewhere near the front of the church, behind him, he heard a door slam. Lyseira was gone.

"I have never seen such disrespect for justice," Elmoor told Helix. "Your parents have clearly failed to instill in you a proper respect for the Church. Your actions reflect poorly on them and make you look a fool." He paused. "And a *guilty* fool at that.

"Bishop Marcus has every right to reject inconstant testimony. Clearly the witness cannot be trusted to speak truth plainly if her story keeps changing.

"Nonetheless, the girl's words are troubling. Bishop Marcus, do you have a response to these accusations?"

"Yes, Father." Marcus was still calm; in the heat of the crowded chapel, he wasn't even sweating. "Lyseira wishes to become an initiate, and has all her life, but lacks – for obvious reasons, I think – the divine boon of Akir. She came to me and said she had overheard the conversation I mentioned. Now that I think on it, she was likely trying to curry favor with me."

To Helix's horror, the judge nodded. *How can he believe that?* The question echoed in his skull, a numb dread seeping into him.

"But the marks on the body, the tracks…"

Marcus nodded. "The girl is no ranger. I don't believe you can take her word as to whether the tracks were on the ground or not. She arrived at the same time I did. We saw the same scene. In my years in the Tribunal I have found many murder sites; I know how to read tracks. There was no horse."

"But the wounds on the body?"

Marcus spread his hands. "The body has not been buried yet, Father. We have blessed it, that it might be preserved as best it can. You're welcome to look at it yourself."

Elmoor considered this, then shook his head. "No," he replied. "That won't be necessary. Please continue."

*This is a farce,* Helix thought wanly. *Akir help me. Please God, I have no one else.*

Marcus nodded to the judge. "Thank you, Father. I have but one thing more–a second witness, who repented to me and sought censure, in the hopes that his soul might be saved. A wiser boy than young Helix, I fear." Marcus pointed to the young man that Helix had seen coming in. The boy was of an age with Helix himself, dirty and unkempt, his hair wild. He stood up, glancing nervously at Marcus.

"This is Nash Dennen, Helix's accomplice in the murder."

Helix felt his guts turn to ice water. All hope slipped away. "This is... madness," he whispered, but Marcus's stronger voice trampled the words.

"Nash, tell Judge Elmoor what you told me."

The young man glanced around the room once, his eyes darting like rats, his hair swinging from his scalp like dirty rags. It summoned a memory Helix hadn't thought of in years, an impression of Rake's greasy, red hair as he hung from a branch in Pinewood forest.

"I don't know why he wanted us to do it, Father," Nash said to Elmoor.

"Who? Don't play games with me, boy. Do as Marcus

instructed you."

Nash's head bobbed. "Sorry, sorry, the man who hired us. He gave me half in front. Tol' me to track this blind man and have done wit' him, you unnerstan." He licked his lips, his tongue flickering like a snake's. "Only I coun't find him, but Master Smith here, he done knew of him. He said he'd go along, even do the job but he wanted half."

"Who is this man who paid you?"

"He live in Newton, Father, not from 'roun here. He never tol' me his name, he din't."

"*Liar!*" Helix screamed. "I don't even know who you *are!"* He sought the judge's eyes, desperate. "Father, I'm sorry, but I swear to you, I've never even seen this boy before! I swear!"

The judge's lips curled at the interruption, but he nodded. "Marcus?" The other bishop lifted his hands in mock surrender.

"That's all I have, Father."

"Very well." Elmoor rose from behind his table, nodding. Helix tracked him like a castaway watching for sign of a passing ship. "You say you swear," the judge said. "We shall see."

Bishop Elmoor closed his eyes and began to pray in the First Tongue, but this time Helix didn't follow suit. As the prayer droned on he looked around, hunting for some way to escape. A soldier stood at every window; two more waited at the front door. And before he would even be able to reach them, Marcus's Preservers would have him.

The numb dread he had felt before blossomed into despair. As he turned his eyes back to the judge he caught Nash Dennen looking at him, a smile clinging to his face like a smear of grease.

As all heads rose and all eyes opened, the judge spoke again–this time in the dark, crawling words of an invocation. They dribbled from his mouth like menace. Helix had heard the words of a miracle before, growing up; for once, the sound gave him relief instead of fear.

*So it's true.* The judge did have the ability to recognize lies. *If only he had used it on Marcus as well.*

Finally, the invocation ended. Helix felt no different, but a guarded sense of hope spiked in his chest. "Speak, Helix Smith,"

Father Elmoor said. "But know that Akir has granted me the ears to divine truth from lies."

Helix rose shakily to his feet. He wasted no time on pleasantries. "It was him, Father, I swear it," he said, pointing at Galen Wick. The Justicar's eyes narrowed as a quiet murmur went through the crowd. "His helm, he was wearing his helm, and I saw the wings under the moon." *In the dark, they looked like demon's horns.* "Justicar's wings. There was only one Justicar here at the time, it was him, he did it. The horse–the horse was there, I saw it with my own eyes, please, can't you hear that I'm speaking truth? Please!"

*Get yourself together Helix! Listen to yourself!*

He pointed at Nash. "I have never seen this person before in my life. I swear. I don't know who he is. I don't know why he agreed to do this, but I suppose Marcus must have offered him a lot of money."

A sharp, scandalized murmur rippled through the crowd. "You will watch your tongue, Smith," Marcus snapped.

Helix whirled on him. "You wanted him dead, but you were scared to do it in public, scared to even *arrest* him where people would see. He'd been talking about you, and people believed him. *I* believe him. Just look at this trial! It proves everything he ever said! So instead of giving him a trial you had him murdered in the night, and did your best to find someone to blame it on."

"I said, watch your tongue."

"Marcus," the judge snapped, and Marcus fell silent. "Are you finished, Master Smith?"

*I've said everything that matters,* he thought dizzily. Terror, rage, and courage fought in his belly like starving wolves over a piece of meat. *If he can really hear the truth, he's already heard it.* He nodded, sinking back to his chair.

"Very good," the judge said at once. "Akir has revealed your words to me as you have spoken them. His justice is limitless. Know that when you speak to a holy judge, your words are truly heard." He looked once at Marcus, his gaze boring into the other priest's eyes before returning to Helix.

"You lie."

Helix's heart lurched. "No," he said.

The judge continued as if he hadn't spoken. "Marcus, Bind the boy and have him returned to his cell. He will be taken to Keldale on the morrow, where, in the name of Akir, he will be executed for the murder of Matthew Rentiss."

At once, Marcus began his black chant. Behind him, Galen Wick smiled.

"*No!*" Helix screamed, jumping again to his feet. "I didn't do this! It was
him! He killed him in cold blood! You should be Binding *him!*"

"*Ayen get sil tar'r, vor kel rushtar'r.*" Marcus's words slithered through the air, crawling into Helix's ears. His muscles tightened as if in the grip of death. *In the name of Akir,* the words whispered to him, insidious and black, echoing Elmoor's pronouncement. *No!* he tried to scream, but his tongue betrayed him; it wouldn't move.

*In the name of Akir,* they hissed, and suddenly he remembered Matthew's voice, quiet and firm.

*They do not speak for God.*

Helix hurled the blackness away.

"He was right!" Helix cried. "We didn't want to believe him, but he was right! The Church is corrupt! You don't serve Akir! You feared what would happen if Matthew were to have a say in a trial–the word that would spread. People were already listening to him! They already know you're liars!" The words poured from him like a waterfall.

"Marcus!" the judge snapped as he rose to his feet. "I said Bind him!" He began to pray; an instant later, Marcus took up the invocation again. Then, every cleric in the room spat darkness.

"I'll be as loud as he was! You think it's easy as killing one blind man?" Helix's hoarse shout barely carried over the sea of shadowed words. They were cresting, rising over him like a tidal wave. "Many heard him! Many heard–!"

Then the blackness crushed him, and he plunged headfirst into darkness.

# Chapter 6

## Before the Storm

*i. Seth*

It ended up being the most boring summer he could remember.

Helix and Syntal were grounded, forced to help in the smithy for weeks. Lyseira suddenly had to help The Abbot a lot more, and was never around. Angbar disappeared, his parents probably scared he'd get in extra trouble because he was a nog or something. Iggy was around, and Seth tried to play with him a couple times, but he was older and a little boring.

Seth's parents hadn't punished him, and as far as he was concerned, he hadn't done anything wrong. Baler and his friends had deserved everything they'd gotten. But by the time summer ended, he wished he could take that afternoon at the tree house back, just so everything wouldn't be so *boring.*

When the rain came, it was the most exciting thing he'd seen for weeks.

It pummeled the village for two days. Despite his best-mannered requests, Mom and Dad refused to let him outside to play in it. The wall near his bed had a little gap between the logs, and he spent hours with his face pasted against that crack, staring into the gloom like a fish in a jar. Now and then he'd leave to eat, or try to play with his toys, but when the boredom got the best of him he would always return to the view.

Finally, after days of peering, he noticed something. "Hey Mom, look," he said. "The river's almost touching the house."

Mom froze as if he'd said there was a parade of elephants outside. Then she bustled to the wall and pushed him aside so she could peer through. Her face paled.

"*Beryc!*" She steered Seth away from the wall.

He squirmed out of her grasp and stole another look at the rising river. His mom's anxiety had transformed it. Now, it looked like a massive, black snake undulating just beyond the wall.

His heartbeat quickened. Finally, something was actually *happening.*

Dad came down from the loft, and Mom nodded toward the wall. "The river's flooding."

"*Sehk,*" he swore. "I thought for *sure* we were far enough up the bank this time." Seth wondered if he would tell the story again about how Mom and Dad's first house had flooded before they had Seth, and how careful he had been when deciding where to build this one. Dad told that story a lot.

Instead he just looked at them, his jaw clenching as he chewed through their options. Finally, he harrumphed. "Well, there's nothing for it. This place could slide into the river. We have to get out." He shook his head, glanced out the crack himself, and cursed again. "Good thing we never got that window you wanted, Mae. By this afternoon it'd be twenty shells down the river."

He grinned, and she swatted him. "We're building away from the river this time," she retorted, "and it'll be a whole new chance to get a window in."

"Seth, help your mother pack up, *m'sai?* I'll run to the Ardenfells' and see if Ike'll bring his wagon."

Mom sneaked him a kiss. "Be careful."

Dad threw on his coat and opened the front door. A roar of cold rain lashed into the house, biting into Seth's face like a swarm of wasps. Water sloshed over the threshold, running between the floorboards in tiny rivers.

"Look at that!" Seth laughed. He had never seen so much water in his life. He craned his head, trying to see past his father in the doorway.

"Hurry!" Mom called as Dad disappeared into the storm. Then she slammed the door against the wind and started barking orders. "Get your things and wrap them in your blanket, Seth. Bring them here by the stove."

"Is the house really gonna fall in the river?" The thought thrilled him. He just hoped they would let him stay long enough to watch.

"Now, Seth! This isn't a game! Go!"

He tried to hurry, but he had to peek outside a few times when his mom wasn't watching. And while wrapping his toys up in his blanket, he realized his red horse–the little wooden one Dad had given him for his birthday last year–was missing. After a brief but fervent search he found it crammed beneath his bed. All in all he'd managed the task pretty quickly, he thought. But when he returned to the kitchen with his bundle, Lyseira's mom was already there tossing pots and pans into a giant burlap sack, nodding as Dad gave instructions from the doorway. Both of them looked like they'd just swum down the Narrel river.

"Just whatever you can grab, Corla," Dad shouted, the door banging and shuddering in the wind behind him. "Only the important things!"

Ike Ardenfell's wagon was outside, standing away from the house to keep it from getting mired in the thickening mud; Mom had just dropped a glob of dripping clothes into it and was turning back to the house, stretching a sodden blanket over her head.

*No reason I can't go out there too.* Seth braced himself for the cry of outrage, then ducked past Dad and into the deluge.

He could have plunged into a lake. The water pummeled him, drenching his blanket and melting his hair into a sodden mess. He'd never felt anything like it. *Is it possible to drown in the rain?*

Suddenly, Mom drew up short and pointed across the river.

"Beryc!" she called through the downpour. Dad cocked his head, squinting.

"Someone's by the bridge!" she yelled, waving toward the river. Seth shielded his eyes and peered into the storm. He could just make out a wagon drawn by two horses, halted at the bridge's far side. A vague silhouette held the reins in one hand, hunched forward against the driving rain; it cupped its mouth and yelled something indiscernible through the storm's roar.

"Akir!" Dad swore as he finally made out the wagon. He shouted, trying to be heard over the screaming wind. "Is that Runith?"

*Syntal's parents? In the middle of the storm?* Seth marveled. *They wouldn't be* that *dumb.*

Mom turned to the river. "Stay off the bridge!" she called. "It won't hold!" But the driver either missed her warning or ignored it; he grabbed up the reins and started the horses toward the bridge.

Lyseira's mom emerged from the house, the bag of pans slung over her shoulder. "The house isn't safe!" she shouted to Dad. "Just get to higher ground! These are only things–Akir can provide anything you leave!"

Dad nodded, but his eyes were still on the wagon. "What is he *doing?*" He ran past Seth toward the shoreline, waving.

The wagon continued out onto the riverbank. The water came to the knobs of the horses' knees as they stepped onto the far side of the arching bridge, which trembled under the new weight.

Seth boggled, grinning. *I didn't even know it could move like that!* He couldn't wait to tell Helix about this.

"They'll never make it! Are they blind?" Dad glanced up and down the river, then ran to the wagon, where Ike was arranging their things to make room. Ike gave a tight nod and crawled into the wagon, out of sight.

Seth started after his dad, wanting to help, but Lyseira's mom held him back with a hand on the shoulder. "Stay here, sweetheart," she said. "Your parents will handle this."

Ike emerged with a long coil of rope, one end tied in a lasso. He and Dad started toward the bank, Mom following.

"Watch yourselves!" Lyseira's mom called, her hand still tight on Seth's shoulder. He protested, squirming, but she dropped her sack and grabbed him with both hands to keep him still. A frying pan slipped into the mud and filled with rain.

The men reached the sloping bank, where the river frothed at their knees. The wagon had reached the middle of the arched bridge. Even there, at the apex, the water lashed like a beast, whipped into a frenzy by the wind. Ike uncoiled the rope and began casting about for something to tie it to.

"Mae, get back to the wagon!" Dad roared. Seth could barely hear him over the shrieking wind. Mom shouted some kind of protest, trying to get him away from the river's shore, but he wouldn't have it.

With a splintering groan, the bridge tore away from the near side of the riverbank. The horses plunged headfirst into the churning darkness of the river, yanking the wagon's driver after them.

Mom screamed. Her horror resonated in Seth's chest. It punctured some secret barrier there and his excitement leaked away, leaving a hollow dread.

The wagon lurched forward and sideways, shearing off two thin, wooden wheels as it snapped around, and then caught, squealing, against the sodden wood of the remaining half of the bridge. Its cover tore from its moorings and billowed into the air, snagging against the knot of wagon axles and bridge rails. Over the roaring wind, an ominous snapping came from the bridge's remaining anchors.

Seth gaped as he saw someone else–*Syn's mom?* –inside what was left of the wagon. She looked behind her as if to return the way she had come, but the bridge's far end was buried in seething water. She shied away from it, curling into herself.

"She ain't gonna make it," Ike barked. He hurled the rope against the driving rain, threw it as thunder shattered the air. On his third try, it landed just inside the wagon.

Mom and Dad screamed at the survivor to grab on. Ike tried to wind his end of the lifeline around his arm, his head still darting back and forth along the shore for anything to anchor it to.

Syntal's mother seized the lasso just as the bridge behind her gave way completely. Black water devoured her. Wood and stone tumbled away like an avalanche.

"Grab it!" Ike snapped, trying to brace his feet against the loose mud of the riverbank. Dad jumped ahead of him and seized the rope as it snapped taut. Seth couldn't see its other end.

"PULL HER UP! UP!" Dad roared, his veins bulging as he fought the river to drag the woman in. He'd slid even further down the bank; the river snapped at his waist like a pack of wild dogs. Mom sloshed down and fumbled at the rope, trying to help.

"MAE!" Dad screamed. "GET BACK!"

Lightning flashed like a door banging open in the heavens, flooding a black room with an instant of illumination, and Seth saw them both: buffeted by rain, hair plastered to their faces, teeth bared in snarls of effort.

Then they disappeared.

Seth's eyes groped for them–down the bank, into the river–and found only lightning dancing on frenzied waves. Empty rope slithering into blackness.

He lurched toward the bank, screaming; felt fierce hands seize his arms and jerk him back. He roared, slapped, bit. The grasp only tightened. It spun him, forcing him away from the black river, into a hug like a vise. He thrashed, shrieked threats and pleas, strove after his parents with every ounce of his will, but the arms were too strong. He couldn't escape them.

~ ~

The world was darkness and rage; the heat of Corla's embrace. He resisted her until his anger gave out, plunging him into an ocean of frustration; then he collapsed, sobbing, into her arms. Years passed, limitless eons, as the rain pounded against his scalp and poured in torrents down his face. Distant voices – frantic, compassionate, meaningless – echoed around him like the murmurs of unseen monsters.

He felt her arm slide beneath him and scoop him up. She cradled him against her shoulder and carried him through the roar of the river and the booming of thunder. Eventually, she brought him to a warm place brimming with firelight.

"Mom?"

He looked up to find himself indoors. Lyseira stood nearby, her face fraught with worry. "What happened?"

"Seth's parents are gone, kitten," Corla whispered. "The river flooded."

The girl gasped. Her hair was plastered to her skull. "Can we find them? Where are they?"

"No, sweetheart. They're with Akir now."

She covered her mouth. "Oh no… oh Seth, I'm so sorry…"

Seth said nothing. Words were pointless. Impotent. Instead he glanced around him, trying to make sense of the world, and saw a stooped iron stove and a small pantry. The kitchen? He was in the Rulanos' kitchen, while the Narrel river washed away his parents, his house–

He had just seen them. They couldn't be gone. He had *just seen them.* He struggled to get down, to run back. They had to be there.

The sympathy in Corla's eyes arrested him. It was absolute as a tombstone.

She set him down and he bolted for the pantry, fleeing her pity and Lyseira's dismay. Darkness smothered him as he slammed the door, hiding the house he didn't grow up in and the mother that wasn't his.

"Seth?" Lyseira's voice. "Mom, is he–?"

"Leave him be," Corla answered gently. "He's fine where he is. He can stay there as long as he likes."

The words could have been *Bahiran.* They meant nothing.

"What will happen to him?" Lyseira asked. "Where is he going to live?"

"I don't know, kitten. Akir will provide."

"But… who will give him dinner? And tuck him in at night?" Somehow, these words pricked him where none of the others had. His eyes welled; his hands shook as if he were freezing. The comfort of the darkness became a crushing expanse of black water and empty rope.

He latched his eyes to the tremulous line of light that traced the pantry door.

"Well, sweetheart, we'll have to talk about that with The Abbot. I don't think he has any other family to stay with – Mae never mentioned anyone."

"He can stay in my room."

Corla's voice melted. "Oh, sweetheart. That is very kind–"

"He must be so scared."

Lyseira's footsteps crossed the room. Seth curled his knees beneath his chin, recoiling from her approach, rocking, staring at the light.

"You can stay in my room. *M'sai?*" Her voice was the light at the door's edges: trembling and luminous. "I can sleep on the floor.

"Don't be scared."

~ ~

Southlight had a little graveyard, a short way up the west road from the village. Seth had sneaked out there to play a few times; once, he and Helix had gone in the middle of the night. They'd darted around the old tombstones in the dark, daring each other to find a zombie or a ghost. The place had been enticing and sinister, resplendent with mystery, and the midnight journey had been worth the paddling it cost him.

The day of his parents' funeral, the mystery ended.

The sun was cold; it exposed the cemetery, naked and pale, to the grey sky. Death no longer hid behind the inscrutable stones. It had become a bedfellow, as normal as waking every morning. It gazed from the wilting slats of the wooden fence and perched on every coarse tombstone; it reflected in Syntal's leaden stare as she beheld her mother's casket.

The ceremony was for her parents as well as his, though the only body they put in the ground was Syntal's mother's. They had never found his own parents' bodies, despite searching for two days. *Maybe that means they're still alive,* a little voice in his head had whispered, but he knew it was wrong.

If they were still alive, they would have come back to him.

The absence of the bodies made the entire ritual an idiotic waste of time. What was the point of putting empty caskets in the ground? His parents were dead. Never returning. He knew that. Why did everyone always have to talk about it? Was he really the only one who understood that talking about them incessantly would not bring them back?

Abbot Forthin's interminable eulogy only made Seth angrier. The man hadn't even known his parents; Dad couldn't stand him. Seth and his family had gone to temple on Dawndays, like they were supposed to, but they'd always been the last ones in and the first ones home, and none of them went for censure as often as they should've. More than once Dad had said, in the privacy of their home, that the Father probably thought they were all headed to Hel. Now, as the cleric droned on about the sanctity of life and Mom and Dad's many virtues, Seth found himself wanting to punch the old man in the face.

Then came the litany of empty consolations and shallow sympathy, punctuated occasionally by questions about what people *really* wanted to know.

*"What will happen to the boy?"*

*"Does he have other family?"*

It boggled him that these questions could come up. It boggled him that *any* question could still come up. His parents were dead. That was the end; there was nothing else.

But people asked all the same, as if the answers actually meant anything in a world where his parents were gone. They always asked Lyseira's mom, as if she had been granted some authority to answer them, and never him, even though he was standing right there. They only asked, he knew, because they all wanted him gone; everyone thought he was a bad kid, almost as bad as Ellic Baler, and maybe now that he was orphaned they expected he would become even worse.

Corla told them all the same thing: that she would be speaking with the Abbot after the service about adopting him. At this some of them looked scandalized, some of them praised her generosity and giving heart, and some asked if she was sure that was a good idea, being a widow with one child already. She thanked all of them for their concerns or their kind words, but never changed her mind. Their implications about his worthiness didn't faze her.

That meant nothing to him. He hadn't asked for her loyalty. She wasn't his mother.

The next day Abbot Forthin came to the house and blessed the adoption. He and Lyseira's mom talked about Seth's fate as if they were trying to care for a bird with a broken wing. He decided to run away.

But that night as he lay in Lyseira's bed, he replayed her voice over and over–

*Don't be scared.*

–and it was the only thing that kept him from crying.

# Chapter 7

*i. Angbar*

When he'd heard about Helix's arrest, Angbar had rolled his eyes and grinned. They were all growing up now, sure, but Helix would be the last one to start acting like an adult. From strewing fish guts all over the road to throwing rocks in church, Helix had always been a troublemaker. He'd settled down a little when Seth left, maybe. But getting arrested by the Tribunal...

It was the kind of thing that always seemed to happen to him. It would get sorted out, they'd realize he wasn't the criminal they thought he was, and in a few weeks they'd all be at Mellerson's talking about how this kind of *sehk* could only happen to him.

Angbar had wanted to witness the trial, but when the guards at the door refused Helix's parents, he knew there was no chance they'd let in a Northerner. He should've gone home then, but he was too curious. He was working on a play, and he was still kicking around the idea of having a trial toward the end of it, and getting some idea of how a trial actually *worked* would make the piece more authentic.

So instead, he'd gone around to the temple's east side and ensconced himself behind the bushes. He ended up underneath a window which, by some stroke of fortune, sounded as if it were only a few feet away from where Bishop Marcus was presenting his arguments. He pulled out a charcoal pen and a small scroll and waited, ready to take notes for his epic.

He tried to copy down the judge's opening invocation and prayer–it would be golden in a script! –but he missed most of it when the judge started praying in First Tongue. His page was covered with crude, phonetic half-words by the time Marcus began speaking.

The arguments went by faster than he'd expected. The word "commune" was new to him in the context Marcus used it as well. He jotted it down with a question mark by it, making a mental note to ask Lyseira more about it later. *God has spoken directly to him,* Angbar thought as Helix's voice exploded from the chapel, interrupting the bishop. *Yeah, right. You tell him, Helix.* He grinned wryly, shaking his head... but a nagging fear had started chewing at him.

As Marcus went on, Angbar's pen kept scribbling. *It doesn't sound good for him,* he realized. *They're not even letting him speak.* His writing came to a shocked halt when the bishop called on Lyseira to speak, but when she started defending Helix, he resumed. *Cut her off,* he wrote. *No chance to finish. Threw her out.*

*Out,* he realized, and glanced around, getting his bearings. He saw two soldiers dicing at the bottom of the hill, but dark was coming on fast. They wouldn't notice him if he was careful.

He crept around the corner just in time to hear the commotion inside, muted by the stone walls, suddenly burst out. The front door flew open, spewing light onto the dark porch. Two guards emerged, dragging a struggling Lyseira by either arm. They shoved her off the front porch in a mass of hair and flailing limbs. She bounced off the steps and hit the ground.

"Go home," one of the soldiers said as they turned back inside. "Don't make us carry you there." The light pouring from the church's doorway disappeared, devoured by the deepening twilight as the doors boomed shut. The sound echoed down the street like the sealing of a tomb.

Angbar glanced around. It looked clear. He hurried to the steps and found Lyseira sitting in the cold mud of the road, her best Dawnday dress torn and filthy from the fall. A small line of blood trickled from a cut on her forehead.

"Lyseira!" he hissed.

"Angbar?" Her voice was hoarse from screaming.

"Are you well?" He offered a hand and she took it, wincing.

"I think so. But Helix–I think he's in a lot of trouble, they–"

"I know, I know, I was listening at the window," Angbar whispered, pointing. His heart thrummed. *If we get caught out here...* "C'mon."

They sneaked back to the window, where Angbar heard someone–*Judge Elmoor?* – droning on in a language he'd never heard before. *Good,* he thought. *It's not over yet.*

"The miracle of truth," Lyseira whispered. "Thank Akir."

As Helix started speaking, Angbar grimaced. The smith's son rushed through his testimony, muddling his words; he sounded desperate, and to Angbar, guilty. *Slow down, Helix!* He threw a worried glance at Lyseira, but couldn't read her blank stare.

"What does that miracle do?" he whispered. "Will he be able to tell...?"

Lyseira shushed him. As he fell quiet, Helix was sentenced to death.

*No.* His mouth fell open; he felt like he just looked down to find a sword sticking from his gut. It had happened only moments ago. Surely it wasn't impossible to reverse. How could one moment change everything so completely?

Helix roared defiance. His voice held the timbre of sermons or prophecy. Then the dark whispers surged, grinding the boy's protests to silence.

Angbar looked at Lyseira as a general commotion drifted out of the window: chairs being pushed back, people standing, a dull current of chatter. He felt a bizarre urge to smile or laugh. His heart thundered in his chest. "It didn't even sound like him," he said. The absolute irrelevance of the words was almost comical.

Lyseira stared past him, ashen.

"Where did they say they were taking him? Keldale?" More irrelevant words; he couldn't seem to stop them. "We should tell his parents. They weren't allowed inside." Something kept forcing his mouth to talk, some ridiculous urge to stand up and declare, *Well, that's done with, what's next?*

Lyseira's eyes searched the wall as if she were scrutinizing scripture.

"Lyseira?" A wild panic reared, threatened to make him scream, and just as quickly dissolved to nothing.

"The Fatherlord," she said. "He doesn't know." Finally, she met his eyes. "We have to tell him."

The Fatherlord was the head of the entire Church; he was Akir incarnated in human flesh. Even Angbar knew that much. "Ah... *m'sai,* but... shouldn't we tell Helix's mom and dad first? Maybe they can get him out of this." Even as he said the words, he knew they weren't true.

Lyseira shook her head, her jaw tightening. "No. The only one who can get him pardoned is the Fatherlord. He doesn't know Marcus is killing people without a trial."

"Lyseira," he hissed. People would be leaving the church soon. If they wanted to escape the bushes without being noticed, they had to go now. "That's crazy. They're taking him to Keldale in the morning. He'll be dead in days. The Fatherlord lives in Tal'aden! That's not enough time to get a message out. Tal'aden isn't even in the Valley!"

"Then we have to get him out of there," Lyseira hissed back. "We can't just let them kill him!"

"Who, you and me?" He was incredulous. "Against the fifty knights behind this hill?"

"Seth can fight," Lyseira said flatly.

Angbar recoiled from this logic. "Seth can't take on fifty knights!"

"We don't have to fight them all!" Lyseira nearly cried out. Angbar winced and shushed her, glancing up and down the line of bushes. They were still alone. "All we have to do is get him out and…" She faltered.

"And what?" Angbar pressed. "They'll just get him again, and probably take our heads for good measure!"

"And run," she finished.

A grim determination settled into her face. Angbar had seen that look before. He didn't like it.

"Run where, Lyseira? Are you out of your mind?"

She shrugged. "Doesn't matter. Out of here." She paused, her grey eyes chewing through the problem. She opened her mouth, halted again, then said: "We're running out of time."

*This is crazy,* Angbar thought. *Absolutely mad.* The reprimands ground through half of his head like clockwork, but the other half whispered, *If we can get into the woods without being seen, they may not know which way we went.*

"I'm going to find Seth. Go to your house, get what you need. Pack everything you can. Meet us…" Her eyes darted through possibilities. "Meet us behind my house as soon as you can."

*Madness.* They were just a couple of kids. The clerics could use *miracles*.

*Who said I was coming with?* he thought, but what he said was, "I'm going to stop at the Smiths'."

"No!" Lyseira snapped.

"That's his family, Lyseira, they need to know!"

"They'll find out soon enough! I'm not even telling my mom." The words came quietly, heavy with resolve or shame. "It could put them in danger."

"*M'sai*," Angbar said, but shook his head. The noise in the chapel had quieted. People were coming out the front door.

They peered around the corner to see Galen Wick leaving the temple, hauling a limp shadow that may have been Helix. Marcus came behind him, pausing to invoke a miracle of light. It burst from his staff like a sunrise, but didn't quite reach them. It dispelled every shadow in its reach, but made the darkness beyond even deeper.

"Go, go!" Lyseira whispered as the men left for the prison tent.

They ran. It wasn't far from the church to Lyseira's house, but it felt like a thousand miles. The jarring thud of each running step triggered something in Angbar. Suddenly, reality crashed into him like a comet.

*They are going to kill Helix,* he thought. *And if they knew our plan, they would kill us too.* Panic flowered in him, surging through his legs. *Burned at the stake for rebellion, or hung in the public square.*

He had never run so fast.

Suddenly, Lyseira grabbed his arm and pulled him to a stop, nearly knocking him from his feet. He stumbled, his arms flailing, and staggered to a halt. He turned back to her, his breath whistling through his lungs in a gale.

"Go!" Lyseira wheezed, pointing through the village toward his house. "Pack and meet us back here! Be quick!"

He nodded once and took off again. But as soon as she turned away, he drew up behind a tree and halted. After she went inside, he sprinted across the road to the Smith house.

~ ~

Angbar vaulted up the steps and banged on the door. It opened at once.

"Angbar!" Syntal looked surprised, then worried. "What's

happened?"

"Helix." Angbar panted. "I listened in on the trial... They're going to kill him."

Syntal paled.

"I heard it with my own ears. The whole thing was a lie, I'm sure of it–they never meant to give him a fair trial, I don't think." Angbar took a tentative step inside the house. "Where are your parents?"

"At the inn," she said. "Waiting for word." She was shaking. "I have to find them." She made to leave, but Angbar grabbed her arm.

"Syntal. Listen."

Her eyes danced with terror. Angbar lifted a hand, as if trying to calm a wild cat. "Lyseira already has an idea," he said. "She's getting Seth and we're going to try and break Helix free. And run."

Syntal licked her lips; her gaze flicked to the road. "Aunt and Uncle..."

"They can't know. It'll put them in danger. Listen. Lys said his jail wagon is near the road. It's not in the middle of camp or anything. If we go up there tonight–*now*–we can do it."

Firelight from the hearth glimmered like fever in her eyes. *Please, Syn. Please.*

"We'll need food," she said, and ran past him, back to her room. "Find whatever you can."

"Good! Yes. Food." Angbar darted to the kitchen and started grabbing salted beef and jars of jelly, anything he could get his hands on, throwing them in a sack as fast as he could. His heart was an earthquake in his chest.

Syntal joined him in the kitchen, a giant knapsack slung over her shoulder, and the two of them went out through the smithy. Angbar helped himself to a dagger as they passed through, throwing it into the sack along with everything else.

Outside, night had taken full hold. Syntal was at his side, breathing hard, her eyes wide. She was waiting to follow him, he suddenly realized. It was a bizarre feeling. He had never been a leader.

"Uh." He pointed down the road. "We're supposed to meet up behind Lyseira's house."

But they drew to a sudden halt as they came around the porch.

Two soldiers stood before the Rulanos' front door; two more, mounted, stood guard on the road. Their torches threw flickering firelight across the packed dirt.

One of them pounded on the door. "Open in the name of the King!" The words boomed down the dark street like thunder.

Angbar's blood ran cold. "*Kirith a'jhul,*" he swore.

*ii. Lyseira*

Lyseira eased the back door open, wincing as it creaked. She knew her mother would be waiting in the front, to hear about the trial, and she wanted to avoid her. A reckless courage had been driving her since she left the church, but her mother had a way of forcing Lyseira's thoughts to slow down.

Tonight, she couldn't afford that.

She slipped in, leaving the door ajar. It was dark in the tiny common room, but she could see the lantern light reflecting from the kitchen. Her mother must not have heard her.

She crossed the room, bouncing on the balls of her feet. Her heart threatened to jump out of her mouth. Any second, she would hear her mother call her name. Her voice would be lilting and inquisitive, not at all accusatory–and it would send Lyseira leaping through the roof.

The call didn't come. When she reached Seth's door, her hands were shaking so badly she could barely grasp the knob.

She sneaked inside to find him balanced on his right foot, with a stack of books piled in either upraised palm. His left knee was bent so his calf hovered parallel to the floor, his ankle crossing his other knee. As she slipped the door closed, his eyes slid open as if he'd been expecting her.

"Seth," she whispered.

He knelt, setting the books on the floor. "What?"

"They found Helix guilty. They're going to kill him."

"You said he wasn't guilty." He regained his feet.

"He's not!" she hissed. "He was framed! It was that Justicar that did it, but they're blaming it on Helix!"

"How do you know that?"

"Helix saw him. He was sure." She plowed over his question and dove into her plan. "We're going to save him," she said, grabbing his hand. "We're leaving now."

He didn't move. "Did the judge do the miracle of truth?"

"Yes! Of course! But he's lying too, they both–"

The look in his eyes made her stumble. She had never considered the possibility that he wouldn't help her.

As a Preserver, he should be *stopping* her.

"Seth, you have to believe me. Please, listen–Father Marcus, he tried to bribe me. He said he would initiate me if I lied at the trial. It was a lie, all of it–I saw the tracks myself, and he said there weren't any. They were... I don't know, they were in on it together, somehow, Marcus and Elmoor. I don't know why." The torrent of words must have sounded like nonsense to him. She could barely understand them herself.

"Lyseira," he said. "If they found him guilty–"

"They *did it,* Seth! And they're blaming it on Helix!"

He glanced at her hand, still clutching his arm. She let him go and backed away. *He's not going to come. I ruined this, I never should have told him.*

She couldn't believe that. She refused.

"I can explain it all, *m'sai?* I swear. But I need you to trust me now. Please. I know it sounds mad. No one knows that more than me. But Angbar is packing right now, he'll be back any minute, and we're going. Don't–please, at least don't stop us."

He looked at her. "You're sure."

*Oh, Seth.* "Certain."

He went to the corner, where his traveling roll was still assembled, and tossed it to her.

"Take it. I'll make another." He grabbed the blanket and pillow from the bed, started tying them with an old belt.

"Thank you." She didn't know what else to say.

"Get my cloak."

She grabbed it, then a few other things they might need: paper, a quill, a bottle of ink. Her hands moved on their own, while her mind watched.

"There's still a little food in the roll," he said as he finished, "but we'll need more. I'll get some from the kitchen."

Lyseira shook her head. "Mom's there. I don't want her to know what we're doing."

Seth slung the new pack over his shoulder. "I won't tell her," he said.

"Seth!" she begged, but he was already out the door.

"Lyseira?" Finally, the call from the kitchen. Lyseira winced.

They found Mom sitting at the table with half a quilt in her hands, a needle poking from her mouth. "Seth?" she said as her son came in. "Lyseira?" Then she saw the packs, and her brows drew together.

Lyseira had thought she was frightened before, but now she was terrified. She stood in the doorway, silent, as Seth bustled into the room and threw open a cupboard. He loosened the belt on his pack and began loading it with food.

"What do you think you're doing?" Mom said. All trace of kindness had vanished from her voice. This was the *I demand answers and I demand them now* voice. It forced Lyseira's mouth open like a pry bar.

"Mom..."

"Seth, put that down," she demanded. Seth held a jar of pickled beets. He stuffed it into the pack.

"Mom," Lyseira repeated. Her mother's gaze turned, and she finally saw that the woman wasn't truly angry. She was frightened.

Lyseira's resolve shattered.

"We can't let them kill Helix," she pled–not for permission, but understanding. "We have to get him out."

Mom was confused. "They're going to kill him? But didn't the judge–"

Horses neighed outside, and she broke off. Lyseira froze, her eyes latching to the front window. Torchlight played across the front yard.

Mom gave her a short, fierce hug. "Get out the back," she whispered. "Quickly. Be careful." Then she pushed her away and turned to Seth, lifting her head to kiss him on the cheek. "Take care of your sister," she breathed.

He nodded, threw the roll over his shoulder, and strode to the back door, still ajar. "Lyseira," he said.

She took a step toward him, then glanced back. Her mother looked impossibly old.

The door rattled in its frame. "Open in the name of the King!"

"Go!" Mom told her.

Lyseira obeyed.

~ ~

Seth swept out the back door and glanced around before waving her out. He stopped them behind the Tevington house, holding her back with one arm as he checked the street. A pair of horses galloped past, heading for the Smiths'.

"Do you see Angbar?" she panted. "He was supposed to meet us behind the house."

Seth glanced behind and shook his head. "No. We'll get along without him. It's clear." He grabbed her arm and again pulled her into a run.

The houses flashed past. It started snowing. Finally Seth ducked behind a tree, pulling Lyseira behind him. The temple was just across the road. A hulking blob of shadow rested at the base of the hill: the prison tent.

"That one," Seth said.

"Yes." Her stomach was taut: a bowstring ready to snap.

"There are two soldiers at the front, facing the camp. If we come from the back, we should be able to get underneath and inside without them hearing us."

Guards; of course there were guards. They'd been lucky so far, but to sneak right past two soldiers? How–?

Seth's brow furrowed. "But we'll need a key for the wagon. The guards must have one. I think I can handle both of them, if I can surprise them." His tone was clipped, but flat; he might have been discussing the weather. Briefly, Lyseira wondered what he meant by *handle them*.

He shook his head. "But we'd have to trick them into the tent, or someone will see us. And if they make any noise the rest of the camp will hear it. We'll never get out." Suddenly he tensed; his left hand grabbed Lyseira's shoulder, his eyes training on something behind the tent. "Look," he whispered. "There's someone over there."

Lyseira leaned around the tree and squinted through the snow. She could see them: one lithe and low, trying not to be noticed, the other tall and clumsy. Each carried a sack. "Angbar," she whispered. "And Syntal. Who else would be sneaking toward the tent?" An irrational annoyance seized her. "He told me he wouldn't go to the Smiths'!"

Seth glanced at her. "You can't believe anything Angbar says," he muttered. "We'd better grab them before they do something stupid." Then he was gone, dashing across the road for the tent. Lyseira followed. The road was a thousand miles wide, every running step a call for the guards' attention.

They came around wide, catching the other two just as they reached the back end of the tent. "Shhh," Seth whispered. "It's us."

Syntal jumped and spun around, gasping. Angbar yelped like a burnt cat.

Seth glared at them, but before he could say anything a soldier stepped around the front corner of the tent, flooding them with torchlight. "Hey!"

Lyseira froze. *Charge the guard. Run for the woods. Cut into the tent.*

The soldier drew his sword; his partner came around the corner behind him. "That's the girl from the trial," he said. "What–?"

Seth charged.

The second soldier pulled his sword.

Lyseira chased after her brother, her mind alight with terror.

Then the air trembled like a herd of bison was charging across the road. Drowsiness crashed into her. The ground tilted and she staggered, forced to grab Seth's shoulder to keep her feet.

Both soldiers crumpled to the ground.

"Syn?" Angbar breathed.

Syntal had raised her hands. For an instant, her eyes were so vivid Lyseira could see them in the darkness.

*Witch.* The word sparked in Lyseira's mind, trembled at her lips. It was too heavy to speak.

Seth stared daggers. "What was that?" He took a step toward Syntal. "Was that you?"

"Hurry," Syntal said. "There'll be more."

"Was that you?" Seth demanded again. "*What did you do?*"

"There's no time!" she threw back, and Lyseira knew she was right.

"The keys," she heard herself say. It was too much at once: the trial, the verdict, witchcraft. The world had transformed, like a stage with the curtain torn away, revealing madness. She had to keep her focus, or be lost.

Seth held Syntal's eyes. A distant laugh came out of the camp, drifting between the snowflakes. Finally he flicked his gaze away as if sheathing a blade.

"Here." He crouched next to one of the fallen men, lifted the key ring and a dagger, and passed them to Lyseira. Then he pulled out one of the tent stakes and peered underneath. "It's dark," he whispered. "If there were guards, they'd have light."

From somewhere inside, Lyseira heard a muffled voice.

"I'll get him," she said, grabbing the torch the first soldier had dropped. "Wait out here." She lifted the fabric higher and slid the torch underneath, then crawled in.

Helix was hunched in the jail wagon, bound and gagged, his hands tied to the bars behind him. The torchlight glinted in his frantic eyes like moonlight on a lake. He made an unintelligible noise from behind his gag.

A padlock hung from the cage door. Lyseira set the torch in the dirt and started trying keys, forcing herself not to think about what would happen if none of them worked.

The second one did. She scrambled into the wagon and took out Helix's gag.

"Thank Akir," he whispered. "Oh *sehk,* Lys, hurry."

As the last word left his mouth, Syntal echoed it from outside. *"Hurry!"*

Helix jerked as if he'd been shocked. "Syn's here?" he asked.

Lyseira nodded, panting as she worked at the ropes with the dagger. With a final lurch, the bindings on Helix's hands came free. Lyseira started on his feet. "She's watching for guards," she said through clenched teeth. "Seth's out there too, and Angbar. We're getting you out of here."

"Where?" he said.

*Tal'aden,* she thought. "Don't know yet."

"We have to get out of the village. They'll find us–"

"Yeah. I know." Finally, his feet came free. "*M'sai,*" she breathed. "Can you walk?" She hopped out of the wagon, her eyes darting, but the tent was still empty. Helix maneuvered himself to a sitting position, then gingerly pulled himself out and to his feet. He wobbled, clutching the bar behind him, then nodded.

"The torch," he said.

"Leave it."

"*Lyseira!*" Angbar roared from outside.

Her heart leapt into her throat. They'd been seen.

She cut a gash through the tent, and helped Helix through it. Seth had a soldier in a head lock. "Run!" he snarled. He tripped the man onto his back and cracked his head against a rock. The soldier went limp. She didn't see anyone else.

Angbar and Syntal were halfway across the road. "Run!" Angbar shouted. "Run!"

They ran.

A wasp buzzed at her ear, and an arrow thudded into the dirt. She was trying to understand this, to make sense of what she was seeing, when another one nearly nicked her shoulder. Panic lurched in her stomach.

*Akir help us, oh, God.*

She stole a glance back. Seth was just behind her, but there were three soldiers at the prison tent, all with drawn longbows. *We'll never make it.*

At the far end of the road, Syntal stopped and turned. The light from the soldiers' torches danced in her eyes like a warning.

Lyseira pounded past her, then turned to make sure Helix and Seth were keeping up. Syntal gestured as two more arrows shot past, and the air vibrated like a piano string.

Again, drowsiness hammered at Lyseira. Her eyelids weighed a thousand pounds. She stumbled.

At the tent, two of the archers collapsed. The third reeled, his numb hands fumbling his bow, but he kept his feet. His eyes widened.

*"Witch!"* he screamed. He knelt for his dropped weapon.

A sliver of light ripped from Syntal's hand and flashed silently across the road. It hurled the soldier, screaming, through one of the tent posts. The tent devoured him as it collapsed on itself.

Then Lyseira's dropped torch engulfed it.

*"Le'sehk,"* someone murmured, and someone else: "By Akir."

Syntal stumbled backwards and threw out a hand. Helix shouted her name and grabbed her hand, keeping her on her feet.

The camp exploded with shouts and screams; soldiers and clerics poured out of the temple like an army of moths toward the tent's lurid flames.

*"Run!"* Seth demanded. He grabbed Syntal's other arm and nearly jerked her off her feet. *"Now!"*

# Chapter 8

## Before the Storm

*i. Seth*

The flood passed, and the village came together to handle the aftermath. They had to cut down trees, Lyseira's mom explained. They had to clear the debris and shore up the banks so they could rebuild the bridge. They had to look for valuables.

What she meant was: they had to look for bodies.

His heart leapt at the possibility. He had been waiting for it since the instant his parents disappeared.

Finally, he would check the bank where they'd been standing. He would comb the water with his own hands. The other villagers were just their neighbors. He was their *son.*

His longing alone would find them.

But when she left for the day to help at the river, Missus Rulano didn't bring him. Instead, she marched him and Lyseira outside and across the road to the Smith place.

Despair seized him. He nearly ran and he nearly wept. It might have been the warring of these two urges that forced him forward, mute and obedient, into an afternoon of purgatory.

The Smiths' house used to impress him: its great size and fancy décor, its upholstered furniture and multiple glass windows. It made the Rulano home look like a stable in comparison. Now, it was as grey as everything else.

While the mothers exchanged pleasantries, Helix came out of his room. "Hi, Seth." He pointedly ignored Lyseira, who had told his mother about him peeing out of the tree house.

Seth grunted.

"Uh... thanks for helping out at Baler's fort," Helix continued. "We really showed him."

The epic battle with the bullies in their tree house had happened in a different person's life, a thousand years ago. Seth tried to remember why it had mattered.

"Welcome," he finally muttered.

"Hi, Helix," Lyseira said timidly. Helix favored her with a long glare.

Seth caught a glimpse of Syntal peering around a bedroom door before she ducked away. Her shyness irritated him, but abruptly, he remembered her vacant stare at the funeral. *Her parents are dead, too.*

Somehow, that only made her timidity rankle more. He had tried to hide, too; but eventually, he'd been dragged out.

"Syn living here now?" he asked.

Helix glanced back. "Oh–yeah. She has to share a room with Beth."

"You two be good today," Lyseira's mom said. She gave them each a quick hug. "With most of the town helping, we might even get the near shore done today if we're lucky. I'll see you tonight."

"Are you hungry, you two?" Helix's mom asked as she left.

Lyseira answered for both of them. "No, ma'am. Mom made breakfast."

"I see. Well, we've yet to have it here, so I'm going to get it started. You two make yourselves at home."

The day was an endless procession of pitying looks and people walking on eggshells. Helix's mom kept trying to cheer Seth up, which only made him more angry and quiet, and Helix constantly tried to play with him, like the older boy thought it was his duty to keep him busy. Now and then Lyseira would intervene, gently steering them away to give him some space. She seemed to understand what he wanted, and alone among everyone, he appreciated her attempts to help. But she was only seven, and Helix and his mother were sure they knew best.

When Helix's mom served an early lunch of radish stew–a meal Seth had always found revolting–he made up his mind.

Today was the day.

After lunch Helix's mom turned them outside to play. Syntal tried to retreat back to her room, but her aunt wouldn't have it. She sent her out with the rest of them, insisting that she "needed the air."

Helix stared at the grass, kicking idly. Lyseira asked what Seth wanted to do, but he just shrugged.

*What do I want to do? I want to get out of here.* He had no place in mind; he just wanted to escape this one. To get away from the pitying looks, to run until something else grabbed his interest and wouldn't let it go. He was going to do it; the only trick was to avoid being followed.

When the idea occurred to him, he marveled at his own cunning.

"Let's play hide'n'sneak," he said.

Helix brightened. "*M'sai*," he said. "Let's play on teams! We can play girls against boys," he added, glaring at Lyseira.

"I don't want to play teams," Syntal said. "Let's just play normal."

"Just normal," Seth agreed.

The kids pulled grass to see who would be the seeker, and Lyseira came up short. "'Member your mom said we can't leave the yard," she reminded the others as she settled against a tree.

"Hey, that's not fair!" Helix sputtered. "You have to face the house or the tree or something, or you can just look any time!"

"I don't cheat," Lyseira retorted, but turned to face the tree. Helix and Syntal scattered around behind the house to hide, leaving Seth alone in the front with Lyseira, who had her eyes closed.

It was perfect. He bounded across the road, and the thrill of each running step knocked loose an epiphany. He realized exactly where he wanted to go.

*"I can't see you, I can't see you, I can't see you, this I swear,*

*"But I might hear you, I might smell you 'cause of stinky underwear,*

*"Try your best to hide from me, while I say the rhyme–*

*"But do it fast because I'll only say it* two more times!*"*

"Three times!" Helix yelled from somewhere behind the house. "Cheater!"

*I'll be gone when she's done,* Seth realized. *Who knows if I'll even come back. I could leave for good, set out on my own. I could join the Pazervers. If I–*

"Seth!" Lyseira called. The word tripped him; he stumbled to a stop. "You're supposed to stay in the yard!" She waved at him from the tree.

*She peeked?* He couldn't believe it. It was so unfair. Lyseira, of all people? *Lyseira* had peeked?

"Cheater!" he shrieked, so hard his voice broke.

Then he ran.

*ii. Angbar*

He wasn't sure his parents would help with the cleanup. They weren't always welcome when the whole village was around. In the end, though, his dad had insisted they go, and Mom had agreed.

The wreckage along the river sounded exciting–he *really* wanted to see the broken bridge–but they told him to stay home. He begged and wheedled, cajoled and whined. They were steadfast. "Stay inside and behave yourself," they admonished as they left.

There was no chance of that.

Outside it was all blue sky and the buzzing of cicadas. The breeze greeted him like an old friend with a warm hug. And the woods...

The woods had completely transformed for him.

Trees were upended and spilled across one another; gentle slopes had given birth to new ravines and jagged hillsides. Paths that he'd known for years were gone. Every branch was a story of apocalypse.

He pretended he was in the legendary Veiling Green, the forest where no one who entered ever returned. *Maybe this is what it's like there,* he thought: every familiar sight a twisted reflection, like something from a dream.

When the forest surrendered to the vastness of the lake shore, he was amazed anew. Branches and uprooted plants littered the shoreline. Debris and treasure lay everywhere. Wooden boards, dishes, nails, dolls–everything he could imagine, washed downstream from Southlight or maybe even from other villages further upstream.

It was the exclamation point at the end of the storm. All the tales of the storm's brutality concluded here. Excited, he ran to the shoreline.

It became a battlefield, and he was the last survivor of the army that had lost.

Then it was the remains of a city under the lake, expelled from the depths in a violent spasm of dark magic.

He was just becoming a pirate who had devastated an enemy ship and was picking through its beached ruins for booty, when he saw Seth burst out of the woods.

The boy's face burned red; he was panting like a dog. He bent over double, gasping for air, then collapsed to his knees.

"Seth!" Angbar called as he ran to meet him. "What are you doing here? Look at all this stuff! Hey, do you think some of this stuff is your stuff? Because I heard your house fell in!"

Seth's hair stuck to his head like a clump of sweaty seaweed. He was panting too hard to answer Angbar's questions, but he leveled a glare at him that could've melted stone.

Angbar must've been talking too much again–he did that at home sometimes and earned similar looks from his parents–but he was too excited to hold back. "You gotta see it all, it's washed up all over the lake. I think that one might have gold in it–" he started, when Helix, Lyseira, and Syntal came stumbling out of the woods as well.

"Aha!" Helix shouted. "I told you he'd be at the lake!" The freckled boy started running, the two girls right behind him.

Seth bolted to his feet. "Go!" he hissed at Angbar, waving him further down the shore.

"What – ?"

"Just go!" Seth yelled, shoving him hard in the back before running past him. Angbar staggered in the mud, but caught his feet and started running, completely confused.

"What's going on?" he demanded.

"I didn't want... them to follow me!" Seth panted back. He fell into a brisk walk before collapsing again to the mud, his chest heaving.

Angbar stopped with him, and a flash caught his eye on the far end of the lake. *Whoa.* "Did you see that?" Again Seth ignored him, too winded to respond.

Angbar squinted toward the far shore, but the glimmer was gone.

As the others caught up, Seth climbed to his feet. "Well?" he challenged. "What are you gonna do, did you tell your mom, Helix? Lyseira? I didn't want you lot to come with, you coulda just let me go!"

Lyseira shook her head slowly, drawing huge breaths. "Seth," she started, "Mom said–"

It happened again. The sun found a hole in the clouds, the lake lit up like a torch, and the glow ignited a twinkle on the shore. Then the clouds covered the sun again, and the glimmer died.

"There's sumthin' there," Angbar urged. He couldn't make out anything. "Did you see it?"

Syntal tracked his gesture, but shook her head.

"Lyseira chased you," Helix protested. "I tried to stop her."

Seth scowled. "That's fishguts! You were ahead of her!"

Helix shrugged.

"I'm goin'," Angbar said. When the others ignored him again, he started walking. *If it's a huge pile of pirate gold, they'll be sorry.* He saw himself returning to the group, a patch over his eye and a parrot on his shoulder, the richest pirate boy in Southlight. *I tried to tell you,* he'd say.

Syntal caught up to him, leaving the others to argue on the beach. "Do you know what it was?"

Angbar shook his head. "I don't know, that's why I want to go look. I've found all kinds of things down here. There's all this stuff washed up!"

He told her about the treasures he'd found so far, like the little red horse and the magic wand. He was trying to dig the chunk of colored glass from his pocket when he suddenly wondered if he should say something about the accident.

Her parents were gone. She had to be sad. But was there any point in saying anything? All he could think to say was, *"I'm sorry your parents died."* What would that accomplish?

His thoughts roamed back to more pressing matters. How large would the pile of gold be? How much could he buy with it? He would have to share some with Syntal, since she had come with. But not half. He *had* seen it first.

They'd come all the way around the lake. A distant whisper of a child's yell, something about a cheater, floated lazily across the water.

Syntal pointed. "Is that it? Look!"

Something metallic jutted from the mud ahead. It might have had a slight blue tinge, but it was so crusted with filth that it was hard to tell.

"Careful," Syntal warned as he started clearing the dirt off.

"There could be sharp parts."

The thing was huge; bigger than him. As he chipped at the encasing dirt, he saw that the metal was curved.

"Armor!" he cried. "It's armor, look!" He thought this specific piece of armor was called a breastplate, but he wasn't sure, so he didn't say anything. Syntal was picky about that kind of thing.

Reams of mud slid off it as they pulled it from the ground.

"Look at the marks!" Syntal said. Arcane whorls and sigils, the etchings packed with old dirt, laced the metal. "Is that the First Tongue?"

"I bet this belonged to a pirate!" Angbar breathed. "Or maybe *belongs* to a pirate!" A wonderful idea came to him. "I bet his treasure is around here somewhere too!" Then a counter-point: "But what if he comes to find it?"

Syntal traced one of the long lines in the metal with her finger. "I don't think he will. Look."

The plate had a gaping hole in it, twisting inward right by the heart. Suddenly Angbar was sure he could see blood stained into the metal.

"He was stabbed!"

"Maybe," Syntal said. "But where is he then?"

Angbar's gaze went to the water. "He took it off," he said, "and swam to his death." He nodded solemnly. "I bet he got ate by sharks."

"No," Syntal said. "Look here." She knelt at the water's edge, soaking her dress up to her knees, and pulled something small from the shallow water.

"What is it?" He held his hand out, but Syntal didn't give it to him.

"A buckle." She turned it over. The metal was badly rusted on this piece; chunks of it were flaking off in her hands. "He used it to tie the armor on with. Helix showed me in Uncle's smithy."

Angbar looked back to the water. "Syn," he said. "I bet this stuff washed up on shore during the storm! That's why we never saw it before. I bet there's more of it down there too."

Syntal looked annoyed. "That doesn't make any sense. It's big and heavy. It would sink to the bottom."

"You saw how strong that storm was! If it could rip down a bridge, it could wash up a little piece of armor!" Syntal jerked her eyes away. "There's more down there, I bet you! What if this pirate had a sword too? Or gold? Or–"

"It's not a pirate, idiot!" Syntal spat. "There's no pirates in a river! Pirates are in the ocean!"

"You never know if–"

"And if this storm was so strong that it would wash up an armor, why would there be anything on the bottom of the lake still? You're so stupid. It would wash up everything, not just leave some things!"

She seemed really mad, all of a sudden. He plowed on.

"I heard of a wind storm once that destroyed a whole city, a big one like Shientel, but it picked up one cow and dropped him a hundred miles away completely safe and he wasn't hurt at all. So if that can happen–"

"That can't happen, that's just some stupid nog story you heard. Or made up, maybe," she accused, glaring.

That stung a bit. *What is she so upset about?* "I don't make things up!" he sputtered.

"You–"

"Hi Angbar," Lyseira said. She and the others had finally caught up.

"Hey, Seira," Angbar said, grateful to drop the argument with Syntal. "Look what–"

"Wow!" Helix raved. "This was on the shore?" The boy grabbed the breastplate, nearly twice as wide as he was, and held it against his chest as if to try it on.

"Yeah!" Angbar said. It was good to see someone as excited as he was. "A pirate was wearing it and he got stabbed!" Wait, what had he figured out exactly? "While he was on his ship, I mean, and then he fell in and died a hundred years ago. And then in the storm, it got washed up!"

The breastplate slipped crooked as Helix freed a hand for an imaginary sword. He swung it a few times as the decrepit armor slid through his grasp.

Even Seth looked a little impressed. "That wasn't no pirate," he said. "Pirates ain't honor-bull, they don't wear armor anyhow."

"This was a knight's armor," Helix declared. "I could be a knight now."

"You can't be a knight!" Lyseira said, incredulous. "Knights don't pee on people."

"How do you know?"

"Because knights are supposed to be chivalrous!"

Helix gave her a look that said, *You made that word up.*

"I wonder if there's more down in the lake," Angbar mused.

Syntal scoffed. "Would you just forget it? There's not, there can't be. That doesn't make sense."

Seth glared at Syntal. "What do you know?" he snapped. "Like you were ever a knight anyway." He looked at Angbar. "Let's dive down and see."

Lyseira gaped at him. "You can't dive down there! It's dangerous! And the water's dirty, you won't be able to see anything!"

"I can see fine," Seth said, peering into the filthy water. He clenched his teeth and glared at Syntal. "I'm gonna go."

Angbar grinned and kicked off his sandals as Seth pulled off his shirt. Helix took one look at Lyseira, saw her indignation, and broke at once into his wicked smirk.

"You're all crazy!" she said. "Helix, I'm gonna go back'n–"

"What, tell my mom again?" he snapped. "Go ahead, blabbermouth! By the time you get back to my house we'll be done anyway."

"Yeah," Angbar said. "And you can't have any of the treasure if you don't help." Standing in his underpants, he found the lake's breeze a bit chillier.

Lyseira shut her mouth. She was giving up.

Seth sloshed past Angbar. When the water had reached his chest, he took a deep breath and dove. Angbar waded in behind him, but hesitated.

There probably wasn't anything in the lake; it was just fun bugging Lyseira with the other boys. That game was losing its appeal fast, though, in the face of the wind. He found himself hoping Seth would surface and tell them he couldn't see anything, so they could all get their clothes back on.

Seth broke the surface maybe ten feet out, thrashing his head like a dog. "There's something glowing down there!" he exclaimed, and dove again.

*iii. Seth*

An avalanche of silence crashed over him, obliterating Lyseira's nagging and Angbar's prattling. The sun's constant stare shattered into secret, drifting shafts of light. It was an alien landscape, where everything else–every rule, every intrusion–simply ceased.

Here he had no one to appease but himself; no needs to attend but his own. The blind anger that had plagued him for days, the constant desire to *get away*, was suddenly and completely satisfied. He reveled in the water's isolation, drinking it in until he could drown in it.

Far below, fathoms into the lake's darkness, gleamed a beacon. It was shapeless and small, a washed out, bleary glow of blue and white fading to grey. The light was so miniscule that it may have been a trick of his eyes, deceiving him with a phantom of the sun. It was impossible to interpret and impossibly out of reach.

But here, he was sovereign. He dove toward it.

The sun beckoned him back, screaming of folly; but as he descended, its warnings dimmed until the water strangled them. In the ensuing darkness the surreal glow warped beneath him, expanding into hues of violet and green as it fluttered in the lake's currents.

Without it, he would be blind.

Beyond the veil of his grief, that ethereal light clamored with portents. As he dove deeper something rose up in him: a ludicrous, serene hope. *They're alive,* he realized. *Or they're dead, and they'll take me with them. But they are there.*

*They are there.*

His lungs began to ache. It was too late to turn back, but he didn't care.

His chest burning, he came to a wall of rock that ended maybe five feet above the lake floor. Kicking, he swam underneath it. Suddenly the glow magnified, but it was coming from *above* him, behind the rock shelf and upwards. His lungs on fire, he kicked off from the wall and streaked away from the lake floor.

As if in a dream that would not let him drown, his head broke the surface.

He sucked in a mouthful of dank air, gasping as he trod water. A rock ledge jutted from the murk in front of him; he latched onto it, his body in the lake but his head mercifully clear, gulping air like a crying newborn.

When he finally caught his breath, he opened his eyes and forgot to breathe all over again.

He had surfaced in an underwater cave. The light emanated from the glowing patches of lichen on the walls. They were violet and azure, scarlet and veridian.

He pulled himself out of the water slowly, too stunned to rush. The cavern unfolded for twenty feet or more before twisting away to his right. The lichen pockmarked all of it, its light glistening on the rock like the blood of a rainbow.

*Wow.* He was powerless to move, his feet nailed to the stone. And then he saw the skull.

It was old; lichen sucked at its lower jaw like a beard. Years in the cave had made it slimy and dark. A jagged gash high on its crown hinted at a mortal wound.

Death had followed him, even here, but at least he was alone.

Seth cast along the cave floor. There were bones, he realized, scattered throughout the cave as if tossed away by the lake. They were all like the skull: black, grimy with age, overgrown with the weird, glowing lichen.

The reverent silence shattered as Angbar burst out of the pool, gasping for air. Seth felt a sharp pang of resentment. Was there *nowhere* he could be alone?

"That..." Angbar managed between gulps of stale air. "That's dreamoss!" He climbed out of the pool. "I've heard of that! How–how did you... find this place?"

"I just came down, I don't know." The question irritated him. *What do you mean, how did I find it? Didn't you see the glow?*

Angbar nodded. "Me and Helix seen it and went back up. I think Syntal–" His jaw dropped as he laid eyes on the skull. "*Kirith a'jhul.*"

"Yeah," Seth said, dismissively. "Yeah, I seen it already."

Angbar approached it as if sneaking up on a rabbit.

"Watch out," Seth said. "There's more bones."

Angbar marveled at the scattered skeleton. "This is him," he whispered. "This is the pirate! He swam away to die, and got sucked down by the lake. I knew it. He must've been here for–" His eyes suddenly widened. "His sword!"

Seth followed his eyes. A longsword lay in the back of the cave, its hilt protruding from a bright patch of crimson dreamoss. He'd been so dumbstruck before that he hadn't even noticed it.

"Keeps," Angbar said.

"You can't call keeps," Seth snapped. "I got here first."

Angbar broke into a run. Seth gave chase, but Angbar beat him to the weapon and jerked it away.

Unlike the armor on the shore, the sword hadn't rusted. The blade wasn't deadly sharp, but it wasn't dull either, and it was beautifully crafted. Under the guard, draped in rotten shreds of black leather, marched a line of strange, tiny markings. Seth stared, trying to make some sense of them, but they were indecipherable.

Helix climbed out of the pool and came over, dripping. He cast long glances at the moss and the bones, but the sword entranced him at once.

"Let me see it," he said. Behind him, Syntal bobbed into the cave, panting.

Angbar grabbed the hilt, scratching the blade on the floor as he put it behind his back. "No, I called keeps, it's mine."

"No it's not," Seth growled, "because I got down here first and called keeps on everything, especially the sword."

"You did *not!*" Angbar retorted. "You didn't say anything about that until I found it–you didn't even know it was down here!"

"I just want to *see* it," Helix said, still holding out his hand. "C'mon, let me see it."

Angbar sighed, but handed it over. Helix accepted it with the reverence of a cleric handling a holy book. Even wrapping both his hands around the hilt, he couldn't support its weight.

"It belonged to the pirate," Angbar said.

"It didn't belong to a pirate!" Helix scoffed. "Look at it! It's brand new! It looks like my dad just made it today!" He gave it a clumsy swing. The weapon bobbed vaguely toward Seth, who stepped away. "Besides, it was a knight, I told you."

"Maybe it got pazerved by the water," Angbar countered.

"Swords rust in water."

"Well, you obviously don't know nothing about it," Angbar said, and held out his hand. "Now give it back."

*It should be mine,* Seth raged. *I should be down here by myself. This was all here for me. I was the one who wanted to come.* He fought the childish urge to whine, to scream at them to leave. He wanted them all gone.

"Give it to me," Seth said, to rankle Angbar. "I found it."

Angbar turned on him. "You didn't find it, liar!"

"Did too, I was down here first."

"But you didn't even see it!"

"It doesn't matter," Helix interjected, "because it's *mine* now."

Angbar whirled on him, but Helix hefted the sword and arched his brows. His bare chest tensed, showing off the hours spent at his father's smithy.

Angbar glanced at Seth in mute appeal, but Syntal had just walked past them, shivering in the drenched glob of her dress. She seemed small and vulnerable.

Seth followed her.

Beyond the curve, the cave walls drew together into a tiny, lightless crack. A second, shallower pool had formed in the back of the cave. In the shimmering colors of the dreamoss, Seth could just make out a large, leather-bound book at the pool's bottom, wedged between the walls.

Syntal started to tug on it, trying to pry it loose, but she was too weak. Her efforts triggered a new spasm of spiteful anger in him. *Why does she care?* Obviously, any book that had been sitting underwater would be totally ruined. But she wanted it, and suddenly, he didn't want her to have it.

Seth knelt in the pool and grabbed the book by its spine. The thing was gigantic, easily bigger than his own head. Syntal continued to try to pull it free, but it was Seth's sharp, repeated tugs that finally yanked it out. Syntal stumbled and fell to her knees in the water, splashing him in the face.

"Seth!" she accused.

"I found the cave, I get to keep *something*," he snarled.

"What does it say?" Angbar said, hurrying over to see. "Open it!"

Seth tried, but the book was locked with a metal band. There wasn't even a key hole. "Can't," Seth said.

"It doesn't even have a title?" Angbar asked. The cover was blank; there were no markings on the book at all.

Syntal sloshed over. "You can't even open a book?" she spat, and grabbed for it. Seth jerked it away.

"*Se – eth!*" she yelled.

"It's *mine!*" he snapped back.

The girl burst into tears. Sobbing, she ran past him to the front of the cave.

Hurting her had been easy.

Helix looked at him with reproach. "C'mon, Seth. Let her have the stupid book."

Seth shook his head.

"C'mon!"

Seth stared at him.

"What are you gonna do with it anyway?"

"Yeah," Angbar chimed in. "At least give it to me, I can probably read it. You ain't gonna learn to read, I bet."

An angry retort flashed to Seth's tongue, but Helix cut him off by raising his hand.

"Look," he whispered, chewing his lip. "I'll trade you the sword for the book."

"Why do I want your stupid sword?" Seth said. Helix's face went lax with surprise. He finally turned to console Syntal when there was a splash from the pool. The girl had left.

Angbar began pulling clumps of different colored drearmoss from the walls. "I should get going," he said. "I need to be home when my parents get back." Then he darted to the skull and snapped it up. "Ha!" he shouted, and jumped into the pool.

Seth scowled. "I called keeps on that skull!" Angbar's victory enraged him, as if he'd been defeated in some fundamental conflict he couldn't define.

Helix shrugged. "There's nothing else here. Are you coming?"

"In a minute," Seth answered.

Helix grinned. "It's weird down here, isn't it? Like a different world, or something."

"Yeah." Seth stared hard at the other boy, willing him to leave.

"Well..." Helix's smile faded. "I'm gonna go check on Syn. Don't take too long. I might need help getting this sword up."

"*M'sai.*"

Helix lowered himself into the pool. With an effort, he was able to tread water holding the sword. "You know, it's actually not as heavy as it looks." Then he drew a deep breath and stopped kicking, letting the weight of the weapon carry him down.

Finally, silence settled over the cave again. Seth waited for his serenity to return, but the sacred privacy of the place had been violated. The other kids' voices echoed from the walls now, destroying his peace as surely as shrieks.

He had found one quiet place, one sanctum, and it was gone.

Images danced in the shadows. The faces of his parents in that final, eternal instant before they fell in. Mom playing with him. Black water. Dad rehashing some old story. Empty rope.

He became a statue at the water's edge, his drying hair curling against his scalp. Finally, he tossed the book back into the smattering of old bones and jumped into the lake.

He'd never wanted it anyway.

# Chapter 9

*i. Helix*

He flew for the cover of the trees, lashed by blind panic, his lungs burning with the frozen air. He still had Syntal's hand but Seth had pulled ahead, nearer to Lyseira and Angbar. They were invisible, somewhere in the dark. He only knew they were there by their panting.

The tree line had to be a hundred miles away. He would trip and break his ankle before he reached it. He would feel a sudden flower of pain between his shoulders, and plunge face-first into the grass with an arrow jutting from his back. He would catch the barest, fleeting glimpse of that horrible winged helm before a flashing sword struck his head off.

He glanced back. The distant fire was spreading toward the camp; it painted the scene in garish reds and yellows. A swarm of silhouettes fought the blaze. Soldiers shouted contradicting orders. Riders galloped into the village, or out of it. It was chaos.

Then they made the trees.

They crashed into the undergrowth with the noise of an avalanche. He winced, prayed no one had heard it back at the camp, and plowed deeper into the woods. He saw Seth–or was it Angbar? –just ahead and to the right, a lean shadow darting between the midnight boughs. It would be too easy to lose the others, to get split up. *We have to stay together.* He clutched Syntal's hand tighter.

"Wait." It was Angbar, somewhere behind them. *When did he get behind us?* "Wait. Need..." Helix looked back and saw a shadow doubled over, its back to a tree and its chest heaving.

"*M'sai.* Quickly." Seth's voice, without a trace of fatigue. "Does anyone else need a rest?"

Helix sank against an old stump. His legs were burning. He tried to answer, but his lungs wouldn't let him. He waved instead.

"Do... do..." Lyseira fought to catch her breath. "Do you think... they saw us?"

Helix shook his head. "They were... busy... fire." He gestured stupidly the way they had come.

"You're sure?" Seth pressed.

"Pretty... sure."

"Then they may not know which way we went." He paused. "They may not even realize you're gone. They may think you're burning."

*Only my legs,* Helix thought, but he was too winded and too terrified to say it out loud.

"We have to keep going," Seth continued. "We need to get as far as we can."

Helix's legs felt like jelly, but he pushed himself up. Angbar's shadow waved behind them. "C'mon," Helix panted. "If I can... you can."

They pressed on, more slowly now, picking their way through the darkness and the bushes. They came to a frozen creek and Seth led them down to it, using it like a road.

Then a bugle split the air behind them, and they were running again.

*ii. Angbar*

The forest was a nightmare, the frozen creek bed a path to Hel. Somewhere, behind his terror and shock and growing resentment of Lyseira's sense of duty, Angbar filed these metaphors away for future use. *Nothing like real experience,* he mused through the whistling stitch in his side, *to make a text feel authentic.*

But he wasn't a Preserver or a smith's son; he wasn't even as fit as Lyseira, who was always running around town on errands. He was slowing down again. In less than an hour they reached the end of the creek bed, and at the thought of trying to shove through the forest's heavy underbrush again, his legs gave out.

"Sorry," he gasped. "Just... need... break." He couldn't see Seth's face, but he could imagine it glowering at his weakness. Everyone else, on the other hand, sank wordlessly to the ground.

They hadn't heard another horn blast since the first one, but Angbar felt like they could at any second. *What if the next one's closer?* He could make out the shapes of his friends as they caught their breath in the darkness, but he wished he could see their faces. It was easy to imagine that it was already too late, that the silhouettes might actually belong to their pursuers.

"*M'sai,*" Helix said at last. He regained his feet. "Should keep moving."

"No," came Seth's voice. "Syntal, what did you do at the tent?"

Helix's answer sounded like a scowl. "We don't have time–"

"They lost us," Seth interrupted. "They're not right behind us, not yet. And I need to know."

Helix's shadow turned to face another, still crouched on the creek bed. "Syn, you don't have to tell him anything. Let's just–"

"It was sorcery," Syntal interrupted. "It was just what it looked like."

The silence was absolute. Angbar's thoughts whirled in it. *Syntal, a witch?* He shouldn't have been surprised, not after what she had done at the tent, but he'd been able to put it out of his mind while they ran. Now it was here, indisputable, admitted by her own lips.

The Church would want her dead. She could be burned at the stake. She was lucky she'd never been caught.

Finally he heard himself ask: "How long?" The words rippled in the silent dark like pebbles in a pool.

"Since I first cast a spell?" Syntal paused. "A few years. But I had to study the book for years before that."

"I knew it," Helix breathed. At the same time Lyseira asked, "What book?"

Syntal gave a shuddering sigh. Just before she answered, Angbar realized what she would say. "The one from the lake."

"You went back for it?" Angbar asked.

"From the *lake*?" Lyseira said. She sounded confused.

"It was in that cave," Syntal told her. "You never saw it. It was right after my... right after that flood. When Seth came to live with you."

"There was a witch's book in the lake?" Lyseira's voice was dumbfounded and horrified, as if she'd just learned her house was built on a demon's tomb. "I remember you and Seth fighting, but..."

"It was locked," Seth cut in. "I remember. No key hole. Did you break it open?"

"No."

"Then how'd you get it open?"

Silence. Angbar's mind summoned an image of Syntal at age nine performing some dark ritual, her hands slick with blood, a mutilated rabbit on the ground next to her. His stomach lurched. *Ridiculous. Not Syn. Lyseira just told me too many stories from scripture.*

"It opened on its own," Syntal finally said. She drew another wavering breath. "After the Storm."

Helix sank back to the ground. Seth made a noise somewhere between a whistle and a growl. Lyseira said, "Oh, Syntal..."

"I know," Syntal said. "I know. But Lyseira, if you had seen it, you would've wanted to read it too. It's written in First Tongue. I had to learn–"

"You knew about it while The Abbot was teaching you First Tongue?" Lyseira accused, and then sucked in a breath. "By Akir. Is that why you had him teach you? You *tricked* him?"

"If you had seen it–"

"I never did see it, Syntal! You never brought it to the church! As *soon* as you figured out what it was, you should've brought it to The Abbot!"

"He would've just burned it!" Syntal snapped.

"Exactly!" Lyseira threw back.

They were getting loud. Angbar raised a hand no one could see. "*M'sai,*" he put in. "What's done is done. Keep your voices down, at least."

"It's *not* done," Seth answered. "We can still make this right. Where's the book?"

Syntal scrambled to her feet. "No."

"Is it with you?"

Angbar flashed back to the few minutes at Syntal's house, when she'd run into the back to pack some things. The sack was lying at her feet now. She put a foot on it.

"Let me see," Seth pressed.

"You are not touching this bag," Syntal said.

"Seth!" Helix hissed. "Back down!"

*We're dead,* Angbar realized. *We even pulled off the rescue, I have no idea how, but we can't get two miles before we start fighting?*

"I came for you, Helix," Seth said, "because Lyseira was sure you were being framed. I didn't risk her life and my own tonight for a witch. You know there's only one thing we can do."

"We wouldn't even *be here* if it weren't for her!" Helix snarled.

"The Church–"

"*Sehk* on the Church!" Helix hurled at him. "*Sehk* on it! It's a bunch of liars and murderers!"

Lyseira recoiled as if he'd slapped her. They all plunged into a stunned silence.

*He's right, isn't he?* Angbar realized. *They framed him, they wouldn't let him speak at his own trial, they rigged the results and bribed a fake witness just to make him look bad in front of the village.* It was rampant corruption. But how far did it go? What did it mean?

"Helix," Lyseira said. "The Rending opened the book. You know what the Rending was. Too much sin, too much *rev'naas.* A sign of God's displeasure. If it opened the book, that proves–"

"It doesn't prove anything," Syntal said. "They lied about Helix. Why can't they lie about that?"

"About the *Rending*?" Lyseira was incredulous.

"Matthew said the Storm was Akir damning the Church," Helix said. "Not Akir damning mankind."

*Maybe it wasn't either one,* Angbar thought. *Maybe it was just a damned lightning storm.*

Lyseira scoffed. "Of course he did. He hated the Church."

"And with good reason!" Helix said. "Look at what happened tonight! Look at what they did to him!"

"Why would they *lie* about the Rending, Helix?"

Helix had no answer, but after a heartbeat, Syntal did. "So they can kill people like me."

The naked trees rustled.

*That's crazy,* Angbar thought reflexively, but he'd always wondered how the Church knew the Storm was something bad. It had looked beautiful to him. How did they know what it meant?

"Syn..." Lyseira began, but the distant baying of hounds cut her off.

"Dogs," Helix muttered. "Oh, *sehk,* they have dogs out."

"We'll finish this later," Seth promised. "Go."

*iii. Iggy*

He'd wanted to challenge the judge. He'd wanted to demand evidence, or to serve as a character witness at the trial. He'd wanted to go to the Smiths, to offer them what support he could and reassure them.

Instead, he'd done nothing.

When he'd heard about the Tribunal arresting Helix, it was like waking to find his worst nightmare was real. It was the thing he'd feared every day since he'd first heard the wind. The only saving grace was that it wasn't happening to him.

He'd always thought he was a better person than that.

*Get up,* he told himself the evening of the trial. He was sitting inside, whittling a birdhouse, while his parents waited at the inn with the Smiths for word. *Your eyes are normal. There's no way for them to know. Go up there. You at least owe it to him to see what happens.*

He went out to the stable to check on the horses, then to the well for water. The litany of recriminations chased him. *Are you going to spend your whole life this way? Hiding from the Church? Pathetic.*

Snowflakes pricked at his cheek. It was dark, and getting cold. He made his way back to the house, staring at the bucket sloshing in his hands, and the wind whispered, *Fire.*

Startled, he glanced up. Behind the houses just across the road, the horizon was glowing.

*The inn!*

He dropped the bucket and ran, his lassitude finally broken. *Too late.* Dread reared in his chest. It was the inn. He was sure of it. His parents were burning and somehow, it was his fault for not being there.

But it wasn't the inn. It was the temple.

A crowd churned in the road. Some were craning their heads; some were weeping; some were running for water. A handful of mounted soldiers kept them all at bay. Beyond them, the hill was a conflagration.

He fought his way to the front of the crowd. The prison tent was gone, the broken bones of the jail wagon wreathed in fire. Between the darting silhouettes of soldiers with water buckets, he saw a blackened body in the flames.

Helix's mother was screaming.

Iggy was too late after all.

~ ~

The soldiers relented before long, allowing help from the villagers, who ran in with their own buckets. Iggy helped, charging back and forth from Mellerson's well. They got the wagon put out first. As the fight against the flames spread outward, Bishop Marcus and his two Preservers swept into the ruins of the wagon and toward the body.

Iggy backed away, his eyes locked to the ground. He didn't want to look any of them in the eye. *Just in case.*

"Insignia," one of the Preservers said. He plucked a charred piece of metal from the body. "It's a soldier."

"Where's the boy?" Marcus demanded.

Iggy's gaze darted around the site, his heart suddenly pounding. There were other bodies, but none anywhere near the wagon.

"Not here," the other Preserver said after a second search. His face was streaked with ash.

"Galen!" Marcus snapped. A Justicar rode up. "The fire's nearly out. Get everyone who's not still working on it over here. Fan out and search the village. The boy is gone. The fire was a distraction."

The knight nodded. "Goreth and Bennett just returned from the girl's house. Her mother says she didn't come home." He pulled a bugle from his belt and gave a single, sharp blast.

"Find her," Marcus ordered, "and bring her mother to me." He scowled. "And get these people out of here."

"Loyalmen!" Galen shouted. "The prisoner's escaped. He's probably with the girl from the trial, the one with the long hair. They can't have gotten far. Check every room at the inn and fan through the village until you find them. Someone is probably hiding them.

"If you're not wearing a uniform, get to the camp. There is still fire to be fought!"

He wheeled away, then launched into the village.

*Lyseira?* Iggy backed away further still. He glanced toward the inn. *Are they in there?*

A Preserver grabbed his arm. "To the camp, boy," he said. "You heard the man."

*No!* he nearly shouted. *Get your hand off me!* But that would be madness, so instead, he obeyed.

Only a few pockets of fire still burned in the camp; it took a little more than an hour to put them out. When he returned, the soldiers had a trio of hounds in the road.

His heart leapt. They must not have found Helix and Lyseira yet, if they were resorting to hounds. But by the same token, if they were using hounds, they'd find them soon.

A man crouched in the road, a shirt in his hands. The hounds shoved their faces into it, eager and wild, then fanned out along the road. One of them started baying.

*Found it!* she shouted. She was thrilled to be the one. *Northeast! Northeast!*

"She has him," the man said.

*No!* Iggy called through the wind. The bitch snapped her head up.

"They actually ran," one of the soldiers marveled.

"They won't get far," Galen said from horseback. "Go."

Iggy reached for the wind. *Help me. Move the scent.* He closed his eyes, his heart pounding. *They'll see me. Hurry.*

*Northeast!* the bitch shouted again. She was straining at her leash, her master fighting to keep up.

Iggy felt the wind shift as it answered him.

*West!* a second hound shouted, and then the last one echoed him: *West!*

The bitch pulled up short, sniffing in circles.

"Wait," the hound master said. The bitch threw her head back and howled.

*West!*

Then they were away, dragging the hunting party behind them.

*iv. Lyseira*

They broke out of the trees and found themselves in an open field. Seth drove them onward, toward another copse of trees to the north, and another beyond that. They took short breaks only when they had to, and forced themselves to move on. Finally they came to another large wood, and Seth pulled them in.

The hours stretched past. The moon dragged itself west, blinking at Lyseira from between the clouds and the tree branches.

She was nearly numb with exhaustion. She had barely slept the night before Helix's trial–a night that felt now like it had happened in another lifetime, to another person–and she had been on the run for hours. They had all settled into a clumsy rhythm: slower than before, but faster than a walk. *Is it really faster than a walk?* She looked at her legs, chasing the path her brother had left, and felt utterly incapable of judging their speed. They weren't even hers.

At least they had left behind the baying of hounds, and hadn't heard anything else from their pursuers. She thanked God for that, and then something asked her, *Why? Why thank God for that?*

Because He was protecting them. Guiding them. He approved of saving Helix; that was the only reason they were getting away.

*Bishop Marcus is the one who works miracles. Bishop Elmoor is the holy judge. Galen Wick, the murderer, is a Justicar. They're the holy men.*

*God is on* their *side.*

Her eyes played a trick on her in the dark, and a low-hanging branch slapped into her forehead.

"Well?" Helix grunted from somewhere. He'd probably meant, *Are you well?* He sounded too exhausted to get all the words out.

"Yeah," she answered. Her tongue was heavy.

And that couldn't be right. God wasn't on Marcus and Elmoor's side. They were killers and liars, just like Helix had said. *Slay not thy fellow man.* It was the second Sacred Principle. It applied to them too.

Just rotten eggs, that's what they were. The Fatherlord didn't know what they were doing. He was Akir incarnate, God granted flesh. When He found out, He would be furious. He would rein them in.

*If He's God granted flesh, why doesn't He already know?*

She staggered and opened her eyes. She'd nearly tripped over a log. But when had she closed her eyes? Was she sleeping on her feet?

She glanced behind her, then ahead. The shadows of her friends were gone.

"Seth?" There was more panic in the call than she'd expected.

His voice came back. "I'm here." He clapped. She turned toward the sound and saw the shapes of Helix and Syntal lurching through the wood ahead of her. Syntal was leaning on her cousin.

Lyseira put one foot in front of the other.

Maybe He did already know. Maybe He would mete out punishment on His own. But either way, they had to go to Him. He was the only one who could commute Helix's death sentence.

And besides, the Chronicle was filled with stories of people who acted on faith and were rewarded. Akir knew what they were doing or what they needed; that wasn't the point. The point was that they acted on faith. They proved themselves worthy. And when the time came, God rewarded them.

*But Marcus and Elmoor aren't worthy. Why does He still let them work miracles?*

She had worked every day of her life for Akir. She had helped The Abbot when no one else could; she had dedicated herself to the cause of God.

But she'd had lustful thoughts, too. She'd lied. She'd regretted the hours in the temple, sometimes. There hadn't always been joy in her heart. If she was honest with herself, there had been far less joy in her heart the last few years.

*Yes, because none of it counted for anything! All that work, and God never granted me a miracle!*

So that meant she hadn't done it for the right reasons. She'd only worked at the temple, only helped The Abbot, because she expected something in return. She was broken. Selfish.

*Not true! I loved The Abbot! He was like a father to me! And if that's the worst I've done, it's still not murder! It's still not faking a trial! It's not faking the word of God!*

Bishop Marcus had tried to *bribe* her.

She shoved through a wall of branches and stumbled on to sudden, hard-packed dirt. They were on a worn forest path, nearly wide enough for a wagon. The trees arching overhead were the walls of a cathedral. Thin moonlight sifted through their branches like the sun through stained glass.

"I thought... we were... stay off the roads," Lyseira panted.

"Where are we?" Helix said as he and Syntal emerged.

Seth took in the path. "I don't recognize it," he admitted. Even he was starting to sound winded. "We must've gotten... turned around. I don't know this area." He squinted upward, searching for the moon.

Angbar broke through the trees in a crackle of snapping twigs. "Why... stopping?"

"Lost," Lyseira answered.

"Lost?" he aped. "That matters... now?" He pushed on to the road, weaving like a drunkard. "Keep going. Lanterns."

"What?" Helix breathed.

"Lanterns... behind us." Angbar reached the trees on the far side and turned back. He grabbed his knees, panting. "An hour. Two. Thought that's... why... not stopping."

Lyseira turned back. She saw nothing, at first. Then there were two pale smears of light, bobbing through the trees.

*God is on their side.*

"What... doing?" Angbar managed. "Have to... go!"

"No," Seth said. "We should make a stand... here." He unslung both packs–his and Lyseira's–and rolled his shoulders.

"What?" Angbar boggled.

The lantern light was gone, but Lyseira could hear something in the brush.

"They'll kill us!" Helix protested.

The noise was louder. Lyseira searched the woods with her eyes. Still nothing.

Syntal, draped over her cousin's shoulder, staggered to an independent stand. She was wobbling on her feet.

"Get into the woods," Seth said. "I'll take them here... catch up after."

Then Lyseira saw them again, just off the road, but they weren't lanterns at all.

They were eyes.

Something massive leapt from the trees and slammed Helix to the ground, its empty gaze smearing a white glow across the darkness. It ripped into Helix's neck. Syntal and Angbar screamed. Lyseira screamed with them.

Seth darted in and lashed at the thing's face–*Wolf,* Lyseira thought, but it wasn't, it couldn't be, it was *too big* and it had *no eyes*–and it reared back, snapping. Black strings swung crazily from its jaws in the moonlight.

Helix wasn't moving.

"Run!" Seth screamed. He leapt on the thing's back, fighting to get ahold of its jaws. It caught his hand and nearly tore it off. Seth howled. The monster shook itself like a dog, hurling Seth to the road. Its rear claws scrabbled once. Then it leapt at Angbar, spraying frozen dirt behind it.

Angbar swung his travel sack with a scream, smashing the monster in the jaw with an explosion of cheese and jerky and bottled beets. Then he was gone, buried in dirty fur and snapping jaws.

*God!* Lyseira screamed. *GOD!* She was rooted with terror, forced to watch as they all died.

The road flickered with light, brilliant as a lightning strike. It hurled the beast into the road. Syntal advanced on it, pointing her finger.

"*Ves!*" she snapped.

A flash from her finger. The thing rocked backwards, scrabbling for purchase.

"*Ves!*"

The light caught it under the jaw, twisting it sideways. Then it leapt for her.

"*Ves!*"

The flash caught it in mid-leap, flinging it backwards. In the nauseating light of the thing's eyes, Lyseira caught a glimpse of blood running from Syntal's nose.

The beast whimpered.

"Ves!" Syntal screamed, shaking.

The light tore into the thing's haunch, spinning it like a kicked rock. The glow in its eyes died. The road plunged back into darkness.

Syntal clutched her head, sobbing. Then she collapsed.

~ ~

*Arc hound,* some calm, rational part of Lyseira's mind said. *Big wolf. Glowing eyes. Created by the Tribunal. They're everywhere in the Chronicle.*

Ahead of her Seth rolled in the dirt, moaning and clutching at his ruined hand. Somewhere to her right, Angbar sounded like he was choking on his own blood.

Helix was silent.

*No one outruns the Tribunal. They have God on their side.*

She could just make out his body on the ground. "*Helix?*" The scream was raw and horrified, the stuff of nightmares; it took her a second to realize it was hers.

*I brought them here. This was my idea.*

She stumbled to him and fell to her knees. The ruin of his neck was pumping blood into the snow; it formed a puddle of black shadow in the moonlight. He grabbed her wrist.

Abbot Forthin had taught her prayers of invocation, to help her focus while praying for a miracle. She fumbled for one of them, tried to mutter what she could remember.

"*Besh... ket,*" she whispered. Was it *besh-ket?* Or *besk-tat?* "*Ben-tas... tíngala.*" The words were heavy and clumsy on her tongue. She hadn't spoken them in years.

*They didn't work then. They won't work now.*

She grabbed at his neck, trying to stop the blood. It was futile.

A trick of the moonlight made Akir appear at the road's edge, hooded and dour, watching in judgment.

"*No!*" she screamed. Her hands were covered in blood. "No! You don't get to just stand there! I've done everything for you! *Everything!*"

The blood was slowing. Helix's hand slipped from her arm.

"What did you want me to do?" she demanded. "Let them kill him? They are *liars!* You call them your servants? *What kind of God are you?*"

The clouds shifted, and Akir disappeared.

"Helix," she whimpered, "I'm so sorry, oh God, I'm so sorry... please... ah, *God! I've done everything for you!*" The scream raked her throat like daggers. "*You do something for* me!"

Then fire seized her.

It was the fury of the sun, the crippling rush of deep love, the raging of floods. It was thunder and lightning; sex and climax; the dawn of creation. It was God, speaking.

Her blood turned to flame. Her hands were His hands; her voice, His voice. She was nothing before Him, but she would not back down.

He had made Helix's flesh.

Now, He restored it.

# Chapter 10

*i. Iggy*

Sometime after midnight, he finally turned for home. During his time at the camp site, the village had changed behind him.

The inn's door hung open, its light still spilling into the dead street. Willis Mellerson was gone, taken up to the temple for questioning, but there were still soldiers inside. Iggy started to wonder what they were looking for, then put it out of his mind.

Beyond the inn, the village looked like Iggy imagined it ever did in the middle of the night. Except the doors seemed to be closed tighter somehow, the homes practically huddled into themselves. It was just his imagination, he thought, but then he saw Minda Fletchins' house laid open, the soldiers' lanterns bobbing inside. A few houses down, Silla Tevington's home was getting the same treatment. Minda had been sweet on Helix–the whole village knew it–but Silla? All she did was work with him.

He should've gone straight home, but something made him veer toward the Smith place.

*Stupid. Go home. If the soldiers are anywhere, they're there. Don't tempt fate.* He'd already gotten away with talking to the wind not twenty feet away from a bishop of the Tribunal tonight. His heart was still pounding; he still half-expected to feel a Preserver grab his shoulder any minute and demand that he come to the temple for questioning. *Isn't that enough for one night?*

It wasn't.

The Smith house was crawling with soldiers and initiates. Light blared from the windows. Inside, as far as he could tell, everything had been destroyed. Across the street, the Rulano place was much the same. It only looked less damaged because the Rulanos had so much less to ruin.

He searched the crowds for Lyseira's or Helix's parents. For Syntal, or Seth. They weren't there. He remembered the bishop asking to have Lyseira's mother brought to him, and felt a sudden chill.

*What is happening at the temple right now?* he wondered, and then, with a twist of nausea: *Are they doing this at my house too?*

What an irony it would be to survive the night at the temple–to work sorcery right in front of a bishop! –and return home to find they'd actually been looking for him all night.

He turned away, giving the scene a wide berth as he made his way back toward his house. He found the door closed, a single light burning on the front step–probably left by his mother for him.

No soldiers, then. No holy men. *But for how long?* He was friends with Helix. All the kids in the village had practically grown up together. *They'll realize the hounds are going the wrong way, or that false scent trail will end–it has to sometime. That bishop will think back and remember me standing there with my eyes closed. He'll put two and two together.*

That was ridiculous. It was an impossible stretch, to think the bishop would figure out his secret like that.

*Just like it's ridiculous to raid Helix's sweetheart's house, or to assume the man he worked for knew anything. Just like it's ridiculous to tear apart his parents' sitting room looking for clues as to where he went.*

Behind him, somewhere in the village, he heard a wail. Not a shout; not a cry. A *wail,* as wrenching as a funeral. It froze him in the street and triggered a series of brutal calculations in his thoughts.

When it was over, he knew he wasn't going home.

~ ~

He packed from the stable to avoid going inside; he didn't want to explain anything to his parents. He took a few blankets and a few apples. There would be plenty of hunting, so he grabbed his bow.

The horses watched him, snorting in curiosity.

*What are you doing?* Wind asked. She was his favorite. He had gotten to name her.

*Leave master's son alone.* This from Kelter, an older stallion.

He ignored them. The act of packing made him feel conspicuous and guilty. He kept glancing toward the door, fearing that someone would catch him in the act.

*They won't catch me. They'll just catch my parents after I go, like they did with the others.*

The thought arrested him. He thought of his mother, possibly still awake in the house, wondering if he was well.

*I shouldn't tell them anything. If they know anything, they'll be targeted.*

*They'll be targeted anyway,* he answered himself. *I've already seen it five times tonight.*

It was all too easy to picture the soldiers breaking in the door when they learned that he had gone, then dragging his parents to the temple for questioning. The wail he'd heard earlier echoed in his memory, but this time, it was his mother's.

"*Sehk,*" he murmured. "*Sehk!*"

*Ignatius?* Wind asked. She always used his full name. *What's the matter?*

He lifted a hand to quiet her, then dragged it over his mouth, trying to calm down. He couldn't go in there. He couldn't explain to his parents why he was leaving.

But he couldn't stay.

*Are we going somewhere?* Wind asked.

He hesitated. He'd be much faster on horseback, but the animals were his parents' livelihood.

*No,* he finally said. He sneaked her an apple and patted her cheek, wondering if it was the last time he would. Then he grabbed his bag and left.

Outside, he took a deep breath and ducked into the house.

He'd been wrong. It was empty.

*ii. Lyseira*

Helix opened his eyes. He looked at her as if beholding an angel. "Akir has made you well," she said, and left him.

Seth was white and silent, his teeth clenched. Muscles bulged in his neck. His hand was a ruin.

She knelt and made it whole.

The miracle was a blaze that engulfed her. She may have been staring into the sun. She waited for the dancing spots in her eyes to fade, then rose.

"What...?" Angbar started as she approached. His cheek had been torn open. She shushed him and shared the fire roaring through her veins. His eyes burned with wonder as he was healed.

Then she turned to Syntal.

The girl was face-first in the road, her filthy hair splayed in a halo around her head. Blood still trickled from her nose and ears, but her skin was unbroken. Lyseira crouched next to her, and spoke with God's tongue.

The midnight trees became suns. Lyseira fought the urge to shy from the light; instead, she opened herself to it and poured it into her friend.

Syntal didn't move.

"Syn?" Lyseira laid her hands gently on the girl's face and ear. She could barely see now, through the floating sparks in her vision. Dizziness clamored in her skull. She refused it, called on Him again, and poured His will through the girl's limp body.

Nothing.

Vertigo assailed her, and Lyseira rocked backwards. Someone took hold of her, breaking her fall. Above her, through the pounding light, came Seth's concerned face.

"What is it?" Angbar said from somewhere.

"Is she well?" Helix asked.

"Enough," Seth told her. "Take a rest now."

The blaze faded; Akir's hand slipped from hers like a lingering goodbye. She wanted to push her friends away, to spend the rest of eternity with Him, but He had already gone.

*Be at peace.* She couldn't tell if the thoughts were her own, or His. They had become too entwined. *You've called once. You need only call again.*

She pushed herself to her hands and blinked into the darkness. The last sunspots were fading. Behind them, she saw the shadow of Syntal in the road.

"Syntal," she said. "She wouldn't accept it. He offered her healing, and she wouldn't accept it." The girl had been holding her pain too close. The fire couldn't reach it.

"Syn?" Helix dropped to his knees and put his fingers to her neck. The road plunged into a tense silence, broken only by Angbar's panting and the creaking rustle of the trees. He spoke tightly, the words wrapped around a trembling core of panic. "She's alive. Her heart is beating." He looked up. Lyseira couldn't see his face in the dark. "Did that thing attack her? Did it do something to her?"

"I don't know. I didn't see it attack her." She was cloaked in serenity. Syntal was fine; they all were.

God was on their side.

"Did anybody see...?" Helix started, then turned back to his cousin. He smoothed her hair and kissed her forehead. "You hold on," he whispered. "You hear me?"

"She saved my life," Angbar said. "She threw the thing off me, used the magic again."

*She killed it,* Lyseira thought, *but Akir saved your life.* She had never felt so joyous. Every part of her felt like singing.

*He answered. He answered.*

Like a chorus of angels sharing their light, the moon shone again onto the midnight path. It was another sign from God, a mark of his blessing. He was everywhere, she realized now. Everything had purpose.

"I saw too," Seth said. He knelt next to the dead wolf in the middle of the road. "What was this thing?"

Syntal tried to lift her head. She put a hand to her temple, moaning.

"Syn!" Helix took her shoulders. "Are you well? What happened?"

"Just..." She winced, as if the single word threatened to break her. "Too much."

"She needs to lie down," Helix said. "We've been going all night, it's too much, she needs to lie down." His eyes darted along the path as if he expected to find a bed.

"Here." Angbar opened one of the surviving bedrolls. "Syn, here. Lie on this."

"What are you doing?" Seth said. "We can't just make camp in the middle of the road! Someone may come by!"

"She can barely move, Seth," Helix grunted as he helped Syntal to her feet.

"It was an arc hound." In her own ears, Lyseira's voice sounded like prophecy. "The Tribunal sent it. I realized it just before Akir answered me."

Helix looked at her like she had suddenly decided to recite a poem about butterflies.

"It matters," she assured him. "The arc hounds are summoned three times in the book of Second Shendra. They are never sent out alone."

Helix pushed the hair out of his face, his eyes blank. Then he turned back to his cousin, trying to help her over to the pillow.

"Are you saying there'll be *more* of these things?" Angbar demanded.

Lyseira nodded. At peace, she answered, "Almost certainly. But they may not know where we are."

Seth stalked to the wood's edge. "Can't risk it. We need to keep moving. The more distance we get, the safer–"

"No," Lyseira interrupted. She smiled. Finally, she understood what He wanted.

She spread her hands, as if releasing the answer into the moonlight. "We go back." She paused, waiting for them to see the wisdom in this.

Falling snowflakes had never been so loud.

With a trace of annoyance, she went on. "Don't you see? Akir has *joined us!* He is *with us!* Bishop Marcus can't harm us now.

"*God* is with us!"

Even in the moonlight, it was impossible to miss the look Seth and Helix shared.

She fought back a scowl. "He *healed* you," she said. Were they imbeciles?

"Lyseira..." Helix said, and fell silent.

"You saved our lives," Angbar jumped in. "That was incredible. Thank you! I don't think I said that. Everyone's saving my life tonight.

"We might have a real chance to survive this, if you can work miracles."

"It wasn't me," she insisted, trying to make him understand. "Didn't you hear me? I called for *Him*, and He came. He saved us. He supports us. We are working His will. This is..." She gestured at the road, at the woods, at the darkness and the snowfall. "This is *right.*"

Helix and Seth glanced at each other again.

"We can camp just a little ways in to the wood," Seth offered. "I'll keep watch for the night, and we can press north in the morning if she's able."

Helix nodded. "Can you walk?" he asked Syntal.

She didn't answer. "I'll carry her," Seth offered.

"Thanks," Helix said.

"Seth!" Lyseira demanded. "Did you hear me?"

He swept Syntal into his arms and turned back to her. His face, normally unreadable, was pained. "It's not a good idea, Lyseira," he managed. Then he pressed past her, into the wood.

She was stunned. *Not a good idea?* Akir had just saved their lives, all of them. They no longer had to run. "But *God*–" she started, and Angbar cut her off with a wince.

"Lys," he said. "They can work miracles, too." He put a hand on her arm. "C'mon."

She could go back alone. There would be no greater expression of her faith than to walk back to that burning tent by herself. She imagined Marcus ordering her to stop, his invocations falling dead without the fire of Akir behind them.

Angbar was waiting.

She sighed and went with him. The others didn't understand yet, but they would.

In time, they would.

*iii. Helix*

They found a small clearing and set out Lyseira's bedroll. Seth laid Syntal in it. While she rested, they ate furtively of hardbread and cheese.

He kept glancing at her in the moonlight, wondering if she would be well in the morning. *Morning,* he realized, *isn't even that far away.* Something about the idle thought triggered him. His mind exploded with warring revelations, all of them suddenly vital.

*The Church has sentenced me to death!*

*Syntal might be dying!*

*Syntal is a witch!*

*The Tribunal is chasing me through the woods!*

*Lyseira worked a miracle!*

And the last, the most sobering: *I should be dead.*

His throat had been ripped open. It should have all been over, but he was still here.

Lyseira seemed rejuvenated by her miracles, certain that everything would work out, but Helix didn't understand that. They had gotten lucky. They should be dead, every single one of them.

His heart was suddenly racing. It was too much, too fast. Despite his hunger he set down his cheese, his fingers shaking.

"Can we light a fire?" Angbar asked, rubbing his hands together. "It's freezing."

"It's not freezing," Seth answered. "Just cold. No fire; they'll see."

"How much food did we lose?" Lyseira asked.

"I don't know," Angbar said. "Everything I had was ruined. Syn packed a bag too, though. Is there any food in there?"

Helix touched his neck. The flesh was whole. He remembered gasping like a beached fish, fighting the excruciating pain for breath. Now, there was no sign it had even happened.

"Helix?" Angbar prodded.

"What?"

"Is there any food in Syn's pack?"

He had carried his cousin's bag off the road, as Seth had carried her. Coming back to himself, he glanced at it sitting next to him. "Um," he said.

*I should be* dead.

"I don't know. It was really heavy, I know that much." He undid the twine holding the bag closed. His sword was inside.

The sight sucked the breath from his lungs.

"It... she packed my old sword," he managed, and pulled it out. It felt light and easy in his hands. It was sheathed, hanging off a belt–just how he'd left it.

Seth looked dour. "That would have been good to know an hour ago."

*When was she supposed to stop to pull it out?* Helix thought.

*Before or after you started threatening to steal her book?* He said nothing. He was too tired.

"Any food?" Angbar pressed.

Helix rummaged through the bag. She'd packed clothes for both of them, and her book lay at the bottom of the sack, the first thing she'd thrown in. No blankets, no food. It was typical for Syntal; she was always too focused on the things that seemed important to her personally. But he couldn't fault her. She'd brought his old sword.

"No," he said.

Angbar leaned back. "We're in trouble."

"Lys and I packed some, too," Seth said. "We're not in trouble yet. Let's worry about it in the morning. Get some sleep while you can. I'll keep watch."

"You don't have to do that," Lyseira said. "You need your rest, too."

"No I don't." Seth snapped, sharply enough that Angbar glanced at him. "I'm a Preserver in all but name. I'll stay up."

Helix was in no mood to argue. He arranged the bag so the clothes were on top of the book, then tried to use it like a pillow. When he closed his eyes, hysteria perched above him like a vulture waiting for a meal to die. He managed to keep it at bay until the blackness claimed him.

~~

He woke to sunlight streaming through the trees. He sat up, and saw everyone else still sleeping–including Seth, who had sunk to the ground with his back to a tree. His left hand still held a long shaft of wood, which he'd been whittling to a point. His right had dropped open and spilled a knife into the dirt.

Helix had a sudden, sharp surge of panic. *How long have we been out?* He looked up, trying to make out how far the sun had come. As near as he could tell, it was almost directly above them.

*"Sehk,"* he muttered. He gained his feet and they protested with agony. Every muscle in his body felt like a beaten strip of old leather. He was still exhausted.

He shambled to Seth and set a hand on his shoulder. Seth leapt to his feet. He jerked his eyes about him like a cat that had just been spit on.

"What?" he snapped. "What is it? What's happening?"

"You fell asleep," Helix retorted, harder than he'd meant to. Seth looked like he was ready to kill him.

"Oh." He shook his head. "That shouldn't have happened."

Helix shrugged. "We're all exhausted."

"No," Seth said. "I'm going to get us killed if I keep failing like this. It was just like on the road. I was too weak."

"Too weak?" Helix blinked. "What are you talking about? You nearly had your hand ripped off."

"Weak," Seth spat. "I shouldn't have allowed the pain, just like I shouldn't have allowed the fatigue from the travel." He shook his head again, as if suddenly realizing how much he'd said. "You don't... forget it. We should wake the others." He knelt for the knife.

It felt like Helix had accidentally peered through a window and caught Seth dressing. *Is that what it was like for him at the compound?* he wondered. *Is that what it takes to forge a Preserver?*

He felt he should say more, should try to assure Seth that his help so far had been invaluable, but he was already moving away. "All right," Helix said to his back, and turned to Syntal.

Her eyes flicked open when he touched her shoulder. To his relief, they looked normal.

"Did we make it?" she asked.

He smiled despite himself. "You tell me. You scared the life out of everybody."

She sat up and put an experimental hand to her head. "Yeah," she said. "I think so. I feel better."

"What happened?"

"Too much chanting, I think," she said. "The book warned about it." She shook her head. "I'll be more careful. It's midday?" She stood up, deflected the questions of the others, and ducked into the trees to relieve herself.

They broke fast quickly, all except for Seth, who resumed work on his weapon. "What is it?" Angbar asked him around a mouthful of hardbread. "Spear?"

Seth nodded, hefting the half-finished weapon in his hand. "It's just pine. It'll probably break the first time I try to use it." He stared at the spear, considering this, then resumed whittling it. "But if those arc hounds catch up to us, it'll be better than nothing."

*The arc hounds.* Somewhere in the intervening hours, Helix had actually managed to forget Lyseira's warning from last night.

"How many do you think there'll be?" Angbar asked her.

Lyseira wiped the crumbs from her mouth. "I don't know. As far as I know the Tribunal hasn't actually made them since the time of Second Shendra." When she saw the look on Angbar's face, she squeezed his knee. "Don't worry!" She smiled. "Akir will watch over us."

Angbar turned doubtfully away from her. *God,* Helix thought. *Please let her come to her senses soon.*

"Sh!" Seth jerked up a hand. He nodded in the direction of the road and rose, spear in hand. "Heard something," he hissed.

Helix froze and heard footsteps, crunching through the underbrush.

*This is it.* He slid his weapon from the sheath, his heart thundering. He knew precious little about swordplay, but at least he would go down fighting.

The others stood. Angbar grabbed the knife; Syntal trained her eyes on the clearing's edge.

Seth flexed his fingers on the haft of the spear, ready to spring.

"Oh, *sehk,*" Iggy Ardenfell said. "Seth, is that you?"

Helix sagged, dizzy with relief.

"Iggy?" Angbar breathed. "Blesséd *sehk*, we were about to kill you."

"Iggy," Helix finally managed. "Oh, thank God. I thought you were them." He crossed the little meadow and hugged his old friend. Iggy smelled of woods and sweat and horse. "I am so *sehking* glad to see you."

"How did you find us?" Seth leveled at him. He had lowered his spear, but his eyes were heavy with suspicion.

"Luck," Iggy answered. "I was taking the old roads. Didn't want to be seen. Came across that... wolf thing? –on the path just now, and the trail you left in the woods... a blind drunk could've followed that." His eyes flicked from Seth to Syntal to Angbar. "I can't believe you're all here. I thought they'd captured you. I mean, I knew about Helix and Lyseira, but..." He trailed off and shook his head. "Blesséd *sehk,* you lot are lucky. They're going crazy looking for you."

Anxiety squeezed Helix's stomach, forcing the relief away. "What's it like there?"

Iggy squared his jaw. "It's bad, Helix. They're taking in everyone who knew you. Your ma and pa, Mellerson and Silla... *sehk,* Minda."

"What?" Helix rasped. *No... Oh, God...* "Minda? Why? Minda doesn't know anything!" *No one knew anything. I didn't* do *anything.* Suddenly, the other names fell on him. *Mellerson. Silla.*

*Mom and Dad.*

"Oh," he said. His legs carried him to a log, and he sat down. "Oh, *sehk.*"

*I have to go back. They'll let them go if I go back, I have to go back.*

*Why are they doing this to me? I didn't* sehking *do anything!*

"I..." Iggy had gone ashen. "I'm sorry. I thought, you know, I'm your friend too, they'll probably come for me next... so I got out. Last night." He swallowed and shook his head. "I left a note for my parents... I hope they saw it. I told them to get out, too."

"What about my mom?" Lyseira asked.

Iggy's jaw tightened. "They have her too."

Lyseira bit her lip and took a half-step backward, circling her heart.

"When?" Seth threw the word like a dart.

"Last night. Right away, seemed like, as soon as they got the fire out."

"*M'sai,*" Lyseira said. "That's it. We go back." She grabbed her pack and slung it over her shoulder.

Iggy looked apologetic. "Lys... I wouldn't."

"You don't know everything that's happened, Iggy. I worked a miracle last night. God came to me. He'll protect me." Something in her tone sounded weaker than it had before.

She took a step toward the clearing's edge, and Seth grabbed her arm.

"No," he said.

She whirled on him. "What are you doing? He's talking about our *mother!*"

"I know," Seth said, "and you're not going back there."

"They could *kill her!*"

"And if you go back, they'll kill you." His eyes were like steel. "She heard the soldiers, Lyseira. She didn't invite them in and tell them to take you. She told you to run, and she told me to make sure you made it."

Lyseira's mouth worked, her eyes heavy with horror.

"I'll go," Helix heard himself say. He stood up.

"Oh, no," Angbar said. "No, you won't."

"They have my family, they have my sweetheart–*sehk,* Angbar, they have my *boss.*" The words were fuel on a fire, the hysteria from last night suddenly catching flame. "I can't just–"

"They might have my family, too!" Angbar roared. It caught Helix like a slap, stamped out the hysteria as suddenly as a flood. He had never seen Angbar angry. "Who do you think will be most expendable, Helix? Hostages they can use to lure you back? Or a couple of nogs?" He stalked over, trembling. "I did this. I made this choice. I can't take it back. And *you*"–he stabbed Helix's chest with a finger–"are not going to cock it up trying to play hero."

"*Hero?*" Helix aped, but Syntal cut him off.

"He's right. No one should go. Especially not you."

"Syn," Helix sputtered. "Mom and Dad–"

"Mom and Dad wouldn't want you to come back and get yourself killed. And what'll the Church do to me, Helix?"

He glared at her. "They won't do anything to you. You're not coming."

She answered with a level look and a single arched brow. "Then you're not going."

Sehk, Helix thought. Sehk, sehk, sehk. He wanted to scream, or flail, or shove past everyone and run home.

The clearing fell quiet. Iggy's horse stamped and blew. Iggy lifted a hand.

"I got one piece of good news," he said. "They all think you went west for some reason. They're tearing apart the road to Newton looking for you."

Seth chewed on this. "Good," he said, "but that doesn't help with the arc hounds."

"Arc hounds?" Iggy asked. "Is that what I saw...?"

"We need to keep moving," Seth said. "We'll explain on the way."

# Chapter 11

*i. Helix*

They returned to the road and walked.

Seth told Iggy what had happened. The others added as they saw fit, and nothing was left out. Helix said nothing. He felt numb.

His shocked mind had been rushing from one emergency to the next throughout the night, but he'd always been sure, somewhere in his head, that there was an end to it all. He just had to reach it. Yes, he'd been sentenced to death, but even now he couldn't shake the sense that it was all a giant misunderstanding, that it could be somehow remedied. Yes, he was running for his life, but the home he'd left was still there.

Except now, it wasn't. It sounded like everyone he knew had been taken in by the Tribunal. His home was gone. There was no turning back.

His thoughts were awash in little questions. *What are we going to eat? Where are we going?* But lurking beneath them, like the shadows of monsters beneath a lake surface, were the big questions.

*Where is home now? Is there any hope?*

Winter was nearly here. It was already freezing the creeks and stealing into his muscles, weighing him down like a hundred pound pack. *When it comes in force, what will we do?*

*Are my parents still alive?*

He had no answers, but the questions wouldn't stop. He trudged through them until the trees started to thin and Seth called a halt for lunch. The words hit Helix like a hammer, and he staggered to a halt and sat.

"Iggy, help me hunt," Seth said. "We should save what we have while we can."

*I should help them hunt,* Helix thought, just before waking to a firm shake of his shoulder and the smell of roasted pheasant.

"Here," Lyseira said, offering him a piece of steaming meat. He took it and ate, his jaw grinding like an automaton. It was good–*delicious*–the best meal he'd ever had. The taste ignited a renewed hunger in his belly that he hadn't even realized had been there, and his exhaustion faded somewhat to give it room.

The others discussed directions and plans. Angbar mentioned

going to Coram to stock up on supplies. Iggy said they'd do best to stick with the old roads; something about Alynwood giving cover from a coming blizzard. Lyseira suggested a longer-term plan: going to Tal'aden, to meet with the Fatherlord and tell him what had happened. It all sounded equally pointless to Helix.

Someone asked his opinion. He gave them a grunt and a shrug. Beyond the fact that home was gone, he couldn't understand anything.

After eating, he climbed to his feet and winced as all the aches in his legs and back flared to life. Even his arms were sore. *Why in Hel are my arms sore? I haven't been walking on* them.

They made Alynwood an hour before dusk. Between the trees, the old road crawled over hills and ridges. It was nearly overgrown here, sometimes little more than two dull trails of beaten, brittle grass.

But at least Iggy knew where to take them. He didn't know these woods intimately, he explained, but he knew forests, and he *had* been to Alynwood before. If he wasn't confident of the best way through, he did an excellent job faking it.

As the forest's light started fading, Helix noticed a glow off the road ahead.

His stomach clenched; a memory of the wound that should have killed him pricked the skin at his throat. They were all exhausted and half-starved. They had barely managed to survive the last arc hound. If another one came now, or, God, a *pack* of them...

Iggy signaled a halt. "There's a cabin," he said, peering into the gloom. "Lantern in the window." He glanced back at the others, a question in his eyes.

Helix forced his terror down and stared, trying to see through the thin light. Just ahead, a little path wound away from the road and down a hill. At the bottom was a small clearing, and in the back of it stood a cabin, easily the size of the Rulanos' home back in Southlight. A lantern burned in one of the windows.

"We go around," Seth said.

Iggy shook his head. "That storm–"

A rustle of leaves interrupted the argument. A man emerged from the deeper tree cover, moving with the ease of a practiced woodsman. The crinkles at his eyes told of forty or more winters, but he was well built and steady on his feet. A longbow hung from his shoulder. "I thought I heard voices," he said. "Good eve."

"Good eve," Iggy answered.

The man had a warm smile. "Don't see many hunters out this way."

Iggy nodded. "We, ah…" He glanced back at his companions. "We–"

"We got lost," Angbar put in. "We've been in these woods for days, we're starving and exhausted, and we're very happy to see you." He stepped forward and held out his hand. "Angbar Shed'dei, if it please you."

"Blane." He took Angbar's hand. "Haven't seen a northlander 'round here in years."

Angbar grinned and nodded. "As I said, lost."

Blane's eyes narrowed as they fell on the bloody rags of Seth's robes and Helix's shirt. "You've been hurt."

"We were attacked," Seth said.

The ranger's eyebrows lifted. "Attacked? In Alynwood? What happened?"

"Wolves," Seth said, at the same time Angbar answered, "Brigands."

Blane gave a wary smile. "Which is it, then?"

A woman's voice called. "Blane! What's keeping you? I've nearly got your supper up!" A woman of an age with Blane stood in the cabin doorway.

"Some lost travelers," Blane answered.

"Well, invite them in!" she called back, excited. "We've too much stew for the two of us!"

Blane looked them over once more. *We must look a sorry lot,* Helix thought. *Bunch of starving kids, torn half to pieces.* "It'll be cold tonight. We've got food and extra blankets, since the children left. Bandages. You can stay with us the night; come morn, I'll bring you up to the road."

Seth shook his head. "Thank you for the offer–" he began, but Iggy cut him off.

"Too kind. Thank you. We accept."

Blane's wife beamed at them from the door as they approached. "My! So many!" Her smile faltered when she saw the color of Angbar's skin, but only briefly.

"This is my wife, Leese," Blane said.

"Helix," Helix heard himself saying. Their hospitality felt like rain in the desert. He shook Leese's hand. "My cousin, Syntal, and my friends, Seth, Lyseira, Angbar, and Ignatius."

Leese's eyes trained on Angbar. It was plain she wanted to ask about him, but she was too polite.

"I've asked them to stay the night," Blane told his wife. "They haven't had a bite in days, from the look of them, and they're exhausted to boot."

"The night?" Leese said. "Well you'd best go dig up the children's things, we haven't had guests since Zeke left." Blane grunted and disappeared inside.

"You'll have to sleep on the floor, I'm afraid," Leese said as she showed them in. The two windows Helix had seen at the front of the house opened directly into a warm, dark room sporting a massive bearskin rug. A fireplace crackled busily at one end, framed by two rocking chairs. A stag's head was mounted above the mantle; a longbow graced the wall opposite it.

But the first thing Helix noticed was the *smell*, the rich, meaty aroma of a good venison stew. He had never felt his mouth begin watering–he'd thought it was just an expression–but he did then. Potatoes, carrots, onions, gravy… he could pick out each scent as if he were a wolf on the prowl.

"Oh…" Angbar moaned. "Oh, that smells… *delicious.*"

"The floor will be more than generous," Lyseira said. "Thank you so much."

"It's nothing, dear. Akir favors a generous heart." Leese smiled again. "I'm sorry we don't have more chairs, but you're more than welcome to make yourselves at home."

Helix limped over to the hearth as the others trailed in, and slid down the wall to have a seat on the floor. The warmth of the cabin enfolded him. He'd had no idea how cold he was until his flesh started to thaw.

Blane returned and set an armful of worn blankets and pillows on the bearskin. "The kids'," he said. "Not enough for the six of you, but may be if you can double up."

Helix thought his chest might burst with gratitude. "Thank you," he said. The heap of thin pillows looked like the lap of luxury.

"You can thank me by getting a good night's rest," Blane answered. "And complimenting my wife on her stew."

Supper was as delicious as it smelled. Blane and Leese brought the wooden bowls out to them in the sitting room, each on a plate with a steaming crust of bread and a mug of cold water. He devoured his own meal as if it were his last and, with permission, went back to the pot for seconds.

~ ~

When they'd all finished, Blane and Leese settled into the rocking chairs as Lyseira and Seth began laying out the blankets. The sun had set, but the fireplace and the lantern in the window kept the darkness at arm's length. Syntal had fallen asleep, the light from the fireplace dancing across her features like manic shadow puppets.

"Your sister looks exhausted," Blane said as he tapped a small pouch of powdered bloodroot into a pipe.

*Cousin,* Helix thought, but there was no point in correcting him. "We all are."

"Your friend said you'd been in the woods for days."

Helix shot a glance toward his companions, but none of them seemed prepared to say anything. He nodded. "Got lost."

"Where were you headed?"

Again Helix looked at the others. His mind was blank. He didn't trust himself to say anything.

"Shientel," Angbar said, and Helix felt a pang of gratitude to the storyteller.

"And you're taking the old roads?" Blane arched a brow. "Quite a journey. Weeks on horseback, let alone by foot."

"We have family there," Lyseira said.

"All of you?"

"No. No, just… just me." *Leave the lying to Angbar, Lys,* Helix thought.

Iggy smirked. "We came with so she wouldn't get lost."

Blane's chuckle was amiable enough. "Know your way around the woods, do you?"

Iggy shrugged. "Thought I did."

"So these brigands and wolves that attacked you," Blane began, but his wife shushed him.

"Oh, enough already. They're guests."

Blane gave her an irritated glance and clamped his teeth over his pipe, but a minute later thought better of it. "Wolves," he muttered around his pipe. He puffed, took the pipe out of his mouth, and leaned forward. "And you said it was here, in Alynwood? I mean, head into Coram, and you'll always hear a good Wolfwood road story. Since the Storm some fool's always taking the road by Veiling Green and not coming back alive." He waved his pipe dismissively. "Nothin' this far east though."

Helix had heard some of the Wolfwood stories. They were pebbles in the beach compared to all the other tales since the Storm.

"A lot of strange things have happened since the Rending," Lyseira agreed, echoing his thoughts.

"Oh, you hear them tell it at the Coram tavern, the whole world's gone upside down. Winter's summer, summer's winter. Witches everywhere. Tribunal's going crazy. I even heard some stories from *Bahir,*" Blane said, nodding at Angbar. "I'm sure it's all true. We just keep our heads down. Nothing happens out here; that's why we're still here. Ain't that right?" He elbowed his wife, who circled her heart.

Helix knew what he meant. He remembered being terrified, as a boy, when the Church had named the Rending the end of the world. He'd walked on eggshells for weeks, expecting every morning to be his last.

Back then, every sign had been gut-wrenching. The time the sun had disappeared in the middle of the day, he'd been certain it was over. He remembered sobbing in his mother's arms, wondering if he'd been good enough to avoid Hel.

The next day, the sun had risen like normal, and life had gone on.

Eventually, the signs the Storm had brought became... not normal, never *normal*, but at least expected. He didn't doubt the

Church when they said the world was in its last days, but what was he to do about it? Give up? Quit breathing? Everyone had to keep eating; everyone had to keep living. So they did. When the world was ready to end, it would.

"So." Blane settled forward in his chair. "What are you kids running from?"

Helix fought for something to say. The silence in the room thundered with guilt.

Lyseira gave him a nervous smile. "Running? We don't–"

"I'm no fool, girl," Blane said, not unkindly. "You're all torn up, got a hunted look in your eyes. Taking the old roads to *Shientel* of all places?" He scoffed. "It's no difference to me, but you give me your secrets and I'll keep 'em."

"No secrets," Seth said levelly. "Just a run of bad luck."

Blane locked eyes with him as the fire threw crackling shadows across their faces. Finally, the older man chuckled. "Forget it." He got to his feet. "You got your secrets, sure as the sun sets, but Hel, everyone does, these days."

"*Blane,*" Leese whispered. "Language."

"Thank you again for the roof and the meal," Seth said. "We'll be on our way before you wake."

Blane brandished his pipe. "Now, there's no need for that. I said I'd guide you to the road, and I mean to. I'm like to be heading into town in a few days anyway; may as well clear a path up. Besides, between the wolves and the brigands and your friend's sense of direction, you'd probably just wind up here again in a few days."

"Thank you," Helix said.

"Well then." Blane cast a final look over them and nodded shortly. "Good night."

"Good night." Seth watched until the pair disappeared into a little bedchamber, then settled himself against the wall to finish his bread. His jaw worked mechanically, his eyes fixed on the window nearest the hearth. After he swallowed, he said, "Iggy."

The young woodsman looked at him.

"This wasn't a good idea."

"I told you, there is a blizzard coming. You won't be saying that if it hits tonight. You're worried about food? If we get caught in that storm, we're dead."

*Storm?* Helix remembered Iggy saying something about that earlier in the day, but he hadn't been listening.

"The more people see us," Seth pressed, "the more likely some Tribunal Seeker will be to track us."

Helix winced at Seth's raised voice. The two were still arguing quietly, but if he knew Iggy's temper, that wouldn't last. He cut in. "What's done is done. There's no use in arguing now–they've seen us, we're here, and we're warm. There's no harm in taking a rest for the night." Helix dropped his voice even lower. "We can leave in the morning before they wake, if that's what you want, Seth. We're better off staying away from the road anyway."

"I agree," Angbar threw in. He looked at Seth. "And Iggy's always been right about storms. Tell me one time he wasn't." When Seth didn't answer, he finished, "If you do go sleep in the snowstorm, though, I call keeps on your pillow."

Seth curled his lip as Lyseira laid a hand on his arm.

"Let it be," she said. "Akir didn't save us on the road only to have us betrayed by an old man and his wife."

Helix's temper surged at the mention of Bishop Marcus's God. Suddenly he was sick of hearing about Akir's will; to hear the Church tell it, it was Akir's will that he die. "Syntal saved us on the road, Lys," he spat. "Akir has nothing to do with this."

He expected an angry outburst or indignant sermon; instead, Lyseira just raised her eyebrows and glanced at his neck. He felt a hot flush of shame and dropped his eyes.

*That's it. I need some sleep.*

~ ~

In the darkness he saw Marcus pointing at him, Judge Elmoor sentencing him, Matthew saying, "I'm sorry," as blood bubbled from his lips. He saw the smeary white glow of the arc hound's eyes, the sword Syntal had brought for him and the tent she had set aflame.

"You should get some sleep," Seth said, and Helix realized he was staring at the ceiling.

"I can't," he said without turning.

"You will," Seth said. "You were earlier."

He was right. The fire in the hearth was low, and everyone else was asleep. *It felt like I only blinked.* He waited, watching the play of the hearth fire across the ceiling, but every time he closed his eyes the reeling images returned.

He turned toward the window. A handful of snowflakes drifted in the darkness, but there were no torches, no clericlight, no arc hound eyes. Seth's reflection stood just outside the window, gazing in, but beyond it was only night. *They haven't found us,* he realized, and the thought helped to calm him.

*But they will.*

Seth cleared his throat, his eyes scanning the wood. He looked as if he could stay attentive for days.

*I owe him my life. All of them.* It was a debt he could only pray he'd live long enough to repay.

"Seth." His voice was clumsy and loud, breaking the ambience of the crackling fire and quiet snores.

"Yes." Seth didn't turn from the window, but the fire created a ghost of him in the glass. The ghost's eyes shifted to Helix as Seth kept watch on the wood.

"What are we going to do?" The question was packed with need.

The answer was immediate. "I'm going to finish first watch, then wake up Iggy. You're going to get some rest."

"I mean in the morning. The day after. The day after that. They won't stop looking for me. This won't end until they have me."

The ghost's eyes dropped to consider this. "They'll have you more quickly if you're too tired to run."

*Seth, you've changed so much.* The Seth Helix remembered would have charged their pursuers head on. But that had been years ago. The games they'd played as children were a long time gone.

"I can't," Helix said. "Every time I close my eyes I see... everything, that's been happening. My mind, it... just won't rest."

"You've been awake too long, you've got your second wind. Lie there, if you need to. Listen to the fire. You'll sleep eventually."

"But I can't. I can't just lie here. I... I just keep thinking about–"

"Helix," Seth said. The ghost turned toward the wood, keeping vigil as Seth locked eyes with his friend.

"Yes."

Flatly, Seth said, "Don't make me knock you out."

Helix gave a weak chuckle. "*M'sai,*" he muttered, and rolled toward the wall.

*Wait... I wonder if he was actually joking.*

*He's inhuman. I don't even recognize him.*

*He's trying to help. He saved my life.*

His mind picked at the question, and his thoughts finally began to shimmer with encroaching sleep.

*His eyes are blank. They burned the humanity out of him.*

*When Lyseira asked him for help, he came.*

*He made a spear from a tree branch. Like the trees outside. The trees with the wolves.*

*He's a good person.*

*Marcus will kill me.*

*Seth is a Preserver. He's here to track me. He's reporting to Marcus every night.*

*He's marked himself for life by helping me escape. He must still be the friend I knew or he wouldn't have thrown everything away.*

~ ~

"Helix." Something shook his shoulder.

He opened his eyes and saw the dim shape of Iggy's face. The room was black, the hearth empty.

"What?"

"I think I saw something in the woods," Iggy said. "I'm gonna go out–"

A ghoulish light seeped through one of the windows. Helix caught a glimpse of the arc hound's sickly eyes just before the window shattered.

"Arc!" Iggy screamed. He leveled a kick at Angbar, then reached back for his bow. "Arc!"

Seth snapped to his feet. His eyes flashed. Then he leapt at the thing's back, reaching for its jaws.

The other window exploded as a second arc hound shoved through. It braced its front paws in the frame, howling.

Below it, somehow still asleep, lay Syntal.

*"Syn!"* Helix dove for his cousin. The wolf in the window lunged at him. It was all slaver and fangs, nauseous streaks of light. Iggy's arrow took it in the shoulder and it fell back, roaring.

Syntal snapped taut, her eyes darting. "There's two of them!" Helix shouted.

Lyseira was screaming, beating on the first monster with one of their guests' walking staves. The other one would be coming through the window again any second.

"Get away!" Helix shouted. "It's–!"

He caught a flicker of that horrible light before the beast crushed him, blasting the words away. He flailed and kicked and screamed; his hands grabbed something and smashed it into the wolf's head.

The thing scrabbled, trying to get purchase. Its breath was hot ash. Helix bucked, trying to get his knees into the monster's gut. The monster snarled and ripped into his face.

He was screaming. He had always been screaming.

A flash of light hurled the wolf off him. It crashed into the rocking chairs, slapping its head against the brick hearth. Syntal was in front of the shattered window, illuminated only by the creatures' eyes, her hands raised as if she were about to choke someone.

"Again!" Helix shouted, but she was frozen, her eyes glassy with terror. "Syn! Hit it–!"

The wolf bounded once, tore into her arm, and jerked her off her feet. She pitched to the floor, screaming.

Helix tried to grab his sword. It wasn't there. He must've taken it off.

The thing lunged for Syntal's neck. Helix hit it with a rocking chair. The air exploded with chunks of splintered wood. "Me, you *sehk!*" He struck again with what was left. "Get *me*!"

Another arrow flashed. The thing yelped and turned, its muzzle dripping blood. Syntal's throat was in one piece.

*My sword,* his mind screamed, *where is my curséd* sword*?* He cast about and saw a fire poker, crawling with sick light. As he grabbed it, the wolf leapt for Iggy.

The woodsman let a wild shaft loose. It buried itself in the ceiling as the monster smashed him into the wall.

The front door burst in. A third arc hound growled, it empty eyes surveying them as if perusing a buffet.

*No,* Helix thought. *Akir help us.* Then he was lunging to help Iggy. He drove the poker into the monster's back, and ripped it back out. The arc hound shrieked, snapping at Iggy's neck as the woodsman struggled to hold it back.

Helix stabbed again. A thrashing spray of hot blood burst from the creature's flank. It fell, yanking the poker from Helix's hands. The light in its eyes died.

A sudden burst of fatigue threatened to drop him. He staggered backward, abruptly woozy, and Lyseira screamed. She was kneeling near her brother. The first arc hound was dead, but Seth was sprawled next to it, facedown in a growing pool of blood.

Beyond, the last wolf had pinned Angbar to the floor.

Helix lurched that way, shouting. Another burst of light streaked past him, pelting into the monster. It jerked and looked up, but didn't go flying. It didn't matter. The spell had bought him enough time to get there.

Weaponless again, he grabbed a vase of flowers and smashed it into the creature's face, spraying dirt against the wall.

The beast lunged and caught his leg in its teeth. The world ignited with pain. The thing shook its head, trying to tear him from his feet. He grabbed a mounted shelf with both hands, desperate for purchase.

It toppled, showering them with vases and books. An avalanche of knick knacks slammed him to his back. He scrabbled through the debris, frantic for something to stab with. The thing had lost his leg, but he only had a second before it lunged for his neck. Shrieking, he twisted to the side, and the beast tore into his shoulder.

The room rocked with screams and instructions.

*"Shoot it, shoot it!"*

*"Helix!"*

*"The knife!"*

An arrow bit into the wolf's neck and it recoiled, ropes of flesh dancing in its jaws. Another of Syntal's spells lanced into it and it heaved against the wall, its eyes still alight. Then Seth appeared behind it and jerked its head back.

"Helix," he grunted, his muscles bulging and his jaw locked.

Helix's left hand was still floundering in the debris of the shelf, but his right had somehow managed to close on a dagger.

"Kill it," Seth said, and Helix stabbed.

The monster wheezed and jerked, spattering blood, but Seth had it locked. Its growl died and its eyes faded, smothering the room in darkness.

Helix dragged himself out from under the body and knelt on the floor. The darkness shivered with murmurs and panting.

"Is everyone well?" Lyseira's voice was just this side of hysteria.

"My face," Helix said. In horror, he felt the words seeping out of his cheek. The side of his face was burning.

A chorus of muttered complaints echoed him. Everyone was alive.

"Where…" The pain in his cheek seared the word to ash, but his outrage resurrected it. "Where in *Hel* is my sword?"

He heard the tinny clink of a lantern, followed by the soft *whoosh* of it igniting. A flickering light revealed Blane and Leese, their eyes wide with shock. The room plunged into silence.

The cabin was a wreck. The two windows facing the front were shattered, and a light snowfall gusted in to the room. The stag's head lay upside down in front of the fireplace, spattered with blood and ash. Both of the rocking chairs were in pieces. The rug was torn and bloody, giant gouges had been ripped from the wooden floor, and the shelf on the opposite wall from the fireplace was broken in half, the floor beneath littered with debris.

The hulks of the three arc hounds were the capstones to this masterpiece, spaced almost evenly across the room, each still oozing from its wounds. The one in the middle had a spear jutting from its belly like a grave marker.

"How, ah..." Angbar winced. "How long have you two been standing there?"

Blane glared. "Out," he said. "All of you."

# Chapter 12

*i. Iggy*

Lyseira called a stop just up the road to work her miracles. In the first light of dawn, Iggy watched her prayer mend the ruin of Helix's face. Ten minutes earlier he had seen Syntal hurl light from her hands, and now he could see her eyes despite the near-darkness.

They were both witches under the law of the Seven Sacred Principles, but then again, so was he. Years of indoctrination murmured in his mind, trying to convince him he should be upset, but all he felt was relief that he wasn't alone.

More concerning was the fact that they had all just nearly died.

The fight was already becoming a blur in his memory, a vivid but vague impression of filthy light and gnashing fangs. He still wasn't sure they had actually survived it. *Some of us might not have,* he realized, looking at Lyseira, *if it weren't for her.*

"No more sorcery," Seth said to Syntal. A minute ago he'd been bleeding from a giant gash in his side. Now it was forgotten.

Syntal faced him, a challenge in her eyes. "What?"

"You can't control it."

Helix sighed. "Seth, not again."

"It put one of the wolves to sleep–" Syntal started, but Seth broke in.

"It put *me* to sleep!"

"That was an accident."

"So you admit you can't control it."

"I'm still learning!"

Iggy dug through his memory of the fight. It was like rummaging through shattered mirrors, but he did remember seeing Seth down. *I thought he was dead.*

"No," Seth rejoined. "No more." His eyes darted to her pack, glinting threats. Syntal took a faltering step backward.

"That's not your decision," Helix said.

"Seth," Angbar said, "you realize Lyseira is as much a witch as Syntal. Neither one of them is a priestess."

"The third Sacred Principle–" Syntal began, but again Seth cut her off.

"Lyseira works miracles with the blessing of Akir. You got your power from a *book*." He spat the word as if he'd discovered a fly in his mouth. "It's exactly what they warn about. And not just any book, but a book that opened during the Storm. Do you even think about that?"

Iggy's breath caught. No one had mentioned that before. *It opened during the Storm?* The murmurs in his head grew louder, until he remembered that the morning of the Storm was the first time he had heard the wind, too.

"Seth." Lyseira laid a hand on her brother's arm. "She killed that first arc hound. If she hadn't, we would be gone. It has to be part of Akir's plan."

He scoffed, but he looked torn. "If she can't control it–"

"She said it was an accident," Iggy snapped. He hadn't realized he was going to speak until the words were out. "I had my bow, I had plenty of shots go wide. I easily could've shot you more than oncc. Would you be throwing a tantrum about that, too? I thought Preservers were supposed to be tough."

"That's not the same thing," Seth said, but the fire in his voice was fading.

"Of course it is. I shot arrows into their walls, into their ceiling... I didn't manage to hit anyone else, but that was dumb luck."

"We were all frantic," Helix said. "I don't know about you, but I was scared to death."

Angbar laughed. Helix looked at him.

"Sorry," Angbar said. "I'm sorry, I just... Helix, I think you probably did more damage to their house than the arc hounds did."

Helix glowered. "What?"

"Oh, come on. You destroyed everything you touched. The shelves, the chairs... Hel, even the fire poker."

"I couldn't find my sword!"

"I half-expected you to burst through the wall and leave a Helix-shaped hole behind. Just to do a little extra damage."

Syntal snickered. "They'll never take in wayward travelers again."

"What in Hel, Angbar?" Helix protested, but there was a glimmer in his eyes. "See if I save *your* life again."

"Oh," Angbar said with a taunting grin, "the feeling's mutual, my friend."

Iggy felt himself smiling for the first time in days. It faded fast.

"We need to move," he said. "The blizzard is still coming." He could hear it, barreling toward them from the north like a stampede.

"I don't know," Helix said, eager to shift the teasing to someone else. "You may have missed a guess for once, Igg." Misting snow swirled about them like a flock of fairies. "This doesn't look–"

"This isn't it," Iggy promised. "This is nothing." He'd caught the scent of the storm just after leaving home. He hadn't been sure, originally, whether to try to find the others or just set out on his own. He'd been leaning toward the latter, but this blizzard was the kind that came on suddenly–the kind that killed–and his friends had had no idea.

"How long do we have?" Lyseira asked. She was peering into the tree cover, as if she could read the answer in the clouds.

"Not long. I don't know. If I were guessing, I'd say it'll hit today."

"Make for Coram?" Angbar asked. "Do you think we'll have time?"

"I don't know." Between the wind's whispers, the distant storm's howl could've been a tornado. "We'd better."

*ii. Angbar*

They broke fast a few hours after dawn. It was cheese and hardbread, once again, but even that was running low. Angbar's stomach grumbled as everyone got back to their feet, following Iggy along the old roads.

The silence left him alone with his thoughts. Normally he wouldn't have minded, but in the past he'd always amused himself by making up stories. Right now every story he made ended with murder and brought him back to the wintry road, wondering if his parents were safe.

His brain tried to abstract this question, turning it into the musing of a fictional character. It spun a tale about a young *Bahiri* separated from his parents, wondering if they were still alive, wondering if he had done the right thing in leaving. Then he'd realize what he was doing and stamp it out.

This wasn't a work of fiction. This was his life.

For the hundredth time, he tried to clear his thoughts. He stole a glance behind him and saw Syntal trudging along through the leaves and drifting snowfall.

They'd been closer, once. A couple years ago they'd even gone to the Harvest Festival dance together. Not as a couple–he wasn't really interested in Syntal that way–but as two outcasts, just to prove they could.

He dropped back.

"Well," he said, "*I* thought the lightning bolts were impressive, no matter what Seth says."

Syntal started. A rope of dirty hair fell over her face. She absently brushed it back, smiling.

"It wasn't lightning," she said, glancing ahead at Seth. He was oblivious. "But thank you."

Angbar caught the glance. "He was pretty mad, hm?"

Syntal shrugged. "Everyone lived."

He nodded. "We've been lucky that way so far." They crunched through the brittle leaves. "So... you really learned it from that book we found in the lake?"

She glanced at him. There was some suspicion in her eyes, but she must have sensed his honesty. "Yeah. I really did." She stifled a yawn. "Do you want to see it? I can show you, tonight maybe."

His heart quickened at the thought. "Are you sure?"

"I wouldn't have offered otherwise." She peered at him. "It's just a book. It can't hurt you."

Angbar arched a brow. "Not gonna suck out my soul?" There was an old story, *Iis-alac and the Witch's Book*. A boy stole a witch's book, but when he opened it, it destroyed his soul. Now that Angbar thought about it, he was pretty sure that one came from scripture; he'd heard it from Lyseira.

Syntal smiled. "Not that I know of. That's just a story."

"Yeah," Angbar said, "I thought witches were just stories, too. Now I'm on the road with two of them."

Syntal nodded a concession. The air was thick with bigger questions, but Angbar didn't know how to ask them. Syntal wrestled with another yawn.

"It makes you tired?" he asked.

"Exhausted," Syntal said. "Like you've been awake for days. I think Helix thought there was something wrong with me for awhile; I was always exhausted. But I'm getting used to it, I think. It's a little better today. I just pushed myself too far the other night."

*I'd say so,* Angbar thought. *Lys said your ears were bleeding.*

"I don't know. Lar'atul said 'seek the safehold.' I think that might be a way to chant without getting so tired. I have no idea how to do it, is the problem."

"Lar'atul?" It was a strange name; Angbar had never heard it before.

"Sorry. He wrote the book." She smiled again. "The pirate, remember?"

Angbar frowned. "Pirate?"

She laughed. "You don't remember? You kept going on about how he was a pirate, after we found his armor on the shore. At least, I assumed it was his."

Angbar shook his head. "All I remember is Helix stealing my sword," he said with mock rue.

"I thought Seth said it was his."

Angbar waved it off. "Seth was always trying to rile people up."

"Yeah," Syntal said.

The name hung between them, drifting with the snow. Angbar grabbed one of the big questions and threw it out.

"So what happened?"

"At the cabin?"

"Yeah."

She sighed. "It's hard to explain." She groped for the words. "They were too close, essentially. Seth and the wolf. I couldn't tell them apart while I was Ascended." She shook her head. "I mean, I knew they were both there, but I couldn't split them up. I had to command both of them."

Angbar parsed this. *Ascended? Command?* He opened his mouth to ask about the words, and her meaning hit him. "Wait... you mean you did it on purpose?"

"That thing was coming for me. It would've killed me. It was the only thing I could do."

"But if... couldn't it have killed Seth while he was asleep?"

Syntal shook her head. "No. The chant was going to command them both. And the other wolf was going after Iggy. I knew it would be all right."

A sudden wind came up, hurling a thousand icy knives before it died out.

Angbar swallowed. *No, you didn't.*

*You didn't know that at all.*

*iii. Iggy*

They were surrounded by fields and farmhouses. A half-mile on, Coram's smoke was staining the grey sky black. Iggy had been cautious about leaving the woods, but it was starting to look like the right decision.

Then a leviathan swallowed the sun.

"Take hands!" Ignatius called as he grabbed Seth's hand. He turned back to see Angbar at the rear, sprinting to catch up. The snow devoured him, transformed by the wind into a rain of savage darts, and then Iggy couldn't see anything.

"Take hands!" he shouted again. The storm hurled the words across the plain, roaring. Its fury was incredible, like the full weight of winter expelled from the Earth's lungs in a single, brutal breath.

He had seen Storm weather. He had seen abrupt weather. He had never seen anything like this.

He waited as long as he thought he could, to give enough time for Angbar to catch up to Syntal at the rear. Then, before he forgot which way led to the city, he pulled the group forward.

Snow washed over the road, erasing its edges and flattening the landscape. His face burned with the cold, his cheeks stinging from the whipping snow. He clutched Seth's hand like a lifeline. If he lost it, he might never find it again.

If he squinted he couldn't see, but if he didn't, the snow tried to stab out his eyes. *Did I get turned around?* He tossed his head, looking for the sun, but it was gone. There was only wind and snow.

He remembered a tale Pa had told him, about how Iggy's uncle had died in a blizzard after wandering in a circle around his own home three times.

*Don't,* he snarled. *The city was right in front of you. It's still there. Don't get turned around.* He forced himself to quit searching for the sun, to keep his face turned forward. *It's still there.*

Minutes or hours dragged past. He couldn't see the road. His hand was numb; he thought he still had Seth's hand, but he wasn't certain.

"Is everyone well?" he shouted. The wind killed the words on his lips.

*It's been too long,* he realized. *I should have seen something by now. A building, a signpost.* The air was too cold and too fast; he couldn't breathe.

How stupid, he thought, to get this far and die in the snow.

He closed his eyes and tried speaking to the wind, but it was enraged. It was like his father, when he was drunk; it couldn't hear his whisper over its own screaming. So he stopped talking, and just listened. Maybe the wind's shriek would tell him, if he could just hear its words.

He let it knife through him until he heard fire.

*Behind us. It's behind us.* He turned and peered into the roiling white. Nothing. But he had heard fire.

Blindly, he lurched toward it.

*Never turn in a storm,* Pa had said. *Never turn when you can't see.*

A crouching giant loomed in the darkness: a building. The lights in its windows were fireflies wrapped in gauze. "There!" he might've shouted. He could only hear the storm.

When he turned the knob, the door flew in and cracked against the wall. Warmth and brightness assailed him.

He stumbled into them, still alive.

"Is everyone well?" he called back. Seth came in behind him, pulling Lyseira. Iggy didn't realize he was holding his breath until Angbar came in at the end of the chain. *Thank Akir. Oh, that was close.*

"Close the door, then," a small woman behind the counter called. "Hard enough keeping it warm without the door open."

Angbar complied. A sign above the door said: *The Wagon Wheel.*

"Right then," the innkeep said. "I assume you'll be renting a room?"

*iv. Helix*

The room was warm, with a window and two beds. Angbar was in a steaming tub, groaning extravagantly as he thawed. They had all eaten hot food tonight. Compared to Helix's days in the jail wagon and then on the road, it was the height of luxury. He should've been relaxing.

He couldn't.

They had scraped together enough coin between them to cover another meal each and two rooms for two nights. When it was over, they would have nothing. Angbar had talked about performing in the common room to earn a few extra heels; Seth had spoken candidly about stealing food. Iggy seemed to think that once the storm had passed, they'd be able to live off of the land.

None of them were good options. In truth, they had nowhere to go. The fire crackling in the hearth and the inviting feather beds only drove this reality home. They weren't respite; they were illusion. Beyond them were more freezing nights on the road, going nowhere.

"Helix," Angbar moaned from the tub, "oh, it's wonderful."

"*M'sai,*" Helix told him. "I heard you the first seven times. Hurry up so I can take my turn."

"It's still going," Iggy said from the window. The view was black and swirling; the glass shuddered in its frame. "Probably will be until morning, at least, maybe longer."

*I hope it stops by the day after tomorrow,* Helix thought grimly, *or we'll be back in it.*

He turned to the bag Syntal had packed for him. He'd been wearing the same clothes for... seven days? Eight? He wanted something clean to wear after his bath. He pulled out a haphazard bundle of shirts, and Matthew's letter fell out of them.

It looked absurdly out of place: a relic from an ancient age. A hundred years ago, Matthew had said, *Promise me.*

Helix scoffed and shook his head, but something in him said, *I wonder if his wife even knows yet.*

*I wonder what they'll tell her.*

That was ridiculous; there was no doubt what they'd tell her. They'd say Helix Smith had murdered her husband and gotten away with it.

*No! I tried to* save *him!* His outrage was as futile now as it had been at the trial, but he couldn't stop it. It wasn't enough that they had tried to kill him. It wasn't enough that they had taken his parents and his girlfriend and his home, that he would never sleep in peace again. They were going to lie about him to Matthew's wife, too.

"Do you think word has gotten to Keldale?" he said.

"About you?" Angbar was standing now, the water streaming off him. "About the trial?"

"Yeah."

"Not in this," Iggy said. "No one's traveling in this." He considered. "I suppose it depends on how much time they wasted looking for you on the west road."

"Why would that even matter?" Helix wondered aloud. "How is it possible that they don't know where I am, right now? Marcus can just Commune with Akir to find me."

"You said he lied about that," Angbar answered as he dried off. "If he lied about what the Communion said, maybe he was lying about being able to do it at all."

He threw it out casually, but the idea made Helix's head spin. He had never considered the possibility. *How many lies did they tell?*

"Let me get dressed and get some fresh water," Angbar said. "Then it's your turn."

*v. Lyseira*

Lyseira had figured it out. She knew what Akir wanted.

She had acted on faith and her sense of justice when she'd saved Helix, and Akir had rewarded her with the power to keep herself and her friends alive. All the signs since then–Iggy's arrival in time to save them from the blizzard, their encounter with Blane that gave them a place to sleep for the night–were His hand, sheltering them and leading them onward. Even the news of her mother...

Lyseira's thoughts stumbled as she thought of Mom. *They took his fingers,* Matthew had told her, *his tongue, and his eyes.* What were they doing to her mother?

*I never meant any harm to you,* she wanted to tell her. *I didn't know they'd come for you.* God had tried to warn her, with His message from Matthew, but she hadn't seen it.

She hadn't seen it.

There was a sob in her chest, clawing to come out. An image of Marcus, smug as a hawk, came to her.

*You,* she seethed. The sob died; its dry bones turned to tinder. *You think you can get away with this? Akir will take everything from you.* She drew a shuddering breath, a fire smoldering in her belly, and picked up her scattered thoughts.

Even the news of her mother had served to help her understand. They couldn't go back, not by themselves. But Akir didn't want her to simply run away. He wanted the sinners punished.

Her first instinct–to tell the Fatherlord about Marcus and Elmoor–had been the right one. When He knew, He would serve justice.

A knock came at the door. "It's us," Seth said.

She glanced at Syntal, who had just finished brushing her hair. The other girl nodded.

"It's open," Lyseira called.

The boys filed in. Seth crossed to the window and checked the lock while the others took up places against the wall.

Angbar drew a deep breath. "Let me be the first to congratulate us all," he said, "on smelling much better." A rumble of laughter came from the floor beneath them; there was some kind of show happening in the common room. He glanced at the floor, startled.

"Listen," Lyseira said. "I know what we need to do. When the blizzard lets up–"

"I'm going to Keldale," Helix broke in.

Lyseira stumbled, her speech forgotten. "What?"

"It might be dangerous," Helix said. "I might not make it out. I don't know. But Matthew gave me a letter before he died, and I swore I'd get it to his wife. She's in Keldale."

Seth glowered. "So hire a courier."

"We can't even afford food. I can't afford a courier." Helix waved. "And that's not the point. The point is, I need to see her. I need her to know I didn't do it."

Lyseira's mouth was moving, but it wasn't saying anything. "Helix..." she finally managed.

"She might be in danger, Lyseira. They killed her husband, and you heard what Iggy said they did to our families."

"But Keldale is huge," Lyseira said, her wits returning. "*Basica Tenuor* is one of the biggest temples in the Valley!"

"It's a huge risk," Seth agreed.

"*M'sai*," Helix said. "Let me start again." He put up his hands. "*I'm going.* I'm not asking anyone else to come along. It might..." He sighed. "I should probably split off anyway. I'm putting you all in danger right now."

"*Now?*" Lyseira aped, incredulous. "It's been dangerous from the start!"

"Fine," Helix said. "Then maybe it's time for it to start getting safer for the rest of you."

"Helix," Angbar cut in, "why are you doing this again? We already talked about this. We risked as much as you did. There's no going back, not for any of us."

A forlorn wind rattled the window. Another round of laughter roared beneath them.

"Please," Lyseira said. "Just... I've been thinking a lot, too. And I did save your life. Will you listen?" If she could just explain it, he would understand.

Helix's jaw was set. He glanced at the wall, then waved her on. "*M'sai.* But I know what I need to do."

"*M'sai.*" Lyseira stood up. "I know it doesn't feel like it, but Akir has been guiding us since the start. Marcus and Elmoor are corrupt–we all know that. I think this... *all* of this... might be happening because God wants them to get caught. He wants them to know justice."

Helix was still frowning, but he twirled his finger. *Go on.*

"You're still talking about going to Tal'aden," Angbar said.

"About talking to the Fatherlord."

Lyseira met his eyes. "I am. It's not easy to know the will of Akir, but think of everything that's happened so far. Iggy showing up just in time to save us from the blizzard. Akir granting me the miracles that have kept us alive. At every turn, He's been with us. I think I was wrong to want to go back–I'll admit that. But He's urging us on. He wants justice."

The distant crowd laughed again. Someone hooted.

Helix sputtered. "A minute ago you were scoffing at Keldale because it has such a big temple. Tal'aden has the biggest temple in the *world*."

"That's different," Lyseira pointed out. "The Fatherlord is in Tal'aden. He's the one who needs to know."

"Lyseira..." Helix rubbed his temples. "You don't know that He'll help us. Matthew thought the Church was corrupt through-and-through."

"The signs–" Lyseira started.

"What if you're misreading the signs?" Angbar said, not ungently. "I understand what you're saying, but it seems to me the only clear sign we have right now is that Helix's letter from Matthew suddenly fell out of his travel sack."

Lyseira choked back a curse. *That's just a coincidence,* she wanted to snap, but even she could see that was useless. The same argument could be made about everything she said. She knew she was right–she *knew it*–but how could she convince them?

"Do you have anything to say?" Seth said, looking at Syntal.

She was sitting on the bed, her book open in front of her. "I'm going with Helix," she said, without looking up.

"It would take months to reach Tal'aden on foot," Iggy said. "You'd freeze to death before you got there. We need to figure out how we're going to survive this winter. All these other ideas about justice and what-have-you need to wait."

Angbar held up a hand. "What if she's willing to help us? Matthew's wife? What if she's able to put us up for the winter?"

"She thinks Helix killed her *husband,*" Seth said.

"No, she doesn't." Helix glanced at Angbar. "Not yet. And she *was* his wife; she probably has no love for the Church herself."

*And that's a good thing?* Lyseira wanted to retort, but she held her tongue, fuming. She was losing this argument.

Iggy considered. "Really, where else can we go? We need shelter, and soon. If she won't help us, at least it'll be warmer inside the city walls." He clucked. "But I don't even know how we'd make that trip, Helix. The roads are going to be impassable, and even if they weren't, Keldale is weeks away on foot."

"Well, we can't stay here," Helix retorted. "We can't afford it. Day after tomorrow, we're back on the road."

~ ~

After the boys left, Lyseira leaned against the door and tried to keep her anger in check.

*I should go to Tal'aden myself. Seth would come with me.* Iggy's arguments about the winter struggled to be heard in her head, but she ran over them. *The Fatherlord will help us. Why can't they see it?*

But it was reflexive outrage, and in her heart, she knew it.

She looked at Syntal. The girl was still on the bed, her palms open and blazing with light. Her eyes were becoming more real by the moment.

Lyseira glared, irritation grating at her. *I wonder when she started doing that.* Lyseira had spent years trying to summon light. It was one of the simplest miracles an initiate could work. *Was she in her room with light coming out of her hands during all those nights I tried? Was she able to do it the whole time we were both learning First Tongue from The Abbot?*

The jealousy was so fierce it startled her. "You shouldn't do that here," she snapped. "Someone could see."

"I have to practice," the other girl answered. The light made the black of her hair even deeper.

"Someone will notice your eyes," Lyseira pressed. "Stop."

The light winked out. Syntal stood, staring at her feet.

*Quit being petty,* Lyseira told herself. Suddenly, she felt like an ass. "Sorry," she said. "I'm sorry, I–"

"Sh." Syntal's eyes were glued to the floor.

Lyseira followed her gaze, expecting a bug or a mouse, but saw nothing. She glanced a question at her.

Downstairs, another burst of laughter dissolved into scattered applause and cheering.

Without looking up, Syntal said, "Someone's chanting downstairs."

*Chanting?* "What do you mean?"

"Sorcery."

"How do you know?"

Syntal shushed her again, then started for the door.

"Syntal, wait. Are you saying there's a *witch*–"

Seth was standing guard in the hallway. Syntal hurried past him and toward the stairs. He threw a look at Lyseira and followed.

"Syn!" Lyseira hissed.

The lights were down in the common room. A makeshift stage had been set up at one end, and a man was crouched at its edge, holding a hat.

"Thank you," he said as someone threw in some coin. "Too kind." He had close-cropped black hair, tinged with grey, and a long, sharp face. The goatee only made it seem longer.

A sign had been posted on the wall behind him. It read, in glittering, grandiose lettering:

*Marlin the Magnificent.*

"You were so funny!" a young woman exclaimed as she approached. "The pigeons... how did you do that?"

He winked. "Oh, my dear, a good magician never reveals his secrets."

"Him," Syntal whispered to Lyseira. "It was him."

Lyseira balked. "He was doing it in front of everyone?" How stupid could someone be?

"Yes. I could feel it upstairs. And look at his eyes."

Lyseira peered, but she could barely make out the man's face in the dark, let alone his eyes. "What about them?"

"Exactly," Syntal said.

Lyseira glowered, annoyed by the cryptic answer, but then she caught the other girl's meaning. If Syntal was right and he *had* been working real sorcery, his eyes should have been unmistakable. *So why aren't they?*

Marlin glanced at them with a lingering grin, full of crooked teeth. His face abruptly sobered. "Joe, take the hat," he called. A younger man scrambled forward and did as he was told. Marlin jumped off the stage and swept toward them. Seth took a protective step forward.

"Are you a fool?" Marlin demanded. "Are you trying to get yourself killed?"

"I–I felt you chanting from upstairs," Syntal stammered. "I came down–"

"Keep your *sehking* voice down!" He turned, flashed a broad grin at his patrons, and gave a short wave. The smile died as he turned back. "Get out of here, before someone sees your eyes. Someone who's not too thick to understand what they mean."

Syntal blanched, but regained herself. Her face hardened. "Not until you tell me why your eyes are normal."

Marlin scoffed and looked at Seth. "If your friend doesn't learn some common sense, she won't be long for the world." He turned away, but Syntal's next words stopped him.

"I'll tell them what you are."

He spun back. "You wouldn't dare. They'd burn us both."

She changed tactics. "*Please*. My home is gone. I'm being hunted. I *need* to know how you do it."

A flicker of sympathy crossed his features and was gone. He cursed and shook his head.

"Master Marlin?" his apprentice called from the stage. "All finished, here."

Marlin waved him off. "How old are you?" he whispered.

"Seventeen winters," Syntal said.

He cursed again and glared at her. "Room seven," he finally said. "Upstairs. One hour." He paused. "Do you have a book?"

Syntal nodded.

"Bring it," he said, and left.

## *vi. Iggy*

The next morning Iggy found himself at the counter near the kitchen, waiting for the food he'd ordered and wondering if things would ever be normal again.

Their situation had changed abruptly last night when Syntal returned from her visit with Marlin. Apparently the older man had been interested in some of Syntal's spells, and had offered to pay handsomely for them. Syntal now had three horses with tack and two golden crowns: enough animals to carry them all to Keldale, and enough money to cover breakfast with plenty to spare. Since he was least likely to be recognized, Seth had nominated Iggy to come downstairs and get food for everyone.

Which was all wonderful, but it did leave Iggy unsettled. When he'd left Southlight, he'd been worried for his own safety. He'd wanted to get away from the Tribunal, certain they'd come after him next. He had ended up chasing down his friends to warn them about the blizzard, but since, things had spiraled out of control.

Syntal was a witch, and Lyseira too–though she seemed loath to admit it, Angbar was right when he said her miracles condemned her in the eyes of the Church. Now there was another sorcerer, and they were accepting his payment to help them get where they were going.

Iggy had wanted to get away from sorcery and strange eyes and the Tribunal, but every morning, it seemed like he was sinking deeper into all three.

*And what of it?* he accused himself. Maybe this was where he belonged. He could talk to *animals,* for the love of Akir.

*You can also heal, just like a priest,* his mind whispered, but he shut it out. He didn't like to think about that.

"How was the trip from Keldale?" the innkeep asked, catching Iggy's attention.

"Been better," the young man at the next stool answered. He took a long draught from a steaming mug.

"You head that way often?" Iggy asked. Some news of the route could be helpful. *Just don't attract too much attention,* Seth admonished in his head.

"Now and again." The other man looked at him. He had inquisitive eyes and sharp features, but the curl to his hair gave him a boyish look.

"Oh now, Harth's just being coy," the innkeep said to Iggy. "He lives up there."

"Is that right?" Iggy looked to Harth. "What brings you down?"

Harth took another drink and wiped his mouth. "Just a little business. Got in yesterday–just beat the blizzard. Why? Heading north?"

The innkeep disappeared into the kitchen, and Iggy hesitated. In his head, Seth glared. *Don't say too much.* "Got family comin' down this way," he said, feeling pleased with himself. "Was just hoping you might be able to tell me how the road was, with the blizzard and all, but if you got in yesterday..."

"I wouldn't know. I came the long way. But you can expect your family to be delayed–even if the blizzard didn't catch them, the Church did."

Sehk. *How did he know?* Iggy fought to keep his face casual, but couldn't resist a quick glance around the common room. It was nearly empty.

"Easy," Harth said, chuckling. "I only mean they're stopping everyone on that road–headed north or south. Or so I've heard." He leaned forward and whispered, "That's why I skipped it."

Iggy said nothing. He suddenly felt like this conversation had been a very bad idea. *How long can a few flapjacks take to fry?* he wondered.

"If your… *family* were interested in avoiding all the trouble of the north road, though, they could go 'round, down through Fors and then east, into Coram. That's the way I came. Avoided most of the storm, too."

"You took the Wolfwood road?" Iggy asked, surprised. The road ran right along the cursed forest's tree line for miles north. It was practically legendary. They said the Storm had turned the wolves of the wood mad. They killed any travelers who came too close. The old Wolfwood road had been abandoned for years.

Harth spread his hands. "It's not always the safest route, but its reputation is worse than it deserves. Someone dies on that road, it's because they did something stupid. The wolves won't give you any trouble if you keep your distance. Usually. More importantly"–he actually winked–"they don't ask any questions about where you're headed or what your business is.

"Besides," Harth went on, "that blizzard barely grazed the

Wolfwood road. Most of the way is clear."

The innkeep slid two plates of flapjacks and sausage onto the counter. "More comin'," she said.

"Thanks. I'll bring these upstairs." Iggy jumped off the stool.

"Your family familiar with Keldale?" Harth asked.

Iggy debated his answer, and finally nodded. "Well, sure. It's their home. They've lived there as long as they've been alive."

"Ah. Nothing to worry about then. I was just gonna mention they might not even be able to get out of the city right now. There's some kind of big Church event happening soon; they're watching everything. If your folks needed any help, I was gonna offer to hunt them down when I return. I know the city pretty well; I grew up there. They wouldn't be the first ones I've shown around." He shrugged. "But if they know their way around..."

Rev'naas *take it,* Iggy thought. He glanced around again and leaned in. "You spend a lot of time getting people around Church patrols?"

Harth matched his low tone. "A lot."

"How much?"

"Three shells a head."

*Eighteen shells. That's almost everything Syntal has left.* "There's six of us," Iggy said. "Do it for fifteen?"

Harth gave him a mirthless smile. "Nope."

*I tried.* "Deal."

# Chapter 13

*i. Angbar*

The sign was like something from a story, one of the scary ones the kids would tell on the Night of *Rev'naas.* It was old, battered wood, jutting from the bare earth like a splinter, written in faded red paint.

*Danger–wolves.*

The road beyond was thick with dying autumn grass. It wended closer to the tree line as it ran north, until maybe a hundred paces of frozen earth separated the two.

Veiling Green, sometimes called Wolfwood, was a sea of dark firs beneath a grey sky, stretching endlessly away toward the mountains of the Tears in the west. Trees whispered like devils as they rustled in the wind, the shadows between their trunks thick as midnight.

Lyseira cast a final doubtful look back at Iggy. *"We won't get twenty paces in Keldale without a guide,"* Iggy had said, and Angbar had agreed. She'd been the hardest to convince, but ultimately she'd gone along with the vote.

They rode north and passed an old campsite, where a travel sack hung impaled on a tree; it flapped in the wind like a flag. "Leave it," Harth called when Iggy made to check the site for supplies. "It's been there for weeks." A mile on, Angbar saw the hulk of a broken-down wagon forty paces off the road. The winding grasses in its axles seemed to be hauling it slowly toward the trees.

*What happened to the people?* Angbar wanted to ask, but he didn't want to hear the answer.

"Stay on the road," Harth warned them more than once. "You notice how all the dead camps and broken wagons are on *that* side?" He jerked his head toward the wood. "Stay on the road."

*If the Church is right about the Rending,* Angbar thought that afternoon, *I wonder if this is what everything will look like at the end.* He imagined a world consumed by *rev'naas,* all the people gone and the buildings overgrown, invisible monsters lurking behind every tree. The Storm had already reclaimed the Wolfwood road. Maybe it was just a matter of time until it got everything else.

*ii. Iggy*

They camped on the east side of the road, away from the wood. After being woken for third watch, Iggy sat huddled in the dark, alone with his thoughts, waiting for dawn. When it finally spread over the plain, his blood ran cold.

The wolves had crept from the wood in the night. They were perched halfway between the road and the forest, sitting like soldiers at attention, their eyes trained on him. Their line stretched as far along the road as he could see.

*Wolves!* Panic sparked in the horses. *Run! Wolves!*

*No!* Iggy whispered. *Wait!* There were enough of the wolves that if they decided to attack, they would overwhelm the little group in seconds. *Don't shout. Don't move. Do nothing.* He froze and watched them, like his mother had always told him to do as a child when a bee landed on his arm.

*You're mad!* his mount said.

*They haven't attacked. If they do, then you can run. Let me think.*

The sun crawled higher. In its light, the wolves' eyes flickered like fireflies.

Finally, slowly, he rose. The line didn't move, but their eyes followed him. He cast his own gaze to their feet, trying to appear submissive.

*We mean you no harm,* he said through the wind.

Their ears flattened; their nostrils flared. One, a lithe grey with a ring of black around its neck and chest, pawed at the earth, whining.

*It speaks,* one of the animals murmured. It was impossible to say which one.

*It lies,* said another. *Tall-walkers always bring harm.*

*Stay away.* The warning rippled through their line like a growl.

*We will,* he returned. *I promise. We're just using the road.*

*There is no road.* A huge white, its face twisted by an old burn across one cheek, took a step forward. *Only a scar, slowly healing. It is ours.*

Iggy nodded, keeping his eyes low. His instincts screamed for him to wake the others and run. But he had never seen anything like this, and he couldn't let it alone. *Why are you doing this?*

The white's eyes narrowed.

*You invite trouble by attacking travelers,* Iggy pressed. *It's not the way of wolves to attack men for no reason. Why are you doing this?*

*We do what we must,* the white said, but another answered, *We guard the wood.*

The wolf to its left snarled and nipped it in the ear. It recoiled with a yelp.

*The wood?* Iggy asked.

The white gave a low growl. *Ignore the pup. She's a fool.*

*We need the road,* Iggy said. *A storm has blocked the other paths. We'll leave your wood alone. You have my word.*

*The word of a tall-walker is nothing. Be gone.*

*Not mine,* Iggy insisted. *I swear, I wish you no harm. I will keep my pack away from the wood–*

*Be gone,* the white snarled, *or we will bleed you!*

Iggy took a step back despite himself. Then he met the white's eyes. *No.* He stepped forward again. *We will take this road. We will leave your wood alone. And if you attack us, one of us will escape, and we will tell the other tall-walkers that your wood has treasure.*

*Your flesh will be sweet, man-speaker.*

*Do you know what treasure is?* Iggy locked eyes with the beast, staring it down, willing his hands not to shake.

*Gold,* the wolf said. The word was clumsy.

*Yes. Gold. And tall-walkers will do anything for gold. They will come here in numbers, from all around. You won't be able to stop them. I will see to it myself.*

The line erupted in protests.

*It lies!*

*Our pack is larger than theirs!*

*Bleed them now!*

The white gave a sharp bark, and the clamor fell away. Behind him, Iggy heard Seth leap to his feet.

"Iggy? What–?"

Iggy shushed him and waved a hand. "Be still. Be quiet."

"How long have they–?"

"Hush!" he snapped over his shoulder. His gaze never left the white. *You see?* he said. *I can control my pack. Can you control yours?*

The white bared its fangs; its gums were a splash of red, dark as blood. Iggy felt the need to swallow, the need to blink, and fought them both. Instead he showed the barest hint of his own teeth.

*Watch them,* the white finally said. *If they cross the scar, take the horses first.* He returned to the line and sat, then lazily scratched behind his ear.

Slowly, Iggy exhaled. "*M'sai,*" he said aloud, still not willing to risk turning away. "They won't attack us. Wake the others."

"How do you know that?" Seth said.

"I stared the white down. He's the alpha. Did you hear the noise he made? As long as we don't stray to their side of the road, they won't risk it."

Seth scoffed. "Iggy, look at that. I've never seen... you can't know that."

"Harth." Iggy knelt and shook their guide awake. "Harth!"

As the man's eyes came open, Iggy shushed him. "Careful. Quiet. They're not attacking. We have to get moving."

Harth sat up. His eyes grew wide. "Blesséd *sehk,*" he muttered.

### *iii. Angbar*

Angbar rode where they told him and kept quiet like they said, but he was resolute: nothing anyone could say would convince him this was a good idea. They might have faced down arc hounds and survived an onslaught from the Tribunal's archers, but riding all day fifty paces from a line of rabid wolves was scary in a way nothing else had been.

*Not rabid,* he tried to tell himself. *Iggy said they weren't rabid.* His eyes stole a glance at the wolves before jerking back to the road. *They're not frothing. Hel, they're not even* moving.

That may have been the strangest part of the whole thing: the way the animals just *watched.* They reminded him of soldiers, following their general's commands. Now and again he would see a smaller group of ten or twenty race past from the rear of the line headed toward the far end, presumably to maintain the illusion that the line went on forever. Otherwise, none of the beasts moved.

*Maintain the illusion...?* he accused himself. *They're* wolves! But it was impossible to draw any other conclusion: the beasts were blocking the little group of travelers from the wood.

As far as Angbar was concerned, they were welcome to it.

After dinner, Harth helped himself to a flask and crawled into his bedroll. Helix passed out near the fire, his back to a tree. Angbar was laying out a blanket of his own when Syntal crouched next to him. She had her book.

"Did you still want to see?" she asked.

They set up another small fire, separate from the main camp. Seth's and Lyseira's eyes chased them.

Syntal laid out a blanket. She handled the old book with a caution verging on veneration. The cover was dark leather and unmarked. A metal band had held it closed once, but now it dangled open.

*There's no clasp,* Angbar realized. Where the two strips of metal should have had some kind of interlocking mechanism, the metal was sheer. It might have been sliced in two by a knife.

"That's incredible," Angbar breathed, running his finger along the smooth edge. "That happened after the Storm?"

"Right on the marking." Syntal pressed the two pieces together. They formed an engraving of a symbol Angbar didn't recognize, like a stylized *h*. The break in the metal had split it, leaving half on each side.

"What is it?"

"It's a First Tongue word. *Salgo.*" Her eyes left him, ranging into the past. "It means 'begin,' or 'speak the truth.'"

Again, that reverence in her voice. Looking at her, he felt as if he had stumbled into a temple.

The pages were thin and yellowed. Angbar couldn't read the words, but they still surprised him. He had expected clean margins and even script, like the time Lyseira had shown him some pages from Gilleus, the first book of the Chronicle. This looked more like a journal. The text was sloppy, written at long, loping angles; there were scribbles in the margins and whole pages left nearly blank.

"It was so hard to translate," Syntal said as if reading his thoughts, "because Lar'atul was such a sloppy writer. Learning the language was hard enough, but then for everything to be so sloppy, too..." There was a tone of grudging admiration in her voice, as if she could complain about the author's illegible writing, but she could never hold it against him. Like she was talking about a friend, or a favorite teacher.

"It looks... almost like he was in a hurry," Angbar said.

"He was."

Angbar glanced at her, curious, but she didn't share her meaning. "Here." She pulled a sheaf of loose papers from the middle of the book. "These are my notes. I translated most of it. I don't really need these anymore, I understand the ideas now, but I've never..."

She licked her lips and looked at him. Her eyes were striking in the fire light. Not from chanting–not this time. Just because fires dancing in emeralds would make anyone's heart skip. Her raven hair swallowed that same light, like the space between the stars.

She was exotic and tempting, a creature of darkness and mystery.

*Uh-oh.* Angbar took a sudden interest in a blade of grass. *Where in Hel did* that *come from?* Hopefully, she wouldn't be able to make out his blush in the darkness.

"I've never shared this," she said. "Not with Helix, not with anyone."

*Well, no,* Angbar wanted to say, *that would be stupid. No one likes to get killed.* His tongue wanted to haul off on him, to blab nonsense until her pretty eyes went away. He wrestled it down and said, "I understand."

He'd been friends with Syntal his whole life. He thought of her more like a sister than anything.

Didn't he?

Even when they'd gone to the Festival dance together, it hadn't been romantic. It couldn't be, not this far south. A *Bahiri* with a pale girl? Just going to the dance had been risky enough. Everyone knew they'd always been friends, and he'd still gotten a few evil eyes. It could never be more than that, even if he wanted it to be. And he didn't. He never had.

*Kirith a'jhul,* she was gorgeous. How had he never seen it?

She was looking at him. He looked back, losing himself, just for a second, in her eyes.

Wait. She had asked him a question.

"Ah... *m'sai,*" he said, nodding gravely.

"You're sure?" Her brows knitted. "You seem..."

"No, no–sorry. I just... the wolves, you know, they're all just sitting there... it's playing with my head." *Shake it off, Angbar.*

"Yeah. I can't wait to get out of this place. I hate those things." She took a deep breath. "*M'sai.* It works like this.

"There's something that tells everything what to be. How to act. It tells the dirt to be dirt, the grass to be grass. It tells the fire to be hot."

"Like God?"

Her expression fell. "That... that's exactly what I was talking about. *M'sai?* God doesn't come into it."

"Ah–sorry."

"If you want to go running off to Lyseira–"

"No, no! Sorry." He mimed clapping a hand over his mouth. "Go ahead. I'm listening."

She looked annoyed, but there was something else in her eyes: fear.

*This is hard for her,* he realized. *Really hard. God doesn't come into it? No wonder they're burning witches.* She had taken him aside to share her deepest secret, and he was acting like an ass.

He sighed. "I'm sorry, Syn. I'm just nervous. I want to hear, *m'sai?* I'll behave." He squeezed her hand and repeated her own words. "God doesn't come into it."

*You just did that so you could squeeze her hand,* something whispered in the back of his mind. *You sly dog.*

She looked pensive, but she went on. "Lar'atul calls it 'the Pulse.' When you hear it, it'll make sense. It sounds like a heartbeat."

He swallowed his questions.

"It's telling the stars to glow. It tells people when to live and when to die. It... it's *everything.* And we can't hear it most of the time. But if we Ascend, we can hear it, and it's so beautiful. When you're Ascended, you... you're just..." Her hands floundered, searching for the words. "You know *everything.*"

It was easy to hold his tongue now; he had no idea what to say.

"The book has these chants." She turned to the back, to pages lined with the neat script he'd been expecting. "They're not First Tongue–they don't make any sense until you Ascend. But when you do, you can speak them. They're commands. You can speak like the Pulse speaks. You can tell the fire to be hotter, or the stars to glow brighter–"

"Or an arc hound to go to sleep?"

She gave him a radiant smile. "Yes! Right! Or..." She pointed at her eyes and quirked a brow; the smile melted into a crafty grin. "Make your eyes dull."

*Your eyes,* he stopped himself from saying, *are not dull.*

"It doesn't last long. I have to remember to do it before I chant for it to work, but that..." She gestured, excited. "I never would've figured that out. I always just thought the glow was something that happened. It never occurred to me that I could stop it." She glanced an apology at him. "I mean, your eyes don't *glow*, really, but that's how I think of it."

"Right."

"And I mean, if it can do that, it's... it can affect *itself*, then... I wonder if there's anything it *can't* do."

Again, he didn't know what to say, so he contented himself by watching her smile.

"And really, Lar'atul would say there's not. There's nothing it can't do. That's why they–" Her excitement died. She had the look of a girl backing away from a cliff. More subdued, she said, "Well, it has more to do with us. How much *we* can stand. He said there were people that could do incredible things. Make mountains fly. But you can only Ascend for so long before it hurts you."

"Like the nosebleeds?"

"Well... yes. And worse. I think there's a way around it, though. Remember the safehold?"

Angbar didn't.

"Lar'atul wrote something about a safehold. 'Seek the safehold.' I think it's a... mental trick, some way to keep your mind held steady, even when you're Ascended. But I haven't figured that out yet, so chanting is still a risk." She fixed her eyes on him. "*M'sai?* It's dangerous, every time."

*How dangerous is it?* he almost asked. *What can happen?* But he wanted to say something that would make her smile again; he wanted to see her eyes ignite.

"I'll be careful," he promised. "Show me how?"

It worked.

*iv. Lyseira*

"She's teaching him." Seth's eyes were trained on the other fire, where Syntal laughed and shoved at Angbar's shoulder.

"I know," Lyseira said. She wasn't sure what to say, or what to think, and her recognition of that fact only paralyzed her more.

"She shouldn't," Seth said simply.

*No,* Lyseira wanted to agree, *she shouldn't.* For a dizzying instant, the truth was laid bare: she was a fugitive from the holy Church, traveling with a witch. It turned her stomach.

Then context came crashing back. *A witch I've known since childhood,* she insisted. *A witch who has saved my life, and is doing the right thing.*

Lyseira had seen the signs that the world was crumbling since the Storm. She'd seen the sun stay up until midnight. She'd seen the crops die in the fields. Her faith in Akir's plan had kept her grounded through all of it. But the stories of witches had never been real for her.

That couldn't happen in Southlight, not in her home town–but it *had* been happening, for years.

It gave her a jolt; made the consequences of the Storm real in a way nothing else had. The world wasn't just crumbling, its natural laws breaking down as it came to an end. It was *changing*.

If Syntal could teach Angbar to do what she did, then maybe it was something anyone could do. Was that the way the world would look, in its final days? She imagined a riot of lawless witches, able to kill on command, the Church unable to stop them. Maybe that would only be the final step. Before it would come more animals revolting, like the wolves. The ground opening with flames. Night become day and day become night.

Everyone knew the Storm heralded the end. But no one knew what that end would look like.

*That's not true*. An idea seized her. *God knows.*

Of course. She had been spending all her time trying to read signs and figure out what He wanted, but she could work miracles now. She should ask *Him*.

Seth stood, his eyes trained on Syntal and Angbar. "I'll be right back."

She took his hand. "Seth–don't. Leave them alone."

"Why?"

"Because you'll fight. You'll wake up Harth." *Because I don't know what's right and wrong anymore.* "I don't want him to know."

"They shouldn't be doing it right in the open like that." He frowned. "They shouldn't be doing it at all."

"I know. But..." Witchcraft was one of the greatest sins. Would they have sat by while Syntal slowly murdered someone ten paces away? Would that have been any less of an abomination? She didn't have a good reason for him. She wasn't even sure she was right. "Please."

The distant baying of wolves rolled over them. The call was caught by a second group, this one nearer, and then the line of animals near the road took it up. Harth and Helix stirred.

"S'all right," Harth mumbled. "They do that."

As the noise died, Seth pulled away. "I'm going to patrol the camp. You should get some rest. Morning comes soon."

She watched his back as he left, fighting the urge to apologize. When she had the fire to herself, she turned and knelt.

"Akir," she murmured in First Tongue. "You answered me when I forewent the rituals, so I'm foregoing them again. I'm seeking Communion."

It was ludicrous. An old voice, a contemptuous voice, whispered, *Who in Hel are you? You're no one.* She ignored it.

"You sent us out here. I know You did. You've saved us more than once, and I've felt Your fire." *It was glorious.* "But I need Your help. I don't know where to go. I'm human, and I'm failing. If You've given me signs, I can't see them. I want justice for Fathers

Marcus and Elmoor. They're blasphemers, lying in Your name. Is that what I should seek?"

In the empty darkness behind her eyes, her heart drummed.

"I feel like it's the right choice, but I can't convince the others. They think I'm mad to seek Your avatar in Tal'aden. Are they right?"

Nothing.

She hadn't expected the sky to open. She hadn't expected to be seized by fire. But she had expected *something.*

*Maybe silence is an answer as well. Maybe I just need to listen to it.* Did that mean Tal'aden was the wrong course? That stung–it meant she had gotten it wrong–but it was also a relief. Seeking the Fatherlord would be terrifying. But where should they go, then? Winter was coming on fast.

She drew a shuddering breath. "Helix is taking us to Keldale right now. Matthew's widow is there. Helix wants to tell her about him. Angbar thinks maybe she can help us for the winter, find us a place to stay. We don't know anyone else. Is that the right course?"

She was certain He would answer now. There were no other choices left.

A wind sliced through her coat and died away. Behind her, the fire crackled. The earth was hard and cold beneath her knees.

The silence wore on her certainty, melting it into apprehension.

"Akir," she begged, "Syntal is a *witch.*" She kept her voice quiet; the other girl could speak First Tongue. "She is over there, right now, teaching Angbar to do what she does. Right now. *Please.*"

A heartbeat.

"We need You! Why would You save our lives just to watch us freeze to death out here? Please!"

There was a tear on her cheek. She slapped it away.

"You said all I had to do was call again! Well, I'm calling! We need You! Please, where should we go?"

In answer, the wolves wound up again, howling. The ethereal noise swept over her like a shiver, alien and crawling.

She felt like a jilted lover.

*Calm down,* she told herself. *Maybe I just can't hear Him.* Not all clerics had the gift of Communion. Maybe she lacked it.

Scripture said that most mortals would be destroyed by the voice of God, if they were to hear it. Maybe He was sparing her.

The howling of wolves made the excuses ring hollow.

"*M'sai.* You won't answer, or I can't hear You. I understand. I have faith that You'll guide us and see us through safely. I don't need to know Your plan to believe in it. I accept Your will."

She stared into the darkness, fighting her disappointment. Was He even listening? Was she out here, freezing, talking to herself?

He had answered before. Why wouldn't He answer now? Had she done something wrong?

She closed her eyes again and reached for His fire. Creating light was the simplest miracle a priest could perform. Just because she couldn't hear Him didn't mean He was gone. She wanted to make sure He was still there, that He hadn't abandoned her. She had never made light, but now that she could call on His fire, it should be trivial.

Her eyes lurched open. The fire was gone.

"Akir," she muttered, "please. You said I could call. You said You would be there."

She tried again, fumbling for the flames like a blind girl striking flint.

*It works for Syntal every time,* something insidious whispered. It had Bishop Marcus's voice. *Every time.*

"Answer me," she begged. "Please, Akir, don't leave me out here alone." The flint was dead in her hands.

*You're still a failure.* Marcus was dispassionate. He might have been remarking on the weather. *You always will be.*

"No." He wasn't gone. She could prove it. There was one miracle she knew she could work.

She tore off her coat and grabbed a broken stick, her heart pounding. The wind lanced through her shirt like it was paper.

She raked the stick down her arm. A bright line of blood and pain bloomed in her flesh. She dropped the stick and clutched the wound, opening herself to flames.

And watched as the blood welled through her fingers and dripped to the ground, cold.

*v. Helix*

A homeless man slept on the cobblestones beneath a red awning. Seth knelt, as if to offer him some coin. Three Preservers emerged from an alleyway behind them.

Seth rose as they approached. The vagrant scrambled away. A Preserver leveled a kick at Seth's stomach that sent him staggering. The other two fell on him and grabbed his arms.

It was over for him–for all of them. They had to run. They'd been found.

"Helix."

His eyes opened to the glaring sun.

"You were having a nightmare," Syntal said.

Helix stared at her. The awning was gone. The ground was frozen dirt, not cobblestone.

A dream. He'd been dreaming.

"Sorry," he mumbled as reality soaked in. "Dream. Sorry."

She nodded and took a spit from the fire. "Here. Have some rabbit."

He sat up, struggling to get his bearings. The light was wrong. Was it morning? Or afternoon?

The meat chased the nightmare away. As he came back to himself, he asked, "What time is it?"

"Morning," Iggy answered.

Helix glanced east. The sky was still dim there.

The sun had risen in the south.

It made his stomach twist, like he was suddenly standing sideways. The faces around the campfire were as grim as his own.

The air buzzed with questions. Would the sun rise in the east again tomorrow? Would it rise again at all? Did it mean something? But no one asked them, because no one knew.

It could mean this was the last day of all things. It could mean nothing.

Harth finally broke the silence. "So what's your business in Keldale?" he asked. Everyone looked at Helix.

Harth followed their eyes. "Ah ha," he said to Iggy. "So you were just the front man?"

"It's..." Iggy started, looking uncomfortable.

"*M'sai,* Iggy," Helix cut in. This had been his idea; he should own it. "I can tell you once we're through the gates."

Harth clucked and shook his head. "That's not a smart way to do it. Keldale's got three main gates, and other ways in besides. If you're looking to make this quick, tell me where you're trying to get first, so we can go through the closest gate the first time."

"What difference does it make?"

"It can make a lot of difference," Harth said. "Best to avoid the Church's districts as much as possible, and this time of year you'd be smart to avoid the poorest blocks too. There are parts of the city where the Church doesn't keep order–they just keep them contained."

"Why does that have anything to do with the gate?"

"Because, if we go through the wrong gate, an area we'd rather avoid may lie between us and wherever you're going. Isn't that the reason you wanted a guide?

"Listen. Let me rephrase. I'm not asking you what your business is, just where you need to go. I don't give the guards any names. If I can help it, I don't see the guards at all. I have as much to lose getting seen by the wrong guard as you do." He considered. "Probably more."

"I doubt that," Helix muttered.

Harth shrugged. "If you don't want to tell me, you don't have to tell me. But if we get inside and you wind up knifed in Stones district because we went in through the wrong gate, don't complain when I rob your corpse. That blade of yours would fetch a pretty penny."

The camp fell silent.

"City humor," Harth said, spreading his hands. When no one responded, he shook his head. "Serious lot, aren't you? Listen, if you get knifed I'll be dead right next to you. It's the district gangs'll be robbing both our corpses. But we'll still be just as dead."

Helix shot a look at Iggy. *Are you sure about this?*

Iggy glared. "I don't think your jokes are very funny."

"You'd be surprised how often I hear that. Now, are you going to tell me which gate we're taking, or leave me to guess at it?"

Helix sighed. "It's an orphanage. I don't know what it's called."

"There're a few orphanages in Keldale," Harth said. "Lot of dead fishermen with kids since the Storm. Do you know who runs it?"

"I think her name is Lorna."

Harth started. "Lorna Rentiss?"

That sounded right. "I think so."

A shadow stole over Harth's features. "We're not going there unless you tell me what this is about."

Iggy straightened. "You said no questions."

"That was before," Harth snapped. He looked around the circle, his gaze lingering on Seth. Suspicion sparked in his eyes. He stood up, his hand dropping to his weapon's hilt.

"Don't," Seth said evenly.

"You're a Preserver," Harth said. "*Sehk,* I am such an idiot."

"I'm not."

"What is this about?"

"We're not going to tell you," Iggy insisted. "That was the deal."

"Then you're on your own." Harth grabbed his pack and made for his mount.

"I paid you eighteen shells–!" Iggy started.

Helix shouted over him. "We're not with the Church! Would you just calm down? We're not!" He snorted. The idea was laughable.

Harth turned back, his eyes flashing. "Start talking, right now, or I get on that horse."

"We–" *God.* How much could he tell him? *This whole sudden outrage could just be an act.* He had a sudden, vivid picture of Harth selling them out at the city walls.

But if it was an act, it was the best show Helix had ever seen.

"If I tell you," Helix said, "you tell me how you know her."

"*Talk,*" Harth snarled.

"Her husband's dead," Angbar cut in. "The Tribunal killed him. We're going to tell her."

"It doesn't take six people to deliver that kind of message," Harth said.

Angbar shrugged. "And yet, here we are."

"When?"

Angbar glanced at Helix. "A fortnight ago?"

Helix nodded.

"What happened?"

"They came to arrest him, and caught him trying to leave the village," Helix said. "They rode him down and stabbed him. I saw it from my window."

Harth searched his eyes. "*Sehk,*" he finally said.

"I worked at the inn in Southlight. He stayed there. We talked a lot. His wife needs to know, and I wanted her to hear it from me."

Seth and Angbar were throwing him looks, but there was no need. He wasn't about to say more.

"*Sehk,*" Harth said again. "He was never careful enough, but he always seemed to..." He was shaking his head. "I *told* him to shut up."

"You knew him?"

Harth gave him a look. "Everyone knows Brother Matthew. The Tribunal Bishop turned apostate? He's a legend."

He made it sound like Southlight had been the last place on Earth to learn about the man. *Maybe it was.*

Harth relented. "All right. Yes, I knew him. He caught me on the docks when I was twelve, stealing fish. He should've had my fingers. Instead he took me to Lorna. I grew up with them." He sighed. "This news will kill her."

"She has to know. I didn't want her to hear it from the Church."

Harth's eyes softened. "That counts for something.

"But I'll tell her. She should hear it from–"

"No," Helix said. "I'm sorry, but if you want those shells, I tell her."

Harth glared. "What are you not telling me?"

Helix met his eyes with silence.

"We've told you enough," Iggy said, "when the deal was 'no questions asked.' We're not coming to hurt her. That should be enough for you."

Harth hesitated, sizing them up. He pointed at Helix. "See that you don't. I've got friends in Keldale. If she's hurt, you won't leave the city alive. None of you."

Seth and Iggy bristled, but Helix nodded. "You have my word."

Lyseira stood. Her look said, *If you're done comparing cocks, can we get going?*

They broke camp. After packing, Helix watched Harth work.

*I hope he knows what he's doing.* The man's casual threat to kill them all should have bothered him, but it didn't. Wouldn't he have done the same, if some strangers had wanted to meet his mother?

"It's a punch in the gut, ain't it?" Iggy said.

Helix realized he'd been staring south, at the blurry disc of the sun breaking the horizon.

"Yeah," he agreed. "Hope it's back to normal tomorrow."

Iggy grunted. "At least the wolves cleared out." He was right; the line of animals was gone. Another inexplicable omen.

They regained the road, headed north. He glanced behind and saw grey sunlight on empty field.

Maybe the sunrise had scared them off.

~ ~

It was eleven days to Keldale, with the sun rising in the east and each night growing colder. A couple hours out, Harth pointed to a distant wood. "If something goes wrong at the gates," he said, "meet up there."

*If something goes wrong at the gates,* Helix thought, *I doubt anyone will be alive to make it.*

That afternoon, the walls of Keldale rose in the distance. It had been years since he'd seen them. Last time he was here, he'd had twelve winters behind him and was riding with his father.

The wall must have been thirty feet high, cobbled together from great blocks of stone that had stood for hundreds of years. Broad sheets of ice clung to the rock. An occasional soldier passed on the walkway that ran atop the wall.

*With archers on that wall they could take down anyone.* He remembered Seth getting attacked in his dream, and shuddered.

"*M'sai,*" Harth said. "Everyone listen." He brought his mount about and beckoned the others to gather around him. They had finally reached the broad road which circled Keldale, allowing easy travel from one gate to the next. There was snow on the road, but it was hard packed.

"I'll lead us up, and I'll do the talking. If I say something you don't understand or know to be false, just go along with it. Yes?"

They answered with scattered murmurs of assent.

"If luck is with us, the guards won't even question us–they'll just wave us through. Once we get inside, I'll take you to Lorna." He glanced at Angbar. "Pull your scarf a little tighter there, Angbar. We don't need any questions about nogs if we can avoid them."

The walls unfolded on their left as they skirted the city to the southern gate. The Sunrise sea glittered in the east. On a clear day, Helix remembered, he'd been able to gaze out at the hazy form of the Grand Isle; maybe even pick out a few of the Fisher Isles, dotting the waves like a fleet of tiny ships.

Today wasn't clear. The sky was wintry ash from horizon to horizon, the sea a grey mirror below.

Then he caught sight of the gate, and his reverie ended. There was only a single guard there, but he was armed.

Helix's heart started hammering. *What if he has my picture? What if word's already come north?*

*That's the whole reason we took the Wolfwood road,* he reminded himself. *It'll be fine.*

*This was my idea. I talked everyone into it.* At the time, finding Matthew's letter in his pack had seemed like providence. It had given him something to work for, somewhere to go. Now, his rationale was growing thinner by the step.

*There was nowhere else to go. Remember?*

*Maybe. Maybe freezing in the woods would've been better than getting caught.*

"Evening," the guard called. "More pilgrims, eh?"

"Is it that obvious?" Harth answered as they cantered up.

"Come up the south road?"

"North," Harth said. "Marshedge. Just trying to avoid the crowd. North gate's crowded."

"Smart," the guard said. "We don't get many at this gate. Half the pilgrims coming north probably froze in the blizzard. Two heels a head."

Harth counted out the coins.

"Where you staying?"

"With family," Harth answered.

"Lucky for you. Most of the inns're filled up anyway." The guard dropped the coins into a clanging metal bucket, and waved. "Go on through. The book's been in purification for eight days. It's at *Basica Tenuor*."

"That would've been my guess. Thanks."

The gate was already standing open. At Harth's signal, they rode through.

*We made it.* Had it really been that easy? Helix wanted to glance back, to make sure the guard wasn't following them, but he stifled the urge.

They came onto a broad avenue, bristling with clanging bells, shouting merchants, and the neighing of horses. Hawkers and beggars dotted the street corners like pigeon droppings. Street urchins dodged through the crowd, carrying messages or picking pockets. A haze of fish stink hung in the air, nearly, but not quite, masking the stenches of sweat and horse dung.

Harth sucked in a deep breath through his nose. "Home at last."

"Pilgrims?" Helix said. "What was that about?"

Harth glanced back to make sure everyone had come through, then started through the winding streets. "Some holy book–Chronicle, I think?"

"Second Joshua," Lyseira said. "Must be. I knew the new book of the Chronicle was almost finished, but..." She shook her head. "We heard nothing in Southlight."

"Everyone in Keldale's gone mad for it. It's always busy, but nothing like this. Pilgrims coming from all over the Valley."

"I might've been one of them, if I'd known." She looked at Helix. "The Abbot would have loved to see this. It must be Second Joshua. Father Forthin always wondered if Archbishop Joshua was going to live long enough to have a second book named for him."

"Here," Harth said, nodding toward a small alleyway.

They turned into a narrow gap between brick buildings. The roar of the main street fell away. A hundred paces on, the alley broke away into two more side streets. After that the little alleys devolved into a maze of rundown buildings and cobblestone paths, the only landmarks being an occasional snow-crusted fountain or sleeping vagrant.

Helix tried to keep track of the turns, and failed miserably. "This doesn't look like the best area," he muttered as they passed a broken lantern post.

"Not far now," Harth assured him.

They emerged onto another broad avenue, painted a bloody red from the sun in the west. Harth marched his horse into the crowd and turned east. The street sloped downward. In the distance, tall sails bobbed at port, stained by the sunset.

"There," Harth said, pointing at a narrow, one-story hovel sandwiched between two larger shops. He kicked at an urchin who had managed to brush against his boot. "It's bigger than it looks. You can't see the back from here."

A pool of filthy children milled about in front of the little building, playing hop-box on the sidewalk as the crowd churned around them. One of them, a boy no older than seven or eight, ran up.

"Harth!" he shouted.

"Julius." Harth gave him a smile.

"We're playing hop-box!" the boy announced.

"I see that. No money in hop-box though. How'd you like to make a little coin?"

"How much?" Julius answered at once.

"Normally I'd say a copper heel, but since I haven't hired you in awhile… we'll call it two." Harth dismounted.

"Uh huh," the boy said. Harth knelt and gave the child the coins, then rumpled his hair.

"This is it?" Helix asked as everyone climbed off their horses. The dilapidated building was not what he had expected.

"This is it," Harth said. "Wait here." He ducked inside.

The kids pulled Angbar into a game of hop-box. Iggy followed Julius with the horses.

Helix's heart started a long, slow crawl up his throat. He was here. He had dragged everyone along. Any minute, he would meet Matthew's widow.

*What in Hel am I going to say to her?*

"Let me talk to her alone," he said. Syntal nodded, her face grave, but Seth shook his head.

"We still don't know what you're getting into here. There could be a Justicar in that building."

"If there's a Justicar in that building, bringing you with me won't change anything." It would almost be a relief, to get caught. No more freezing nights, no more wondering where they would spend the winter. A quick death, and an end to it. Helix shook the morbid thoughts out of his head.

"I want to meet her too," Lyseira said. "We've come all this way. I want her to know..." She took Seth's hand. "Just give him a few minutes."

They waited. Angbar pulled Syntal into his hop-box game. Iggy returned with the boy.

*What's taking so long?* As soon as the thought occurred to him, he knew.

"He's telling her," Helix said.

"Probably," Lyseira answered.

Finally, Harth emerged from the doorway, his face ashen. "Helix. She wants to talk to you."

~ ~

The door opened into a cave-like pantry hall, its cubby holes burgeoning with clothes, bandages, and grain. The city's din fell away. The smell of fish gave way to a subtle, homey incense.

The short hallway spilled into a well-lit kitchen with one large table and several smaller ones. A woman stood near the counter. She had a tangle of auburn hair tinged with grey, and a brown dress of heavy wool, dotted with food stains. Her eyes were red and haunted.

Suddenly Helix felt like a fool for coming here. A callous, selfish fool.

"This is him," Harth said.

"Helix Smith," he tried to say, but his voice broke and he had to clear his throat. She shook his hand. Her hand felt small and cold.

"Harth told me about Matthew." Her voice was brittle. She

wouldn't meet his eyes. "Thank you for coming to tell me."

"There, ah..." He dug awkwardly in his pouch, feeling like a buffoon as his fingers sought Matthew's letter. "He wanted me to give you..."

He found the envelope, rumpled and stained, and held it out to her. "Here. He asked me to give this to you. I think he... I think he had some idea."

Lorna's eyes flicked across her husband's last words to her. She sank to a chair.

"He always said I'd know," she said to the empty air. "That was how he... put me at ease, whenever he left. 'You'll know, Lorna. I'll make sure.'" Her face turned quizzical, as if she'd just spotted an owl in her house. "Was that supposed to make me feel better?"

Harth put an awkward arm around her shoulder.

"He loved you very much," Helix said. "He... when I told him he was in danger, the first thing he asked about was the letter. It was everything to him. He wanted... he made me promise to get it to you."

Lorna was nodding, her hand over her mouth, staring at the wall.

"All right," Harth said. "You've done what you came for. You can go."

Helix wanted to nod and back away. The force of her grief shoved at him. He felt like an intruder at a funeral.

He was still standing there.

"Missus Rentiss," he heard himself saying, "there is something else."

Harth glared, his nostrils flaring. *No,* his eyes said. *That's enough.*

"Mama Lorna?" A little boy stood, forlorn, in one of the doorways. "I can't find my slate."

"Go outside, Joseph," Harth said.

"But my slate has–"

"No buts, go outside. Just for a little bit. Find Julius. All right? Go ahead."

The boy turned doubtfully toward the front door. When he heard it click closed, Helix drew a breath. "They... I saw them kill him. I tried to help him. And they..." *God help me.* "They arrested me.

They said I did it."

For the first time, Lorna looked at him.

Harth cursed.

"They staged a trial," Helix hurried on. "They had a lot of very convincing fake evidence. They even had a fake witness. They tried to get my friends to testify against me. They even said they'd had *Communion*. But if they asked God, He was lying. I swear. I didn't do it. Bishop Marcus–"

"*Marcus?*" Lorna seized on the name. "Marcus was there?"

Helix nodded.

"Did he do it?"

"Not himself. It was a Justicar, Galen Wick. But I think Marcus gave the order. I think they wanted to make it seem like it was some two-heel crook that did it. So Matthew... so he wouldn't look like a martyr."

"They sentenced you?" Harth said, carefully.

Helix nodded. "To death. But I didn't do it, I swear. I–"

"Then how are you here?"

"We... my friends got me out. We escaped."

"Got you out of a *Tribunal prison?*" The words dripped with suspicion.

His heart thundered. Harth's threat–*If she's hurt, you'll never leave alive*–suddenly buzzed in his ears. "I'm telling the truth," he swore. It sounded like he was begging.

"And they just let you go, is that it? Tried you for murder, then shrugged it off when you got away?"

"Harth," Lorna said. "Enough."

"No, of course not!" Helix snapped. "They chased us!"

Harth looked to the ceiling. "*Sehk'akir*. You *sehking* idiot."

"Harth!" Lorna barked. "Hush!"

Harth fell silent, but his eyes were sparking.

"I believe you." Her voice was hoarse with weeping, but there was strength behind the pain. "Marcus has hated Matthew since the day he married me. And framing it on you... it's exactly the kind of thing he's known for. He'll come here, to tell me himself. I'm sure he will. He'll want to see–"

"Mama Lorna?" Joseph was back. "Rinnie won't let me play–"

"*Outside, Joseph!*" Lorna ordered over her shoulder.

*He'll come here,* Helix thought as he watched the boy disappear.

*Sweet God.*

Matthew had said, *Do you have any idea the things I've seen the Tribunal do to children?*

"I'm sorry," he said to Harth. He felt sick. "I'm sorry, I didn't think... I never wanted..."

"They saw you at the gate," Harth muttered. "If he shows a drawing of you..."

God, he was a fool. "We need to leave. I'm sorry, Missus Rentiss." *I'm so sorry.*

"Where will you go?" she said.

He turned for the door. He was a creature of flame in a pile of tinder. Everything he touched would burn.

"Stop!" Lorna shouted. "*Rev'naas* take it! Stop and turn around!"

He spun back, his mind screaming, his muscles twitching. *My mom and dad. Minda. God, Minda.*

*Don't you understand?* he wanted to shout. *I have to get away! I have to* get away *from you!*

"I have room for three of you," Lorna said. "In the morning–"

"No." Helix's head was shaking on its own, threatening to bounce off his shoulders. "No, we shouldn't have come here. We need to go."

Harth was nodding.

"Go where, son?" Lorna's voice was heavy with compassion. "You can't go home. Do you have anywhere?"

"We'll find something, camp in the woods, or Shientel..." *Tell the Fatherlord!* a delirious voice gibbered. *Make everything better!*

"You'll freeze to death," Lorna said evenly.

"We can't stay here!"

Lorna clapped her mouth shut.

*Why does she want to help me?* something inside him howled. *Why can't I let her?*

"Listen to me. My husband... it wasn't chance that he picked you. It never was, with him. He knew you would come here. He was blind, but... he could see things. Akir gave him a gift."

Helix shook his head. The words were gibberish.

Everyone he knew was turning to ash.

"Stop." She had his shoulders. "Listen."

*She learned ten minutes ago that her husband is dead, and I'm making* her *console* me. The thought struck him like a slap.

She held his eyes. "Listen. He would not have sent you here, if he thought it would put me in danger. Do you hear me? He could *see things.* If you spent any time around him, you know that."

Finally, her words penetrated. *He gave me the letter the day he came to Southlight. He knew.*

*From the first day, he knew.*

"Now. You tried to help him. He sent you here. That's all I need to know. We'll figure out the rest. *M'sai?*" Her voice was hoarse, her eyes searching his. "Do you hear me?"

"*M'sai,*" he breathed. The panic receded, tugging at the hem of his mind.

"*M'sai.*" Her face pinched. She pulled him into a hug. "Oh, you poor thing." Her voice was hot against his ear, trembling with shared pain. "I'm sorry."

# Chapter 14

*i. Iggy*

Iggy had never been in a city as big as Keldale. He didn't like it. The walls were too close, the crowds too thick. In some of the narrow alleyways, he could barely see the sky. It made him feel imprisoned. Or entombed.

Helix, Seth, and Lyseira had stayed at the orphanage, but Lorna hadn't had room for all of them. She had offered to put them up at the Keg and Kettle, an inn off the central square where Harth apparently had some connections to the owner. Iggy had expected to finally catch his breath in the square, but when Harth led them there, it was just as bad as everywhere else.

The square was huge, and even in the cold and with night coming on, the merchant stalls clamored with customers. A swarm of pilgrims took to their knees in prayer, facing west, toward the temple. A pocket of town guards drifted through like a lily pad on a pond. Rising from the center of the cacophony was a statue of a man on a rearing horse, his noble eyes fixed on the coast.

When they finally reached the inn and Harth showed them to their room, Iggy was fighting for breath.

"You well, Igg?" Angbar asked. "You look terrible."

Iggy nodded, but he felt light-headed, the room spinning around him. He put a hand to the wall. "Yeah, just... need a minute."

"*M'sai,*" Harth said, sweeping in and closing the door behind him. "Aron only had one room open, so you're sharing it. It's got two beds, at least."

Syntal staked out one of the beds, wincing as she took the pack from her shoulders. Angbar drifted to the other.

"Aron is an old friend of Matthew's. He knows me. You can trust him. If you need something, talk to him. If he tells you something, believe it."

Iggy nodded. When he stopped, the room kept moving.

"I didn't realize your friend was wanted by the Tribunal for murder when I took this job." Harth looked at Iggy. "Eighteen shells? It should have been eighteen *crowns*." He pointed out the window. "The whole city is crawling with pilgrims and clergy. With luck, no one will recognize you. Stay inside. Don't leave your room unless you have to. I'll be back tomorrow. If I can talk any sense into Lorna, you'll be out of the city again tomorrow night."

That sounded wonderful to Iggy, but Angbar frowned. "What? Where will we go?"

Harth shrugged. "Not my problem. But it's not safe here. Not for you, not for Lorna. Keep your heads down."

He left.

Angbar made an incredulous noise. "You sure know how to pick 'em, Igg."

"Iggy?" Syntal said. Iggy looked at her. She was very far away. "You should lie down." The words echoed down a tunnel.

"*M'sai,*" he said, and took her advice.

~ ~

In his dreams, he was flying.

The wolves' wood unfolded beneath him, spreading to the horizon in a sea of snow-drenched treetops. *Wake up,* it called in his mother's voice. *Come home.*

She had given birth to everything; she was the soil and the sun and the rain. Her heartbeat thrummed in the air, a pulse like the rhythm of the sea. He yearned for her. Her branches reached to embrace him.

But on the ground, the wolves watched. Their eyes were glittering and black, full of enigma. He could feel their relief at his passing. They wanted no men in their home.

*I'm not like the others,* he wanted to say. *I won't harm your young. I won't take your home.* He wanted to make peace, but he wasn't one of them. He didn't belong.

*They don't understand,* his mother said. *They think they can't trust you.*

The trees fell behind him. His mother's heart ached, her pulse deep and sad, and he wanted to weep. Beyond, he saw the human roads. He veered above one that led east, and remembered walking on it. It had seemed benign.

Now he could see it was a scar, gouged into his mother's flesh. Its desecration stretched nearly to the sea. At its end was the city: a festering sore.

Its pillars of smoke rose like blood leaking into the sky; every building was a knife in a wound. The wall turned his stomach: tree and rock, murdered and carved to meet the desires of their killers.

He wanted to stop, to turn back, but his flight carried him in, to a place rife with horrors.

Tree and grass were torn away, the soil entombed in dead stone. Humans crawled across his mother's diseased flesh like maggots. Chimneys jutted toward the sky, hissing smoke and malice.

These were his people. This was his place.

He woke surrounded by the corpses of trees. Most had been butchered, their bodies nailed together to provide him a place to sleep. Some fed the fire in the hearth. It crackled and spat as it devoured them.

*I started that fire,* he remembered, and felt his gorge rise.

"Iggy?" Angbar's voice came from a bed on his left: a cradle made of bones.

Iggy lurched to his feet. The eyes of wolves stared at him from the darkness. *Now you see the scar,* they accused. *Now you know.*

"Iggy?" Angbar sounded annoyed and sleepy. He didn't notice the sputtering cries from the fire. For him the burning wood didn't stink like a slaughterhouse under the sun.

Bile rose in Iggy's throat. He reeled toward the door, threw it open, and bolted down the stairs. The inn was a nightmare, a structure built of corpses. Every corner accosted him with new atrocities.

He burst through the front door and onto the cobblestone street outside. Freezing air hit him like a waterfall, and he gulped it as if he were dying of thirst. It was sweet and caustic, burning and pure. He gasped like a man flagellating himself.

The inn's door groaned closed behind him.

The town square sprawled in the dark, exposing him to the midnight wind. He shivered and turned away, but he couldn't go back in; he would rather freeze than inhale the stench of burning trees.

*I am here,* his mother said. *Between the scars, even here, you can find me.*

He followed her voice into a nearby alley and curled up on the frozen stone. He lay there, his body quaking from the cold and the horrors, until the heartbeat came over him again. It was gentle and powerful: the mother's pulse heard from the womb.

*Shhh,* she whispered. Her fingers were in the breeze, caressing his forehead. When she held him, he warmed. *Shhh. Rest now.*

Her voice drove away the horrors. He burrowed into her arms, and slept.

*ii. Helix*

Helix woke staring at a ceiling he didn't recognize, in a room he'd never seen before. Filmy morning light trickled through the patched windows and crept over peeling walls. Outside, he saw children chasing one another through a narrow alleyway. The air smelled of salt and fish.

*The orphanage.* He sat up, remembering. *Lorna insisted we stay.*

He must've slept in his clothes. He barely recalled coming to the bed, let alone falling asleep.

He padded to the door, where the hallway greeted him with the rich smells of frying tula fish and fresh bread. He turned toward the kitchen.

*A month ago I would have been waking up to the smell of Mom's wheatcakes and sausages. Now I can barely remember where I am each morning.*

He rounded the corner to find Seth and Lyseira in the kitchen, eating.

"How late is it?" he asked as he approached the table. "You should've woke me."

"Oh, there's a few hours 'til highsun," Lorna said. She gestured at a chair. "Sit. I made you breakfast."

Helix sat. Lorna's eyes were still bloodshot. She shouldn't be making him food. "You don't have to do that," he said, and she ignored him, casually filling a plate with hot bread and two tula strips.

"Eat," she said.

Courtesy gave way to hunger. He grabbed a fork and stabbed a piece of fish. "Where are all the kids?" he asked.

"I asked Harth to bring them outside. It's cold, but not too cold to play, yet."

The food was delicious, but thinking about the children made his stomach twist. *If Marcus learns I was here...*

"I spent a lot of the night in prayer," Lorna went on, "and I think I can make room for your friends for the winter. Winters are never easy, but I believe Akir sent you here for a reason."

Lyseira looked at him; was there a glimmer of hope in her eyes? *She probably thinks this is another divine sign, just like everything else.* Helix wasn't convinced it was.

*But we can't go home. I don't have any other family, and even if I did, it wouldn't be safe for them to harbor me.*

His throat clenched. *Exactly. It wouldn't be safe.*

"You would have to stay hidden, but Marcus would never think to look for you here. In the spring, you could get out of the Valley–make for Ornbridge or Chesport, somewhere distant–and start again. With luck, the Tribunal will assume you died in the wild, over the winter."

"I can't..." Helix's voice broke. What she was offering sounded like heaven. *A chance to stop running. A home for the winter. Even never leaving the building, at least it would be warm.* "I can't ask you to do that."

"You aren't," she said. "I'm offering."

"We'd never make it that far in the winter, Helix," Lyseira said. "It kills me to say it, but I don't see how we have a choice."

"Of course we have a choice," Helix said. "There has to be somewhere else we could go."

"Where?" There was an edge to Lyseira's voice that hadn't been there before, the same brittle fear that he felt every morning. He wondered what had changed. "We can't go home. Our families–"

"Our families have been taken by the Tribunal," Seth said. He looked at Lorna. "Which is exactly what will happen to you if Marcus finds us here."

"You remember Leese and Blane, Lyseira?" Helix said. "The cabin in the woods? There could be an arc hound on its way here right now. There are kids here. Can you imagine–" He cut off as a picture tried to form in his mind. He didn't want to see it. "I'm sorry," he said to Lorna. "It's... I can't believe you're offering. It's too kind. Matthew told me what a wonderful soul his wife had, and it's..." He shook his head. "But there's no chance. Harth was right. I never should have come here in the first place."

The silence trembled with premonitions.

*That's it, then. We'll be caught, or freeze, or starve.* His chivalry would get him killed. But he still dreamt about the night Matthew died. When he closed his eyes he could still feel the hot gush of the man's blood against his hand.

He wouldn't bring the same fate to his wife.

Lorna's jaw tightened. "*M'sai.*" She sucked on her bottom lip, her eyes searching the table. "Wait here." She disappeared into a hallway.

Lyseira looked stricken. As soon as Lorna was out of earshot, she said, "I don't understand. We came with you here because you thought it was our best chance. Angbar thought she might be able to help us, and he was right! And now you want to leave again? For what? Helix, we have *nowhere to go!*"

Retorts clamored at his tongue, but the fear in her eyes killed them. "I know," he said. "I'm sorry."

"I know staying here is a risk, but she's willing to take it! And leaving again..."

She didn't have to say it; Helix knew. Leaving again meant being hunted. It meant being hungry and cold. It probably meant dying.

"We should split up," he said. He was both relieved and horrified to see Seth nod behind her. "You take Syntal and the others and head for Shientel, or back to Coram. It's me they're after, and you've done enough."

"And let you wander off to die? No!" Lyseira's lips pinched, quivering. "What in Hel did I do this for?"

Lorna crossed the room to the front hall, where she opened the front door and called for Harth. When she came back with him, she set a bag in front of Helix.

"Here." Her face was hard with resolve. "You're taking this."

"What is–?" he started.

"Twenty crowns," she said.

He coughed. Harth said, "What?"

"If you won't stay here, you'll need money to survive the winter. Harth can take you to the bazaar and then bring you to Shientel." She looked at Harth. "Can't you?"

"Where were you hiding twenty crowns?" Harth sputtered.

"*Can't you?*" Lorna repeated.

"Well, of course I can, but–"

Helix pushed the bag away. "I can't take this. This must be years of savings for you, I–"

Lorna grabbed his hand and shoved the bag into it. "If I send you out that door with nowhere to go and no money for supplies, I might as well kill you myself. I won't do that. Stay here, or take the money."

"I..." *Thank you,* he wanted to say, but his throat was suddenly too tight to speak.

"Don't you have some friends in Shientel?" Lorna asked Harth. "For the right price, someone who might be able to put them up for the winter?"

"I–well, yes, probably. It won't be cheap."

Lorna nodded. "*M'sai.* Then we have a plan."

~ ~

Harth disappeared for a couple hours. When he came back, their plan had flesh on its bones.

"We're in luck," he shouted over the dull roar of the kids having lunch. "A friend of mine will be on the south gate tonight just after sunset. I talked to him. Should be no problems. I stopped by the Keg and let the others know we'll be by for them tonight. We keep quiet and keep our heads down, we'll be back on the road by evening."

*Evening,* Helix thought. The idea of sleeping on the road again so soon left him bleak. He shook it off. *What's done is done.*

"Right now we'll head up to the bazaar and get you supplied, then come back and wait for sundown."

"Shouldn't I stay here?" Helix asked. "If someone sees me–"

"I don't think they're looking for you yet. I've asked around. *Quietly,*" he added, as he noticed the look of horror on Helix's face. "Akir, Helix. I'm not new to this."

"Still," Seth said. "There's no need to tempt fate."

"It's the Beggar's Bazaar," Harth said. "Church doesn't come around there. And if he's going to get seen, I'd rather have it be as far from here as possible. Besides, if someone in the city could recognize him, I don't want it happening at the orphanage."

Helix didn't want that either. He nodded.

A scruffy boy with a wild cap of blond hair bounced off his leg, laughing. Another boy chased him, this one older, his hair stringy and red. A powerful memory of Rake, the bully from his childhood, rocked Helix. He put a hand on the redhead's shoulder. "Leave him be," he said. "He's smaller than you."

"Sit down, both of you," Lorna ordered. Then, to Helix: "Get plenty of blankets and food. Get a packhorse, if you can. It'll be two weeks to Shientel on the Fisher's Road. They'll be cold."

"Mama Lorna, can we go out and play?" Helix recognized Julius, the boy who had stabled their horses the day before.

"No, you may not, it's snowing outside."

"But I'm all done eating!" he whined.

"That has nothing to do with it. You go out there now, you're like to freeze a leg off."

"Julius could stand to lose a leg," Harth mused. "I wager he'd eat less." Julius glared, and Harth gave him a mock glare in return.

"*M'sai,*" Lorna said, turning back to Helix. "Be quick. I'll see you back here."

*iii. Lyseira*

Lyseira understood why Helix wanted to leave. She even knew he was right. She just didn't care.

When they had saved him, she hadn't had a clear plan. She'd expected to get him out and get away. A short time after that, she'd expected everything would be resolved somehow. Goodness would prevail; the wrongs would be set right.

Reality had not followed this script. It had seemed like it might–especially when Akir had finally granted her the miracles they needed to keep everyone alive–but the miracles were ended, now. She didn't know why. And it was becoming more obvious everyday that it would be months or years, if ever, before Helix's name could be cleared.

*Not just his name. My name, Seth's... all of us.* Syntal would probably never be safe again.

Lorna's offer had struck Lyseira in a sore place she hadn't realized was there. The prospect of *home* was an aching wound in her chest. On the last leg of their journey toward Keldale, her nightly prayers had given way to meditative memories of her mother. *I miss you, Mom,* she'd whispered into her blanket. *And I'm sorry. I'm so, so sorry.*

Lorna was the first person who had known everything about them–all their reasons for running–and kept her door open. Lyseira's gratitude to the woman was paralyzing. No, it was more than that. It was desperate. She could've clung to her like a drowning girl.

*And dragged her down with me.*

"Here," Harth said. He angled right, guiding them off the busier main street and into a narrow, shaded alley. "It's not far, but stay close. Look..." He gestured emptily. "Look like you belong."

A verse from the book of Solac whispered to her. *"He is your strength when you are weak; He is your hope when you are lost. Lay all burdens at His feet, that they may be borne away."*

She had lived her life by that verse. She had always had faith, or striven to. When she had felt His fire, she'd thought it was a vindication of all her choices, a promise that He was with them. But if that was true, what did it mean now that He wouldn't answer her?

Above, she could just glimpse the ashen sky between the rooftops. *Where did I go wrong?* she asked it. *Please! I want to do Your will, but how can I when You won't answer me?*

The answer was the same as always: silence. It settled into her stomach like a black pit.

*Even silence might mean something,* a dogged voice insisted. In years past, she would've gone to The Abbot for help deciphering it, or her mother.

They were both gone now.

"*M'sai,*" Harth said. The murmur of a crowd echoed from the twisting alley ahead. "Make it quick. Helix, you stay with me for clothes and blankets. For Akir's sake, keep that bag close. You blink and someone will nick it. Seth and Lyseira, pick up food and supplies. And keep your eyes open for a packhorse. And tents."

Lyseira glared. Harth pretended he knew what he was doing, but she suspected he just enjoyed acting the boss. She was sick of being bossed around by a street thief. "If you get the horse, let us know," she said. "Otherwise, we'll find one."

The bazaar was a half-dozen blocks' worth of fish and vegetable stands, leatherworkers and blacksmiths, guides for hire, map-sellers, and as far as Lyseira could tell, everything else anyone could possibly try to sell. Hawkers crowded the streets, stamping their feet in the cold and blowing into their hands, and there were more *Bahiri* than she had ever seen in one place in her life.

Unlike the open square she'd been expecting, the shop stands were mostly set up between the buildings: sagging ruins that might have been living apartments once. It was filthy and loud, but at least it was enclosed. The idea of shopping in a wide open square had made her nervous.

"There." Seth nodded at a vegetable stand. They drifted that way, the crowd jostling them like shifting ocean currents.

"Seth," Lyseira said. "Do you think we did the right thing?"

He answered as though he'd been waiting for this question for weeks. "I don't think Helix killed Matthew," he said, his eyes navigating the crowd. "I don't understand why they sentenced him. I think you're probably right, that the Fatherlord should be told. There are some bad apples in the Church sometimes, though it's rare."

*He didn't answer the question.* "Why did you come with me? It could cost you everything."

"It probably has." His face was unreadable. "When I go back... I'll be a traitor."

"Then why?" she pressed.

"You asked me. You needed me." He flicked his eyes toward her, once. "You're probably the only person I wouldn't have refused."

*But* why*?* she wanted to demand. *Why, when I had no place in the Church and you had no reason to believe me?* She wanted him to say he had faith in her, that he thought she could hear the voice of God. She wanted to know that he didn't spend his nights wondering if she had lost her mind.

She wanted more than he could give.

They joined the milling throng around the vegetable stand, inching closer as the front row of people moved on.

"It doesn't matter now." He surprised her; she'd thought he was done talking about it. "We're here. We've made our choices and we can't give them back. You're worried about Mom?"

His casual concern pricked her. Her eyes welled, the pit in her stomach suddenly doubling. She nodded, fighting to keep her composure.

He took her hand; squeezed it once. "Me too."

They waited, alone in an ocean of people. She closed her eyes and focused on the feel of his hand in hers. With the skill of long years of practice, she wrestled her doubts down.

When she opened her eyes, something had snagged his gaze. At the far end of the street, a couple of young men were harassing a homeless man beneath a red awning. They were arguing. One of them shoved the vagabond to the ground.

"I'll be right back," Seth said.

She kept his hand. "Does it matter? It's nothing to do with us." The words were like grease on her tongue. They made her queasy.

*Mind your brother's sin,* The Abbot whispered. *In all things, seek the righteous path.* The girl she had been in Southlight wouldn't have hesitated to help a stranger. But now...

Now she was someone else.

*Well for* rev'naas' *sake, we can't help everyone in Keldale,* some part of her retorted. It sickened her to know the voice was her own.

"It'll be our problem if they attract the guards. Wait here."

He pushed his way through the crowd. She went after him.

"Enough," he called.

The thugs snapped their heads toward him. The bum curled into a ball on the ground.

"Leave him alone." Seth's voice was like distant thunder, echoing with threats. They broke and ran.

Seth approached the beggar, still huddled on the ground. "Are you well?" His tone was flat, devoid of empathy. "Did they harm you?"

"My knee..." Even from behind her brother, Lyseira caught the stink of sour ale. "I think they broke my knee."

Seth scowled. "Let me see it. Hold still." He reached toward the man's leg, feeling along it for signs of injury. "You're well."

"No, my other leg–please, the Church won't heal it without a donation."

Seth grimaced. "You have your life. Be happy with that."

The beggar's eyes trained on something behind them. Lyseira turned and saw three Preservers stepping out of a nearby alley.

Her pulse doubled. She dropped her eyes, trying to look inconspicuous, and willing her brother to do the same. *They have no reason to talk to us. Just turn and go back to the stall. They'll walk right–*

"Seth Rulano," one of the Preservers marveled. "In Keldale."

She looked up. *They know him?* Fear thrashed in her stomach, screaming for her to run. *It might not mean anything. We might be all right.*

Seth straightened and gave a short nod. "Dessic."

The man who had spoken was the tallest of the three, nearly a head taller than Seth, and whip-thin. "You're not marked."

"I've yet to pass the trial. Master Retash sent me to my sister to study."

Dessic absorbed this. His companions exchanged looks.

"You would blame your desertion," Dessic finally said, "on your master?"

"I didn't desert," Seth said evenly.

"Yes, you have. Master Jokan has said it."

"Master...?" Seth blinked, confusion stealing into his eyes. "No, Retash–"

"Retash has been detained," Dessic said, "for treachery of his own. Even if you spoke truth, nothing he's done could pardon you." He held out a hand. "Come. Master Jokan requires your return."

"*Detained?*" Seth's eyes darted. "For what?"

"That's not for me to say." Dessic gave a sharp nod to his companions. They fanned out, moving to flank Seth.

"Dessic," Seth said, taking a step backwards, "you misunderstand."

Dessic cocked his head as if he would listen–then skipped forward and leveled a kick into Seth's gut that buckled him like a rag doll.

"Seth!" The shout burst, unbidden, from Lyseira's lungs. Dessic glanced at her as if taking note of a bug.

The other two Preservers grabbed Seth's arms, twisted them behind his back. With a short jump, Dessic snapped a kick at Seth's chin.

But this time Seth was ready. He ducked forward and under the kick, surprising the attackers who had his arms. One of them lurched forward. Dessic's kick took him in the neck. He collapsed, gurgling.

*Bind them,* Lyseira thought. *I can Bind them, like Marcus did to Helix.* She called to Akir, frantic.

He ignored her.

The second of Dessic's companions still had Seth's other arm. Seth chopped at his hand, precisely as a viper, and the Preserver's wrist shattered. He recoiled.

He didn't scream.

*God help us,* Lyseira begged. *Please, damn You, what did You send me here for? We need You!*

Dessic slid sideways. Seth moved to follow him. The Preserver he'd turned his back on, the one with the broken wrist, spun into a kick–

–and fell, a dagger suddenly sprouting from his neck.

Dessic danced backward. His companions were dead. His eyes flashed calculations.

Then he crouched and leapt backward, fifteen feet up, to land out of sight on the building behind him.

Seth tensed as if to launch himself after him.

"Seth!"

Helix's voice. Lyseira's stomach sank. *Get out of here!* she wanted to shout to him. *Get back! They haven't seen you!*

Harth appeared from nowhere, his cloak swirling. "What in Hel happened?" he hissed. "I told you–*sehk*." His eyes lit on the body of the Preserver Dessic had kicked. "How many?"

"Three," Seth answered. "You said they never came here."

Harth held up a hand. *Quiet.*

"I saw this," Helix said. "I *saw* this! They know we're here, they're coming, we have to get out!"

The crowd was murmuring.

"...the Church..."

"...attacked those Preservers..."

"...after that boy..."

Someone broke from the crowd, headed for an alley. Lyseira watched him run, wondering what it meant.

"This way," Harth snapped. "Now!"

Lyseira caught a glimpse of one of the dead Preservers, facedown, his blood spreading between the cobblestones like a branching river.

Then they were running.

# Chapter 15

*i. Iggy*

He dreamt that he woke to the sight of a weed, forcing its way between the cobblestones and drinking in the sunlight. It was a picture of defiance. It was life in the grave.

Then he woke to a kick in the back.

"Up," a man barked. "Out of here."

He scrambled to his feet, the alley spinning as he shed his sleep. The man who'd kicked him grunted and disappeared into the swirling eddies of people in the square.

Iggy put his back to the wall, trying to collect himself as nausea swirled in his stomach. He closed his eyes to get away from the city. But even with his eyes closed, the smoke scratched inside his nose. The wall behind him bulged with death.

A night of sleep had done nothing to change his–*What? Hallucinations? Revelations?* He had hurled the cover off a bed to find it crawling with maggots, and no one could see them but him.

*Help.* It was an empty plea, aimed at no one. *Please help.* He would go mad like this. Perhaps he already had.

And then he heard her pulse, steady and warm and certain. He clung to it like a child that had found his lost mother. *Even here,* she had said. *Even here.*

He was weeping.

*You've lost your mind,* some distant voice said. It was numb with disbelief, marveling as it watched him unravel. *Do you even remember what's happening? Harth told you to stay inside, and you slept in the alleyway. Harth asked you to lay low, and you made a stranger kick you awake.*

He had to get back upstairs. Angbar and Syntal were probably worried about him. But at the thought of going inside again, a wild scream thrashed in his belly. He couldn't face it.

*Face what?* the voice demanded, incredulous. *Brick and fire wood? What is* wrong *with you?*

*I don't know,* he answered. *I don't know.*

The wolves had called the road a scar, and now he understood what they'd meant. *If I spoke to them now, they would recognize me. Let me in. I could sleep between the trees.* He wanted that. In that instant he wanted it more than he'd ever wanted anything.

*Shhh,* his mother whispered, hushing him through the wind. *Shhh. All in time. Your friends are worried.*

He sucked at the air, trying to calm himself. It tasted of filth and ash.

*Even here.*

He gathered his courage and turned back to the inn, slogging through madness.

~ ~

The common room was gorged with human bodies, the air rancid with the stink of burning. He marched through it as if wading through mud, bounded up the steps two at a time, and threw the door open without knocking.

Syntal started. "Iggy!"

"We thought you were caught! *Sehk,* where were you?" Angbar hissed, jumping to his feet.

"I just... needed some air." It sounded flimsy, even to him. "I wasn't feeling well." He wasn't ready to explain further. Even if he had been, he wasn't sure he could.

"Were you outside all night?" Angbar pressed, incredulous. "You must have frozen half to death–"

"I'm well," Iggy snapped. "Forget it happened." Angbar fell silent, his face painted with questions. Iggy glared at the hearth. "But we're not keeping a fire. When this wood is gone, don't throw in any more."

Angbar gaped. "Are you mad?"

"I don't know."

"Iggy," Syntal said, "It's freezing. We need the heat–"

"It won't be that cold today. And you won't need the heat. There are three of us in here. This room is so small we'll keep it warm just by being here.

"*No fire*."

He took a seat by the window, ignoring their stares and trying not to shake.

~ ~

He dozed.

The room stayed warm. His thoughts rich with dreaming, he realized that the air was doing it. Comforting them. Why wouldn't it, after he had stopped the fire? They could be at peace, nature and man. His mother knew this. Maybe he could learn it too.

An argument in the alley woke him. His dreaming clarity blurred, dissolving into absurdity. The room was warm because there were three people in it, all the windows were shut tight, and the sun was up. The air didn't care whether or not any wood was burning.

*For the love of winter,* he reprimanded himself, *it's* air.

Syntal and Angbar were sitting on the bed, busying themselves with Syntal's spellbook. Iggy glanced at the sky. It was nearly highsun. They must've been working at it for hours.

Syntal was lecturing Angbar. She sounded exasperated. Iggy ignored her and let his eyes drag closed. He was drifting off again when he heard her say something about a pulse.

"What?" He started awake, the word jumping from his lips, and looked at her.

"I was talking to Angbar," Syntal said.

"*M'sai,* but what did you say?"

"She said I shouldn't be trying to figure out what the words mean, I should just be listening for the Pulse." Angbar shrugged. "I'm listening, I just don't hear anything."

"You can hear the heartbeat?" The words were out before he could stop them, before he could think about what they admitted.

Syntal looked at him as if he'd appeared from thin air. "Sometimes," she said slowly. "Only when I'm chanting. You..." She peered at him. "Why? Have you felt it?"

*Yes,* he wanted to say, remembering the heartbeat he'd heard in the alleyway. Sehk, *I thought I was going mad.* But he swallowed the words. They were too dangerous.

Instead, he stood up. "For how long?"

Syntal drew herself up. Her eyes said, *You didn't answer me.* "Five years? Six? You've never heard me talk about it with Angbar before?"

*Syntal can hear it? What does that mean? What does that make me?* "I just never heard you."

"Well, *sehk,*" Angbar said. "Maybe you should try, Iggy. You'll probably have better luck than me." He glanced at Syntal. "Though I think I might have felt something that last time. Just a little twinge."

Syntal waved him off. "You've had all morning." She nodded toward the book, sitting on the bed between Angbar and herself. Her eyebrows quirked a question at Iggy.

Iggy grunted. "No thanks."

"If you've felt it," Syntal said evenly, "you want more. I can show you."

*She really has heard it,* he knew at once. *And she's right. I can either do it now or later, but I have to do it. I have to know.* He forced himself to shrug, as if he had no idea what she was talking about. "Nothing better to do."

Syntal pointed at the book. "There are words here, in First Tongue. Can you read First Tongue?"

"No," he said, relieved and disappointed at the same time.

"I'll read them for you, then. I'll speak them, and you repeat them. They make a pattern, a beat. That beat will become the Pulse. They help you to hear it."

"*M'sai,*" he said. "I'll give it a try."

He knelt next to the bed, and the heartbeat returned.

He didn't just hear it; he *felt* it. It was in the air. It was in his blood. It was even in the dead, nailed wood.

*(Even here)*

It was wild and free, a heartbeat echoing his own. Hearing it was like rounding the corner to find an old friend. He felt a relieved smile pulling at his lips.

Syntal hadn't said anything. He raised a hand, signaling her to leave off, when she spoke.

"*Moshka do* vér *te*." The words scraped against the Pulse he was feeling, their accents falling in the wrong place. "Go ahead," she said. "*Moshka do* vér *te*."

"Mosh*ta*...?" It wasn't what she had said. The words had their own rhythm, and it wasn't the Pulse's rhythm. He knew; he could feel the Pulse beating a counterpoint to his own heart.

"No, *moshka do* vér *te*."

The Pulse was a symphony. Her words were a cacophony of drums, banged out by a child. *Hush,* he wanted to say. *I can't hear it when you do that.*

"Listen. I'll say the whole set of mantras a few times so you can get a feel for the cadence.

"*Moshka do* vér *te. Satchka se* shér *le. Paela sen* ér *re. Voran sah* rér *de.*"

Her voice screeched; it was fingernails on a slate. *Stop,* he wanted to say, but found himself too aghast to speak.

"*Moshka do* vér *te. Satchka se* shér *le. Paela sen* ér *re. Voran sah* rér *de.*"

The Pulse could be quick or slow, agitated or calm–just like his own heart. Its tempo changed with its mood. But Syntal's voice was unceasing and mechanical, the words growing steadier with each repetition.

To his horror the Pulse shifted, just slightly, to accommodate them. Its color and beauty fled as the tempo changed, leaving only grey.

"*Moshka do* vér *te,*" she droned. "*Satchka se* shér *le.*"

Her voice was obscene. It thrust between the Pulse's accents like rape. The symphony dissolved into shrieks of discord, matching Syntal's demands so that its suffering would ease.

Her face lit with joy.

"There," she said. "I can feel it. Can you?"

"Stop." Iggy clenched his eyes shut, tears burning behind them.

"I have." Her voice was a monotone of rapture. "Once you can feel the Pulse, you don't need to keep saying the words. I could chant right now. This is what Lar'atul called Ascension. Look."

Syllables tumbled from her mouth. She put her finger to the bedspread and drew a mark. The spell seized the cloth and violated it, forcing it to shed light.

*It was already dead,* Iggy gibbered. *It's already been murdered, and now you're... you're...*

Her name glowed on the bed sheet like an open wound.

"This is one of the simplest chants I've found. I can draw anything, but the mark doesn't stay. It'll glow for a little bit and then–"

"*Stop it!*" Iggy hissed. The horrors of his dreams were nothing compared to Syntal's vapid desecration.

"It's all right!" She was smiling as she raped his mother. "This–"

He lunged at her, shoving her to the floor. The mark disappeared. The Pulse's symphony burst back around him like a dam had broken.

"Iggy!" Angbar jumped to his feet. "What are you doing?"

"Never do that again," Iggy snarled. "Do you understand me?"

The girl clambered away from him, scooting up against the wall, her eyes dancing with panic. She jerked her hands up, ready to chant.

"Do you even understand what you're doing?" he roared.

"Oh, *Kirith,*" Angbar said, exasperated. "You sound like Seth! If you didn't want to do it, why didn't you just say so?"

*You're killing it!* Iggy wanted to scream. *You're like a disease to it! Can you even feel that?*

She couldn't. She was trembling, her lips parted in fear.

A knock came at the door. "It's Aron," a muffled voice said. "Let me in."

~ ~

*The innkeeper,* Iggy remembered. *Harth's friend.*

Angbar glared a warning at Iggy and held up a finger. Syntal got to her feet, glowering.

Angbar opened the door.

"Harth came by," Aron started as he swept through, then suddenly fell quiet. "Everything well in here?"

"Fine," Iggy said, when the other two looked at him. The word made him sick. He wanted to shake Syntal by the shoulders, make her promise to never chant again.

Aron closed the door. He was skinny, maybe a few winters short of thirty, with a tight cap of sandy hair. "I heard you shouting from the hallway."

"Won't happen again."

Aron considered this. Finally, he repeated, "Harth came by. Asked me to keep you in your rooms until sunset. He'll be back around then with your friends and your horses, and he'll show you out of the city."

"What?" Angbar said. At the same time, Iggy said, "To where?"

"I think he said Shientel."

"*Shientel?*" Angbar said, incredulous. "That's weeks away!"

Aron shrugged.

"What happened to staying with Lorna?" Angbar pressed. "Can't she–?"

"Look," Aron interrupted, "all he told me was he needs to get you out tonight. He knows the city; if I were you, I'd take him at his word."

Angbar sagged. "*Sehk,*" he muttered.

"I've got a performer coming tonight. He usually packs the common room. I'll hold a table for you by the door. You should be able to wait there until Harth comes."

Syntal was quiet, looking away to hide her eyes; Angbar looked stricken. He'd obviously been expecting something else. Staying in Keldale for the winter, maybe, their running days at an end.

Iggy thought of getting outside the gates, of escaping the open wound of the city, and had to force himself to be still. It might have been madness, but he could hardly wait.

*ii. Lyseira*

"Here." Harth had led them through the labyrinthine alleys to a crumbling structure with a missing door. Now he indicated the stairs in the back of the place. "Down."

The steps descended into the smell of rot and old fish, growing darker and colder as they went. "It's dark," Lyseira muttered as she neared the bottom.

"We can light a torch later. Keep moving."

She *was* moving. She was sick of his orders. *We didn't ask for this,* she wanted to snap. *You said the bazaar was safe.*

"Here," he said again, tapping at a doorway. "In here." She could just make out the others as they filed in, feeling their way with their fingers. The walls were cold and sticky. Harth closed a door, clapping a lid on the last bits of grey light that had chased them down the steps.

The darkness bristled with the sounds of their panting: fevered and frightened.

Harth lit a torch, turning his face grim with shadows. "This should serve until sunset. Then we stick with the plan. I'll go back to Lorna's, get the horses–"

"What happened?" Lyseira demanded. "You said the bazaar was safe. Why was the Church there?"

"Ask him," Harth said, nodding at Seth. "Who were they?"

"Students," Seth said. "They took the Trial at the same time I did. I beat them all in sparring. Separately," he conceded.

"What were they doing here?" Harth pressed.

Seth shook his head. "I don't know. They looked surprised to scc me."

Harth grunted.

Lyseira was shaking; she was terrified and furious. Akir had abandoned her again. But this time the need was as real as it had been on the road, when the arc hound had attacked.

She had called, and He had left her to die.

"We're relying on you," she snapped at Harth. "If you say a place is safe, all we can do is take your word for it. We listened to you, and almost got killed. Do you have any idea what you're doing? Are we even safe here?"

"No, you're not safe here," Harth threw back. "You're not safe anywhere, least of all in Keldale, because your friend over there is being hunted by the Tribunal for murder."

"I thought that was your job! Keeping heretics safe!"

"Tithe-dodgers and blasphemers. Not escaped killers."

"I didn't kill anyone!" Helix barked.

"It doesn't matter!" Harth retorted. "Don't you get that? You–!" He cut off, shaking his head. "Forget it. I'm going back for the horses. We wait here 'til nightfall, then with any luck–"

"I'm coming with you," Helix said. "I have to talk to Lorna again."

Harth stared at him. *Are you mad?*

Helix hurried on. "I saw what happened today. In a dream. The red awning. I saw it. Just like she said Matthew–"

Harth was shaking his head. "No. You wait here."

"No! I have to ask her–"

"*God!*" Harth cried. "Are you damaged in the head? You're being hunted by the *Tribunal*. You should be on a ship for *Bahir!*"

Helix fell silent, his mouth gaping.

"Instead you trick me into thinking you've got some petty squabble with the Church? You come to Keldale, and bring your *sehking* problems to my foster mother? A hundred people saw me kill a Preserver today! Do you know what that *means?*" His neck bulged, a vein there flickering in time with the torch's shadows. He clapped his mouth closed and held the torch out to Seth, who took it.

"Sit down," he hissed. "Shut up.

"And don't. Do. *Anything.*"

The door slammed behind him like a tomb.

*iii. Angbar*

The common room churned with laughter and conversation. A haze of pipe smoke roiled near the ceiling.

As Aron had promised, the table closest to the door remained empty. As he guided them through the crowd, the lanterns suddenly flickered and dimmed. A voice boomed from the stage.

"Good eve, fine ladies and gentlemen of Keldale, the greatest port Or'agaard has ever known!" The crowd applauded.

*I know that voice.* Angbar craned his head, but the stage was dark. He elbowed Syntal and whispered, "Was that Marlin?"

"Here's the table," Aron said. "Keep your hoods up and your heads down. When you see Harth, go." He disappeared, and they all took a seat.

"Tonight you will see acts that defy reason! When you return to your families and try to explain what you've seen, you'll be forced to tell them... it's unexplainable!"

A half-circle of floating, colored lights winked to life at the rear of the stage, illuminating the silhouettes of Marlin and his apprentice.

The crowd cheered again, and Angbar joined them. "That's impressive, huh, Igg?" he said, but the woodsman had put his head in his arms, facedown on the table. Normally Angbar would have prodded him, but now he just shook his head. He had no idea what had gotten into Iggy today, but he was in no mood to poke a sleeping bear.

He took a sip from the mug Aron had left, looking around. The rippling color from Marlin's lights warped the faces in the crowd, making Angbar's head swim. *Or maybe that's all the bloodroot smoke,* he mused. He glanced at Syntal, and she gave him a smile.

For just an instant, he imagined that he had invited her here. That instead of waiting for a man they barely knew to help them escape the Tribunal, they were simply enjoying a night together. He smiled back.

*I should take her hand.*

*Don't you dare,* a voice said. *People might not notice a witch sitting by the door, but a nog and a pale girl holding hands? The* best *thing that comes out of that is getting beaten to death.*

*For the love of winter, no one's going to see. It's dark, we're in the back of the room, it's perfect.*

*She doesn't want to hold your hand, you idiot. She doesn't think of you that way.*

*How do I know that unless I try?*

*This isn't a date, moron! Have you forgotten–*

The internal argument died. There was a priest in the crowd, staring at the stage with a look like he'd just bitten into a lemon. His Preserver sat next to him.

*Oh, God.*

"Syn!" Angbar whispered.

She leaned in toward him. She'd gone to take a bath last night; she still smelled like lavender. "I Ascended to make sure. Yes, he's chanting. He must've done it in the dark, before anyone could–"

"No!" Angbar nodded toward the cleric. "Look!"

Syntal followed his eyes and paled.

"What do we do?" he said.

"We'd better get outside."

*Good idea.* Angbar nudged Iggy, but suddenly the lanterns

flared, flooding the room with light. The crowd *ooohed.*

Angbar froze. Suddenly, it felt like every eye in the tavern was on them.

"Only the beginning," Marlin promised. "Can someone help me? Who has the courage?" A handful of audience members made their way to the stage, to scattered applause.

The Preserver scanned the room, an owl watching an open field.

"Wait," Syntal whispered. "That Preserver–"

"I see him." Angbar shrank into his cloak, wishing he could pull his hood over his face entirely.

"Brave souls," Marlin announced as his volunteers lined up. "Now, are you all rested? It's the night of Meadows. You plan to stay up, yes? Drinking and watching the show?"

"And whoring!" one of the men slurred, his eyes glassy with drink.

"Of course!" Marlin cried. His assistant, a small, furtive-looking man, tossed pillows to the floor behind them. "And your name would be?"

"Robert!" the man said.

"You can last all night, then, Robert? You wouldn't be much good if you couldn't."

"I'm all man," Robert roared, grinning at the crowd and raising his arms. The audience hooted and banged their cups.

"He's all man!" Marlin announced. "He can go again and again, yes? He can hold his drink, he can have wench after wench! His stamina knows no end! Well, let's put this to the test for all of them! Here is a beautiful woman." Marlin gestured, and his assistant tore the drape from a painting of a scantily clad redhead. "And here are our men!"

Angbar felt a familiar wave of drowsiness roll over him from the stage. The four volunteers collapsed.

Marlin's assistant spun the painting around. On the other side, the redhead was pouting.

"It's true, what the clerics say on Dawnday!" Marlin cried over the roaring audience, chuckling. "The flesh is weak!"

"*Enough!*" the priest shouted, shooting to his feet. His Preserver rose with him, sinuously, like a panther stretching.

The crowd quieted. Marlin froze, his eyes glittery with surprise.

"I am Father Calfon," the priest said. "Many of you know me. And I am *appalled.*

"We are in the last days! You *know* this! We have seen the tide stop and the sun rise in the south! We've seen fishers catch nothing but weeds for days! And this *warlock* comes to you, hiding in plain sight, casting his spells while you laugh? Akir *weeps!*"

Iggy finally looked up, his face ashen.

Marlin raised his hands. "Father, I assure you. These are only tricks. Convincing, yes, but tricks." He pointed at his face. "Look at my eyes. Aren't they plain? I would never–"

"Silence," Calfon snarled. "Your lies won't save you."

Marlin's jaw dropped, incredulous. "The eyes don't lie, Father! Look–"

"You!" Calfon stabbed a finger at a man that had been sitting with Robert. "You laughed when your friend fell. Go try to wake him, and see how much you laugh then."

Angbar glanced at the door. It was a thousand miles away now.

The crowd parted to let Robert's friend through. Calfon's Preserver followed him.

"Robert," the man said, shaking his friend's shoulder. "Robert." He didn't wake.

"It's just a trick." Marlin's chuckle was more of a wheeze. "He'll wake in a moment."

"Robert!" the man shouted. He shook his friend again. Nothing.

"He's dead!" someone screamed. A murmur rippled through the audience like an electric charge.

"He killed them!" someone else shouted.

Marlin's apprentice darted for the stage door. The Preserver glided in and jabbed him once, precisely, in the neck. He crumpled.

"Stop them!" Calfon screamed, pointing. "They're trying to escape!"

The audience erupted, a dry field struck by lightning. The front row surged to their feet.

Marlin screamed chants. Some of the attackers collapsed, asleep, but the rest crashed onto the stage. He scrambled backward–into Calfon's Preserver, who jerked his arms back. His last chant died on his tongue.

"Drag him out!" Calfon shouted. "Burn him! *Burn him!"*

The mob echoed him.

Angbar looked at Syntal, frozen to her seat in terror. "We, ah… we'd better go."

*iv. Lyseira*

"This can still be easy," Harth said.

It was sunset, and they were in the alley behind the building, mounting up. He'd returned with their animals and one extra: another gift from Lorna, its saddlebags loaded with food. They were riding one to a horse until they reached the inn.

"Aron will have your friends waiting by the door. You just wait outside, I'll duck in and get them, and we'll be on our way to the south gate. As long as no one recognizes any of us, my friend at the wall will make sure we get out."

He sounded confident, but his constant glances down the alley gave the lie to it.

"Getting through the gate will be just like on the way in. Stay behind and let me do the talking. Keep your hoods up and try to look poor."

*Shouldn't be hard,* Lyseira thought grimly. "You're sure the south gate will be safe?"

It was hard to tell in the gloom, but she thought he was glaring. "I thought we already talked about this. You're not safe anywhere. But if Jacob's there, he'll get us through."

He clucked and brought his horse about. For once, he led them down the main thoroughfares rather than keeping to the alleys and side streets. *It figures,* Lyseira thought. Tonight of all nights she would rather have skulked between buildings like a thief.

"Please just get us out of here," Lyseira mumbled–to Akir, to Harth, to whoever was listening. The city had turned sinister, bristling with threats. She was no longer sure Akir would save them when they were outside the gates, but she didn't care. She just wanted to escape.

"Almost there." Harth frowned. "What is *that?"*

The rooftops near the inn were dancing with firelight. There was a roar, too: a hundred people yelling. A cold hand gripped Lyseira's insides.

"Go," Helix said. "Faster, we have to get–"

"No!" Harth snapped. "Stay behind me. If we..."

Then they gained the square, and words failed him.

The mob was a thrashing ocean of blades and bodies, of torchlight flickering in frenzied eyes. In a depression in the middle of the square, someone had built a pyre of butchered wooden shop stalls. A Preserver was wrestling someone onto the central post.

*Syntal,* Lyseira thought. *They found her, she wasn't careful enough, it's Syntal.*

Helix's face was grey, his jaw slack.

*We have to save her,* she realized in despair. *We have to try.* They wouldn't be leaving Keldale alive after all. They couldn't let her burn.

But then her eyes focused, and she saw it wasn't Syntal.

It was Marlin.

"Heads down," Harth said. "Keep moving."

It was Marlin, the chanter they'd met in Coram. The Preserver was tying him to the post. His eyes were rolling with terror. She couldn't hear his screams over the roar of the mob.

Her relief made her sick.

She turned away, keeping up with Harth, skirting the square to make their way to the inn.

*They're going to kill him.*

*There's nothing I can do.*

*They're going to kill him!*

*Maybe he deserves it! He's a witch!*

*Like Syntal? Like Angbar, soon? Would you let them die?*

*I don't even know him! I can't risk my life for–*

*That doesn't make it* right!

She drew to a halt and turned. There was a priest on the pyre now, shaking his fist and shouting. Lyseira didn't need to hear him to know what he was saying.

*This is wrong. This is* wrong.

*There's nothing I can do!*

The Preserver left the mound, but the cleric remained. He held his hands out, palms down, praying. Flame leapt from the wood. The pyre flowered into inferno.

Marlin's scream was like nothing she'd ever heard.

"Lyseira, come." Seth was tugging on her arm, but she couldn't look away.

*Is this Your will?* she demanded. *It could have been Syntal up there! Why do You give them everything they ask for? Is this Your will?*

The crowd roared. Those in the front stumbled back, recoiling from the heat. The priest's eyes were embers, his smile lurid in the flames. The fire couldn't touch him.

He stepped out, unharmed, as Marlin shrieked.

"Lyseira," Seth insisted.

*Akir wants him to die,* Marcus whispered. *He's not just letting him burn–He* lit *the* fire*!*

*Now get out of here. He's your God. Obey His will.*

She hesitated, horror grappling with outrage in her blood.

Then she kicked both heels into her mount. It reared once, protesting, and launched toward the mob.

*No,* she snarled. *I have a will of my own.*

"Lyseira!" Seth barked. "No!"

She felt like she was standing at a cliff's edge as the wind whipped around her, staring at her own death. *You made me what I am. You know I can't leave him!* she screamed. *You know I can't watch them do this. You* made *me!*

Cobblestones flashed beneath her; when she reached the mob, she would die. It wasn't too late to stop.

*Are You even worth it?* she demanded. *A God that orders murder? A God that laughs as He burns innocents? Who are You? I thought I* knew *You!*

Fifty paces. Forty. She could still turn back. She could still leave Marlin to die. She owed him nothing, after all.

And when she turned away, who would she be?

Suddenly her rage fled. She was naked and weeping, and all was silence.

*If You love Your daughter,* she pled, *keep her safe now.*

Ten paces. It was too late to turn away. She had dropped over the cliff, begging her Father to catch her.

He didn't.

He gave her wings of flame.

*v. Helix*

Lyseira hurtled toward the mob, her hair a banner flying behind her. Helix wanted to speak, to scream, but his throat was closed. The world went still as he waited to watch her die.

Like a tree stump split by an axe, the mob parted. She shot through the gap without slowing.

"*Lyseira!*" Seth screamed. He vaulted off his horse, sprinting after her.

"What in *Hel!*" Harth roared.

Helix pointed, dumbly. "Lyseira..."

"*Come!*" Without waiting, Harth kicked into a gallop toward the inn.

Sick with terror, Helix followed.

*vi. Lyseira*

Her blood burned. Her heart sang. The people in the mob dove away as if she were a lightning strike.

She finally burst into the shallow space around the pyre, and her horse shied from the fire, whinnying. The priest she'd seen earlier stood twenty paces away, his face painted with shock. Even his Preserver looked surprised.

God had sent her for Marlin. She ignored them.

When she started for the pyre, the priest bellowed at her, pointing. The crowd didn't move; they were riveted. But the Preserver charged her.

She turned to him and prayed for Binding. The answering fire in her veins made her want to roar. He staggered. She started to turn away, certain he would fall.

Then he caught his feet and came on.

*Impossible.* Akir was with her. *How–? Why...?*

The Preserver leapt and spun, his kick flashing toward her neck like a scorpion's stinger.

Seth hurtled into him, slamming him to the ground.

*Seth,* she heard herself saying. Her tongue was fire in her mouth.

"Go!" Seth grunted, trying to hold his opponent down. The Preserver back-handed him, hurling him away, and snapped to his feet. "Go!" Seth shouted again, scrambling to block him.

Lyseira ran for the pyre, and Marlin's screams. The fire was livid and hungry; anyone sane would shy from its glare.

But she would not waste His gift. She embraced the flames, and they engulfed her.

*vii. Angbar*

They had made it out of the inn, just ahead of the tide of rioters, and crept into the alley to wait. The roar of the mob had grown ever more horrific, until the wash of firelight had come, and the screams had started.

Now Syntal was on the ground, her head in her hands, rocking. He wanted to hold her, to console her, but his own horror paralyzed him.

"Syn!"

Angbar jumped at the sound, his heart quivering like a rabbit. Harth and Helix were galloping toward them, two extra horses in tow.

*Oh, thank God,* he thought.

"Helix!" Syntal jumped to her feet. "We didn't know if–"

"Get on," Harth demanded. "We're going."

"Where's Lyseira?" Iggy said. "And Seth?"

"They went to help Marlin," Helix said.

Angbar's mind went white. "They... what?"

"They're dead," Harth snapped. "Come on!"

Iggy glanced at the pyre, then back to Harth, his jaw slack. "They're... in *that?*"

Syntal ran to the mouth of the alley, her eyes wide. Lyseira flickered inside the pyre's flames like a wraith: majestic and terrible.

"Blesséd *sehk,*" Angbar breathed.

"We can't just leave them–" Iggy started, and Harth's face flushed with rage.

"Get on the *sehking* horse!" he hissed.

Iggy jerked, then glared. "*Sehk* on you!" he snapped.

There were two Preservers near the pyre, sparring. One of them was Seth. Father Calfon, the priest who'd incited the mob, advanced on them.

*I don't know how they got in there,* Angbar thought, *but there's no way they're getting out.*

Harth had lost patience. "Stay if you want. I'm leaving. Our window is closing fast, and I'm not dying for this." He wheeled his horse toward the far end of the alley–

–and drew up as a cluster of clerics and Justicars cantered in.

He spat a curse and spun back toward the square. At the mouth of the alley, Syntal was chanting. Father Calfon spilled to the ground.

When Syntal turned, her eyes were more real than the fire.

"No," Harth breathed. "Oh, God–"

"Syn!" Angbar called. "Your eyes–!"

From behind them, a Justicar roared. "Witch!

"*There's another witch!*"

*viii. Lyseira*

The heat billowed over her face; the flames licked at her hair. She was walking unharmed in a dragon's throat.

She picked her way across the shifting wooden boards until Marlin hung before her, shrieking, sizzling like a pig on a spit.

He was *melting.*

His bonds flaked to ash as she sawed them open. He collapsed, tumbling down the pyre: a piece of roasting meat. She chased him and dragged him roughshod out of the fire, then started beating the flames out with her cloak.

The crowd was still holding back. Something–Awe? Fear? God? –held them. And the priest had fallen; she didn't know how.

But his Preserver was still trying to get past Seth. He wheeled toward him in a series of spinning kicks. Seth ducked the first two, then blocked the third with his forearm and pushed, staggering his enemy. He pressed the advantage immediately, dancing forward to take the fight away from her.

She tore her cloak away. Marlin had stopped burning, but his skin crackled and smoked. His body was a ruin. The smell was nauseous.

But he was still breathing. She leaned over him and called on her God.

Night became day; the stars burst into suns. Marlin was nearly gone–nearly–but there was a sliver left, a spark of life. She seized it and stoked it, refusing its death by infusing it with holy fire.

His blackened skin sloughed away. His breathing evened. Pink and raw, he opened his eyes.

She sagged backwards, her head spinning with heat and brilliance. Marlin said something she couldn't understand. Her ears were ringing.

The Preserver was still coming.

He darted sideways, sliding like a snake. Seth spun in to intercept the attack, landing a solid blow to the shin. But when he moved to follow up the strike, the Preserver flipped extravagantly backward. He launched himself easily ten feet up and back, his robe snapping behind him as he twisted in the air.

He landed clutching a wicked barbed chain. Its full length clattered to the stones behind him.

Through the clamoring stars in her vision, Lyseira saw Seth glance left and right, his eyes dancing with panic.

The Preserver swung the chain. It whipped around once, twice–then leapt, snapping like a viper.

Seth dove beneath it, rolling forward. As he came up, he drove his fist into the Preserver's gut. The man hurtled backward, bowling into the gawking crowd.

The chain skittered across the cobblestones.

Seth ran back to Lyseira. "Go!" he roared, pointing at the horse.

"You take the horse!" Lyseira said. "Take Marlin and–"

Seth lifted her into the saddle, an argument she could not rebut. "I'll catch up. Get on," he ordered Marlin.

The Preserver scrambled from the mob, his eyes blazing. As

Marlin climbed onto the horse's back, Lyseira prayed again for Binding. Her enemy stumbled once and shook his head.

Then he kicked into the air, hurtling toward them like a falling star.

Seth slapped the horse's rump, sending it into a panicked gallop.

"Seth!" Lyseira screamed. She craned her head back to see her brother launch upward and smash into the Preserver. They spun in the air as they bore down, clutching each other like dancers.

Then they crashed into the churning mob and were gone.

*ix. Angbar*

The three Justicars charged.

Iggy drew his bow, smoothly nocking an arrow. Helix leapt down and pulled his sword, scrambling in front of his cousin. Syntal stumbled backward, eyes wide.

And Angbar froze. His friends' reactions played out like a conversation overheard in the next room: vaguely interesting, but ultimately irrelevant. With brutal certainty, he realized he was going to die.

The first knight smashed into Harth, shoving his mount against the wall and nearly spilling him from his saddle. The second flinched as one of Ignatius's shafts ricocheted off his helm. Helix gutted his mount with a lucky swing, and he tumbled to the stone.

The third came for Angbar.

He charged across the cobblestones, a vision of flying death. The wings on his helmet splayed out like a bird of prey swooping down for the kill.

*This is what Matthew saw when he died.*

Then a flash of light caught him in the shoulder. He snapped sideways, yanking his horse off balance. With a shared scream, they both collapsed.

Harth was locked in a clumsy grapple with the knight that had pinned him to the wall. Iggy aimed his bow at them, flinched, and switched targets to the clerics at the far end of the alley. The shots went wide.

Syntal chanted again, and the priests he'd shot at pitched from their horses like sacks of wheat.

Harth shoved his attacker away. The Justicar clutched at a dagger sticking from his neck. His horse reared, its eyes rolling.

The last Justicar, near Helix, was pinned beneath his animal. Helix stumbled away from him and clambered back to his horse. "Syn!" He circled in front of her and pulled her into the saddle. "The south gate!"

"No!" Harth wheezed. He was holding his side; blood seeped from his fingers. "The plan's changed. I'm not bringing this *sehk* to Jacob." He winced. "Angbar, with me."

Angbar had lived. Somehow, they had survived an attack by three priests and three Justicars. It had happened too fast. Was it really over?

He climbed up, behind Harth. They tore down the alley. Angbar glanced back to make sure the others were coming.

Behind them, bathed in bloody torchlight, Calfon's mob spilled into the alley. *They saw us,* he thought numbly. They were waving torches or weapons; some threw stones.

*Thank God for the horses.* As the mob fell behind, Angbar turned forward again.

They slanted west, onto a broad street. People dove out of their way.

They were in a canyon carved of buildings, towering on either side. Alleys gaped like mouths, echoing with bloodlust: the splintering cries of bugles, shouts of "This way!" or "The west gate!" An instant of relief seized him every time they passed one, but another gap always loomed ahead. The next one leered with torchlight–more than any of the others.

*Look out!* he tried to scream, but the words froze in his mouth.

Harth had seen it. He screamed something incoherent and leaned forward, pushing them faster. Angbar should've done the same. Instead he twisted to gaze into the alley.

As it flashed past he saw a still portrait of a horse bearing Lyseira and Marlin, galloping their direction. A trio of riders in pursuit, with torches. Behind them, three archers. And two arrow shafts, one of which shattered the illusion of a picture as it tore the hairs from his head.

He yelped and ducked, far too late to save his life if the arrow had been a degree to the right. "Lyseira!" he shouted to Harth. "In the alley! They're chasing her!" If Harth heard, he gave no sign.

Angbar glanced back to see Lyseira and Marlin burst into the street, falling in with the others. The torchlight from the alley behind them grew until the three riders exploded from it, banking to keep up the chase.

He was powerless. He had no weapon, and couldn't aim it if he had. *Harth will lose them before we reach the gate. He has to.*

Turning forward again, that hope died. The west gate loomed. The portcullis was closed. Ten soldiers blocked it.

"Halt!" one screamed, hefting his weapon.

*"Witch!"* Harth shrieked. "Behind us! Help! God, help!"

Angbar's stomach dropped. "What? What are you doing?"

"What do you think?" Harth snapped. They shot past the soldier who had shouted the warning, and the other guards closed to protect them.

*x. Helix*

Harth disappeared behind a wall of guards, and Helix sucked air as if he'd been kicked in the gut. *Traitor!* he screamed in his head. *You* sehking–!

A hail of arrows rained from the battlements. He just had time to see Iggy, ahead of him, go down before his own horse tumbled forward, snapping its leg. His face smashed into the frozen cobblestones; a knife of pain flared in his jaw.

He dragged himself clear of his animal and staggered to his feet. Half of the soldiers at the gate swarmed forward, three falling on Iggy before he could gain his feet, the other two rushing at Helix. Syntal snapped a chant, and a bolt of light hurled one of them back, cracking his skull against the wall. The other soldier fell back, eyes wide, just before she treated him to the same.

Iggy thrashed beneath the swarm of soldiers. Helix exploded into them, his weapon flailing. One of them fell back, clutching at his chest. The other two retreated a step, and Helix caught a glimpse of the bloodied mess that had, a moment ago, been his friend. Then an arrow tore into his thigh, dropping him to his knees, and a second speared his shoulder. Behind him, Syntal screamed.

The shots had come from the gate, not the battlements. Three of the five soldiers still guarding the portcullis had drawn shortbows.

"Syn!" Helix called. "At the gate! Archers!"

They were nocking new arrows. Taking aim. The gate was just behind them. *So close,* Helix thought.

Then Harth grabbed an archer from behind and locked an arm around his neck: his victim jerked and pitched forward, coughing blood. Angbar tackled one of the others and they toppled into the last, making his shot go wide.

"Syn!" Helix shouted again. He cast about and saw her. One side of her face was a sheet of blood. An arrow jutted from her ribcage, another from her chest. She spat a spell and staggered once, then collapsed.

Three of the remaining four guards at the gate crumpled. The last was scrabbling with Angbar. Harth knelt, grabbed his hair, and expertly cut his throat. Angbar scrambled backward, his face covered in blood. Harth disappeared into the gatehouse.

A moment later, the portcullis began a ponderous climb upwards.

A second flurry of arrows lashed from the battlements. Helix staggered for the gate, trying to reach cover, but something struck his head. The street lurched sideways. Angbar caught him before he fell.

"Stay here!" his friend shouted, and Helix stumbled against the wall. Behind a crimson curtain, the world spun and caught, spun and caught. He closed his eyes to escape it, but even the darkness whirled. His leg felt too thick, crammed with pain; his shoulder sparked with agony whenever it moved. He heard screaming horses and the whistling of arrows.

*I need... to do something.* Syntal was out there. Iggy and Lyseira. They needed him.

He opened his eyes and saw Iggy crawling toward the gate, leaving a smear of blood across the stones. He wanted to help him.

The darkness grabbed him, pulling him into a black spiral. The world retreated, and he fell... until fire caught him, and warmth flooded his limbs.

Lyseira was before him, a smear on a window pane. His eyes wouldn't focus on her.

"Can you stand?" she said, from a million miles above.

He could. She turned away, and slowly, images crystallized around him: Lyseira praying over Iggy, Harth cutting some of the soldiers' horses loose, Angbar helping Syntal mount up.

Harth gestured at the portcullis, which was just high enough to ride under. "There are still archers on the walls," he said. "I blocked the door. It should hold them up there, but they'll fire at us. We've no choice. We have to get out of here."

The door blocking the archers gave a sudden jerk; the tip of an axhead peeked through the wood. On the street, a host of new riders careered toward them.

Beyond the wall, a long, snow-shrouded road stretched into the dark.

"This will never work," Harth muttered, and kicked his mount into a mad charge through the gate.

# Chapter 16

## Before the Storm

*i. Syntal*

When Uncle Kevric had told her that her parents were gone, a pit had opened in her belly. It was black and bottomless. There was nothing inside, forever.

But she had tiptoed around it. All summer she'd been waiting for her parents to take her home. She had turned her back on the pit, and kept on waiting.

At the funeral, the pit had widened. She'd nearly fallen. But they'd only buried one body, and it was unrecognizable. The ceremony had felt like a rehearsal.

She hadn't cried. There was no need.

Any day now they'd find out it was a mistake, that the wagon lost in the flood hadn't been her parents'. Any day, Uncle Kevric would get word from Dad, asking him to bring Syntal home. Any day, she would hear a knock at the door and find them standing there, beaming and open-armed. Dad would say, "There's my girl!" and Mom would crush her in a hug and marvel at how much she'd grown.

But every night she fell asleep in the Smith's house, that hole gaped a little wider. Every morning she woke alone, it turned a little blacker. She was still balancing, but it was hard, and when Seth stole her book in the cave–the book *she* had found, that *she* had been trying to pull out–her footing slipped.

He had pushed her in.

She clawed for the lake surface as the darkness pressed in. It was everywhere. It was unrelenting. When her breath ran out it would suffocate her.

Rage pounded in her constricted lungs; grief burned behind her eyes. The sun stretched down, its arms shimmering in the lake's depths, and she reached for it like a sinner for deliverance.

But when she finally broke the surface, its empty light changed nothing.

Lyseira splashed down the beach, hitching up her hem in a futile effort to keep it dry. "Syn?"

Syntal made the shore, quivering. Getting out of the lake didn't matter. The pit still had her.

She thrashed against it like a girl in flames. "That Seth is such a bastard!" she exploded. "I *hate* him!" Her voice splintered on the last word, which broke and fell to ruin–like everything else on the lake shore.

Lyseira boggled. "What happened?"

*What do you think happened, you idiot? My mom and dad are dead!* The thought was an arm shooting from the depths, grabbing onto her ankle, tugging her down. She slapped at it, frantic. "There was a book I found! *I* found it! I dug it up! And he *stole* it!

"He can't do anything with it! He said there's no words on it and he can't get it open, but *I* could get it open! He just doesn't want me to get anything because he's an idiot! He can't even *read* anyway!"

Lyseira looked confused. "But... why would–?"

"How should I know?" Syntal roared. Her rage was fire in the darkness. When it was hot enough, she could forget; it buoyed her to the pit's lip, where she scrabbled for purchase. "How should I know why an idiot does anything? I can't help that he's so stupid!"

Lyseira's face flickered between sympathy and indignation. "Hey! That's not fair."

Syntal glared. "Yeah?" she seethed. "What would *you* know about it? You can't read either."

"Can too!" Lyseira protested.

"You?" Syn snapped. "You're practically still a baby! You–"

"Hey, Syn!" Angbar called from behind, oblivious. "I brought you some drearmoss."

He looked like a drenched cat as he splashed through the surf, his hair plastered to his skull, nude but for a pair of bedraggled underpants. Several globs of drearmoss hung from his waistband. He was grinning like a fool. The absurd sight would've made her weak with laughter an hour ago.

Now, it was just stupid.

"See?" He offered one of the globs: violet, her favorite color. In the cave it had been lustrous, shimmering with riches. The sun robbed it of its beauty; left it limp and pale.

"Why do I want your stupid drearmoss?" she sneered.

Angbar shrugged. "I just... thought you'd like it. It's not a big deal." He fed the moss to the waves, and they dragged it down.

He sloshed past her and up to Lyseira, already jabbering about everything he'd seen in the cave, waxing reminiscent about the skull that had slipped away on his swim out. Syntal hated him. She hated both of them. Why didn't he ever shut up? Why didn't Lyseira ever take her side? They were all Helix's friends, anyway. Not hers. They'd never be her friends. And now she was stuck with them forever. Because–

She gasped for air, thrashing. That hand had her ankle again, pulling her down.

Helix splashed out of the lake, struggling manfully with the sword. He threw a consoling look at Syntal, but said nothing.

When Seth came up, he didn't have the book.

"Where is the book, Seth?" she asked, struggling to keep her voice level.

Seth shrugged as he waded to shore. He wasn't looking at her. Fury swelled in her breast like an ocean storm.

"Did you leave it in the cave?" she demanded. He shrugged again.

"Seth!" Lyseira cried, affronted. "That's not very nice! If you didn't want it, why didn't you just–?"

Seth whirled on Syntal. "What am I gonna do with a book? I can't read, 'member?" He spat in the mud and grabbed his shirt.

Syntal gaped. He had *left it.* After all her begging, after Helix had offered to trade...! He *knew* she'd wanted it, and he'd still left it.

*He must think I'm a sissy. Is that what he thinks?*

He was staring at her, his expression empty but his body nearly crackling with contempt.

She would be *damned* if he got the last word on this.

She splashed back into the lake. The others shouted after her. *You think I won't go down there alone?* The thought was searing. *Watch me, you bastard.*

The water closed over her, and she was back in the dark.

She shot down to the rock shelf, glided beneath and around it as easily as an otter. Her lungs were just starting to burn as she bobbed into the cave.

She hauled herself, dripping and gasping, onto the ledge. The cave's silence thundered around her, leeching her anger away. As her eyes adjusted to the chamber's dim light, the lumps of shadow pocking the floor slowly coalesced into scattered rock and bone.

The light from the dreermoss was sterile and alien. Crimson was just as cold as violet, both frozen on the wall like a discoloration of the stone. Behind her, water lapped against rock. It sounded like a panting beast: something hunched in its lair, waiting for prey. The bones littering the cave suddenly became the remnants of its last meal.

A sick worm of fear wriggled through her. She fumbled after her earlier rage like a chilled traveler trying to light a campfire, but the wood for that fire was sodden. It wouldn't spark.

*There's nothing to be scared of,* she told herself. *It's just a stupid cave.* What kind of baby would go back just because she was alone? She imagined emerging from the surf above, shamefaced and empty-handed, a helpless victim of Seth's persecution.

That *is not going to happen.*

The tinder sparked. The fire caught. Its heat forced the fear back, and in its light she searched for the book.

She crept deeper into the cave, toward the little pool in the back where she and Seth had fought. She became aware that she was taking shallow breaths, ginger steps–trying to keep quiet even though there was no one to hear. *Stupid,* she accused herself, but kept doing it. She rounded the bend, saw nothing, and sneaked to the pool she'd found the book in.

It was empty.

The sight of the shallow basin made her suddenly imagine returning to the first pool, ready to leave, only to see that same blank rock wavering beneath the water. She would discover, too late, that the cave was a trap; that the monster in the darkness had sealed off all escapes.

She swallowed thickly and turned away. The dreermoss was dimmer, she suddenly noticed–it had been dimming steadily since she came back. *Maybe it's just the bait. Once the prey is here, there's no need for it, and the lights go out.*

Once again, fear thrashed in her belly. Again, she reached for the fire of her anger. *Where is that cursèd book? Did he throw it in the lake?* That was a wretched thought. If he had dumped the book, she would never find it. He would have beaten her twice: once when he made her run away crying, and again when he watched her swim back.

The fire leapt and crackled. *That* sehking *bastard!*

She darted back around the cave's single bend, her anger finally roaring hot enough to burn up her fear of making noise. She cast about that first, long passage again, furious at the thought of him besting her, *willing* the book to be there...

And there it was, at the far end of the cave, right next to the first pool. So close, she had gone right past it.

A grim satisfaction seized her. She lumbered into a run, her drenched dress chafing her calves–and her foot exploded with pain.

"*Sehk!*" she screamed as she tumbled to the stone. She hurled herself around, wincing at the throbbing pain in her toe, and fumbled for whatever had tripped her. "God *sehking* damn it!"

She scrabbled at the ground like something feral, her rage building toward cataclysm. She burned to find whatever had tripped her and throw it, to watch it shatter on the cave wall, or maybe smash it with another rock. She would crush it for hurting her, she would *destroy* it, she–

"What–?" It was smaller than she'd thought. Some kind of weird, smooth stone, like an agate, but perfectly rounded. "Curséd thing," she insisted, but her tantrum was fading, eclipsed by curiosity. She ripped a patch of yellow drearmoss from the cave wall and leaned in close, panting with spent anger.

It wasn't a stone at all. It was a simple, black ring, wedged hard into a crack in the ground. It was beautiful in the drearlight, gleaming with enticements.

She worked her finger underneath it, scraping her nail against the stone. It took several minutes of heaving and cursing to finally drag the thing loose. At last, though, a circle of perfect darkness glimmered between her fingers.

She felt a flush of pride. Because of her tenacity, she'd found a new ring *and* gotten the book back. *Idiot,* she thought, picturing Seth standing on the beach and thinking he'd gotten the best of her.

Then she realized how to really get back at him.

The ring kept slipping off her finger, so she popped it in her mouth before grabbing the book and jumping into the pool. When she cleared the rock ledge, she kicked upwards and outwards–away from the others.

She swam below the surface until her chest threatened to implode. When she finally went up for air, she cast about, gasping. She could just make out Angbar and Seth on the shore. They hadn't seen her. She turned, and pushed away.

The book grew heavier with every kick, and each gulping breath threatened to make her swallow the ring. Finally she bobbed to shore and crawled up, her limbs aching. When she dropped the book, it thudded like an anchor. Her arm groaned.

She couldn't see the others anymore. Maybe they'd gone down to the cave, looking for her, or maybe they'd gone back to tell someone she was gone. Through her exhaustion, Syntal felt a surge of vindication. Either way, when Auntie learned that Seth had made her run away, he would be in a whole pot of trouble.

She spat out the ring and hung it loosely on her thumb, but even this small movement made her wince from the pain in her arms. She lay against a tree and let her overworked muscles rest. *There's no hurry,* she realized. *The longer I take to go back, the more trouble Seth'll be in.*

She slid her eyes closed, waiting for her muscles to relax. The sun glowed red behind her lids, bathing her with infinite warmth. She let herself sink into it, reminded of winter nights spent curled up on the floor in front of a blazing hearth at home, her parents chatting idly as her mother caressed her hair.

Her eyes jerked open, suddenly brimming with tears. She blinked hard, trying to think of something else. *Don't cry. Don't cry.* Her father had always told her that crying never changed anything. She could see him now. *You have to get up and do it, not cry about it,* he always said.

But he'd never said what she was supposed to do if he died.

Her stomach dropped. She reached for that image of him, stern and loving at the same time, and saw the edges fraying to black. *Daddy!* she called, she *screamed,* but the picture disintegrated in the rushing darkness of that endless pit. She was falling, and all her rage had been an illusion.

She had never stopped falling at all.

~ ~

She woke, still alone, to a lake shining with streaks of red and orange.

Her head had splintered and been sewn back together; her eyes stung from sobs; her clothes had dried into a chafing shell.

At last, though, the sudden storm of grief had receded. It had scoured her raw and left her empty, but the emptiness was better than the crying. She *hated* crying.

Climbing to her feet, she groaned in agony: every muscle was exhausted and stiff, especially her right arm, which had been clutching the book as she swam. She had fallen asleep with the arm curled against her in a tight V. Now, when she tried to straighten it, it screamed in pain. She had heard of muscles cramping before, but she had had no idea how much they *hurt.*

The book, still lying in the nearby grass, may as well have been a mountain. It was all she could do to keep her arm cradled, to keep the pain a distant whisper. The idea of trying to pick the book up was ludicrous. Here, in the silence of the early evening and far away from her anger, it seemed a miracle she had ever lifted the thing to begin with.

She sighed, frustrated, and glared at her crippled arm. In the dying sunlight she caught a glimmer of blackness against her thumb. *The ring.* She had gotten that, at least.

She barked a joyless laugh. So that was it. All that work, and stubbing her toe, and fighting with Seth and Lyseira and Angbar... for nothing. The rage that had driven her back to the lake's depths had dissipated; if anything, she only felt stupid now for acting like such a child. Her dad would've been disgusted–

*No. No, no, no, no....*

Syntal backed carefully away from the thought. *Something else. Anything else.* She tried to straighten her arm. The backlash of pain sizzled her thoughts clean and reduced her to whimpers.

"Syn?"

Her breath caught; she whirled toward the sound and saw Helix.

"Akir, are you well?" He trotted toward her. "The whole village is out looking for you! Are you well?"

"I..." She didn't know what to say. She was fine, of course. *Did he say the whole* village *is looking?* "My arm hurts."

He had been about to hug or grab her; the words halted him. "What's wrong? How did you get all the way over here? Mom and Dad are going crazy. What happened to your arm?"

Mom and Dad. *He means Uncle Kevric and Auntie Bella.* "I... I just..." Sudden fear seized her. *What if they find out I wasn't really lost? What if they find out I did it on* purpose*?* Would they even let her stay with them? She had nowhere else to go, if they decided not to keep her. They wouldn't turn her out for being a brat, would they?

*What if they do?*

"I just went back to get the book." She nodded toward it, still resting in the grass. "I just didn't want to lose it. But when I came up, I... I got turned around..."

"Akir!" Helix swore. "Thank God you're well. Seth was scared you drowned in the lake."

That surprised her. "Seth?" she repeated, numbly.

"Yeah. He's swimming around out there right now, he's almost as crazy as Mom and Dad. He couldn't find the cave, though. He must've dived down a hundred times by now."

*Seth* was diving, looking for her?

"Come on." Helix took hold of her good arm. "I gotta get you back to Mom and Dad, they're going crazy."

"No!" Syntal pulled away. The thought of their faces, the thought of *Seth's* face, made her feel like a fraud. *Seth will know,* she thought, *even if Auntie and Uncle don't, Seth will know right away.*

"Syn?" Helix's face was tight with confusion. "Come on! They're going *crazy*," he repeated.

"No, I know, I just..." She looked at him, the cousin she had always thought of like a distant brother, and the words spilled out before she could stop them. "I did it on purpose. I was trying to get Seth in trouble. I didn't mean to fall asleep, but... I swam away on purpose." She wanted to say more, to offer some justification or defiance, but the sudden torrent of words dried up. All she could do was wait for his reproach.

Helix was dumbstruck. "You were *hiding*?" His mouth worked, but no sound came out.

"I know, I'm sorry, I didn't mean to scare anyone..." She trailed off. Scaring someone was exactly what she had meant to do.

He stared at her for another instant, then guffawed.

"Oh my God!" he nearly shouted, before quieting his voice and glancing furtively up and down the lake shore. "Syntal, that is *brilliant!*"

Syntal blinked. *You aren't mad?*

"Mom and Dad will *kill* you, though. I mean, pissing on Ellic Baler is one thing..." He gave his old, evil grin. "*Rev'naas* take that," he said. "All you did was put Seth in his place. I can keep a secret if you can."

Gratitude welled up in her. *Are you sure?* she felt she should ask, but she was too scared he'd change his mind. "*M'sai.*" He hadn't simply accepted her deviance. He had actually *admired* it. A timid smile tugged at her lips. "But what are we gonna do?"

Helix surveyed the lake shore again, making sure they were alone. "Well, most everybody is over on the Pinewood side. Me and Seth came over the river, but he's swimming all around the lake right now, looking for you." He winked.

"He won't be able to find the cave, I don't think," Syntal said. "The light from that weird moss was getting darker. I think maybe it doesn't glow at night."

Helix waved her off. "He'll be fine. He can be a stubborn idiot but he won't drown himself or nothing.

"So really all we have to do is go around the lake, and we'll tell everyone the truth–that you got lost coming out of the cave, and got scared and fell asleep, and I found you... what?"

She had started shaking her head. Even with an accomplice, she couldn't face Auntie and Uncle. Not yet. "My arm really hurts. It's messed up from swimming with that stupid book. I want to go home." *You'll never be home again*, something inside tried to whisper, but she ignored it. "Can't we just go home, and you can tell them I'm safe?"

"I don't know, Syn," he started. "They're really going cr–"

The wild fear in her eyes cut him off. He sighed.

"Yeah. *M'sai.* Let's go home. You can get to bed. I'll talk to 'em.

"Besides," he added as he grabbed the book, "you know they'd probably take this away if they found it, and bring it up to The Abbot. After all the *sehk* you went through for it, that don't seem fair to me."

He loved swearing like that, when his parents weren't around. He sounded casual and empowered. She suddenly loved him for it.

Mute, she followed him up the lake shore.

Nightfall had sneaked up on them as they talked, transforming the lake's burnished gleam into an endless expanse of cold glass. They picked their way over the ruined shore, speeding up when the clouds let the moonlight fall, slowing when they crowded it out.

"You really got them, though," Helix marveled. "Seth for sure, I think he felt really bad."

Syntal snorted. "I'm actually surprised. He was being a horse's ass in the cave." She enjoyed the words' mature taste–they were an adult's comment, worlds beyond the tantrum she had thrown earlier. "I honestly didn't think he was even gonna care."

She could hear the grin in Helix's voice. "Well, *m'sai.* Lyseira was maybe the most upset at first, but you know how she is. She makes you think of things you didn't think of." His voice held a note of rueful admission. "She probably got to him, but he would've felt bad anyway, I think. He was mean, yeah, but he doesn't want you to *drown* or nothin'. He's still Seth. He's just kind of an ass since..." Helix glanced back at her. "You know."

The words were barbed. She handled them carefully. "Yeah."

"But still. Leaving the book there was just a *sehk* thing for him to do." He glanced at it, heavy in his arms. "Does it even open? What's so great about it, anyway?"

The question took her by surprise. She didn't have a ready answer. "Nothing, really. I just wanted it."

But that wasn't true. She had always loved books. Her mother was a schoolteacher, and had already started teaching Syntal to read. More than once, Syn had picked a book from the shelf and asked Mom to show her how to read it, and they had settled in at the table together and worked over the words. It made her feel grown up and smart. Every bit of casual praise from her mother was priceless as a jewel.

*"Where did you get this?"* she could see Mom asking, her eyes lighting at the sight of the massive book. *"My goodness!"*

*"I found it in Southlight,"* Syntal would answer, feeling a quiet thrill at her mother's interest. *"I thought we could look at it together. It's too big for me to read by myself."*

*"Too big for you? Oh, I don't know about that."* She would have that secret smile in her eyes, that smile that said, *You are my daughter, and you can do anything.*

The smile that Syn would never see again.

She stumbled to a halt. Her vision blurred; a hint of freefall fluttered in her stomach. She drew in deeply of cool, black air, shivering on the lip of the pit, fighting for balance.

"Could we open it, you think?" She turned carefully away from her mother's memory and focused instead on Helix. A black wind rushed from the pit, leaving her chest tight and hollow. "It's closed. There's no clasp. But there must be a way to get it open."

He couldn't have understood how badly she needed him, but again, he responded. "Well... yeah, Syn. Of course." His easy agreement–so casual, so crucial–grounded her. The wind from the pit lessened.

Helix shifted, working his shoulders against the book's weight. "It's a heavy bastard though, ain't it? Come on, let's get home."

He had moored a little raft on the riverbed. It bore them across the high Narrel. When they reached the far bank, he set her book on the raft and dragged it toward home.

The village was black, punctuated only by the occasional lantern glowing in a window. One of these burned on the porch of the Smith home, throwing long intimations of loss into the dark.

"Maybe we can try to cut the band open with Dad's smithing shears," Helix whispered, the porch steps creaking as he climbed, "but not tonight. I gotta get the raft back to the river, in case Seth needs to use it, and find Mom and Dad–"

"Wait!" Syntal hissed. He was about to bring the book in the house. "They'll take it!"

He glanced at his arms, as if he'd forgotten the book he was holding.

"We've gotta hide it!" she urged, but had no idea where. She scanned through a mental map of the house, and came up empty.

Helix's brows furrowed. He crept back down the steps and skirted the porch, beckoning her to follow. He stopped at an old, bowed slat of wood in the porch's side, as forgotten by the light as the cave beneath the lake had been.

"Don't tell anybody." His shadowed face was grim. "*M'sai?* No one else knows, not even Seth, or Iggy–*no one.*"

"*M'sai,*" she nodded.

"Always double-check, make sure no one saw you. You never just come down here to play around. It's not for hide'n'sneak. *M'sai?*"

"*M'sai.*" She had never heard him so grave. "I promise."

He unhooked the warped board and led her, stooping, beneath the porch. As he replaced the board behind them, gentle awe stole into her chest.

Lantern light drifted through the porch slats, striping the soil with cloudy light. She smelled dank earth and mushrooms, saw the skittering shapes of centipedes. The close, comforting weight of solitude embraced her.

It was a realm apart, a place of aching stillness.

The silhouette of an ancient crate rested against the house's foundation. Next to it, she caught a faint shimmer from the sword Helix had found in the lake.

"I'll put it here." Helix's words were the barest wisp of sound; they could only be heard here, in this hallowed space. He sneaked to the crate with the book. "You can come find it whenever you want. Just don't let anyone see you."

"I won't." The promise was little more than a silent exhalation.

He guided her back into the open night. "I gotta get back and tell Mom and Dad you're well," he said as he replaced the bowed board. "You are well, right? You can open the door to the house, and whatnot?"

She nodded.

"*M'sai.*" That evil grin flashed. "Get inside, you sneak."

As always, despite herself, she felt an answering smile break across her own face. Sentiments clamored for purchase on her tongue: *Thank you*, or *You saved me.* Perhaps, *I was all alone, and you led me home.*

Or simply, *I love you.*

But she could articulate none of these, and by the time she realized how much she wanted to tell him, he had gone.

# Chapter 17

*i. Lyseira*

She remembered Seth putting her on the horse, with Marlin behind her. She remembered careening through the nightmare streets of Keldale, reaching the gates to find them barred, and seeing her friends drowning in blood. She remembered calling on Akir to heal them, even though she was already near-blind.

After that, there was only holy fire.

Divine flares still dotted her vision; her blood ran sluggish, in streams of cooling lava. But she could hear her friends' voices over the sighing of branches. They were in a little wood.

Grimacing, she counted the shapes of their heads in the dark. *Six,* she thought around the fires in her mind. *We're all here.*

But no, that was wrong. Seth wasn't there.

She'd traded him for Marlin.

Angbar said, "Why are we stopping?"

"Seth," Harth said. "Lyseira said he'd be here."

*I did?* The thought trembled in the furnace of her mind before flashing into fire. "This is where you said we'd meet," came a voice from her throat, "if we ran into trouble. This is where he'll come."

She turned to look at Marlin. "Are you well?" she heard herself asking him. He didn't answer. He was staring into the gloom like a man on the gallows.

She had surrendered everything–even her life, even her *brother*– to save him, and he wouldn't look at her.

*I did what I thought was right. I did what I had to do.* And Akir had been there. He had split the crowd, protected her from the mob. He had let her walk through *fire*.

But now she had breathed so much holy flame that her mouth tasted like ash, and they were still being hunted by every priest and soldier in Keldale. She had surrendered everything to God–that hadn't changed–but she was empty. She had no more strength to channel His will.

*Was it worth it? Was it the right thing to do?* Like the ones before them, these thoughts flickered to smoke. It didn't even matter now.

They would die here, or they would survive the night. It was in

His hands.

*ii. Iggy*

*I'm alive,* he told himself, but he couldn't believe it.

Surely he'd died inside the gates, when the soldiers had fallen on him and the world had shattered into crimson shards. He remembered dragging himself toward Helix, certain of the end, and then nothing–until Lyseira's hands had gripped him, and he had woken free of pain.

Then came the flight through the wilderness, a nightmare of shrieking bugles and buzzing arrows. Their pursuers were everywhere, they must have outnumbered them five to one, and there was no cover on the plain–until his mother had heard his panic and a snowstorm had burst from the sky. She had thrown a blizzard around him like a cloak, hiding them all and sending the arrows wide.

*I'm alive,* he repeated, his mind grey with fading panic. *I'm here.* They'd made it to the little wood Harth had pointed out on the way in.

"Syntal's a witch," Harth's silhouette said. "Lyseira's a witch. Helix is wanted by the Tribunal. What else? I swear to Akir, if there's more, you are telling me now."

"Nothing," Helix said.

Harth fumed, pacing. "This is madness. Just... we're just *sitting* here. They're going to find us. We can't just–"

"Leave if you have to." Lyseira's voice was heavy as lead. Keeping them all alive must have nearly broken her. "I'm waiting. He said he'd catch up."

This argument had been going for ten minutes, buzzing around Iggy's head like a fly. He wanted to swat it.

"Where are you planning to go, anyway?" Angbar said. "You said Shientel was out of the question."

"It is!" Harth snapped. "It's the first place they'll look! They probably have pigeons flying that way right now!"

*Unlikely, in the blizzard,* Iggy thought, but he didn't say it. His shock at his own survival had left him languid. He was drifting beyond his body, floating above the discussion like a specter. None of it mattered. Didn't they see that?

They were alive because the *plains themselves* had helped them. The sky and the wind and the snow had reached out to shelter them.

It changed everything.

"Then where?" Angbar said.

The snow pattered against the trees. "I don't know." Harth had never sounded so lost. "But it's stupid to just sit here."

"We can't go back," Helix said. "We can't go to Coram. We can't go home." His voice faltered. "We... God." The rest of his words hung in the air, unspoken: *There's nowhere. It's only a matter of time.*

Their escape from the gates might have been a miracle, but it was for nothing. They were out of options.

Iggy wasn't sure he believed that. Not after a snowstorm had answered his cries for help; not after the dreams that had sent him reeling into the alley the night before.

*There's food and water all around us. There's shelter in the trees.* He remembered sleeping in the alley, his mother's embrace keeping him warm. If he asked it, she might do the same for all of them.

*I can't tell them that. They'd call me a lunatic.*

He wasn't even sure they'd be wrong.

Branches snapped in the undergrowth behind them. Harth's shadow jerked up a hand. "Shhh."

Lyseira ignored him. "Seth?"

Seth stumbled into the little clearing, leading a horse. He was limping.

"Oh no." Lyseira hurried to him, but she was nearly as unsteady as he was. "Are you well? Let me–"

The shrill scream of a bugle cut her off. Iggy leapt on to his horse. "Go!" he hissed. "Now!"

~ ~

Somehow–because they were too weak to argue, because there was no time, because he was the first to ride–Iggy became the leader.

He shot away from the horn blast, his friends behind him.

He pushed through the trees as fast as he dared, ricocheting off the wood's yawning threats like an acorn dropped into a stampede. Lights atop a ridge forced them north. An impassable ravine turned them southwest. As it fell behind them they reeled around again, chased by another horn blast.

Suddenly, the trees broke.

The moon gazed through a hole in the clouds, illuminating a sea of snow splayed out to the west. Iggy hesitated.

*It's too open. They'll see us a mile off.* And the snowfall had ended; their tracks would be plain as day.

The others came to a stuttering halt when they saw him hesitate. Their animals stamped and panted.

*Help us,* he whispered to the plain. *Help, like you did before.* If he was wrong, if he was talking to himself, his madness would kill them all.

He snapped the reins, pushing his mount into the open. The clouds surged, dimming the moon and bringing another bout of snow. A sudden, driving wind swept all sign of their passage from the plain.

The bugles called twice more, but they were quieter each time. *They're still in the wood,* he hoped, *chasing each other in circles.*

An hour passed, then two. He realized his mare was quivering. They had been pushing hard for too long. His panic would run her to death if he didn't get it under control.

"Shhh," he whispered as he brought down her pace. "*M'sai, m'sai.*" He scratched behind her ear. "You've done well. So well." They had already lost one animal escaping the gates. He felt a flash of self-hate. *She didn't ask for this. No one accused her of murder.*

"I'm sorry for this, girl," he whispered. "I wish there was another way. When this is over, I'll bring you wherever you want. I swear."

Suddenly he could hear his mother's Pulse again, wrapping them like a blanket. "Do you hear it? Can you feel that?"

He closed his eyes and willed the sensation to flood over her. Her muscles relaxed as relief stole into them.

"Why are we stopping?" Harth said.

Iggy jerked to look at him, and saw his mount in the gloom. She was exhausted. "The horses need rest. We can't push them like this all night. We have to slow the pace."

"We don't have time."

"If we ride them to death we'll be dead anyway. Give them rest."

He jumped down.

"What are you doing?" Harth demanded, a quiver of hysteria in the words.

*Stop,* he said to the other horses. The words were the rustling of twigs, the hush of the falling snow. *Breathe. We rest.* "We rest."

"Iggy?" Angbar prodded. "They're still behind us."

"Just trust me." *Trust me.* He scratched Harth's mare on the cheek. She felt steadier than his own–she was more accustomed to flight and combat–but she was still exhausted.

Iggy opened her to the Pulse, and flooded her with relief.

"Can we wait until we're safe to feed them sugar lumps?" Angbar's voice held the same shivering edge as Harth's. He slapped the reins, but his mount harrumphed and stayed still.

Iggy visited each of the horses, assuring them he would keep them safe, opening them to rejuvenation. He had to look ridiculous, but he didn't care. *We stole these animals and forced them to run all night.* He would not allow them to be run to death.

"*M'sai,*" he finally said aloud. His delay had cost them precious time. "Let's go."

The night unfolded. Just before dawn, he caught a glimpse of a distant light behind them–a light too clear and smooth to be a torch.

"They're behind us." Lyseira sounded numb. She might have been commenting on a sandwich. "That's clericlight."

*We can outrun them. Their horses haven't had any rest.*

*Neither have ours!* something in his mind protested. *Scratching their ears is not the same as letting them rest!*

He had the sudden, dizzying sense that he was dreaming. The last two days had left him in a world he couldn't even recognize.

"Get to high ground," Seth rasped. His voice was a tattered flag, torn but still flying. "Have to fight."

Iggy looked at the others. Lyseira had healed most of them enough to ride, but she was barely holding on. Syntal could manage nothing until she rested. The two girls were the only reason the group had survived as long as it had, and both of them were nearly comatose. There was Marlin, but the man had said nothing since they'd left the walls; his eyes were dull with cooling shock.

If they fought, they would lose.

Iggy shook his head and pushed on. "No. We have to outrun them."

"It doesn't matter, Iggy," Helix said. "There's nowhere to go."

*He's right,* Iggy thought. *If the Church doesn't kill us, the winter will.* They couldn't go home, and they couldn't go to Shientel. But his mother lived in the trees. She could shelter them, if he could only find a place the Church couldn't follow.

His breath caught.

"*Rev'naas* take this," Harth growled. He yanked a dagger from his belt and peeled toward a hill.

"No!" Iggy rebuked him. "With me! I know where to go!"

*Now run,* he whispered to the mounts. *Run!*

~ ~

They shot like lightning across the plains, a froth of shattered snow in their wake. The storm was abating; anyone who found their trail could easily chase them. It didn't matter. They would make the Wolfwood road before their pursuers caught them. Beyond that...

*Maybe they'll catch up in time to find the wolves fighting over our carcasses.*

Iggy shook his head. Everything was different now. Before, he had simply spoken with the beasts. Now, he *understood* them.

*They called the road a scar.* Just like in his dream. He knew how they saw the world. He'd seen the horrors they'd seen; he wanted to escape those horrors as badly as the wolves did.

Instead of threatening them, maybe he could offer protection. Aid for the winter. Something. They had to listen.

There was nowhere else to go.

The mounts slowed to a steady gallop, keeping their pace better than Iggy could've hoped, but the flicker of clericlight still chased them. When the sun rose it died away, replaced by a distant, churning cloud of snow.

After sunrise he risked another stop to invigorate the horses, as he had before. Then it was flight, and more flight. Snow gave way to frozen earth as they crossed the edge of the blizzard's path. Finally, a few hours after highsun, Wolfwood's broad shadow burgeoned in the west.

"Ignatius." Seth's eyes were vises, locked on the horizon. "Where are we headed?"

"Safety," Iggy grunted, ignoring the question. He whispered to the mare, *We make for the wood, and safety.*

Her shock hit him like a punch to the gut. *The wood isn't safe! It's cursed, guarded by wolves!*

Iggy struggled to calm her. *Don't fear. I'll speak with them, just like I spoke to you.* The animal crackled with anxiety. *Please. Haven't we come this far? I haven't forgotten my promise. But we aren't safe yet. Not quite.*

*Please.*

*You don't understand,* she whimpered. *The wolves won't help you! They are servants of the dark wood!*

Iggy's blood ran cold. *Servants...?* What did that mean?

*Does it even matter?* The riders from Keldale had to have their trail. They couldn't turn back. North and south along the road were equally futile.

He had to pray she was wrong.

*I won't force you to enter where it's not safe,* he tried to persuade her. *But we have to try. Death's behind us, coming fast.*

The mare wasn't soothed. Her fear shuddered in her muscles like a spasm. But she did as he asked.

The great wood grew, a giant emerging from the fog. When he saw the line of wolves, he quailed.

Part of him had been hoping they wouldn't be there, that their bizarre cause had somehow been appeased. Instead, there were even more than before: their line stretched along the edge of the forest to the limits of his sight. They sat bolt upright, their eyes alert and cold.

*It won't work.* He was suddenly certain of this. He felt closer to them than he'd ever thought possible–they had the same *mother*–but it didn't matter. One look at their eyes killed his hope.

"Iggy," Harth said.

Iggy silenced him with a hand, fighting to keep the despair from his face. Something else caught him, something he couldn't have seen before the nightmare dreams and insights of Keldale. An echo of the Pulse near the animals, deadened and grey.

*Just like at the inn.* It was like rounding the corner to find your parents being crucified.

He was starving and spent, his body lurid with saddle sores. His crippled mind struggled with this insight like an ape with a book, trying to figure out what it meant.

*They hunger.* The mare's plea shivered with panic.

"By Akir." Harth drew up, his eyes riveted to the wolves. "So many."

"Why stopping." Lyseira might have been talking in her sleep.

Iggy glanced back, looking for some sign of their pursuers, but there were too many hills. They could come over any one of them without warning, at any time. It was too late for second guesses.

He swung down, his legs wobbling like sodden branches. He'd brought them here. He had to try. "Wait here."

Seth shook his head. "Iggy–"

"If we get into the woods, they can't follow us."

"We don't have time for this!" Harth snapped. "These are *rabid wolves*! You can't–!"

"They're not rabid," Iggy threw back. "They'll–"

*They'll listen,* he'd started to say, but the words shriveled on his tongue. His friends were looking at him like he was a stranger, a madman with Iggy's face. *They won't understand.* The old terror of being discovered froze him.

Beyond the nearest ridge, a cloud of dirt was churning.

"Please," he said. "Wait." He turned his back on their outrage and went to the wolves. They rose as he came, the air suddenly humming with growls.

*You,* said the wolf with the burn on its cheek. It was the white he'd talked to on the way north. *You lied.*

It must have ranged miles north to meet him. It had to be a good sign. *We need to enter the wood,* Iggy whispered.

*No. Turn back.*

*We're hunted. We've nowhere to go.*

*You may not enter here.* Slaver glittered between its teeth.

*We won't harm you. I know you now.*

*Turn back!* It tensed to leap. The motion rippled through the pack as it followed his lead.

Iggy fumbled for something that would convince it. *Please,* he begged. Behind him, hoofbeats thrummed in the air. The Tribunal was coming. *Please.* An epiphany sparked, and he grabbed it.

*Our mother sent me.*

The white's growl stopped. It looked down. A whimper stole from its chest.

But when it looked at him again, its eyes glinted with murder.

*I don't want to kill you,* it said. *But I will. Turn back, or be slaughtered.*

The Pulse echoed between the words, tainted with grey.

*By Akir,* Iggy realized. *The mare was right. They're compelled.* His mind whirled.

*We can help you,* he said. *My friend knows this magic. She might be able to–*

In his urgency, Iggy took a step. The spell suffusing the wolves flared.

*No!* the white shrieked, but the sorcery seized it. Its next call crackled with frenzy.

*Slaughter them! Keep them out!*

They leapt as one: a wall of slavering fangs that shot through the grass like wildfire. Behind Iggy, the horses screamed. He turned to run, panicked–and his mind went blank with horror.

A squad of horsemen had crested the ridge.

He screamed a warning, but his companions mistook it. Seth dropped to the ground, eyes trained on the wolves. Syntal rose her hands, somehow mustering the strength for a final chant.

His stomach roiled as the Pulse shuddered behind him. Even at the edge of death, her magic repulsed him.

Then the enchantment on the wolves spasmed. Syntal's magic seized it, writhing and thrashing. The transformed spell blasted through the wolves like an invisible lightning strike. It punched Iggy in the back, sent him sprawling to the frozen ground.

The white's voice became an echo, grey and mindless. *Spare the chanter's pack. Allow them no harm.*

They thundered past him, splattering his face with grass and frozen dirt. As he struggled to his knees he saw Harth wheeling about to escape. Behind him, a soldier raised his sword. It flashed in the winter sun like a guillotine's blade.

Before he could swing, the wolves had him.

A breaking wave of teeth and claws crashed into the city soldiers. They screamed, slashing at the onslaught. Some turned to flee, and the avalanche of beasts tore their mounts' legs out beneath them. The road became an ocean of fur and blood.

Seth leapt to Lyseira and snapped a wolf's neck. It didn't fight back; the spell wouldn't allow it.

The sight triggered Iggy's voice at last. "Seth, no!" His friend snapped his gaze up, wild with the fever of combat. "They defend us! Look!"

Seth froze, trying to comprehend him–and a bugle call split the air. A second squad broke the ridge, this one with Preservers and clerics.

"Into the wood!" Iggy screamed. His eyes darted for his mount, but she had fled. "Follow me! Into the wood!"

His companions launched past him, Seth slowing just enough for Iggy to swing up behind him. They thundered toward the tree line, chased by the screams of soldiers and wolves alike.

Then they gained the trees, and the cursed forest swallowed them.

# Chapter 18

*i. Angbar*

Oh, the stories he could write now.

Weeks ago, when they'd first escaped from Southlight, he'd caught himself putting the events into a story; constructing an epic from the stuff of his own life as he ran. He'd been appalled. *This is no story,* he'd told himself. *Be serious.* Now, as branches slapped at him and the boughs of Veiling Green choked out the setting sun, he was doing it again. This time, though, turning everything into fodder for his epic wasn't appalling him. It was keeping him sane.

The hate in the eyes of the mob. The fire leaping as it devoured Marlin. The flashing arrows from the alleyways, the wolves crashing over the road, the–*oh, God*–the blood at the gates.

All of it held at arms' length, like an enraged dog snapping at the end of its leash.

*They tromped through the trees, nearly delirious with exhaustion*, he thought. *Still, somehow, the wolves left them alone. The Tribunal was nowhere to be seen. They had survived another night.* He blinked as he stared at the trees, fighting to stay upright. *He didn't even care. His eyelids had anchors tied to them. He was sore down to his bones. All he wanted was sleep, and to get off that curséd horse.*

"Here," Iggy called from ahead. They'd come to a little stream. A doe and her fawn bounded away. There was no snow on the ground. Angbar stared, waiting for these impressions to become something that made sense.

Seth swung down and helped Lyseira, then Marlin. Syntal crumpled when her feet hit the ground; Helix tried to hold her up and nearly went down with her.

*Need to help them,* Angbar thought, but instead he just stood there. His legs felt like jelly. Had he dismounted? He didn't remember dismounting.

"Is everyone... is everyone well?" Lyseira aimed the question at the trees, staring like a blind woman. Her hair was wild with sticks and char.

"We're all here," Iggy said. Angbar remembered watching him disappear beneath an avalanche of hacking swords, and felt a scream boiling in his throat. He grabbed the memory and stuffed it into the story to get away from it.

*His companion was dead. He'd been sure of it. But the girl with the long hair had healed him. Her God was as powerful as she'd always said.*

"Wasn't there a pack horse?" he said, surprising himself.

"Lost." Harth's voice was like lead. "Going out the gates." He blinked and looked at Helix. "Do you still have the money?"

Panic flickered in Helix's eyes. He was sitting with his back to a tree. He twisted to look at his belt, searching with his hands, and heaved a sigh. "Yeah," he managed. "Yeah, I still have it."

*How are we going to make camp without the pack horse?* Angbar said. Or meant to; his tongue never actually moved.

He realized he was sitting down now, his saddle sores blaring.

"What's your plan?"

The words froze everyone. They were the first Marlin had uttered since Keldale.

He was leaning against a tree, draped in rags and a blanket Seth had found for him. Without his hair or goatee he looked naked and old. "Do you have one?"

He was glaring an accusation at Lyseira. She stared past him, heedless.

*Yeah,* Angbar answered. *We're gonna die in the woods.* It was funny in his head. Something told him it wouldn't be funny out loud.

"I..." Helix stammered. "We have to... I have enough money for..."

"I'm talking to her," Marlin snarled. His voice was raw: burlap scraping over rocks. "Hey!" He snapped his fingers. "Did you have a plan when you charged into the fire?"

Lyseira started. "Me?"

Marlin scoffed, shaking. "*Sehk'akir*. Yes, you! You're the witch who charged the fire!"

Seth bristled. "Watch your tongue."

Marlin ignored him. "Did you have a plan?"

Lyseira's mouth worked. Nothing came out of it.

"You're going to die here," Marlin said. "You brought me out here to die."

"You were going to die in that fire!" Iggy snapped, incredulous. "You want to go back?"

"You have no idea what you've done. They won't stop until they have you."

*Some change of pace that'll be,* Angbar thought.

Iggy glowered. "You should be thanking her!"

"She's a *child!*" Marlin threw back. "You all are, and stupid ones at that! I gave you that spell," he seethed at Syntal, "so you could hide. Do you even understand that? How did you expect to survive this? They'll find you, and they'll gut you. All of you."

He threw out a hand in disgust and turned away. Lyseira stared at his back as if it were covered in maggots.

Angbar glanced at the others, dumbstruck and slack-jawed. Only Syntal seemed to have the right response: she lay down and passed out.

Shrugging, Angbar followed her lead.

*ii. Iggy*

He woke to a horn blast, sharp as an accusation, and bolted upright.

"Up," he said. The Tribunal was in the woods. They'd gotten past the wolves. They were coming. "Up, come on, we need to get moving."

Seth was by the fire, the only other person awake.

"The horn–didn't you hear the horn? Wake them up, come on!"

"No horn," Seth said. "You were dreaming."

*No horn.* He waited for his frantic heart to slow, searching the tree cover for some sign of the sun. There was light bleeding through the branches, but it was still low. Morning, then–unless the sun was moving backwards today.

Iggy rubbed his forehead, the horn's blare still echoing in his ears, and narrowed his eyes at Seth. "I said no fire."

Seth gave him a flat look. "We'd all have frozen to death in the night without it. It's winter. There's no choice."

*The forest won't let us freeze. It brought us here.* He could say the words. He might even mean them.

He could also just say, *Help me, Seth. I've lost my mind.*

The fire made him nervous, but there was something different about burning dead branches from the forest floor. No one was murdering trees here. The disgust that had seized him in Keldale left him alone.

He shrugged and went to relieve himself. When he came back, the others were awake.

"I told you," Harth was saying, "Shientel is out of the question."

"It's the only place Lorna's money will do us any good," Helix countered.

"It's the first place they'll look," Harth said.

Marlin sat hunched on a log, picking at a piece of bread. Iggy caught himself glaring at the man and looked away before speaking. "We can go anywhere the forest goes. Shientel, or the foothills of the Tears. Even around the Tears altogether. Head up toward Tal'aden."

"That'll take weeks on foot," Harth said.

"We have the horses," Angbar said.

"There are no roads!" Harth snapped. "The horses are just a liability until we get clear of the trees."

"We tried Keldale, Helix," Lyseira said. Her eyes were clear this morning. A night of rest had done her good. "It's time to go to the Fatherlord."

Helix's face fell. "Lyseira..." he started.

Seth shook his head. "Things have changed," he told her. "You stopped a witch-burning. Everyone saw Syntal. We've no chance of getting anywhere near the Fatherlord. We'll be arrested the instant we enter the gates."

Lyseira shook her head, stubborn. "He needs to know–"

"About the bad apples in Southlight?" Helix broke in. "And the priest that tried to burn Marlin, was he a bad apple, too? How about the ones that are still chasing us, the ones that might be in the woods right now? Them too?" He snapped his mouth shut, fuming. The fire crackled. "The *whole Church* wants us dead, Lyseira. I'm not going to Tal'aden."

"Then where–?" Lyseira demanded, but this time Harth cut her off.

"You really want to go to Tal'aden? Are you mad?"

"You're not coming!" Lyseira snapped. "We're done with you."

"Damned right I'm not coming. You'll freeze to death before you even–"

"Then shut your mouth!"

Harth's eyes flashed. "You would be *dead* if I hadn't–"

Angbar shot to his feet. "Enough! Hush! They might be in the woods right now!"

Everyone fell silent, glaring. In the back of the group, Marlin rolled his eyes.

Something about that triggered Iggy's tongue. "Southwest," he said. "We'll head to the edge of the Valley. Shientel's not safe, Keldale's not safe, Southlight's not safe. We have to get out of the Valley. From there, everyone can go wherever they think best."

Harth scoffed. "That's *weeks away!* We're gonna freeze–"

Iggy spoke over him. "You want to go back to the road?" he demanded. "You?" he spat, looking at Marlin. "Then go. Get out of here." He stalked to the fire and doused it. "But southwest is that way, and anyone who comes with me can get there."

~ ~

His scolding got them in line. They followed him as he picked his way through the wood, but he could feel them fraying behind him. Southwest was as good a direction as any, but really, Harth was right. They all were. There was no good choice. It would take weeks to reach the mountains of the Tears, with every night colder than the last.

*Just keep them moving.* While they were moving, they weren't fighting.

As highsun drew close, he started watching for a place to halt for lunch. A stream, maybe, or a meadow where they could see the sky for a time. He spotted a small stand of butterwoods dotting the banks of a creek. Butterwood was a rare tree here–except for their camp the night before, most of what he'd seen was spruce–and its broad cover had kept the ground free of snow.

"Here," he said. "Lunch."

*Yes,* something told him. *It's a great place for lunch, just like it was a great place to camp last night.*

His stomach flipped. *We've been hiking west for hours. This isn't the same place. It can't be.*

The others filed past him. None of them said anything. He put the similarity out of his mind, but when they started hiking again, he watched for landmarks.

Like the ravine they followed for a half-mile. The thin, frozen stream at its end. The fallen butterwood, two hours out.

At dusk, he started watching for another camp. He found a creek dotted with butterwoods.

"Iggy," Syntal said. "Is this–?"

"Shhh," he said. "I have to think."

"Circles?" Marlin sneered. "We've been running in *circles?*"

"I said shut your mouth," Iggy snapped. *Think, think, think.*

He closed his eyes, reflecting on the day's hike. After lunch he had changed course, but he'd still recognized the landmarks, and now he was back where he started.

The Church had to have gotten past the wolves by now. They could be here any minute.

*What did I do wrong?* he thought, fighting down his panic. *What am I missing? How–?*

He reached for the Pulse. It would give him his bearings better than any landmark. Every time he tried to focus on it, though, all he felt was a twinge of stale grey.

When he realized what was happening, his fear ruptured. Anger boiled out of it like pus from a boil.

"A spell," he spat. "There's a spell on the wood. Marlin's right; we've gone in circles all day."

"A spell?" Lyseira parroted, as Angbar said, "How do you know?"

"I just–" He snapped his mouth shut. *Careful.* "I don't get lost easy. Never have. It's..." An excuse came to him, and he grabbed it. "It's Veiling Green. Remember the old stories? It has to be why no one ever gets out."

As the words passed his lips, he realized he believed them.

He'd never actually thought the old stories were true. After the

Storm, nobody ever told them. No one got lost in Veiling Green anymore. No one could get past the wolves to even try.

A chill stole through him. He'd led them into a spider web, and now they were trapped. *The wolves tried to warn me.*

"Those are just stories," Harth said.

"Did you watch the moss?" Helix pressed. "The moss grows–"

"Yes, I watched the moss!" Iggy snapped, insulted. "And the sun." *And the Pulse.* "Come on, Helix. It's *me.* I'm telling you, there's something about the forest." His mind spun. Suddenly, he desperately wanted to find a wolf. *Are they actually trying to protect people? Do they know about this?* It sounded like a million other stories he'd heard after the Storm–a cursed forest, where no one who entered escaped alive. But it wasn't. That legend of Veiling Green was as old as he could remember. His dad had talked about it when Iggy was little, before the Storm.

*Then why did the wolves start guarding the borders* after *the Storm?*

The others were arguing: Harth insisting they head back to the road, Helix pushing to try again, Lyseira trying to calm everyone with her certainty that Akir would provide. They were a cloud of gnats, swarming in his ears. He couldn't think.

The Pulse deadened, the grey deepening. Syntal was chanting.

*This was a trap,* something gibbered in his mind. *It was her, the spell responded to her, she led us here! She tricked us! She–*

"Hush." Syntal stared into the trees, the fingers of one hand outstretched. "Iggy's right. There *is* a spell." Her eyes, green and vibrant in the dusk, searched the air as if reading invisible script. "Marlin, can you see it?"

"I know which chant you're using," he said, "but you didn't share it with me. Remember?"

She ignored him. Dead leaves crunched beneath her as she pivoted, her gaze locked on the trees. "It's everywhere," she breathed. Was there a trace of admiration in her voice? "It's... in the trees, floating–" She cut off. Her eyes widened.

"There's something out there."

Iggy followed her stare, but saw nothing.

"A light." She squinted into the dark. "I think it's... I don't know."

He glanced at her again, then back into the trees. He tried to hear the Pulse, and found only rushing grey.

"By Akir," Syntal whispered. "It's beautiful. Can't you see that?" She took a step forward.

"Syn." Helix took her shoulder. "Just wait. *M'sai?* What's out there?"

"A light. It's a light. You can barely see it through the trees, but..." She peered, her head bobbing. "I can get us there."

"There's no light out there," Seth said flatly.

"I used a chant. I never knew what it did before. But when Iggy said there was a spell, I tried it... I can see it now." She lifted a hand, staring at her fingers. "I can see it now." She flicked her gaze to Iggy, marveling. "It's all over you. No wonder you got lost. It doesn't want you to find it."

"Syn," Helix said. "You're not making any sense."

"You can't *see* it, Helix. But I can."

Helix ran a hand over his mouth. His eyes searched Iggy out, their meaning plain.

*Has she lost her mind?*

"We have to go there," Syntal said. The others exchanged glances.

"No." Marlin scoffed. "No, this wood is cursed, and you have no idea what you're dealing with." He turned. "You're fools. All of you. I'm going back."

"You aren't," Syntal said. "You'll get lost."

"I know how we came in. I'm not a fool."

Her head drifted when she shook it, like she was trapped underwater. "The spell will take you."

*She sounds mad,* Iggy thought, and another thought chased it: *She sounds just like I would, if I told them what happened in Keldale.*

"*M'sai,*" he said, his heart galloping. "Syntal, I'm with you."

"Iggy–" Seth began.

"No. I tried, Seth. There is something in this wood. You can't just hike it. I believe her."

"Just because she's seeing something with her magic, doesn't mean we should chase it down," Seth pressed. "What is it? Does she even know?"

"It doesn't matter." Syntal looked at him. "There's no other choice."

"Can you... walk away from it?" Harth asked. "Just... instead of taking us toward it, put it behind you? That would get us out, wouldn't it?"

She turned around, then shook her head. "The spell's on me, too. If I'm not looking at the beacon, I'll get lost."

"It's a beacon now?" Seth said, his eyes dark.

Syntal glared. "If you don't believe me," she said coldly, "try to get out on your own."

"All right," Angbar said. "Enough. It's dark, it's getting cold. We're not traveling any more tonight. And hey, at least we *know* this is a good camp site." The joke fell flat. "I'm starving. Let's eat. We can decide in the morning."

~ ~

Dinner was tense and quiet. Iggy took first watch. When the others were asleep, he crept around the fire and woke Syntal.

"Iggy?" she said, peering at him. "What's wrong?"

"Nothing." He sat on a log. "I need to talk to you."

She sat up, shivering, and pulled her blanket around her neck. "Aren't you cold?"

He realized he wasn't. His breath bloomed from his mouth in clouds, but he didn't even have a coat. "I'll get a blanket later. I want you to tell me what's going on."

She shook her head. "What do you mean?"

He hesitated. "I know you know more than you're telling us."

She drew back. "Oh?" she said, defensive. "And how do you know that?"

"Too many coincidences."

"*You're* the one who brought us to Wolfwood."

He said nothing. She watched him, her face flickering with shadows.

"You saw the spell," she finally said. "At the road, with the wolves. Didn't you?"

He swallowed and raised a hand. "I..."

"I saw you drop. I thought I'd hit you with it, at first. But I didn't. You saw what happened. It must have knocked you over."

"What did happen?" he pressed.

"I was right, back at the inn. You *can* feel it."

"What happened at the road?"

"Why haven't you told anyone?"

He rubbed his temple. This wasn't what he'd wanted.

"Iggy? Tell me. I sit here everyday with Seth's eyes burning into my back. You can hear it too, and you say nothing?"

"I don't," he snapped. "I don't say nothing. I try to help... when I can. I stood up for you last night. Remember?"

She stared at him, her eyes cold.

"It's... it's different for me." *What you do makes me sick.* "I don't have to chant. I don't have to say *mantras.* It just comes to me. I can hear it when it wants me to hear it. But I don't have to tell anyone. I don't have..." He groped for the words, gave a weak chuckle. "I don't have *light* shooting out of my hands. I can keep it a secret."

"Must be nice."

He flinched, then recovered. "It is. It is nice. I would like to keep it this way. I don't..."

*I don't know what it means. I don't know what it makes me.*

He met her eyes. "Please."

She sighed. "*M'sai.* You want to know what happened at the road?" She shook her head. "I have no idea."

She must have read the disbelief in his eyes. "I tried to put a few of them to sleep, and something happened to the spell. It transformed. I don't know how. I've been trying to figure it out."

"You didn't... do it on purpose?"

She scoffed. "If I could've done it on purpose, I would've done it on the way up."

He believed her. But she was hiding something.

"You know more than that," he said. "This light you saw in the trees... what is it?"

"I don't know."

He peered at her. "You have a guess."

"Maybe. But I've got my own secrets, Iggy." She rolled away, burrowing back into her blanket. "And I'm much better at keeping them."

# Chapter 19

## Before the Storm

*i. Syntal*

The book became everything.

Her parents were dead, haunting her dreams like specters, and the once-familiar walls of her aunt and uncle's home had transformed to prison cells. But under the porch was a secret, an impregnable mystery, and it consumed her.

She sneaked beneath the porch–always quiet, always unseen–whenever she could to look at it. She found a mark on its metal band, a sort of stylized *h* that she thought she recognized, though she couldn't remember from where. Sometimes Helix came with her, and he tried everything to get the book open, straining at the cover until his freckles blared like trumpets. He even snatched Uncle's smithing shears. When they failed to break the clasp, he got her permission to try cutting the cover itself. It was brittle leather, faded with age, but the shears couldn't even scratch it.

"It's some kind of magic," Helix panted after one of these sessions, his hair awry with sweat. "I bet you a hundred crowns. It has to be."

He sounded frightened, though he tried to mask it. The prospect frightened her, too. Everyone knew the story of Iis-alac and the witch's book.

But every night, the book glowed like a beacon in her dreams. Her mother sat with her secret smile, watching.

Summer came to an end, borne away by drifting golden leaves. Autumn brought rain and cold, and Auntie's increasing insistence that Syntal stay indoors. She was forced to think on the book instead of touching it, and finally, she remembered something about the symbol–something critical.

It was in First Tongue, the language of scripture.

~ ~

Abbot Forthin was old and dour. He scared her. On Dawndays, he always looked like he hated everyone; like he could see what they were really like inside, and it disgusted him.

But he was the only one in the village who might know what the symbol was.

She wrestled with this problem until the answer found her. The Night of *Rev'naas* was coming. The temple Keeper always gave a sermon that day, and at the end, everyone had to go up, one by one, for censure. She wouldn't need an excuse to talk to him. She would just have to remember to ask about the symbol while she was up there.

When the day came, service was the same as always. The temple Keeper–Father Samuel at her old church, Father Forthin here–came up and spoke with all the temerity of a wash rag. She fought to stay awake, speak when she was supposed to speak, and sing when she was supposed to sing.

She stared out the window, watching the sun hover when it should have been pushing toward noon. Her right hand idly twisted the black ring she'd found. It was still a little big, but she kept it on her thumb, and it usually stayed on when she put it there. *Maybe the ring has something to do with it,* she mused for the thousandth time. *It was in the cave, too.* But she'd inspected the ring inside and out, and there were no marks on it–it was just a plain, black ring. She and Helix had both tried to find some place on the book or its band where the ring might fit as a key. There was nothing there.

Father Forthin was telling the story of the demons, the same story Father Samuel always told on the Night. It was from the Chronicle, somewhere. An army of devils had come to Or'agaard, and the Fatherlord had cast them out. It was an exciting story, and scary if she thought too hard on it. Luckily, Father Forthin shared her old Keeper's knack for making everything boring.

"But the greatest of the devils," Forthin droned, reciting from a huge book laid open in front of him, "whose name shall not be penned, resisted him, saying: 'Art thou mad, great one? Truly, the Father of Heaven and Earth has given you this power to rebuke us, and we cannot resist it.'"

Syntal stifled a yawn.

"'But while your threat may frighten me, the evils of men grant me infinite courage. While your words may wound me, the black souls of mortals invigorate me without cease. While your rebuke may destroy me, the sins of your followers shall birth me forty times again.'"

*Sins,* Syntal thought. She'd complained to her father, once, about how boring Dawnday sermons were. *Keep listening,* he'd told her. *One day, they'll make sense.*

Abbot Forthin closed the great book and circled his heart. The congregation did the same, then rose. She found herself alone in a sudden forest of legs and pews, staring at the floor. The old cleric's voice, disembodied and grey, sought her out.

"For forty winters I've given the Night sermon, and you all know what to do. Keep your young ones inside. Keep the lights low. Await the dawn. Pretend you don't hear your kids, telling each other scary stories." A quiet chuckle murmured through the crowd. "But it's not just rote, or it shouldn't be. It *means* something, my children. Tonight is a night to reflect on our sins."

If her book had a mark from the First Tongue on it, she suddenly realized, it was probably just an old book of scripture.

The thought made her sag. She couldn't believe she hadn't thought of that earlier.

*It can't just be a book of scripture.* It had been in the water for a long time–years, maybe–and it never got damaged. The cover couldn't even be *cut.*

*Just more proof that it's scripture.* The voice in her head was Lyseira's, grating and smug. *There's a miracle on it, keeping it safe.*

She wished she could show it to Angbar. He'd have some good ideas.

"All of us experience hardship, and all are eager to lay the blame for it on Akir. But the lesson of the Night of *Rev'naas* is simple: we are to blame for our own hardships."

The words trickled past her musings and snagged in her mind. Something about them made her look up.

"Our *rev'naas* creates evil, just as the Unnamed Devil said. And what creates *rev'naas*?"

*Sin,* Syntal thought again. This time the word felt like a thorn.

"Our sins. Every lie, every skipped tithe, every lustful thought. People ask, 'Does Akir hate us? Why does He bring illness? Why does He bring floods?' But the story of the Unnamed Devil answers these questions. Akir doesn't bring us calamity. We bring it on ourselves."

Floods?

Why does He bring *floods?*

A black horror stirred in her chest, flicking its tongue like a serpent.

She had skipped censure. She had told lies.

Once, she had found a silver shell–*a whole shell*–and hadn't asked her parents to break it into heels so she could tithe from it. She always told herself she'd forgotten, but that wasn't true.

She'd chosen to keep it.

*Why does He bring floods?*

That beautiful image of her mother sitting at the table, smiling her secret smile, dissolved into a memory of her casket.

"Oh," she murmured. Her eyes were burning.

"It's easy–so easy–to think, 'This one won't matter.' 'I'm only human.' But when we hurt others, we hurt ourselves."

*When we hurt others.*

She saw the rock she'd hurled at Ellic Baler, that day at the tree house. She saw the blood burst from his head, heard Helix demanding, *What'd you do that for?*

Auntie had tried to send her to censure for that. Syntal had refused. *I'll go when I get home,* she'd said, but even that had been a lie.

A month later, her parents had drowned.

"Let us recite the Seven Sacred Principles," Father Forthin said. The people around her answered in one voice.

*"Obey the word of the Fatherlord, for He is Akir in the flesh.*

*"Slay not thy fellow man.*

*"Seek not the power of your Creator, save with His blessing and through the hand of His Church.*

*"Do unto others as you would have them do unto you.*

*"In all things, seek the righteous path.*

*"Carry the scripture of your God into all the lands and hearts of men.*

*"Mind your brother's sin as you would your own."*

She should be speaking, reciting the Principles with the others, but her tongue lay dead in her mouth. It was just another sin, heaped atop the others.

The recitation ended, and the Father prayed.

"Al'Akir above, who is Father and Guardian, Savior and Punisher, bringer of all things righteous, I beseech thee to hear my mortal voice.

"The Night of *Rev'naas* comes soon, and your wayward children need guidance. Some are being punished even now, Father. They know their sins. They suffer with their guilt, with their misery and pain. Their *rev'naas* weighs on them.

"Find their hearts. Work in them, that they might seek censure and lay bare their faults. Let them be washed clean of *rev'naas*."

*Washed clean.* The words were an impossible promise. If she had sought censure sooner, before the flood, then maybe...

Her heart twisted. Why had she been so wicked? Why hadn't she listened?

*But Akir is* God, she pled with herself. *If He can cleanse me, maybe they'll come back.*

The body they'd buried was unrecognizable. Maybe it hadn't been her mother. Maybe the whole thing was a trial from Akir, meant to show her how wicked she was and force her to repent.

She had learned her lesson. Maybe He could spare her now.

The prayer ended. The villagers started talking or filing toward the exit. Only a few trickled forward to the altar, where Abbot Forthin stood waiting.

"Where is everyone going?" she said, grabbing her aunt's hand. "It's the Night! Everyone has to go up!"

Auntie glanced down. She looked pained, like an adult who knew she was breaking the rules, and had to try to explain it. "Not everyone always goes, honey," she said. "The Abbot doesn't..." She touched Syntal's cheek. "Are you crying?" Her faced melted with concern. "Oh, honey–"

"I have to go up!" She shouldered past her and pushed into the aisle. "I have to!"

"Syn?" Helix asked, but she ignored him and kept her eyes nailed to the floor. Her cheeks burned. Censure was supposed to be private, between priest and sinner, on every day of the year but this one. *That's why we all go,* Dad had told her more than once, *so no one is singled out.* But here they didn't all go. Here, she had to go alone.

If she had killed her parents, maybe she deserved it.

She was the last in line. Every eye in the temple bore into the back of her head as she waited.

"Syntal Smith," the Father finally said. Her new family name left her ears ringing. "Speak to me," he said, beckoning.

"I..." Her tongue betrayed her. It wouldn't move.

"Tell me," he said again. His hand cupped her chin, tilted her eyes to his. The compassion she saw there jolted her.

"It's just my parents." She couldn't trust her own voice. It was a writhing snake, trying to escape. "I hurt Ellic Baler real bad, but I didn't mean to. I really didn't."

She searched his eyes, desperate for some sign that her appeal would matter. They didn't change.

"But I think... I heard what you said, and I... I mean, what if I...?"

Something–some final brace against her horror–gave way. She felt it disappear, swallowed by the dark as surely as a bridge falling into the river, and an anguish she had never known thundered through the gap.

"It was my *rev'naas*, Father! I should've gotten censure! I did all these bad things, and I never got censure! I want... is it too late? I want it! Please! I would've been better if I knew! I just didn't know! I swear, but I just... it's too late, because they're dead, and I can't... I *can't...*!"

He knelt, shushing. "Child, no. No, no, no. Here." He pulled her close. "Hear me. No censure today. You lost your parents. That's censure enough for one childhood."

He put a hand on her forehead, clammy and trembling.

"Father, help this girl," he prayed. "Cleanse her soul of the evils she's invited. Bring her peace in this time of repentance and grief, that she might resist whatever new darkness will come."

She closed her eyes. His prayer was hot against her face, foul with his breath. She was desperate to believe in its power. But when his hand left her head, her pain only deepened, festering in her chest like an infection.

Her parents wouldn't come back. What kind of baby would ever believe they could?

"You are cleansed, child," he said. "Go and work the will of Akir from this day forth."

Absolution slipped away. The Abbot was grave, his eyes watchful, as if he knew she still suffered.

The illusion of restored innocence was all she had. Dreading that he might press her, she turned to escape.

Her vision snagged on the bookshelf. The symbol from her book was on one of the spines.

"Syntal?"

She glanced at him, then back to the shelf. Before the Father could speak she blurted, "Is that First Tongue?"

He followed her pointing finger, taken aback. "Which? The one at the end?"

"The first one."

The Abbot searched her face. "Yes, of course."

"What does it mean?"

His eyes narrowed; for a heartbeat, she feared he would ask why she wanted to know.

"That's the book of Gilleus, the very first book of the Chronicle," he finally said. "The word is *salgo.* It means 'begin,' or 'speak the truth.'" He gave her a small smile. "For Gilleus, it means both of these, hm?"

*Salgo.* It meant nothing. It did nothing to unravel the book's mysteries.

In her mind, her mother's smile faded. Syntal was stupid after all.

"Go on now," Father Forthin said. "I believe your mother's waiting outside."

This jerked her back to reality. *What?* She reeled. *How...?*

When she realized what he meant, her confused hope shattered. The familiar weight of her guilt fell on her, and she turned to find her aunt.

~ ~

When the sun set, Auntie Bella locked the doors and lit a single candle in each window, dousing all other lights as the Canon commanded. The family ate dinner in cold silence as flames flickered in the sills.

After, Auntie put her to bed in Beth's room. Beth was Helix's older sister. She hated having Syntal in her room. She was always giving her mean looks and kicking her out.

"Sleep well," Auntie said, tucking the blankets under Syntal's chin in the wan light of the window candle. She gave her a gentle kiss on the forehead and left.

Her godparents murmured in the hallway. The door to their bedroom clicked closed, leaving only black silence.

Her sins started whispering.

*If I had told the truth about the time I lost Mom's ring, would she still be alive?*

*If I had held that rock instead of throwing it at Baler, would the storm not have come? Maybe if I had agreed with Lyseira more quickly, and offered to help him sooner?*

*If I sin again, will I lose Helix, or Aunt and Uncle?*

Sometimes, in the Night stories, people were so wretched that demons manifested in the flesh to claim them.

The door creaked open. As if summoned by her thoughts, a shadow leaked through.

Her heart froze. She jerked a finger toward her heart, clawing out a circle as if it had some power to protect her.

"Syn? Beth?" Helix's voice floated from the devil's shadow.

"Helix!" Beth hissed from her own bed. "Are you sure they're asleep?"

A lantern lit with a soft *whoosh.* Helix's grin swam out of the dark, draped in flickering shadows.

"I heard 'em snorin'," he whispered. "They're out."

Beth chewed her lip.

"They don't care anyway, long as we're quiet."

"All right," Beth said. "Come on."

A sliver of dread pricked Syntal. *They're gonna tell Night stories.*

Her parents had told her Night stories once. Nightmares had

tormented her until dawn; eventually she had fled to her parents' bed, shivering. Every year since, they'd promised not to do it again.

But her parents couldn't protect her now. In this house, their promises meant nothing.

"Can we skip stories this year?" Syntal said. She sounded like a baby. She hated how desperate she was.

Helix's face fell. "Skip *Night stories*?"

"We always tell Night stories," Beth said.

"I know, but I'm just... I'm really tired. I want to go to sleep."

"Then go to sleep," Beth retorted.

"Well..." Helix looked torn. "Just, maybe be quiet. For real, quiet."

"I will be," Beth said. "But we're definitely telling stories, 'cause I heard one that really happened. In Coram."

*That's a real town.* Syntal had heard adults talk about it. And if the town was real...

*The stories aren't true, kiddo,* Dad used to say. *It's just fun to scare each other sometimes.* But he was dead now. His consolation was an echo from a ghost.

Beth told them about a family of four, and the screams that came from their house. The doors that rattled, and the red light shining through the walls. The family was never found.

She told about a boy and his father. The boy was murdered, but the father still heard him screaming in the hallways.

Then came the young mother. A demon came to her dreams, pretending to be God. It made her kill her baby.

Syntal huddled beneath her blanket, each new story like the lash of a whip. She asked Beth again to stop, but by then the girl smelled blood. She tried to get to sleep, but when she closed her eyes, there was nothing but Beth's voice.

When Beth started nodding off, Syntal begged Helix to leave the lantern.

"Sorry, Syn." He sounded like he meant it, but that only made it worse. "I'll get in trouble."

When he left, darkness swallowed her.

Demons clawed at the window. From beyond them came a distant, dying scream. *Branches,* she told herself. *Wind.* But these were only words. They were no defense against horror.

She was rigid and sweating, her eyes fixed to the low-burning candle in the window.

Then she was running, and something was chasing her.

Its breath was hot on the back of her neck. She was pounding up the road toward home, but home was gone, and all she could see was the Smith house. She shrieked for help, but no one came. They had left her to her fate. After all, she was the one who chose to be out in the Night.

She was the one who had killed her parents.

*I didn't kill them!* she screamed, but no one heard; no one believed her. She didn't even believe herself.

She reached the house, bounded up the stairs, but her first step onto the porch plunged through rotted wood. She pitched, flailing, into the dirt beneath.

She saw Helix's sword, but it was rusted and useless. Her book perched on its crate like a queen on her throne.

Above, her predator loomed: black smoke, with bleeding red eyes. It hissed an accusation at her, so true it made her sob. She scrambled to her feet, lunging for the book. A word burned in her mind, but it was too alien. It slipped through her thoughts and into the dirt.

As she fumbled, the beast poured itself through the hole, violating the sanctity of the place beneath the porch, filling it with darkness. She wanted to scream, but couldn't. She was staring at a black ceiling. *Where did it go? Oh God, where* is *it?*

She sat up, throwing wild glances everywhere. She saw a guttering candle in the sill and felt sheets soaked with sweat.

*Sheets. A pillow.* Somehow, she was back in bed. Where was the thing that was hunting her? Was it gone?

She wanted to wake Helix, to crawl into bed with Aunt and Uncle. Even call to Beth. But she deserved none of those things, and her clenched throat would not allow them. Instead she threw the blankets over her head. It was a mistake.

When she took her eyes from the window, it boiled over with terrors.

~ ~

Dawn crowded in gently, a whisper of grey at the window that slowly bloomed into a pale aura. When the sun's long caress touched her bed, she hurled the blankets away and sat up, her heart finally slowing.

Her nightdress clung to her like seaweed, heavy with sweat; her bed reeked of stale fear. She listened–for retreating devils, for God's judgment, for Beth or anyone else who might be awake–and heard nothing. She was alone.

Quietly, she set her feet on the floor. She might have stepped barefoot onto a frozen lake. The breath curled from her lips. Her sweat-soaked shift began to freeze, and she started shivering.

The violence in her muscles drove out the last of her terrors. She dug out her warmest clothes, relishing their dryness as she pulled them on. Geese flew by outside, honking, but the sound only enhanced the morning's repose. The world was frozen. Waiting for her.

With the sudden certainty of a prophet, she knew why.

The bedroom door slid open at her touch; the hallway beyond flowed past her like a dream. Outside, the wild morning air shimmered with mist. The surrounding houses were islands, floating in a sea of clouds.

She stole across the porch and down the steps. Hoary morning grass crackled between her toes. At the old, bowed board she cast about, looking for someone who might see her–but this was her dream, her destiny, and it preserved her from intruders. Reassured, she entered the secret realm beneath the porch.

The sun's blurry light shivered between the shadows of the porch slats. The stillness amplified the sanctuary's beauty. It left her heart aching as if she had come to a temple, but there was no shame for her here. Instead, her breath burned with exhilaration.

The crate rested like an ark against the house's foundation, her book atop it. She drew it down, and its solemn weight triggered a final assault from her nightmares: a memory of a demon, pouring itself beneath the porch like blood. Even then, she'd known the book was her salvation. But in the dream she'd been a victim. The word she needed had escaped her, and everything she feared and hated had caught her as a result.

She was tired of being afraid.

She was no longer dreaming.

*Salgo. It means 'begin,' or 'speak the truth.'*

The book was on its spine, the ancient symbol facing her. She traced it wonderingly with her finger.

"*Salgo,*" she said.

And the world obeyed.

# Chapter 20

*i. Syntal*

Asleep in Veiling Green, she dreamt of shattering skies.

A flash of scarlet glimmered between the porch slats; a ripple of emerald bathed her face.

She emerged to find Thakhan Dar crowned with lightning: violet and azure, ivory and pitch. It leapt around the peak like a litter of puppies. A bolt tore loose, bounding overhead in a streak of green fire. Another followed, splashing her with silver. Their colors flickered in the mist.

Then silence fell like a shadow, and the sky exploded.

Lightning slashed the dawn to ribbons. Blue and red and gold crashed mutely into each other, birthing new hues. It was beautiful and primal. It was furious and limitless.

It was hers.

A savage joy ignited in her breast, burst from her in laughter. The sound sparkled in the silence.

"What then?" Angbar asked.

The dream shifted; she was in her room. Helix's friends were with her.

She'd had this dream before. It was comfortable, but bittersweet. The others were listening; they cared what she said. Their eyes were empty of judgment.

That was how she knew it was a dream.

"Then the book was open," she told them, still smiling. "Then I read what Lar'atul wrote, and learned to chant."

"Weren't you scared?" Seth asked.

No. She wasn't scared. The Storm had taught her how to *stop* being scared.

With the clarity of dreams, she told them.

"After my parents died, everyone called the flood 'the storm.' Do you remember that?"

They nodded. Of course, they all remembered.

"It was a legend. No one had to explain what storm they were talking about. They were talking about the one that drowned my parents.

"But the morning I opened the book, that changed. There was a new storm. It replaced the old one with something amazing and beautiful. Now when people say 'the Storm,' they're talking about what I did. Don't you see?

"I made 'the Storm' mean something wonderful."

They smiled at her. They all understood.

All but one.

"*Wonderful?*" Marlin accused. "You brought the end of the world."

"It's not," she tried to say. "The Church says–"

"People have starved to death. The sun rises in the *south.*"

"I know." She hesitated, flustered. If anyone could understand, surely he could. "But it's not... I don't think..."

"You don't *know.*" He glared, eyes flashing. "You're playing with fire." Smoke curled from his chest. He was smoldering.

"*Fire.*"

~ ~

She woke shivering, staring at a butterwood tree, and waited. It was always like this after a nightmare, and she'd had many. She waited for her eyes to accept the reality of the sun, for her groaning limbs to report that yes, the ground was solid. She waited for the sounds of camp–for her cousin's earnest whispers or Angbar's nervous laugh–to draw her back to the world.

The sun soaked in. Her leg reported a rock lodged against her knee. But the camp was silent. She sat up to find the fire dead and everyone asleep–even Seth.

*I'm the first one awake?* she marveled. She was *never* the first one. *Shouldn't someone be up all the time?* Seth talked about watches every night, but she couldn't remember who was supposed to be on third last night.

She crunched through dead leaves and undergrowth to her cousin. "Helix," she said, touching his shoulder. "It's morning."

He didn't stir, but Seth's eyes snapped open.

"What happened?" he demanded.

"What?" Syntal said. "What do you mean?"

Seth ground his teeth. "It was my watch. I couldn't have fallen asleep."

*Well, apparently you did.* She bit back the comment, but it gave her a guilty flush of pleasure to see Seth fail at something. *Seems you're not as perfect as you think.*

"Where are the horses?" he said.

*Horses?* Syntal started to nod at the tree, where Iggy had tethered the animals the night before, and froze. The tethers were empty.

"Where's Marlin?" Seth growled. Syntal followed his eyes.

The magician was gone.

*No.*

*Oh, no.*

"Up!" Seth barked, shoving Iggy with his foot and moving on to Lyseira. "Quick!"

Helix roused, blinking. "What? What is it?"

"Marlin," Syntal told him. "He took the horses."

Helix boggled. "What?"

"I was on second watch," Seth said. "He chanted me. He must have."

Everyone was awake now, climbing to their feet, checking their things.

*My book,* Syntal realized with dread. *Oh, God, my book.* She darted to her bedroll. Her sack was a twisted mess, tangled with her blankets just as she'd left it last night, and the book was still in it. He must not have been able to get it without waking her.

She sagged, her heart thundering. The book was everything.

"The money." Helix's voice was grey. He held a pair of cut leather strings in his hand. "He got the money."

Harth stalked across the clearing and grabbed Helix's hand, staring at the strings as if reading the stars. Then his eyes darkened. "Where is he?"

"Gone," Seth said. "It was second watch. He's got hours on us."

"Do you know how much money that was for them? *Twenty crowns?*"

"Maybe," Lyseira stammered, "Helix–maybe you dropped it? Or animals chewed it off?"

"It's cut," Harth retorted. "Not chewed. And Marlin's gone.

Don't be a fool."

Lyseira glared, but the barb struck her. She said nothing.

"I'm going after him," Harth said. Seth nodded.

"You can't," Syntal said.

"Iggy," Harth continued as if she hadn't said anything, "can you tell which way he went? You're a tracker, right?"

"You *can't*," Syntal said again. "The spell will take you."

Harth whirled on her, his jaw quivering. She met his eyes. There was anger there, but there was even more confused fear–an emotion she knew well. She waited, staring him down.

"Wait," Angbar said. "Wait, wait, wait. Can't we just stay here? Won't the curse just force him in circles, like yesterday?"

Everyone looked at her.

*How should I know?* They had never trusted her–not even Helix–and now, they expected her to know everything? She was an *expert?*

*I've read one book,* she wanted to snap, *written in a dead language, by a man with terrible handwriting.* Seth was glaring a challenge at her. *You were ready to burn it when we left.*

But Seth hadn't asked her the question. Angbar had. His eyes were the only ones without an accusation.

She drew a deep breath. The frozen air burned her throat; gave her the strength to shove her old pain aside. "I don't know. You lot look at me like I know everything." *Like I cursed the wood myself.* "I don't. I'm guessing. *M'sai?*"

Angbar nodded, his face soft with empathy. Most of the rest of them glanced away, chastised. Seth's glare remained.

"But my guess is no. He won't come back here." Before Angbar could voice his question, she went on. "We were following Iggy yesterday. We went in circles because that's what the spell did to *him.* I don't think... I don't think it would affect everyone the same way."

That was probably true. When she chanted slumber, some people slept longer than others; others somehow resisted the Pulse's command altogether, and didn't sleep at all.

But the truth was, she didn't want to wait. She wanted to hike to that beacon. The only other thing that had ever been so enticing was the book itself.

"She's just guessing," Seth said. "If we went in circles yesterday, there's no reason to think–"

"Yes," Angbar interrupted. "She just said that. She still knows better than you."

"I'm going after him," Harth repeated.

"Didn't you hear her?" Iggy said. "You'll get lost."

"She just admitted she doesn't know that for certain."

No one was looking at her now. She was just an oracle to them: a curiosity to be prodded for answers and then argued over.

Angbar threw her an apologetic look. He knew what they were doing. She caught his eyes and shook her head. *Forget it.* It had always been like this, for both of them.

She twisted her ring and waited.

The argument raged on. If Marlin didn't come back, where else could he go? Was it possible he could get out?

No, she told them. The curse would have him, and he didn't have the spell he'd need to see past it.

They didn't hear her. It was too much money. He had half their food. They had saved his life. How could he do this?

"I don't know what it means," Lyseira finally cut in. "I saved him. I don't know why he'd do this." She blamed herself for what had happened–Syn could see it in her face. "But we have to listen to Syntal. She's the only one who knows the way out of here."

"We don't know that it leads out," Seth urged.

"I know." She touched his shoulder. "I *know that.* But it's the only chance we have."

Harth was quiet, his mouth a pale line. "No. Even if we get out of the Valley, without any money, we're dead."

Helix nodded with him, ashen. He loved Syntal; but he didn't *trust* her.

"Enough," Iggy said. "No one's chasing him without me, because no one else here will be able to track him." He looked at Helix and Harth. "That means no one's chasing him, because I'm going with Syn." He began to gather his things.

"Iggy–" Harth started.

"*No.*" Iggy turned on him. "I'm sorry you didn't know

everything when you signed up. I don't think we even knew it all. I didn't mean to get you into this, not like this. But we're not in Keldale anymore. You're not in charge." He glanced at Seth. "Neither are you."

Seth's face was like stone.

"Don't you see?" Iggy went on. "We never should have come here. I was wrong to bring us in." He shook his head. "It was stupid. Those stories–all those old stories about people never coming out–they're *true.* And the next one is going to be about us.

"The Tribunal, all that *sehk*–it doesn't matter. You're worried about food? Our food will run out even faster if we waste it going nowhere. We have to pray it lasts until we reach Syntal's beacon, whatever it is.

"We follow her, or we die. Does that clear things up for you?"

~ ~

She didn't need the mantras anymore; she hadn't used them in years. Ascending, now, was as simple as twisting a key.

She unlocked her mind, and felt reality fall away beneath her.

The world became a web of concepts, succinct and intricate. There was no dirt under her feet, only hardness and friction and millions of pinpricks of life. There was no air in her lungs; there was wind or stillness, sustenance or death.

The Pulse thundered. All these truths echoed its commands. As always, she yearned to lose herself, to drown in insights.

That, Lar'atul had warned, was the danger.

She chanted, the words flicking from her tongue like darts. Her voice *became* the Pulse. She ordered her eyes and thoughts to align anew; to see differently.

Then she Descended.

Mundane reality crashed back. The world became pretense and nonsense, shallow as a sheet of parchment. She shuddered. Every time, the loss was vicious: as acute as her parents' funeral.

The others watched expectantly. To them, she knew, nothing had happened.

*None of you understand,* she wanted to accuse. *None of you know what it's like.* They had no idea what the world even was. They were blind people, all of them, living in caves.

"*M'sai,*" she murmured. "Follow me."

With her new sight, she scanned the trees. The curse was draped over the branches, drifting in the air like a cobweb. It caught in her companions' hair and tangled in their minds. *This way,* it might have whispered. *You are lost.*

*Who could have done this?* she wondered. If the spell covered the entire wood, it had to be enormous. It wasn't natural–the spellsight made that clear–but where had it come from?

Part of her couldn't help admiring it. It put her own sorceries to shame.

She pivoted, searching, until she caught a flicker of light from deep in the wood. It throbbed like a heartbeat, barely visible one second, brilliant the next. *There.* It had to be miles away, behind countless trees, but somehow she could see it.

*Definitely a beacon.* She started walking.

The curse swirled like disturbed mist, dragging at her feet and snaking into her ears. She was suddenly certain she'd forgotten something back at the camp. Her legs were tired; she wanted to rest. She was thirsty. She had to go back.

*No,* she told herself. *I'm not stopping.* Gritting her teeth, she waded through the curse as if it were a river of mud.

"Syn," Iggy said. "That's the way we came in."

Annoyed, she looked back. His face wore a shroud of grey mist. "I have to keep my eyes on the light," she said. "Don't make me keep turning back."

~~

The spellsight wouldn't last forever. She had to concentrate on it, and the effort wore on her. It was like walking with her arms held out straight, for hours. At the same time, every glance away from the beacon emboldened the curse, giving it the chance to snarl her thoughts.

These things were making her slow enough, but every other step was plagued by a stumble in the snow or a rocky patch of earth.

Worse, the others forced her to halt again and again as the curse tricked them into wandering away.

The constant distractions gnawed at her concentration, chipping away at her mind like a sculptor's chisel. The seed of a headache formed in her skull.

"Syn," Helix asked when they paused for lunch, "are you well?"

"It's tiring." She tried to reassure him. "But I'm well."

"If you need a break, or a nap..."

His concern was comforting. He didn't trust her magic–he never had–but he still cared for her. She nodded. "I'll tell you."

The hours crept past. Inside her snow-soaked shoes, socks clung to her feet like moss. Her vision turned blurry, the beacon becoming a smear of light behind the trees. Her headache grew to a roaring throb.

She lifted an arm to wipe her nose. Her sleeve came away dark with blood.

Then she was falling.

"Syn!" Helix and Angbar towered above her, tall as the trees.

"No... no more," she managed. "Too much."

"She's bleeding," Helix called to the others. "We have to stop."

"Stop?" Seth sounded incredulous. "There must be two hours of light left. We can't waste them."

"She needs rest!" Helix threw back.

She let the spellsight go. Releasing her mind's hold on it felt like uncurling a fist that had been clenched for days. She winced, moaning.

The curse's grey tendrils disappeared from sight.

"It's the witchcraft." Seth's face crowded into her vision, glaring down. "You must know it. The sorcery's doing this to her."

Angbar gaped at him. "Her *sorcery* is the only reason we're alive, fool!"

Helix laid out a bedroll for her. She crawled into it, left the argument behind, and plunged into darkness.

~ ~

The pain was gone in the morning. It always was.

Since they'd left Southlight, she had pushed herself further than ever before. She could chant or focus until her eyes bled and her muscles screamed, and a night of rest would always refresh her. But there was a line she couldn't press past. Beyond it she wouldn't be able to rest, because she'd be dead.

She'd glimpsed that line at the edge of the wood, when she'd chanted her last slumber spell at the wolves. She didn't want to find it again.

Harth caught her alone as the others broke camp. "Are you certain of this?" he muttered. Iggy's challenge yesterday had left him subdued; he'd hardly spoken since. "Every instinct I have is telling me to turn around. But I'm trying to trust you."

She gave him a wan smile. "I'm certain," she lied. "There's no other way."

She Ascended and slipped back into spellsight, a horse getting fitted with a bit. She set out, Seth's ire burning between her shoulders.

The ache in her mind returned slowly, creeping over her like a shadow. After lunch, her vision blurred again, and the nosebleed started. She pressed on. By the time dusk stole over them, she wondered through the constant scream of pain in her mind if she was going blind.

"Enough," she whimpered, sinking to her knees. "Enough." She slept.

The next day was the same, only colder. And the day after that. They took to walking with blankets draped over their shoulders, shivering as they stumbled through the snow.

The beacon didn't look any closer, but she told the others it did. The curse wasn't just trying to turn them around; it was wearing on their resolve, convincing them with every passing hour that they were wrong to follow her, that she was delusional. She had to do something to combat it; something to reassure them.

By the fourth night, even Angbar was doubting her.

The next morning, they ran out of food.

"It's all right," Iggy said. Unlike everyone else, he seemed *stronger* each morning, as if the forest's grueling trials rejuvenated him. "I've been watching. There are still berries on the bushes, and plenty of rabbits."

Her hollow stomach gave the lie to his confidence. He talked of food, but what he had was words.

They couldn't eat words.

*We're going to die here.* A wind cut through the trees, making the curse flutter and dance. *We're going to die.* They had talked about it–Harth had glibly mentioned *freezing to death* a hundred times–but now, she truly imagined them all collapsed beneath the trees, too weak to continue. Iggy's bizarre optimism would chase them as they fell, making vapid assurances until the snow covered them.

*No. I won't let it happen. I'll Ascend–I'll* rewrite what hunger is *before I let it happen.*

But there was no chant for that. She couldn't just command anything. She needed a chant, and she had no idea how to craft them.

Her sorcery was everything, but in the end it would fail her.

Ascension beckoned; an infinite, perfect world of ideas. Maybe she didn't know the chant she needed, but the Pulse could do anything. Maybe, if she was desperate enough, she could figure out Lar'atul's "safehold," and plumb the depths of the Pulse for answers. And if she couldn't...

She steeled herself, drawing defiance around her like a blanket.

If she couldn't, she would hurl herself into the Pulse anyway, would push until her mind snapped and left her body behind. If there were revelations to be found, she would find them.

She turned her back on Iggy's surety and trudged through the snow. The others followed. Highsun came and went, and Iggy distributed the berries he'd managed to pick. There were a few for everyone. Eating them felt like spitting on a bonfire.

Then, without warning, the trees gave way.

She stumbled into a meadow. An oblong stone building hunched in its center, at the bottom of a shallow depression. Fingers of browning vines clutched its walls, dragging it into the earth with the slow determination of centuries.

She was so prepared for failure that she wondered if it was a trick of her mind. But the beacon was here, throbbing in the meadow's heart like a toothache. It was on the building's only door.

"*Kirith a'jhul,*" Angbar breathed.

As she left the trees, the curse ended. Its whispers ceased so abruptly she nearly stumbled.

"Syn?" Helix said. Turning back, she saw the curse retreating from all of them. Its grey tendrils halted at the tree line, curling in an invisible breeze.

"We made it." She could barely believe the words herself. "It's gone. Can't you feel that?" A whisper of relief tingled in her mind, like the first hint of warmth in a limb gone numb with cold. "We made it."

They filed into the clearing. Despite the cold, despite the danger, she had a sudden, potent memory of their days as children, exploring Pinewood forest. The days when Southlight had been a haven, not a prison. The days when her mother still smiled.

"What is this place?" Angbar marveled, his voice a whisper. "It's so *old*."

The edges of the hollow were too steep to climb down safely, but at the far end from the building, a path led down. Syntal picked her way toward it. "I don't know." There was no reason to think the building had food inside–it looked as ancient as a tomb. But it could provide shelter from the snow. Maybe they could start a fire inside it, without being seen, and keep the heat enclosed.

And the Tribunal had no chance of finding it. The curse ensured that.

A spark of quiet hope, a thrill of vindication, stole down her spine. *We may survive this.* She grappled with it, trying to keep it on a leash. The door still had a spell on it–the beacon, at least, if not something else. They were still surrounded by a curse. She had to be careful. But her sudden optimism would not be stifled.

*We may survive.*

The path was a line of worn stones, bulging with snow and tufts of dying grass. It sloped down the basin toward the old ruin. A row of statues, their features worn into smooth stone, lined the path on either side. Some of them listed. One had lost its battle with the ages and snapped in half, its legs still jutting from the ground in surprise.

The crumbling stones beckoned. She started down, her eyes locked on the light welling from the building's entrance: the light only she could see.

Seth called for her to wait. She ignored him. The faceless statues watched as she passed them, their admonitions meaningless.

The ruin grew as it approached. It was taller, down here, than it had looked from above. She reached the door and hesitated. The beacon was brilliant now, shining like the sun.

Shuddering, she reached toward it... and felt only cold stone.

"By Akir," Lyseira breathed from somewhere behind her. "Can you read it, Syntal?"

*You don't "read" a spell,* she thought, irritated. *I can barely look straight at it.*

Lyseira drew up next to her and touched the light. "That... I think that's First Tongue."

*First Tongue?* For an instant she was even more annoyed–then she realized what Lyseira was seeing. She squinted, peering past the pulsing spell to the door itself, and saw markings.

A triangle was carved into the stone, its tips capped to form smaller triangles in each of its corners. The entire shape encompassed a cross. Beneath was a line of First Tongue script, caked with dirt. Lyseira scrubbed at it with the corner of her blanket.

"Safe... hold?" she read, "of the Faithful."

"*Safehold?*" Angbar echoed from behind them.

"Let those who are... guided, and those who have..." She leaned in, peering. "*Come before...* find rest in the arms of Akir."

*Seek the safehold.* Syntal felt faint, as if she suddenly stood atop a mountain peak.

*It doesn't mean anything,* she told herself. How could this be what Lar'atul had meant? He said to seek it, not stumble across it by accident.

*But I didn't stumble across it,* she realized. The beacon flared, rippling with insights. *I didn't.*

*He led me to it.*

"Syn," Angbar said. "Wasn't that what–?"

She batted a hand at him, shushing. Her mind whirled. This was it? It was a place, not an idea?

*This* was the safehold?

"'In the arms of Akir,'" Lyseira repeated. "He brought us here." She released a breath, a long exhalation of relief that smoked upwards. "Oh, thank Akir. We're safe. He did this." She was smiling, tears in her eyes. "He did this."

"Lyseira," Helix said, "we don't even know what this building is."

"It's safety," she said. "It's a blessing from God."

"How do we get in?" Angbar said.

Syntal pushed her hands against the stone, experimentally. It slid inward so smoothly she nearly stumbled. A rush of warm, stale air rolled over her.

Within, the sliver of light from the doorway fell across a book.

It rested on a stone pulpit, facing the door. It was unmarked, its cover bound in black leather, sealed with an unbroken band of metal. Sparks flickered in its pages like lightning behind storm clouds.

"A Church entry," Lyseira breathed. "It has to be. I wonder–"

"It's no holy book," Syntal whispered. *Not to you.* She stepped in, and her shadow fell over it.

"Syn," Helix murmured. "That looks like your book."

She ran a finger over the cover, her heart in her throat. *Another book? Why?* The first one had brought the Storm. By opening it, she had changed *the sun.* Something inside her screamed for caution, begged her to let someone with more wisdom make this decision.

"*Salgo,*" she whispered at the band. Nothing happened.

"Syn," Angbar said. "Do you think Lar'atul put it here?"

She focused her spellsight on the band. There was a truth there that made no sense, a command from the Pulse she would never have guessed.

It was alive.

*What does that mean?* Her mind reeled. *Alive? How?* It was a piece of metal.

"Enough," Seth said tightly. "Leave it." Suddenly he was next to her. "It's a witch's book." He grabbed it, made to wrest it away.

"*Ves,*" Syntal snapped.

A flash of white sparked from her finger, hurtling into the band like a knife. The metal died with a whispered shriek only she could hear. It fell open.

And the Pulse roared.

Colors exploded from the book, thrashing upward. The walls quaked with panic; the air trembled and screamed.

Outside, the meadow rippled an unearthly orange. Above, a blue bolt ripped away to the east.

Then the sky detonated with lightning. It flashed every color known. It flashed colors that had been forgotten. It lanced through the clouds and shattered the sky, strobing the forest floor with madness.

# Epilogue

*An excerpt from "Musings: A Commentary on the Kespran Chronicle," by Angbar Shed'dei*

I've been asked if we knew what the lightning meant. "You must have," people say. It's too frightening to imagine that such incredible things could happen in ignorance. People want order, they want things to make sense. They want to believe things happen for a reason.

We tried to figure it out. We fought, of course. Seth was furious. All of us were terrified, but to this day, I think none of us were more frightened than he was.

Opening the second seal changed everything in ways we couldn't even conceive of, but when the Storm ended, the world looked as it always had. It was more real, more vibrant. As beautiful as Syntal's eyes. But fundamentally, it was still the world we knew, and our situation hadn't changed. We didn't have time to figure out what the Storm meant. We were still starving and cold and lost. We had to find a way to survive, so we explored.

The Safehold saved our lives that winter.

I learned, years later, that it had once served as a sanctuary for the persecuted. It was built as a place for hiding. A hot spring kept it warm; we didn't even need a fire. It had rooms for everyone, austere and quiet. And Lar'atul's wardbook was only the first of its treasures: Lyseira lost herself in its library that winter, sparing Harth and I untold hours of lectures as Syntal taught us to chant.

There was no food, but Iggy was true to his word. I don't know how hunting pained him, his new relationship to the world being what it was, but he did it. He kept us fed.

After running for so long, we were happy just to rest. We burrowed in, and rode out the winter. They were hard months, and cold, but I still think on them. They were good. Maybe the last good months we had.

What did the Storm mean?

None of us knew for certain, not even Syntal, but she had a better idea than most of us. She said when the clerics saw the Rending, they were scared. They saw something they didn't understand–something that *threatened* them–and they called it the end of the world.

But they were wrong. The Storm wasn't the end of the world.

It was the beginning.

## Acknowledgements

This one was a doozy.

Thank you, first and foremost, to the original children of Southlight: Joy Nicolai, Ethan Mills, Jason Parviz, Jerry Murphy, Matt Giesler, Jason Formo, Mike Lonetti, and Jason Tabor. Thank you for coming with me to this incredible place, and helping me realize just how great it could be.

Extra thanks to Jason Parviz, for having the temerity to review all kinds of late-stage revisions.

Thank you to Adam Paquette for creating, so brilliantly, a window into a world I had imagined since I was eight.

Thank you to Ryan Holthaus and Ethan Mills for countless hours on (and off) the playground, talking about Axist, Eminallies, and Kesprey.

Thank you to my beta readers: Karen Welter, Tony Tavegia, Joy Nicolai, Jason Parviz, Ethan Mills, Ryan Holthaus, and Senja Nicolai. Your feedback was invaluable, even when it was expressed in carefully neutral terms. I got the hint. Two more full revisions were warranted.

Thank you to all the agents who turned the early version of this manuscript down. You were right; it had a long way to go.

And thank you to my wife, Joy. I dedicated this book to you, but that isn't enough. You saw me through countless hours of agonizing and despondence. You weathered my most dizzying highs and blackest lows. You were the first and truest believer.

The look of wonder you had after your first reading is one of the greatest achievements of my lifetime. I love you.

## About the Author

Adam J Nicolai lives near Minneapolis, Minnesota, with his wife, Joy, and their two children, Isaac and Rydia. His first novel, *Alex*, was a Kindle Suspense bestseller. His second, *Rebecca*, was a bestseller in Kindle Lesbian fiction. Both are psychological thrillers.

He has been working on the world of *Children of a Broken Sky* since he was eight years old, and is delighted to share it with you.

The sequel, *A Season of Rendings,* will be available in 2014.

## Glossary

**abbot** - A title of great respect in the Church; the next rank above Deacon; the last rank before Bishop.
**Abbot Forthin** - An elderly man, Keeper of the temple in Southlight, of the Order of Apostles. Known to the villagers simply as "The Abbot."
**Alynwood** - A small forest to the north of Southlight.
**Angbar Shed'dei** - A *Bahiran* boy who lives in Southlight with his blood parents. 18 winters, dark of hair, eye, and skin.
**Archbishop** - The highest rank of priest, second only to the Fatherlord. Each of the seven Archbishops represents one of the four orders within the Church.
**Aron** - Innkeeper of the Keg and Kettle in Keldale. Acquainted with Harth Silwen.
***Bahir*** - The nation to the north of Darnoth, beyond the Plains of the Fahrnar.
**Baltazar Godson** - The first Fatherlord.
***basica*** - First Tongue for "temple." Now used as a title or honorific for temples of great note.
***Basica Sanctaria*** - The holiest of temples, where the Fatherlord holds residence. Located in Tal'aden. Sometimes called the Crystal Tower.
***Basica Shientel*** - The temple in Shientel, the largest in the Valley of the same name.
***Basica Tenuor*** - A large temple in Keldale, where new books of the Chronicle must undergo a cycle of purification.
**Bella Smith** - Helix's mother and Syntal's aunt; wife to Kevric.
**Beth Smith** - Helix Smith's sister by blood.
**Binding** - A miracle which paralyzes its victim.
**bishop** - A position of great authority in the Church. Bishops typically administer Church business for entire regions and report directly to the Archbishops.
**Bishop Marcus** - Bishop of the Tribunal, whose domain is the Shientel Valley. Severe. First name Gilead.
**blackweed** - A healing herb, used for packing wounds.
**Blane** - An old woodsman who lives in Alynwood with his wife,

Leese.
**Blessday** - The seventh day of the week, on which Akir created all men and beasts. Considered a day of rest.
**bloodroot** - An herb, typically smoked.
**Caleph Sera** - The current Fatherlord.
**Canon** - Half of the holy scripture. Eight books devoted to defining the Seven Sacred Principles.
**Chronicle** - Half of the holy scripture. A series of history books stretching back thousands of years.
**circle the heart** - A gesture intended to ward off evil spirits, profess one's love for the Church and Akir, or indicate finality. It involves pointing to one's forehead, then bringing the finger down and circling the heart.
**Cleansing** - A painful process by which a cleric of the Tribunal attempts to purify a sinner's soul. Often fatal or debilitating.
**clericlight** - Holy light created by a cleric's miracle.
**Communion** - A miracle which grants the power to speak with God.
**Coram** - A town north of Southlight.
**Corla Rulano** - Lyseira and Seth's mother; a pious but pragmatic woman.
**crown, golden** - Currency of Darnoth. Twenty are worth a single star.
**Darnoth** - A kingdom on Or'agaard, located south of *Bahir.*
**Dawnday** - The first day of the week, on which Akir created the sun and stars. A holy day.
**Day of Banishment** - The day after the Night of *Rev'naas.* Called "The Day."
**deacon** - A "rank and file" priest; a cleric who is no longer an initiate.
**Dessic** - A student at the Preserver compound in Newton, who trained with Seth. Now a Preserver.
**Fatherlord** - The ruler of the Church, to whom kings bow. A mortal vessel for Akir's spirit on Earth.
**First Tongue** - Called "the tongue of the first clerics." An ancient language now used mainly in religious ceremony and for penning scripture.
**Fisher Isles** - A series of islands populated by fishermen, in the

Sunrise Sea.
**Galen Wick** - A Justicar who accompanies Bishop Marcus to Southlight.
**Gideon Elmoor** - Bishop of the Order of Judgment.
**Gilleus** - The first Archbishop of Scripture, for whom the first and second books of the Chronicle are named.
**Grand Isle** - A large, unsettled island, three days' sail from Keldale.
**Harrowing** - The tenth month of the year, marking autumn's midpoint.
**Harth Silwen** - A secretive resident of Keldale, often hired as a guide. Brown of eye and hair.
**heel, copper** - Currency of Darnoth. Fourteen are worth a single shell.
**Hel** - A place of eternal damnation, reserved for the greatest sinners and those condemned by the Church of Akir.
**Helix Smith** - A boy from Southlight, 17 winters, red of hair and brown of eye. Syntal's brother by adoption.
**highsun** - noon.
**High Tongue** - The modern tongue of Darnoth, originated by nobles.
**hotsick** - Delirium and fatigue caused by exposure to heat.
**Ignatius (Iggy) Ardenfell** - A young man of 19 winters, dark of eye and hair. A woodsman and son of a rancher in Southlight.
**Iis-alac** - A character in a story from scripture. A boy who opens a witch's book without permission and loses his soul.
**initiate** - One who has been ordained as a member of the priesthood, typically very young.
**Isaic Gregor** - Firstborn of Lucas Gregor's two sons, and heir to the throne of Darnoth.
**Jacob** - A friend of Harth's in Keldale, who guards the city's southern gate.
**Jan Gregor** - Lucas Gregor's second son.
**Jokan** - A master Preserver at the Preserver compound in Newton; a rival of Retash.
**Julius** - A boy at the Rentiss orphanage in Keldale.
**Justicar** - A holy knight.
**Keeper** - a priest who administers a temple, typically of the Order of

Apostles.

**Keldale** - A sprawling port city in the Shientel Valley, on the Sunrise Sea.

**Keswick** - The capitol city of Darnoth, home of King Gregor's throne.

**Kevric Smith** - A blacksmith of some renown who has fallen on hard times. Helix's father and Syntal's uncle.

**Lar'atul** - A powerful chanter and Tei'shaar, long dead.

**Leese** - A woman who lives in a cabin in Alynwood with her husband, Blane.

**Lorna Rentiss** - Matthew's wife, who runs an orphanage in Keldale.

**loyalman** - Colloquial term for any soldier or knight that swears fealty.

**Lucas Gregor** - King of Darnoth.

**Lyseira Rulano** - A pious girl from Southlight, 16 winters, grey of eye and long of hair. Wishes to be initiated as a priestess. Seth's sister by adoption.

***m'sai*** - First Tongue. Literally "very well." Generally used to express casual agreement.

***manna*** - First Tongue word for the holy bread created for Church ceremony.

**Marlin the Magnificent** - A magician who performs unexplainable tricks.

**Matthew Rentiss** - A blind man from Keldale who was once a bishop of the Tribunal.

**Minda Fletchins** - A pretty girl from Southlight. Helix's sweetheart.

**miracle** - A supernatural feat worked by a follower of Akir. A host of miracles have been documented, including those of Binding the living, invoking flame, and calling forth light, but the most well-known are those that heal the sick. The third Sacred Principle forbids the invocation of miracles by anyone outside the Church.

**Mountainday** - The fourth day of the week, on which Akir gave form and depth to the Earth.

**Newton** - A small town in the Shientel Valley, known primarily for its training grounds for Preservers.

**nog** - A derogatory term for dark-skinned Northlanders (*Bahirans*).

**Or'agaard** - The world, sometimes called the Earth, extending from edge to edge.

**Order of Apostles** - Of the four orders of the Church of Akir, that most concerned with spreading the word of God to foreign lands, establishing new temples, and maintaining and expanding existing temples, as well as collecting tithe and monitoring the populace.

**Order of Judgment** - Of the four orders of the Church of Akir, that most concerned with the administration of laws, the determination of guilt or innocence, and the reconciliation of the king's decrees with the Seven Sacred Principles.

**Order of Scripture** - Of the four orders of the Church of Akir, that most concerned with keeping record of all events and scribing their observations in the current book of the Chronicle, which will eventually become part of scripture.

**Ordlan Green** - A massive forest in the far northwestern corner of Darnoth.

**Pinewood** - A small forest at the southeast end of the village of Southlight.

**Preserver** - A monk devoted to the protection of the Church and its members, capable of great feats of physical prowess and extremely skilled in combat.

**Redleaf** - The eleventh month of the year, marking the end of autumn.

**redwarts** - A disease that causes the victim's flesh to erupt in scarlet pustules, accompanied by fever and hallucination; often fatal if not healed.

**Rending, The** - The Church's term for the Storm, naming it the herald of Or'agaard's final days.

**Retash** - Seth's master at the Preserver compound in Newton.

***rev'naas*** - First Tongue. Literally "darkness within," referring to the concept of sin and the notion that all men are sinners.

**saltleaf** - A wild herb, renowned for its unique flavor.

***sehk*** - First Tongue word for excrement. Survives in common use as an all-purpose curse.

**Seth Rulano** - An apprentice Preserver of 17 winters. Dark of eye, with no hair. Lyseira's brother by adoption.

**Seven Sacred Principles** - The divine commandments by which all God-fearing people abide.

**shell, silver** - Currency of Darnoth. Seven are worth a single crown.
**Shendra** - The second Archbishop of Scripture, for whom the third and fourth books of the Chronicle are named.
**Shientel** - The capitol city of the Shientel Valley, carved into the base of the Tears.
**Shientel Valley** - The southeastern part of Darnoth, bounded by the Sunrise Sea, Thakhan Dar, and the mountain range called the Tears.
**Silla Tevington** - A girl from Southlight who waits tables at Mellerson's.
**Southlight** - A tiny village in the distant southeastern corner of the Shientel Valley, in the shadow of the mountain Thakhan Dar.
**star, platinum** - Currency of Darnoth. Rare and valuable.
**Storm, The** - A severe but silent lightning storm. In its wake, the sun would sometimes fail to rise, crops would suddenly sprout or wither overnight, and peasants discovered the power to work witchcraft.
**Summermorn** - The sixth month of the year, marking the start of summer.
**Sunrise Sea** - The ocean beyond Darnoth's eastern shore.
**Syntal Smith** - An orphaned girl who was adopted by the Smiths in Southlight. 17 winters, green of eye and black of hair.
**Tairen Sea** - The ocean beyond Darnoth's southern shore.
**Tal'aden** - The Holy City, seat of the Church's power.
**Tears, the** - The mountain range that marks the northern and western boundaries of the Shientel Valley, in the southeastern corner of Darnoth.
**Thakhan Dar** - A towering mountain in the southeast of the Shientel Valley. Its peak is shrouded in clouds.
**Tribunal, The** - Of the four orders of the Church of Akir, that most concerned with hunting, imprisoning, slaying, and Cleansing the wicked.
**True Hearing** - A miracle to discern truth from lies.
**Veiling Green** - A legendary forest that bewitches travelers who enter. After the Storm, sometimes called Wolfwood.
***Ves*** - A chant which invokes a flash of light and can kill the weak.
**Willis Mellerson** - An innkeeper from Southlight.
**Wolfwood** - Another name for Veiling Green, so given for the

wolves that surround it since the Storm.
**wurmroot** - A healing herb, known for dulling pain and clotting blood.

www.ingramcontent.com/pod-product-compliance
Lightning Source LLC
Chambersburg PA
CBHW030821310726
48980CB00006B/583/J

* 9 7 8 0 9 8 4 9 2 6 4 2 8 *